SCIENCE AND SORCERY IV

By Jeffery Scott Sims

Published by Dyrezan Press

"Critical Information," "The Spirit of Lenny Gilk" and "A Curious
Incident at the Office" first appeared in *Strange Mysteries*; "The Advent
of the Exterminators" in *I, Executioner*; "The Seal of Jacob Bleek" and
"The God in the Machine" in *Chaos Theory: Tales Askew*; "The Nasty
Club" in *Malicious Deviance*; "Peril in the Red Zone" in *M-Brane*;
"Expedition ZB-12" in *Bizarrocast*; "A Critique of Vorchek's
Holobiologia in *Mad Scientist Journal*; "A Tale of Dyrezan" in *Voluted Tales*;
"The Saturday after the End of the World" in *Nihilist Sci Fi*.

Terror creeps from the darkness!

The fire had burned low. He saw mostly by torch light. There crowded the denizens of the forest, clad in pathetic and shredded rags, a dozen or more, engaged in the dismembering and devouring of the late Herr Katzmann. So much had Bleek been forewarned, or logic entailed, yet it was not this gruesome confirmation that staggered him. It was, rather, the aspect of the ravenous creatures that shocked.

Human they may once have been—they, or their fathers—but these dwellers in the Black Forest, these forsaken servants of Helvetius or their spawn, had deteriorated into things uncanny and unclean, repulsive shamblers with grotesquely manlike features protruding from unnaturally hairy faces. Their ruthless master had conjured strangely and well, creating for his cruel utility these nightmarish horrors, horrors that tarried abominably on Earth long after their prime necessity had ended. Now they turned from the red, sodden wreckage on the floor, their forms thin and wiry, hairy and befouled with gore; flexed their lips to show crimsoned fangs, and advanced.

Jacob Bleek bellowed in terrified rage and mortification, roared out a mystical curse that called upon the most vengeful demons, thrust at his attackers the blazing torch. They shrank back, barking like wolves at the flame, and he deduced their instilled or adopted dread of fire; recalled, too, that they had made no overt move by day. So it seemed to his generous hopes, but they did not flee, instead attempting to edge at him from the sides, the mark of savage cunning.

Beyond them he quickly noticed a yawning opening in the floor, where a trap had been raised near the fireplace; the tunnel of which Helvetius' shade spoke, through which they gained surprising access to Bleek's unfortunate traveling acquaintance. Wherever it led, that passage might have been on the Moon for the good it did him. The house's door, as well, was barred by the maddened, frothing monsters. Bleek backed up the stairs, reached the upper level. The creatures crept after him in a body, seething up the steps as a fleshy, furry mass.

From "The Dwellers in the Black Forest." Read this and many more tales of horror in *Science and Sorcery IV*.

CONTENTS

INTRODUCTION

At last it's here, *Science and Sorcery IV*, my latest collection of tales old and new. This one ranges widely, from grim horror to exotic fantasy to mind-bending science fiction. Several stories star some of my more popular and enduring continuing characters.

Within these pages you get a heaping dose of Professor Anton Vorchek, he surely good for what ails you. That investigator of strange mysteries had an interesting literary development, commencing as background reference in certain works—"Holobiologia" being a fair example—before exploding onto the scene as hero in his own right. "Peril in the Red Zone," also included here, marks his meeting with Theresa Delaney, subsequently his valued (if querulous) assistant.

Jacob Bleek, my longest running and gloomiest character, shares a couple of his magical exploits this time around. That cold and cunning medieval sorcerer scarcely measures up to the Hollywood definition of hero, his saving grace being that his opponents tend to be a great deal nastier and more deserving of comeuppance.

I include the original space adventure of Captain Avatar, that laid-back journeyman of the cosmos. A simple premise animates his tales: in an infinite universe, there are no rules; *anything* may happen. And no matter how weird the events, Avatar has seen it all before.

There's also an early chapter in the Dyrezan saga, the unfolding history of a mighty lost civilization of wizards and warriors. All the above share the volume with a bunch of one-off stories, a little bit of everything for everyone. There are even some verging on the comical—a peculiar strain of humor, to be sure—for those desiring a break from soul-shattering fright.

Have fun, and thanks for stopping by.

Jeffery Scott Sims
May 5, 2022

Expedition ZB-12

The orbital survey of the unknown world complete—gravity check normal, atmosphere safe, oxygen content excellent, radiation danger nil, etc.—the spaceship *Halcyon* set down at a carefully chosen prime location. "Now commences," announced Commander Avatar to the crew over the intercom, "the business of our expedition to this planet, provisionally designated ZB-12." Crisply he told off duties to his four mates. Harry Benson, the strapping technologist, and Agatha Morgenstern, the elderly physicist, would accompany him on the initial scouting of the site, while mild little Waldo Ventura of life sciences, the combination zoologist and botanist, along with lovely Sylvia Fremont, the psychologist, would hold the fort and continue instrument readings. "Yes, sir," they responded one after another. All were space novices, quite willing to accept the guidance of Avatar, an old hand at cosmic exploration. "I advise extreme caution," said he, "until we know what we're dealing with here." The commander and his two companions descended the elevator to the great lower door, where at the press of a button an electronic ramp extended to meet the ground.

The *Halcyon* had landed in the middle of a broad green lawn, beautifully manicured save where the ship's exhaust had damaged the turf, which surrounded a large, isolated building exactly resembling an English country manor, with two stories and countless windows, of the period 1840-1910 in the old style calendar. Beyond in every direction rose rolling hills with pretty woods and meadows and ripened fields and occasional huts. Results of the survey from outer space had indicated the presence of much bigger groupings of artificial structures, including fair-sized cities, but the commander had wisely decided to investigate a lesser location before tackling the greater. In this his crew members had concurred. As Avatar pointed out yet again to Benson and Dr. Morgenstern, upon descending and planting his firm boots into the soft, luscious grass, "We can't afford to take chances. There's a lot we don't know about this place; specifically, the fate of the *Tartarus* expedition, which preceded ours. We know from their single transmission that they touched down in this general vicinity, but

1

everything after that is blank mystery. We must seek to resolve that mystery, if we can." He patted the sonic blaster on his hip. "Let's be ready for anything."

Indeed, the current expedition had been partly formed as a rescue mission, sent to find survivors of the first. As the trio, dressed in their heavy flight suits, marched across the lawn toward the manor house, Benson advised, "We should treat the inhabitants as hostiles until we learn otherwise. This is a big world, and there's obviously somebody here, no matter what the instruments say." "Inaccurate," replied Dr. Morgenstern in her quiet, thickly accented voice. "I have confirmed my readings from space, checked and double checked them. Sentient organisms rate zero, as do coherent electro-magnetic emissions. Despite appearances, there is no higher biological form, as we know it, on this planet." Avatar shook his head, muttered, "There must be something. In the absence of enemies, our own people should be somewhere about." He knew, however, that the good Doctor's readings hadn't disclosed human presence either.

They marched down the tidy gravel walk to the house, mounted the limestone steps to the porch, stood before the polished, double wooden doors between marble Corinthian columns. Commander Avatar knocked, received no response, drew his blaster and said, "Let's go in." A door opened at the turn of a knob, then both swung easily inward. They entered, he leading the way. They passed into a warmly lighted hall, from there into a grand drawing room on the right, also well lighted by silently burning gas lamps on the walls. "Either the lamps have just been filled," noted Benson, "or they fill themselves. It looks like the owners just stepped out for an afternoon stroll."

They beheld a wide space redolent with antique charm, marked by beautiful furniture, a marble fireplace stacked with ready logs, ornate ornaments, fine paintings and delicate hangings on the walls. Avatar scanned the room with his alert eyes, then trooped through examining blind spots, rapping on panels and peering up the fireplace chimney. He satisfied himself that nothing lurked. Benson threw himself down on a plush sofa, exclaimed, "This is the good life. I wonder if there are really cigars in that box." There were. He bit off the end of one, prepared to apply flame. "Don't be stupid, Harry," snapped his leader. "It might be a trap." Benson rolled his eyes and retorted, "Set by whom? We're all alone, remember?" He lighted up, puffed, sighed happily. Dr. Morgenstern fingered the quaint blue china on the mantel. "These would make valuable additions to my collection," she said. Sylvia threw herself down before a grand piano and plunked merrily at the keys.

Avatar got them moving again, led them back into the hall and on a search through several other rooms. They studied the vast kitchens with their massive iron wood-burning ovens, investigated the pantries—fully stocked with delicacies, raw but fresh, and warm, newly baked bread—probed a couple of sitting rooms, perused the servant's quarters, then mounted the spiraling staircase to the upper floor, where they peeked into a handful of magnificent bedrooms. Benson took it upon himself to check out one more room in a practical manner. "The plumbing works great," he declared.

"The place looks safe enough," Avatar grunted. "We can go over it completely with all personnel. This will make an excellent base of operations. I can bring in Ventura and Dr. Fremont, along with necessary supplies. We'll establish camp right here, get to work in the morning." He radioed to the ship.

The three returned to the *Halcyon* in order to help with the unloading. A mechanized trolley remotely controlled conveyed all necessaries to the steps below the porch, while manhandling carried them into the drawing room, where they were deposited in heaps. "It's a wonderful place," cried Sylvia, upon viewing the interior. "It reminds me of a fancy hotel, or a museum. So, what's the set-up?" "There's rooms for all upstairs," Benson pointed out. "We can operate in style." "I wouldn't mind a real bed," said Waldo meekly. "It's been a long time," said Dr. Morgenstern, "since I had a room to myself. "Adjoining rooms, then," agreed Avatar.

So they settled in for the night, as evening drew upon them. Outside all was darkness, save for the stars scattered across the night sky and the faint gleam of landing lights at the foot of the spacecraft. Within all was light and warmth and conviviality. The fire crackled soothingly. The astronauts relished the comfortable appurtenances of unlikely civilization. They lounged on sofas, sprawled in chairs, chatting amiably or reading selections from the volumes in the impressive library. These books were all eminently readable, for those so inclined; none quite wholly familiar, but suggestive of the quality and style of the Dickensian era, if not earlier. They ate well. Foodstuffs from the ship—healthy and nutritious, but unappealing concentrates—were ignored in favor of what the kitchen larders offered. They dined, in the appropriate hall with its wondrous big table, on steaming roast beef and hot bread and butter and cooked vegetables and fresh fruit, all prepared by the two ladies, after ceremonious taste-testing by their commander. He judged the repast

3

suitable and safe, at which they indulged until they could eat no more. They had dressed for the occasion, raiding the numerous closets of their appealing attire. Everyone found something to fit. Afterward Avatar and Benson amused themselves with billiards in the game room, where the two men fought an evenly matched set. Then Benson talked their third male crew member into a round, insisting they play for credits on pay due them. His intended victim demurred. "Come on, Waldo," said Benson, "take a risk, put up a stake." The life sciences expert warily agreed, got himself soundly trounced for his pains. Sylvia, who had sidled close to the technical man while watching, laughed merrily and exclaimed, "You'd better stick to your butterflies, Waldo."

So went the evening. At the stroke of ten (as determined by the chimes of the looming grandfather clock, rather than ship instrumentation) Commander Avatar ordered lights out. He and the crew repaired to their chosen rooms, he competently examining the locks on all the doors before he allowed his people to withdraw. Satisfied, he turned in himself, secured the latch from within his room, climbed into bed under silky sheets and a deep mound of blankets, read for a few minutes from an intriguing novel, then twisted the brass knob which lowered the gas light. He slept soundly, as did they all.

In the morning, given the absence of untoward developments, Avatar laid out a program for systematic exploration of the property. "We will begin by following the wall," he said, referring to the line of ancient stone which bounded the estate, "and check each outlying structure." Benson argued for hiking down the lane to the south, the graded dirt road which ended near the front lawn, and investigating the little village, noted during landing, which lay that way a mile or two. Sylvia cheerfully volunteered to accompany him. "So be it," agreed the commander. "Carry your radios, stay in touch. Dr. Morgenstern comes with me on the perimeter. Ventura, you stay here. Go over every inch of the house. Check everything we've seen again; skip nothing; open every door and drawer. Oh, and if you have time, collect samples of the plants, too. We may do that ourselves. I'll contact each group on the hour. That's all."

Commander Avatar and Dr. Morgenstern undertook the grand tour of the estate, spending much of the morning carrying out their circuit, then cutting across the land in geometrical segments, then subdividing those. In this manner they explored several square miles of pleasing countryside, entered every dwelling, examined each artifact, without deriving further useful information. At ten o'clock Avatar communicated with Benson, learned that he and his delightful companion were brunching at the village inn. "The fare is superb," reported the technologist, "although we had to serve ourselves." "Be sure to take notes," Avatar growled.

By mid-afternoon the parties had returned. With the crew all together once more and gathered at table, their leader called for observations. Said Benson, "It's a typical farming community, of a period corresponding to that of the house: thatched roofs, dirt streets, implements of iron, brass, and copper, some silver utensils. Sylvia and I ate with the best. Sans company, of course; there's nobody around." "And yet," blurted the psychologist, "I always felt that someone was close by. Everything was pristine, clean and fresh, as if we'd just missed our hosts. You know, it started to give me goose pimples. Even while we ate I began to feel as if someone was looking over my shoulder, or watching us from concealment. There wasn't, though." "She insisted that we make sure," Benson boomed. "So I did," she admitted. "Laugh if you must, but it was getting creepy towards the last. I enjoyed our outing, but I sensed a need to return. It felt good to get away from there, even though we didn't see everything."

"We may investigate further," said Avatar. "I don't make much of subjective impressions. At this stage, however, I'll accept any contribution to knowledge. Waldo, you seem to be faring well. I didn't hear much out of you. Did you experience a lazy day?"

"I can draw you a blueprint of the manor," replied Ventura quietly, "if you wish. Otherwise, I don't know. There are large storage rooms under the house, containing little more than old furniture and used tools. There's what looks like a private museum on the second floor. Remember that room with the suit of armor and the swords on the wall? Well, there's a lot more to it. I suppose it functions as another drawing room, but it's filled with paintings and statues and *objects d'art*. There are more books, too. I enjoyed myself there very much. Also, there's a rubbish dump out back, where trash is burned. I poked through the smoldering ashes, found about what you'd expect, except for this. Harry, I would appreciate your opinion."

Ventura produced the object from the empty chair beside him, passed it to Benson, who examined it critically, turning it over in his hands. "A fragment of metal," he mused, "a bit of machine-worked plating; good sheen, quality construction, some scorching along this jagged edge. I'd say titanium alloy, at a guess; a fair guess. That's not right, though. It shouldn't be right. It doesn't fit."

"Let me see," said Dr. Morgenstern. She held the fragment,

5

soberly studied it. "I agree with Harry. This piece does not belong. It is alien to this planet."

Avatar stared, rubbed his firm jaw. Then he asked the obvious question. "Could this be a fragment from the *Tartarus*?"

Ventura shrugged helplessly. "It certainly opens up dire possibilities. Whichever the case, there's more going on here than we currently recognize."

A certain moodiness reigned that evening. The sense of almost holiday atmosphere, born of delightful surroundings, had vanished, driven by dark thoughts. No one knew what to think, but they all did, according to their natures. At dinner (a roast goose with trimmings) Commander Avatar broached a plan for the following day involving round-the-clock instrument readings. "I should have been on top of that already," he grumbled. "If nothing else, I'm going to sit by the radio in the ship and try to make contact, with the crew of the *Tartarus* or anybody else I can reach." Dr. Morgenstern and Benson wished to search for more relevant artifacts. Sylvia proposed to deduce planetary psychology from the available social-systemic evidence, although she granted that appearances might be deceiving. "Is this real?" she asked, rapping the table top, "or collective delusion, or put-on? It's a tricky problem." All present agreed, but Ventura pointed out, "We aren't losing weight on this fare. It is sustenance. Maybe I should pick these bones apart. I'd like to examine live fauna. It's a pity there are none."

Darkness fell without, the strange stars of that extraterrestrial sky invisible. Apparently clouds had moved in. A partial darkness came within as well. Benson and Sylvia noticed it first, reported to Avatar. "All the lights are out in the back of the ground floor," complained the comely psychologist. "We were amusing ourselves in the kitchen bins and—"

"So I see," snapped the commander. "Harry, wipe the lipstick off your face and give me the details."

"There aren't many," said the technologist sheepishly. "The lamps started to go, gradually. Inside of a minute they were completely out. I came back for a flash, did my best to tinker, but no luck. I thought a gizmo might have malfunctioned."

"What gizmos?" demanded Avatar.

"That's the funny thing, of course. There aren't any. These appliances are good old lamps and nothing more, oil or gas. Somebody didn't refill those; not very considerate, if you ask me."

"I'll pass the word. Meanwhile, keep out of the dark area until morning. We'll investigate then." When he called for sleep time

Avatar insisted on setting a guard in the hall. He stood first watch, then Benson, then Ventura. Nothing happened that night.

With the coming of morning they explored the restricted region, finding nothing pertinent save that the lamps were empty. Refilling them from other, full lamps did not achieve the desired end; they rapidly flared out. "Some kind of break down," concluded Avatar. "Stick with it, Harry. The rest of you have your assignments for the day. Get to it."

All but Ventura had entertaining projects to absorb them. He did puzzle over the refuse of their goose, what little he noted being wholly goose-like in character. He studied blades of grass plucked from the lawn, which under the microscope conformed perfectly to expectations. At loose ends after lunch, he repaired to the fancy drawing room on the second floor, there to indulge his reading, hoping to find something outré in one of those beautifully bound volumes which might provide scientific insights into the mystery of ZB-12. He threw open the big windows, through which the sun streamed from a cloudless sky, and read happily. He learned nothing of consequence, but whiled away the afternoon in contentment. The books, be they histories or novels or religious tracts, were what they should be. Almost everything in this environment belonged, according to its own internal logic.

Dr. Morgenstern made the next discovery. Taking a break from her fruitless search, she went to Ventura's drawing room for relaxation, greeted him casually, and after a bit of chat devoted herself to the glorious collection of antiques. She had never seen such an impressive and tasteful display. Everything was so right, so natural, so becoming; but wait, what was this? One single item in that fulsome array jarred her sensibilities. "Waldo," she called, "come here. Have you seen this?"

She drew his attention to a statue which stood among a grouping of sculptures in the corner of the room, between a rectangular multi-paned window and a massive oak bureau. He looked it over, nodded, said amiably, "Yes, I noticed it yesterday. It's an interesting specimen, I suppose, although I don't know much about that kind of thing. I would call it Impressionistic, or Expressionistic, or one of those terms. I get them mixed up. Is it valuable?"

"That is hardly the point. It doesn't belong in this collection, doesn't fit the milieu. Everything else here is Neo-Classical, Baroque, or Victorian. It isn't marble, or even plaster. This style is radically different, if it be a matter of style at all."

Ventura said miserably, "I don't know what you're driving at. It's an odd statue of a man."

"Yes," said Dr. Morgenstern impatiently, "but what kind of man?"

Her companion gave the thing a more careful going over. It was a strange one: a softly shaped, distorted three-dimensional representation in some glistening substance, the lower portion merely a crude lump without discernible legs, the torso twisted upon itself, the arms buried in the substance and lacking hands, the head grotesque. The skull was smoothly rounded, the eyes hidden beneath a flat shield, only the nose and mouth clearly observable. The teeth protruded unpleasantly.

"You know, that looks like—" He stopped, nervously massaged his receding hairline. "We'd better call the others." The physicist radioed, the others came. They saw, debated, discussed, as an ugly realization stole upon them.

"It's an astronaut," said Commander Avatar, "in the cheap suit that traders often wear. That's a helmet, with face plate, and this stuff over the shoulders could be a bit of flight jacket. This here could be a bent zipper. That's what it is. What's this thing doing here?"

"I don't care for the look on his face," said Benson.

"That is very bad," agreed Avatar. "Professor Fremont, what do you make of that?"

"It doesn't take an expert," Sylvia replied, "to read stark terror on a human face." She shuddered. "He must have died horribly."

"Wait a minute," cried Benson; "Where do you get that from? It's just a statue."

"I'm not so sure. This doesn't jibe with the other sculptures. Come to think of it, it doesn't resemble sculpture at all. Agatha, do you see traces of workmanship?"

"No," said Dr. Morgenstern, "this is not the product of an artisan. I'd call it a sort of physical duplication, something carried through at one stroke, of a piece, you might say." She touched the face, drew back her hand hastily. "It is warm. It radiates faint heat. My God, it's a lifelike heat. Excuse me, I must get out of here." She fled the room. Sylvia went after her.

"It's incredible," said Avatar, "but we can't ignore evidence. This can only be one of the crewmen of the *Tartarus*. Something did this to him. Something messed him up and froze him, or solidified the remains, like a mummy, only it's warm. Good Lord, I can feel it, too. Waldo, shall we treat this thing as living?"

Ventura cringed visibly at the thought. "There's no point in that. He's a casualty. There's certainly nothing I can do for him. We have records in our files, Commander, on the members of the *Tartarus* crew. I can look up those, perhaps identify the man. That will be important to his next of kin."

"Of course. Harry, I want you and Waldo to carry this poor fellow downstairs. I must decide what to do with him. Do we open him up and study, or give him a decent burial? I'll get back with you on that. For now I'll see to Dr. Morgenstern. She seems rather shaken by this development."

"I won't dissect him," rasped Ventura as the pair struggled with the heavy mass. "Give me a frog, give me anything, but not this." As they slowly descended they heard sweet, tinkling music wafting from below. Reaching the lower landing, they stowed their dreadful burden in the kitchen. Joining the others, they found Sylvia playing the piano for Dr. Morgenstern. She was quite good. The music, chosen from the available selections, sounded very much like Chopin, but was not.

"I behaved badly," confessed the physicist. "That—the statue—may mean nothing. There are necessarily puzzles, curiosities open to interpretation. There may be a harmless reason for its presence." She received nods in return, but no one said anything to the point. Eventually Commander Avatar observed, "It's getting dark. I call for an early evening, and an early morning. Let's eat, rest, pull this expedition into shape and make a big day of it tomorrow. We'll find out what it's all about. Every question has an answer, I'm told."

Benson and Ventura had to move the statue again, because the ladies would not enter the kitchen until the thing had been hidden away in a disused bin. That disagreeable chore performed, the women cooked a fat pork roast, and at table that night all present were outwardly convivial. Avatar carved and served. Fine wine flowed, crystal goblets clinked, healths were drunk and toasts dedicated to science and success. Then, at Avatar's insistence, they trooped to their rooms to put this day behind them. No sooner had they separated than the lights went out.

The commander, on watch, banged on their doors and hustled them into the hall, his handheld light stabbing at their faces. He brandished his blaster in the other hand. "It's got to be trouble," said he. "There's dirty work afoot. Flashlights on, everybody." Five beams slashed the darkness. They quickly established that the entire second floor had lost illumination. "Get below, fast," ordered Avatar. "Keep together."

9

They stumbled and stampeded down the stairs, at the foot of which warm yellow light beckoned. There they regrouped, the commander and Benson breaking away to investigate conditions on the ground floor. "Lights on in the kitchen," announced the technologist when they returned, "here, and the adjacent rooms. All others out. The lamps are bone dry." "There's more," said Dr. Morgenstern. "Look out the door. You cannot see the ship." Sylvia clarified, "You can't see much of anything. Fog has rolled in."

"That's not fog," whispered Ventura. "It's darkness, just that, like we're getting inside, an impenetrable darkness. We simply can't see anything. I could almost imagine that the rest of the world has been made away with."

"Keep your imagination to yourself!" shouted Avatar. "I forbid panic. Someone shut that door. Now, into the drawing room. It looks fine." They hastened into the room. The commander paced while the rest sat wearily, tensely. He started to lecture about fact-finding tasks for the coming day. As he did so a subtle sound distracted him, held him motionless. "I hear it," cried Benson. "It's coming from the kitchen. Something's moving around in there."

Avatar barked, "Waldo, check it out." The little man stood abruptly, croaked in a ghastly voice, "You've got to be kidding!" "It's necessary," said his leader harshly. "Take a peek. What are you afraid of?" Ventura obeyed like a rusty automaton, passing hesitantly from the room and out of sight. He returned quickly. "It's dark in there now," he reported. He was unable to expound further detail.

"Then we all go," Avatar said hotly. He looked wild, his eyes darting from one white, impassive face to another. "Come on, we stick together and discover who's in there. It might be"—here he paused, gasped for breath—"it may be someone we need to meet."

And they went. He actually led the way, by choice, his gun held out before, with his team closing up behind, huddled, pressing upon one another. The light was dimming in the hall. "We're still losing ground," muttered Benson. "At this rate there'll soon be nowhere left to us." Said Sylvia, "Shouldn't we be thinking about getting out of here? The ship is starting to sound pretty good about now. What do you say, Agatha?" Dr. Morgenstern said nothing. She seemed almost petrified, propelled forward only by inertia, and that haltingly. "I will decide that in due course," said Avatar, his voice unnaturally high.

Two turns of the hall past family rooms took them into the huge kitchen. Flashlight beams pierced the dark. The sound came again. "It's in the bin," said Ventura, pointing, "where we put the statue."

10

Said his commander, "Open it Waldo." The life scientist inched forward, turned the knob, backed away as the door swung open faster than it should have. The so-called statue emerged, reached for the man with unfolding arms. It had changed, dissolved, shed its semblance of humanity. Little more than a pale, glossy, amorphous blob, it slopped out of the storage space to ooze like gelatin. Ventura shrieked, Sylvia screamed, Benson roared, Avatar groaned. The latter fired once, aimlessly, with his blaster, then all ran. In the dark hall someone cried, "Where's Agatha?" The physicist had gone or disappeared. "Back to the ship," Avatar bellowed. "Here, Waldo, hold it off until we're clear." He thrust the gun at his subordinate, took off with the rest. Ventura stood dumbfounded. Then the thing entered the hall.

The little man jumped, whirled, and ran, losing his way in the darkness. He found himself unexpectedly within a room, endeavored to orient himself as the horror appeared. Ventura struggled clumsily with the weapon, squeezed off a shot. The whitish mass darted to the side of the room, extended rubbery appendages and removed from a wall display a shotgun. To the man's shock and amazement it turned the ancient but deadly looking piece on him. Ventura dove as an explosion stunned his ears and bathed the room in dazzling light. Another blast, and he felt sharp pains burning into his shoulder. From behind a sofa he fired, fired again, then let rip a steady stream of destruction. The far wall erupted and crumpled, as did the monstrosity crouching before it. The shotgun clattered to the hardwood floor, its possessor sagging into a smoldering, stinking, inanimate mass of dripping paste.

Ventura had lost his flashlight, but he got out of that room into the hall, edging past the hideous ruin on the floor, dashed in what he hoped was the proper direction, attained the front door. Looking out he saw far, tiny lights in the strangely dense gloom. He made for them in crazy flight, stumbling against the abandoned trolley, lost the lights to view, cried out despairingly. He knew the *Halcyon* stood no more than three hundred yards from the door. It ought to be there, somewhere, and would be hard to miss if he approached it. He ran in circles, calling to his ship mates, who did not respond. Fortune favored him, however, for presently he spied a single bright light, a strobing light, high in the air. At all speed his short legs would propel him he made for that, soon discerning the dim bulk of the ship with its beacon flashing on top. The ramp was down, dimly illuminated. He dashed up, banged on the hatch. It unsealed with a squeal as brilliant light poured out, helpful hands thrusting forth to drag him inside. The door

11

crashed shut behind him.

So, as Ventura learned, the four of them were safe. "Well done, crewman," declared Avatar. "Your delaying action worked." Dr. Morgenstern was not present, not having been seen since she broke away from the group. "We'll round her up in the morning," their commander assured them.

Reality proved different. Come the dawn the odd darkness passed and a fair sun shone in a beautiful blue sky. The great house stood as before across that well-tended lawn, with the front door closed. The three men ventured forth to seek their colleague, Sylvia remaining to man the ship radio. The party returned shortly bearing a small wrapped burden. "She's gone," Avatar said crushingly. "It's hopeless." Sylvia asked, "What's that you have in the package, Waldo?" He grimaced as he adjusted his bandaged shoulder, replied, "It's one of Dr. Morgenstern's shoes. We didn't find anything else, but it looks bad. You see, the shoe is still full of—ah—of material." Sylvia blanched and turned away.

"I hereby declare this mission a complete success," announced Avatar. "Harry, it's time to rev up the engines and take off. Once in space I'll transmit a full report." "Aye aye, Chief," Benson cried joyously. He and Sylvia left the chamber to assume their stations. Ventura shook his head morosely. "Commander," he cried, "what kind of success is this? We know nothing, we accomplished nothing. We didn't establish the fate of the *Tartarus*, nor make contact with the native denizens. We haven't formulated even a conceivable explanation for what goes on here. Planet ZB-12 is as impossibly strange as it seemed the moment we touched down."

"Your summation is only partially true," Avatar replied thoughtfully. "Come, Waldo, focus on our gains, our advances. The *Tartarus* expedition was a dead loss, while we survive—the clear majority of us, that is—to carry back knowledge of a sort. We can be pretty sure that our predecessors are a write-off, and that dear Dr. Morgenstern is a tragic loss to science and humanity. However, we have our recordings, measurements, and observations, as well as a tale to tell. As for explanations, a tough bird like me, who has seen so much over the years on a dozen worlds, doesn't bother his head too much about those. ZB-12 is what it is; it's a known place on a chart, with certain attributes, not all of them immediately fathomable by us. So be it. The next expedition, armed with our findings, will learn more. I'm perfectly willing to leave that to them.

"Really, Waldo, the longer I've spent in space, the more I've

12

realized that it is a region of mystery piled upon mystery. You must accept that, too. In time you will. The universe is strange, and the farther we venture the stranger we find it. Its rules aren't our rules, and we should never expect to grasp its totality. Seek, observe, analyze; that's all there is to do. In an unimaginably vast cosmos, what else is there to do?"

The Spirit of Lenny Gilk

My friend Lenny Gilk died recently. The San Diego police declared his death an accident, and who was there willing to argue with them? Certainly not I, and I paid very careful attention to the news reports and to the statements of the authorities, who were scrupulous in interviewing anyone closely associated with him. They talked to me at some length, but I told them nothing useful. The case presented no truly unusual features: one night he pitched headfirst over the third-floor balcony of his grand home, expiring on impact with severe brain contusions. That was really all they could establish. The cops wondered if he was alone at the time, or whether someone else had been present who could contribute to their evidential base. No one came forward, and that was that.

Chalk it up as just another hard luck story, if you will, although those who didn't know him wouldn't tend to remember the Lenny Gilk story that way. Wasn't he a self-made man, a man of great fortitude and spirit, rising from humble conditions to make himself the owner and principal stockholder of a stupendous West Coast retail chain? Hadn't "Lenny's" made Lenny rich and famous and happy? Wasn't that the good life? And yet I knew better, to a degree. Sadness lurked in his tale; for all he'd accomplished, Lenny Gilk was never wholly satisfied with life. Perhaps he wasn't what they call a "people person." That might be the answer, although I thought him decent enough, never detecting harsh or crude tendencies in the fellow. He really tried to surmount his origins, seemed distressed that his efforts along those lines weren't sufficient. He married three times, always the wrong kind of women. As he told it, he bent over backwards for them, but it never did him any good. All three took him to the cleaners, he acquiescing graciously. He drew to himself, once he had achieved remarkable success, many acquaintances, few whom he long considered friends. In the end it usually transpired that they wanted a little piece of what he had earned, and little else. That hurt him. In his final years he tended to live solitary by choice.

I liked him. For what it's worth, I liked him, and I told him so often enough. He needed that. My pal Lenny once said to me, "You're the only real friend I've got." That warmed my heart. He meant it, too, a fact obvious to all after he died, when it turned out that he'd left me practically his entire fortune.

Oh, a few odd relatives snagged a bit, grants of cash settlements just for breathing, but I got the rest. Lenny didn't show gratitude by halves when it came to rewarding companionship. We had some fun times, I stuck by him when others wavered, so I got it all. More money than I thought existed in the world, millions of dollars in cash, investments, disposable properties, all mine. That would have been quite plenty, but there was so much more, the tangible, ostentatious proofs of extreme wealth. The big house by the ocean (please call it an "upscale beach front property") dropped into my lap, the keys being delivered to me immediately following the reading of the will. I'd previously had a key made for my own purposes, but that symbolic handing over felt great. It was a fantastic house, a mansion of many rooms, plunked down according to Lenny's exacting specifications in the center of twelve acres of prime real estate. The furnishings were pricey, some of them gaudy, the artworks and other decorations abundant and showy, the conveniences modern and expensively wrought. Four fabulous cars came with the place, each both sporty and foreign, custom built too. I received those keys as well. Lenny left another house, his occasional retreat, a nice cabin somewhere in the mountains of Colorado, but I'd never seen it, and would dump that for the money so soon as I got the chance. Oh yes, there was also the boat. I will have more to tell about that, but let me say now that he had his own private dock on the beach, with a fancy yacht parked in it. The *Mary Lee*, named for his third wife when she was still around. Lenny and I sailed many a fishing cruise in that bus, some of our best moments. Now it was mine.

I remember the day I took possession and moved into the house. It gave me a real kick to vacate my seedy apartment (having already walked away from that embarrassing, disgraceful job) and dive into luxury. I let the staff go first thing, that pretentious housekeeper and her two equally snooty underlings. I intended to hire better; also, I was convinced it was they who suggested me to the police as a character worth bearing down on after Lenny's tragedy, although maybe the boys in blue would have anyway. After all, who gained but me? Accident or no, it was fortunate that I had a solid alibi for the night in question. Now I was rich, made for life, determined to enjoy it all. I tried my dead level best. It's the strangest thing, that my plans went so entirely awry.

15

Believe this: I had nothing on my mind whatsoever, neither the slightest trace of concern nor of doubt. That's why I can't explain ensuing developments in a conventional or rational manner. The big house didn't agree with me. There's the simple statement but, oh my, what miseries underlie it. Things happened from the earliest days, things I didn't wish to believe at first, things which in the end I must. Perhaps it might have been different if I'd retained the staff, kept others around me. I experienced a constant sense of unease whenever there. The place appeared too dark, regardless of the number of lights I switched on, as if I wore sunglasses indoors, and shadows shifted without proper cause. When I sat down in a plush chair to watch television or lounged on the mammoth sofa while flipping through a coffee table book, I felt something creeping up behind me, so powerful an impression that I started and looked about. Nothing would be there, but the itchy feeling at my back remained. It was worse when I moved about the house, from floor to floor and room to room, room after room always the same. I heard creaks like footsteps on the stairs around the hall corner, light steps through the ceiling from rooms above, movement within rooms before I entered them. Imagine my shock when I sauntered into an overly dim hall to see a vague dark shape passing out of sight at the other end. These incidences multiplied, grew wearisome. They wore me down. I tried to blame residual nervousness on my part, failed utterly. My dreams of loud, wild parties evaporated, although I kept telling myself that was the best solution—get people in there, noisy, crazy people—but I dared not extend invitations while such mystery reigned. It scared me to think that others might not see and hear these things, frightened me the more that they might.

One evening it got so bad that I fled, clearing out to bury myself in a hotel room. Me, the king of the palace, scurrying away like a rat to a hole! I sneaked back in the morning, felt queasy immediately that I entered, decided to try something new. A fresh approach this, hopping into the rakish Mercedes and spinning off into the blue. Of course I'd driven all the cars, but this was the first time I undertook a purely pleasurable, open-ended joy ride. It was my last. Somewhere near the heights of the scrubby mountains to the east, just before one comes to the desert, I began to get the foolish notion that I was not the sole occupant of that sportster. What a cruel blow, to realize the car was as bad as the house. My duty as citizen motorist required me to keep my eyes on the road, an awfully difficult mission when my peripheral vision insidiously tricked me into believing that something not quite human sat beside me the whole time. It was only a shape, a fuzzy impression, which I did not see clearly, not once, disappearing every time I glanced that way, but it nearly drove me insane and off the road. I turned around, when I could not stand it anymore, speeding recklessly back to my morbid manor.

And that very afternoon Darlene showed up. I wasn't ever supposed to see or hear from her again—that was our deal—so I thrilled with dread when I saw her lovely but sharp features on the screen of the security camera guarding the front door. Letting her in, I heard all the bad news I feared. The police had leaned on her, astutely endeavoring to break her story. Their pestering annoyed her, got on her nerves. She still had bills to pay, in addition to the fretful attention from the law. She wanted more money. Of course she did, it had to be. It pained me very much that she should reappear, that an unpleasant chapter of my life should open again. With no reasonable choice before me I gave her more money, all the cash I could grab, on the proviso that she leave town and never darken my door again. She agreed merrily, but grinned knowingly as she spoke, and as she drove away I shuddered. She constituted the one weak link in my arrangements, and I knew she would be back when greed resurfaced. I felt sick. Would I have to undertake another special action in order to safeguard my position?

With my future looking shaky I examined possibilities, tried to think, couldn't. The atmosphere of Lenny's house dispirited me. I pondered the notion of cutting and running with the funds I could raise, shelved that for now, but still needed to get away. The boat; now there was something I hadn't tried, a soothing sail of the sort Lenny and I had enjoyed, only this time on my own. The yacht hadn't been out of the dock since I took over. I'd sent away the two Mexicans the former owner kept for crew, and I knew nothing about the sails and all that rigmarole, but I'd operated the engine in former times, was still good for that. I could collect food and wine, sail out into the lonely bay, be at peace with myself for a change.

The yacht wasn't a giant party battleship, rather a relatively modest vessel, stylish and classy, with four ward rooms below and plenty of leg room above. I could handle it on a calm day. The next morning, after a frankly harrowing night (which clinched matters for me; I simply could no longer tolerate Lenny's house), I set out, slipping easily from the pier into the open water. I navigated lazy circles until I felt comfortable with the controls, then set course for the open ocean. Out there for some hours I did feel at peace, as if the plague of occurrences

17

and disquieting impressions had been left behind to be avoided and forgot. When the shore receded to a distant gray line I stopped engines, weighed anchor, set about hustling up a late breakfast.

What came next is not to be understood, merely described. These events marked the beginning of the end.

I cooked scrambled eggs and sausage links, threw in some packaged rolls and marmalade, popped a bottle of wine. Scarcely had I completed preparations, swigging from the bottle as I cheerfully labored, and sat down to my repast when that confounded tingling at my back commenced. I turned, saw nothing, willed myself to eat, jabbed with my fork, observed the grotesque results. The food in my plate began to move of its own volition. The eggs scattered, refashioned themselves into unappealing lumps, united weirdly with the sausages. The rolls rolled, wobbled, broke apart, combined disgustingly with blobs of gooey sweet raspberry. This horrid pageant unfolded before my eyes, the bits creeping jerkily across the china until they assumed an approximation of recognizable form. The quivering mass resembled a crab, a nasty creature that waved at my face crusty stumps of sausage. I swept the plate from the table, sat staring blankly at the motionless debris dirtying the deck. I got up presently, ready to return to the mainland.

There was, sadly, no more grace for me. I did the necessaries, got the engine going and steered a course, and then something touched me from behind, a definite physical contact. I jumped, stepped away, whirled at the bulkhead, saw a misty shape hovering there. I could not see it clearly in that instant, but it did not look like a man, any man, much less the one I half expected. I ran up the stairs to the covered deck. It waited for me there, so I bolted down the passage to the hall between the bed rooms, where it appeared again. By now the thing was coming into focus, the concentrated essence of the pall which had hung over me for so long. I'd heard stories of such cases, never paying much attention, wished that I had, for this was wholly beyond my experience or knowledge. Picture, if imagination dares serve, an object somewhat like a monstrously large, shimmering, semi-transparent pink shrimp drifting with minute gradations through the air. That is how I saw it, how my brain wracked itself to classify the nightmare. There was a bulge of a head with knobby black eyes, a glassy trunk from which short feelers or tendrils waved, and a depending tail which curled at the end without quite reaching the ground. It did not walk or crawl, this filthy image the size of a man, but floated, an impossibility existing within normal space, ever inching toward me, a gradual movement associated with a hateful fluttering sound. I screamed and fled from it, only to meet it where ever I attempted to hide.

There was no escape from that presence while I was trapped on the boat. Afternoon shadows lengthened, transformed into evening murk before I made landfall. During those wretched hours I was hunted like a beast, felt mindless terror as a beast when confronted by that which it may not fathom. The presence never assaulted me—perhaps it could not, although I shrieked and ran madly every time it approached, not daring that particular experiment—but it, as the term goes, haunted, and did its work well. Though my mind could not grapple with the shape it assumed, I knew what it was, even took a stab at guessing why it had reserved its grandest manifestation for the yacht. Naturally so, for it was here in the old times that I'd carried out my mightiest endeavors to gull poor old Lenny Gilk, stupid rolling in dough Lenny, who remarkably believed in me as he had no other man or woman. He fell for it all right; those silly, joyous times on the boat convinced him, may be, and he believed, believed in me.

He believed when he told me that day, told me on board in fact, of the new will. He believed that night a few paltry weeks later when I slipped into his house, let myself in and accosted him by surprise in his bed, coshed him on the forehead as he blinked stupidly at me, then hurled him from the balcony. I left no traces, but of course the police, who are no dummies, had their doubts and theories, harshly grilled me until I produced Darlene, that smart cookie who agreed to provide an alibi, no questions asked, in return for a pot of gold derived from my proceeds.

That should have been that, might still have worked out somehow, only Lenny had believed with all his heart, and having learned the truth in that last moment, it appeared that he could not rest. His rage came back to assail me, and now his mounting, eternal, unquenchable rage assumed ever more hideous forms. By the time I set shaky foot on land I knew I was finished.

In my terrified, or deluded, state of mind I could conceive of only one option left to me, only one decision that could satisfy him. It was ridiculous, I knew; I laughed to myself as I thought of it, shook my head in self-approbation as I entered the house, mounted the stairs to the third floor, sought Lenny's old room, which I'd never entered since that night, and still chiding myself for my nonsensical attitude paced to the deadly balcony. There, I told myself, hearing that abysmal sound of fluttering creeping up behind, I must leap over the edge and dash

19

out my brains on the pavement below. It was the only way.

So I told myself, and so I shall do, this very minute, before the thing touches me again.

An Ending, Orchestrated

So now it was a fight for life and sanity against a remorseless peril which he could still scarcely conceive, much less understand; and he wondered whether he would survive long enough to grasp the explanation for what had happened to him and his world, or if the receding hope of survival could vouchsafe the possibility of answers. It galled him—it terrified him more than anything else—to think that all which had transpired must remain an evil mystery until his dying day, fifty years from now or tomorrow.

Twenty four hours before, Jonathan Blaine assumed that all was right with the world when he told his wife that he was heading out to run a few morning errands for household necessities. It was his day off, nothing was going on around the house, he had the time, and the wife was agreeable, so why not? The shops he meant to patronize were ten or twenty miles away farther into town, but that counted for little in Phoenix, Arizona, where everybody drives all over the spreading urban and suburban city-state to get anywhere. Nothing was close by, nor did it need to be. He kissed his wife, joked with the kids, patted the dog and set off in his automobile on this trivial enterprise like all the others before. Only this one worked out differently, for it was the day that the world changed unimaginably.

Spinning down the broad city avenue (not so much traffic this day, which pleased him) which linked each suburban hub with the next, he felt the ground shake, that minor tremor which first informed him, however slightly, of the advent of the unusual. It wasn't much. A few cars pulled to the side of the road, a few more wobbled, but Blaine kept cruising evenly, albeit at reduced speed. He thought for a second that strange lights flickered into his eyes from undefined sources, that the sky shuddered with peculiar color. The moment passed, with no untoward ill effects, and presently he picked up the pace again with the steadied flow of traffic. He snapped on the radio, expecting some sort of chirping announcement, got nothing but the prattling norm. The tiny earthquake, as he guessed it was, didn't even rate special mention. He could catch the details at the top of the hour.

He made his first stop at a discount department store, engaged in casual chatter about the late occurrence, picked up the family wants— toothpaste, mouthwash, kitchen cleaner in the plastic spray bottle— then pushed on farther into the city maze, arriving in time at his final destination, the limit for the day, the big red stone-faced mall built into the gently sloping hillside where orange groves stood when he was a boy. He and the wife both needed new pairs of blue jeans for the upcoming yard work. It was that season again. There were prickly shrubs to prune, and Blaine had agreed at last to order a fresh load of gravel to spread on the desert-landscaped "lawn". The lady had read of the sale on at one of the mall's big boxes, thus the reason for his lengthy excursion after that common item.

That's where all hell broke loose for him. It really did seem like a scene from a bad horror movie, and nothing more at first, although that was plenty. One moment he was contentedly browsing among the other shoppers, pouring over the wares, keeping in mind always his wife's exacting specifications, and then in the next—when he had completed the purchases and was making for the mall exit—the undead, or the living dead, or the zombies, or whatever the customary term for such grisly conceptions, were all around, shambling, lurching, darting forward with apparently mindless, if murderous intent, and the place exploded into a maelstrom of frenzied screaming and panicky bedlam.

Blaine found it impossible, then or later, to figure out where they came from so suddenly, then because he didn't have a second to think, later because thinking served no purpose. From the grave they came, most of them, judging from their appearance: the pale dishevelment, the indications of incipient rot, the morbid funereal habiliments; yet there were those mixed in among the ghastly throng that looked scarcely human, as if they had been fabricated for the occasion according to the general plan of man without ever having walked the earth as such. What they wanted there was clear enough, because what they did was commence killing the genuinely living folk there and keep killing so long as there was anyone present and within reach. The shoppers fled, dropping their precious packages in little unceremonious heaps, ran for the doors, ran down the vast corridor, ran away from the monstrous staggering creatures or ran straight into them. The things killed, did so in bestial ways, rending like animals with teeth and nails and bludgeoning blows that tore living flesh and shattered living bones. The things did not speak, neither to threaten nor to taunt, but grimly set about their sole goal of making a massacre

22

of everyone within sight.

Only a miracle got Blaine to and out the door. Shouting uncontrollably, his breath crying in the intervals, he pushed and jostled against his fellow men and women who were being torn to pieces before his eyes, slipping once in a moment of delirious terror on the pooling blood from a young woman who was being crudely butchered. She had caught his eye before, a pretty girl then, now an atrocity, her skin being peeled away in damp red strips, her flesh gouged in spurting chunks. Blaine recovered his balance—it had been instant death to have fallen—slammed shoulder first against the plate glass door and gained the outside.

He dashed across the parking lot, weaving between the stiffly mobile corpses, the fresh ones scattered on pavement, the fleeing shoppers. Images assailed him that he could not analyze, the scenes of slaughter certainly, yet others too: the cracked asphalt beneath his feet sprouting weeds, the unexpectedly decrepit appearance of the shopping complex's facade, chipped and crumbling. If the supposed earthquake had caused that he hadn't noticed before, nor did time permit his pondering now. He reached his car at a dead run, flung himself inside, cranked the engine. For a moment of crystallized fear he thought it wouldn't fire, but it did, grudgingly, and he spun round quickly with a squealing of tires and hurtled toward the edge of the huge lot. Near the service road leading into the avenue he paused to take bearings. The aspect of the mall puzzled him. From this remove it seemed still more worn and decayed, as if extreme age had taken its toll within those few minutes. That made Blaine question his sanity, even more than the now distant vista of gory mayhem.

In a fever pitch of terror he pulled into the main street and gunned the car to full speed. Other vehicles sped by, maneuvering dangerously, though not so many as he counted on. Indeed, the traffic, never heavy today, seemed definitely lessened. His vision grew dark with a sky which turned to murk, low clouds and oppressive, and the pressing trees by the side of the road served to further cut down on the fading illumination. He hadn't remembered so many trees so thickly situated along the formerly bright, broad avenue, an expanse of orderly situated trees rather like the olden groves he remembered. He snapped on the radio, hoping for useful, life-saving information, explanations, justifications, received squawking static on every channel he tried.

He pulled off behind an untenanted gas station to call home on his cell phone. It worked, although the sound quality was piteous. His

23

wife answered with a scream, began to babble of her dread and mystification. Blaine cut her short, told her his estimated location, promised to proceed directly home. Then he issued the orders which in his mind the emergency demanded. He told her to wait an hour— no, two—and if he had not arrived by then, she was to collect the children and get them into the other car and take them to the summer house in Payson, there to expect him to join them when feasible. He decided on this, trusting that the madness was local and temporary. He told her he loved her and broke off.

That sad task out of the way, he braced himself for the long haul home, a distance that expanded conceptually as he thought of it. That run didn't seem a minor jaunt any more. Also, he found himself stifled by the thick gloom that weighed upon the scene at noon. The sky had grown dark gray, leaden with more than cloud, as if something vast and amorphous weighed down the sky. The rear lot behind the station, cluttered with trash and unkempt as with long neglect, somehow disturbed him. Yes, it looked long abandoned, corrupted with age, as if forsaken for years. He realized with disgust that bodies were mixed with the debris, far gone with decay, as if they had lain there for a very long time. He couldn't make it out, but just then a half dozen horrors, walking dead and things like vaguely humanoid animals, swung around a corner of the building straight for him, so he skipped the curious ruminations and thundered back into the street.

Blaine figured that in his haste he must have plunged onto a back lane, because once he became fully aware of his milieu he noticed that the road was narrow and unfrequented, empty of other drivers, empty save for a couple of abandoned cars. Also the trees—cottonwoods, tall, fat, densely crowned with foliage—wholly overshadowed the way, which wasn't right at all. He thought those big trees had gone decades ago in the city, he having seen pictures only of their former glory. Here some still were, obscuring the pitiful light, darkly menacing with their jagged arms twisted at all angles. He tried the radio again, couldn't even pick up static.

His progress slowed to a crawl. The decent pavement gave way to broken, pot-holed asphalt, shrank to a single lane between dark woods and spiky walls of underbrush. Thorns and dry branches rattled and scraped against the sides of the car. No amount of hopeful logic could tell him where he was, or how there could be such a place within a normally short drive of the mall. He expected to reach the highway overpass by this time, but it wasn't in sight, nor had it ever, to his knowledge, passed over terrain like this. Came a point at which the steadily worsening lane bottomed out in a wash with running water, just enough to spook him, but he was past caring and splashed through on impulse without incident. On the other side Blaine, after checking the time, called home again to inform his wife that he could not keep the appointment, to inquire of her safety and that of the kids. The blasted thing didn't work, wouldn't start. He cursed, then prayed that they made it unmolested to Payson; prayed, in terrified puzzlement at the thought, that there was still a Payson where they could seek safety.

He continued creeping along the impossible road, crowded by unmanicured growths, dirt now, ungraded, unpleasantly jarring. Strange objects by the roadside nudged his attention, proved themselves on careful examination to be skeletal human remains, clean but only partly articulate. It made no sense. Where had gone the time to produce these hideous relics? How came they here, in this state, within the last hour or so? Was this Phoenix, or Peoria, or Sun City? Blaine didn't believe it. He thought himself in a hateful dream, begged to wake up, failed, felt his breath rasping, his heart thudding unhealthily, knew himself awake. This was the world, simply not the one with which he was familiar. Once the woods and brush drew back, exposing a clearing containing a pathetic lean-to hovel of unpainted boards and tar-paper roof, an apparently antique wagon alongside. An old man stood in the desiccated yard, motionless, staring at him as he passed and paused. No, that fellow was more than old: he looked dead himself, or withered and collapsing like the awful shack. He never moved or once blinked, so that suddenly Blaine took fright and clattered on by. Beyond that peculiar vision Blaine approached another running wash, this one very slight, no concern, but occupied by a trio of peccaries, a bristled, glaring family of the wild pigs who regarded him as an intruder. They did not shy at his approach, but sidled obstinately aside as he dipped through their territory. They shouldn't have been there, but then again, nothing before him should have existed. They fit in quite well, whereas he felt a lonely stranger.

With the increasing darkness his forward movement became ridiculous. His headlights failed to shine. Blaine spent the night in his car edged off the road so far as the harsh scrub would allow, shivering against the untimely chill. He may have slept in snatches, but come the hint of dawn he would not swear to it. He felt tired, ill, feared he was dying, but he didn't, not then. Not a single human being, of any variety, had appeared during that time, nor did any light gleam or move in the dark sky. Wild creatures had called and crept at intervals, but that was all, and he never saw them. With passable light he tried to start his vehicle. It would not. He crept out, beheld the deplorable shell of rust and eaten through corrosion that had been a snazzy coupe mere hours before. The car was dead, like so much else he had known, like everything, perhaps, that he had known. The cell phone was useless, his watch a broken wreck. He observed himself, as he could, noted the rotted shoes, the threadbare attire; everything, everything going, everyone dead or gone and falling back into non-entity and non-existence. He didn't dare look at his face in the car mirror, fearing greater multiplication of the signs of decay.

The road wouldn't have borne vehicular traffic further anyway. Ahead of him it stretched as little more than a walking path.. He imagined that it converted into an animal trail beyond the next rise. Weirdly interested, he ambled to the top, thought that it did narrow ever more, maybe vanishing into the wildly tangled growths. That way, above the trees, he spied the far mountains at the western edge of the valley, looking exactly as he had always known them, save that no radio and television towers stabbed the sky as they had all his life. So it was like that, then.

He hadn't the slightest idea what to do. Blaine sat down on a fallen log, forswearing wrestling with a dilemma which had mastered him. There wasn't anything for him to do. The world had changed, in one incredible day all had been swept away, so far as he could tell. He strove not to think of his family, where they were, whether they were. These ideas were now moot. The world had revolted against him and his kind, thrust them out, eradicated them or rendered them unnecessary, utilizing lurid and incomprehensible means to achieve its purpose. Why or how was altogether beyond him.

Blaine figured somebody was responsible. Yes, that had to be the defined cause. Things like this, he reasoned, don't just happen, can't just happen by themselves. It was all part of a plan, a deliberate scheme in which he and his fellows had not been consulted nor deemed worthy of consultation. It had to be like that. Natural laws don't reshape the grand design on their own. It takes a designer to do that.

All this, he deduced, was truly an act of God, or of some less compassionate entity, one who had had enough of man's reign and chose to teach him a lesson, or simply to put him out of the way; conversely, perhaps that unknowable one had merely grown bored and desired to shake up creation, put it back on a new or different track. Judgment or malice, the result was the same. Blaine knew, beyond doubt, that the old way had suffered destruction past redemption. Just like that, it wasn't there any more. That's the way it can happen, when somebody big is pulling the strings.

He asked himself, should I bow down or curse? Either response seemed pointless. The great orchestrator would have his way. Blaine had his, for so long as existence remained to him. He set out walking, and kept walking, determined to keep moving until the new world should swallow him up or discard him.

A Tale of Dyrezan

It is written in the book of Jacob Bleek that the wizards of fabled Dyrezan once faced a dire peril, one to threatened their fair city with destruction, and those wise and learned men confronted this peril, resolving it after their accustomed fashion with intelligence and vigor, and through their wisdom and foresight thus saved that noble city, guaranteeing its continued existence and glory for a span of years which should strike most as approaching eternity. It is a curious and revealing tale of those elder times, one which it pleases me greatly to present here in my own telling.

As I say, this story derives from Bleek, that reputed sorcerer of yesteryear, an ominous and grim old fellow if the legends gathered about his name be true, who made it his life's work to study and compile all the knowledge of the world and the universe (including much that is horrid or downright evil in content) for his own benefit. What he gained from his endeavors I know not, but he diligently transcribed the fruits of his immense scholarship in what has come to be styled his *Black Book*, and the literary products of his research continue to fascinate scholars, mainly those of an esoteric bent, who have followed in his footsteps; those who crave for themselves his supposed magical abilities, or those (such as myself) who would know more of those mysterious or even seemingly mythical periods of ancient history which have dropped out of the conventional textbooks, if indeed such knowledge ever found its way into those standard volumes. There exists a furtive, though reasonably professional, traffic in Bleek studies, and those of us who have buckled down to that difficult task consider ourselves enlightened and enriched by the experience.

Something must be said about the difficulties of utilizing Bleek's work, for it helps explains how I come to be telling this tale of Dyrezan. There exists no recognized, authoritative text of Bleek; his writings were never formally published during his lifetime, when such would have been possible, due to the secretiveness or indifference of that great wizard. After his death, whenever that was—a murky business at best, for there seems to be no definite record of the event in any annals of former times—what must have been the master copy of the *Black Book*, written in his own hand, was either lost or destroyed. The complete manuscript or manuscripts has never turned up, and at this late date it is unlikely to do so. What we having surviving to the present are extracts from this work, copies of portions made by especially favored colleagues of Bleek who visited him in life, or extracts prepared by Bleek, in his own crabbed hand, which he chose to send to certain of his wizardly correspondents. The latter tend to be highly interesting and suggestive yet uninformative, mere nuggets of tantalization, as if Bleek feared or refused to reveal the profound depths of his knowledge to potential competitors; while the former, on the other hand, tend to be longer and more focused on elements of intellectual magnitude and scholarly merit. There have been various attempts in the past to collate the numerous fragments, short or long, and thereby reconstruct the totality of the original work. These endeavors, some the products of many years' efforts, have all failed. Despite the discovery of considerable overlap among the circulating documents, we who care about such things have grown painfully aware that from all known fragments, however pieced together, we may derive only a crude outline, lightened in spots by flashes of detail, of Bleek's otherwise missing opus. The practical result of this is that individual researchers, academics and collectors, each "own" a part of the masterwork, and many of them have reported with pride on the unique elements, if any, that their cherished copies contain. For instance, a good friend of mine, a worthy gentleman by the name of Professor Anton Vorchek, a man of repute among students of the arcane and the uncanny, has in his private library a contemporary transcription encompassing over two hundred pages of choice material, which he located hidden away within the special collection of a private museum in Brugge. Vorchek has proved a gold mine of Bleek lore, not only due to his astute analysis of the text, but because he has thoughtfully chosen to publish that lengthy extract at his own expense.

I came by a lesser extract, from sources that I am not at liberty to disclose, a small piece of the Bleek puzzle running to a length of twenty-four folio manuscript leaves. The information these pages impart is not entirely novel; a goodly portion of the matters described parallels that found in Burton's synopsis of the 1860s, which most likely stems from a similar source, and there have been uncovered, previous to this time, other fascinating references to Dyrezan; now, however, within my document, we have in its entirety this particular and revealing tale of that great city which reigned supreme in the dim and glorious past of the human race.

It is that tale which I choose to tell, a story hailing, if Bleek be believed, from the wondrous heyday of that amazing city of wizards which flourished in the near forgotten dawn of man and civilization. Many ages ago the city was founded, and for long ages it existed where it was erected by the wise and clever magicians of an elder race who had delved into every secret of nature and supernature. As Bleek (our immediate contemporary by comparison) relates the ancient legend, the artful masters of the earth in those days had discovered a source of incredible mystic power, termed a "vortex," generated by what they held to be the Gateway of the Gods, through which those titanic Entities who govern all things in the universe come and go on Their mysterious rounds throughout the cosmos. This power the wizards learned to tap for their own ends, and they used it to build and maintain a city like none other in the world before or since.

Imagine, if you can, a city built and ruled by brilliant and noble wizards, a city fueled by the energy of the Gods, a city where to desire was to have, for with their knowledge and abilities nothing was denied to the masters of Dyrezan. Does not that sound something like a vision of paradise? Those who dwelt there apparently thought so. The mages fashioned for themselves a dazzling citadel of monumental architecture, a vast metropolis of towers, palaces, walls, monoliths, and statues cunningly wrought of granite and marble, of shining glass, of polished steel spun sheer as cobweb, whole structures faced with indestructible gold. All precious metals were employed in the construction; there were jewels as well, priceless gems inlaid into terraces and crowning spires that gleamed in the sunlight and twinkled like stars by the light of the moon; there were pavements of semi-precious stones, so common as to flag the streets and broad avenues; and yet it was gold that dominated the scene, gold flashing from every exposed surface and comprising the entire facade of the incomparable Temple of Truth, that magnificent domed edifice where even the proud, haughty minds of Dyrezan gathered to pray. Bleek informs us that Dyrezan was known as the City of Burning Gold, for as viewed from a distance (which, oddly, he claims to have done in a vision), from the proper vantage, at the precise moment of dusk when the rays of the sun struck at just the right angle, the whole city seemed to ignite into blazing golden fire. Such was the appearance of Dyrezan.

There is another wonder to add to the accounts of the place. The sorcerer architects, not content to make with their brains and their magic spells a city which reduces all others to insignificance, decided in their uncontested hubris to expend the Godly fuel of the vortex on a feature that would forever confound and amaze all who should pass to see or hear of it by report. By using—perhaps squandering is the better word—the power at their beck, they raised up from the earth all of Dyrezan, from the tops of its needle-like towers to its massive foundations, and flung it into the sky where, as they intended, it would hover majestically for all time, high above the curiously round and regular valley where its stones had first been laid. This they did, and so was born the Sky City of common lore, the basis of the story oft repeated and oft garbled in legends from all points of the globe. Great Dyrezan drifted as on a cloud, looming like a beautiful mirage in the air, while far below the circular valley, enclosed by a ring of jagged, forbidding peaks, was wholly given over to agriculture and animal husbandry in order to sustain the teeming and happy populace.

Oh, could there ever have been such a place? Does myth naturally fabricate wonders and fables because we need them to sustain ourselves, our hopes? That may be, but such is not the view of Jacob Bleek, who claims access to strange knowledge and who prefers, as he constantly insists, to report only verities. The stories of Dyrezan come down to us as fact; fact as those people of long ago knew it, fact as we can reconstruct it.

In the Golden Age of Dyrezan, so goes the tale I report, in that time long after the founding when life there was good and settled and dreamily serene, there lived a most remarkable mage by the name of Osthrakkias. To be acclaimed a wizard in the glory days of the Sky City was a marvel unto itself, for by any conventional criterion all the citizens, even the least, were adepts of the esoteric arts, but as ever in human affairs there were levels of quality and ability and virtue, just as there were many levels to the structure of the fair city. Osthrakkias was the wisest of the wise, the noblest of the noble, and he dwelt alone, with his books and his instruments, in a spacious apartment of several grand chambers atop the highest tower of that cloud-piercing skyline. Never was there a more respected man in all the annals of Dyrezan. His closest colleagues considered him the ultimate sorcerer, a man who could (and had) unraveled every incredible secret that came to his attention, perfecting spells of frightful power over which other worthies faltered. His friends considered him a font of dispassionate benevolence, a truly good man with a just and critical eye for the truth and loveliness and decency in all things and all men. The people considered him a reasonable and solicitous ruler, praising without fail his thoughtful decisions and pronouncements issued during those several occasions when he presided at the august meetings in the Temple of Truth, or dictated sense and wisdom from the marble halls in the Palace of the Eternal Court. All this he did, earning the esteem of his fellows, such that they gave the festive governance of the Chapel of Beauty perpetually over to his care. Never dwelt there a man so popular, unto the point of idolatry, as Osthrakkias.

Of brilliant mind and insights extraordinary, this Osthrakkias was wont to sit comfortably in his chambers, whiling away what free time he had from public or professional duties in the thinking of Deep Thoughts. He would disappear into his high apartment when he could, and when he emerged—when that moment did come—he invariably issued forth bearing in his celestial brain a Great Idea. The Idea was always something, in theory, enormously useful or penetrating, with the subsequent practice always proving him correct. Life was better for everyone because he produced his Ideas, and much cheer would greet the news that he was about to impart yet another. So it happened this time. Osthrakkias made known to those he favored, speaking directly to their minds from a great remove (for very good wizards could do such things as a matter of course), that he had developed an Idea, of the cleverest and most insightful sort, that he wished to formally present to them in council.

Word spread, as it will, of the intimation, and the folk rejoiced in the streets at every level of the city. People danced and caroused in unrestrained merriment, not just because Osthrakkias had formulated an Idea, but because they suspected that it touched upon a subject dear to the hearts of all. It had long been known, and discussed about the metropolis, that he had been pondering, with every spare minute at his disposal, the very nature of the cosmic Vortex itself, the fountain of mystic energy which comprised the life's blood of Dyrezan. Osthrakkias had sought to learn all that could be known on that matter of infinite importance, a matter which other large minds considered humanly exhausted. There was no more that could be learned about the Vortex, they pontificated, no more secrets fathomable by man, even through the cold and clear lens of unleashed sorcery. It could not be done. Only the Gods knew more that the reigning powers in Dyrezan, and They were not inclined to reveal more . . . and yet Osthrakkias announced an Idea.

The great portal opened upon the world where it did because the Gods commanded, and its properties were such as the Gods decreed, and that was the end of it, for the Gods did not submit to question or analysis, nor did anyone know much at all about Them, save for the general assumption that They were "out there," prone to decide and act for Their own ends; and yet Osthrakkias announced an Idea. The builders of the city had learn to tap the superfluous effluvia gushing from the Gateway, and since then the city had sailed the air and the lights had burned and magic become common coin, and no one could add to that; and yet Osthrakkias announced an Idea. What could it be? It must be something wonderful, even by the lofty standards of Dyrezan.

Osthrakkias called a council, and the cream of the select flocked to the central hall of the Temple of Truth on the appointed day to hear his words. None could guess exactly what he would say or what he might reveal, but they, betting on grand discoveries central to their lives, would rather have died than miss the show. Picture the scene, imagine those high walls of white and pink marble, the soaring, curving ceiling of gold under the vast dome, curious fixtures and *objet d'art* of glass through which pulsed strange flickering colors that weirdly illuminated the hall, and the semi-circles of delightfully comfortable chairs, wrought of finely worked stuffs acquired from far regions or conceived in magical laboratories, grouped about the dais which served as a speaker's podium, from which marble steps led up to the permanently flaring blue flame of the sacred altar. This is how I describe it to you, in my words, drawn from Bleek's account of the great day. He tells it differently, as ever, for the erudite wizard of a later age possessed an incongruous poetic bent, composing all of his *Black Book* in the manner of the poet. This makes telling the tale in his words a difficult and chancy enterprise. Investigators of the arcane tend to be lame litterateurs, nor do I except myself, poetic translation not being my strong point. I offer here, in narrative context, a taste of pure Bleek, as best I can manage. Some faults may be his, while most are surely mine:

See the wise ones in the Temple thronging
Drawn by new knowledge for which they're longing
Osthrakkias the Great will this day speak
Unto them granting the marvels they seek.
Marble halls enclosed within golden walls
Echoing to the shouts of sorcerers' calls
Where is the mind who will answer them true
Relating what once the Gods only knew?
Ghostly radiance reveals faces keen
Eager for verities they live to glean

The man emerges from out the curtain
Countenance steady, solemn, and certain.

Thus spake Bleek, and he goes on to do so for page after page of linked sonnets which, in sum, tell you what I condense into a paragraph or two. Soon I will publish the original as it stands, and all can read the tale in its intricate poetic glory. For now I return, without linguistic pomposity, to my version.

Osthrakkias arrived, passing out from, I presume, a draped room at the back of the hall, calmly mounted the dais, greeted his friends and colleagues in his kindly manner, and forthwith began to speak so that he might end the suspense. His researches, he said, had carried him far; covering in detail all old ground, in order to ensure that he missed nothing; calculating fields of force and energy levels as generated by the Vortex, the power which made their city possible; and studying its effects on human mentality (we would say "psychology" today, I think), especially that relating to the enhancement of magical abilities, which were known to be concentrated in Dyrezan like nowhere else in the world. During the course of his research he had noted a curious feature relevant to them all, one which had first entertained him, and then fascinated him with its logical implications.

He had uncovered a peculiar problem which originally formed a digression from his intended work, but which in time drew him to focus upon it to the exclusion of all else. He thought that he had mastered the problem, come to understand it and its ramifications, and out of his boundless love for the pursuit of truth he felt himself obligated to tell all. The analyses he would distribute later; for now, he offered essentials.

The issue before them, intoned Osthrakkias, dealt with the nature of the energy generation and utilization powering the city and, most importantly, maintaining it aloft in its ostensibly precarious position far above the curious valley of its birth. Of course they all knew from childhood the traditional answer (he nodded, acknowledging the murmurs and stirrings among his audience), that the founders had constructed great powerhouses fueled by magic which funneled the necessary energies where desired, thus creating the mighty force serving for all profane purposes. This beneficent task had been achieved far back in the mists of time, at an epoch so remote that those founders were often deemed demi-gods themselves, and since their mechanisms and spells had functioned flawlessly throughout the eons, no one had ever paid much heed to the processes involved, other than to note that they worked and were readily sustained. But how, he asked

34

the wizards in council assembled, did those processes work? What were the real world connections between the Vortex on the one hand, and the ancient machinery and incantations on the other, that drove the engine of Dyrezan and made the whole system go?

He, Osthrakkias, could tell them. He knew the answer now, had checked and double checked his findings, and could vouch for them He had revealed an answer so simple, so elegant, yet so unexpected, that he amazed even himself with his supreme cleverness. The founders of Dyrezan, those heroes of dim antiquity, in their cunning and through their enormous magical skills, created for all their descendants to come a grand illusion, a mental trick on a massive scale, not unlike, save in degree, the games of misdirection employed by false magicians of other peoples who practice in order to amuse and confound. The Vortex was not, per se, the energy source of the city. It enhanced the magic of the wizards, to be sure, and it heightened and enlightened their minds, definitely, but it did not—could not— produce the base, materialistic power needed in the real world.

The powerhouses, he explained, were a fraud, mere empty boxes and tubes and wheels of noise and motion, pleasing images run by trivial spells of a lingering form. They accomplished nothing of consequence other than to create belief in themselves, the belief that the mechanisms performed a valid task. The founders had thereby labored to create a mythic system of free power which would be maintained solely by the devoted, unthinking beliefs of the teeming, magically stimulated brains to come in all future generations. The people thought the lie (he used that word, according to Bleek) in their conscious minds, and in their dreams they accepted the lie without question. The dreams were everything, for there lay the real secret of Dyrezan's greatness; only a constant stream of blind, heartfelt dreams and the mindless beliefs they embodied could make Dyrezan live, thrive, and soar. In fact, Osthrakkias thundered, Dyrezan was upheld by nothing but dreams; in fact, by nothing!

There was commotion in the great hall, much spontaneous movement and an upwelling of confused and fretful noise. The gathered crowd of mighty minds did not react with glee, or warm approval, or quiet approbation to this amazing pronouncement of their hero Osthrakkias; indeed, there reaction proved quite otherwise, scarcely in tune with their responses to former revelations from the grand sorcerer. Harsh shouts arose from the milling throng, snide catcalls and grumblings, finger-pointings and even raised fists. Jacob Bleek describes the scene at delicious length, complete with hostile quotes from the lesser worthies present. One may question how our author-poet comes by the exact words, if they are meant to be such. I suspect that Bleek takes certain literary liberties, as the authors of former times were wont to do, in order to clarify the tale. One declaration, in the poet's rhyme, from a noble gentleman named Zaragor, sums up the intellectual distress of that moment.

Accord not to mental virility
That which reeks of rancid senility
A truth that defies all that well is known
And accepted by one cracked brain alone.

Clearly the respect felt by so many for the august scholar dwindled at a rapid rate. His supposed discovery antagonized his peers as could no other claim. Firstly, it flew in the face of tradition, by which so much of the ancient history of the land was retained; secondly, it seemed to conflict with reason, which truly did matter a deal to the wise minds of Dyrezan; thirdly . . . well, what if—yes—what if it were true? If by some grotesque chance Osthrakkias really had hit upon something, what would it mean to all concerned? The wizard claimed that only magic-cloaked, dream-inspired belief prevented the Sky City from tumbling to a horrific and messily final fate. What would be the result, cautiously whispered several of the attendant minds, of abjuring that belief and thereby suppressing those dreams?

Cooler heads recommended that Osthrakkias return to his books and his charts, recalculate his formulae and dissect again his evidence, perhaps taking a very long time at it, if necessary the rest of his life, however incredibly long that might be. This suggestion they advanced as a sort of friendly compromise. Osthrakkias would have none of it. I, for one, detect something rather unworldly in the character of that great fellow, an unwillingness or inability to grasp the magnitude of the hornet's nest he stirred up. Their notions he rejected with scorn, demanding that his findings receive customary scrutiny, that the results of the analyses be published to all as was long standing convention. That had always been the way, and it was his way still.

Not so for the majority of his audience, who were eventually forced by his obstinacy to unorthodox measures. Cabals and committees formed within the ranks, where ideas and possibilities were bruited, and ere long they reached a collective decision. Osthrakkias would be restricted, under guard, to his tower chambers, for the duration of what was now termed "the crisis." A panel of three would be elected to investigate the astonishing claim, keen men who would pore through the accumulated documents and diagrams of relevance, and who then, under conditions of extreme secrecy, would report their findings to the Grand Council in the Temple of Truth.

So was it done. Osthrakkias was led away, protesting the indignity visited upon his person and his brain, while three men were chosen to follow in his intellectual footsteps, men of minds not very inferior to that of the great man himself. They were Baldon, Malachet, and Yuregias, reputable scholars and noblemen, brilliant, cunning, and patriotic. They would uncover the facts in the case, and act rightly according to their results.

This they did. The complete notes of Osthrakkias they seized and conveyed to a sanctified chamber into which none might enter or even approach, save the chosen three of solemn dedication. They entered into that place, wise Baldon, Malachet, and Yuregias, and they commenced their crucial enterprise. While all without waited tensely through endless days, those men within studied, analyzed, discussed. They deciphered afresh the moldy documents of ancient times that first sparked the interest of Osthrakkias; they unraveled scrolls which contained hints of the forgotten knowledge of lost eras; they consulted charts engraved on plates of gold, charts portraying the strange linkages of energy and power which flowed from the Gateway of the Gods; they compiled data on and examined technical details of the weird instruments that, as all had presumed, tapped that flow; they broke down into logical components the aged network of spells which held together the system of their lives, and they recomputed equations of impossible complexity explaining, to the very wisest, the reality underlying all things. When all of this monumental study was complete they took to their beds and they slept, and they dreamed many dreams, and when they awoke they conferred among themselves and analyzed those dreams, and deduced many important insights therefrom. This they did and, having pondered long, one day the three strode forth, announcing to the Commander of the Guard that they desired to be taken at once to the Temple of Truth, there to make their report before the Assembly, and this was done.

The three were led into one of the great halls, where their audience of the wise and holy awaited them. Those many had waited long, with their breath held in their mouths, for all present knew how vital would be the result of the special report; and here, Bleek tells us, at this point something curious happened. I would expect (surely you would as well) a series of great speeches at this juncture, in which every man of knowledge and wisdom would deliver at sonorous length the fruits of his studious endeavors, or his earnest reaction to same. Nothing of

37

the sort occurred. The three wizards stepped up before the dais, encompassed by their seated brethren, and then Malachet stepped forth from his companions, held his head high, gazed directly into the staring eyes of the reigning Council Leader, and he—barely so, almost imperceptibly—nodded. As Bleek has it:

No grand wild rant solemn Malachet gave
For the method had been forehand arranged
No need to rock the hall with a mad rave
To confess truths abhorrent and deranged.

The Leader nodded once in return, the slightest inclination of his noble head, and with that all was known and acknowledged, and the three were dismissed. Yes, it had all been planned well, and no man present on that day would ever have to admit that any revelation of a startling nature had been passed on or established as verity. Officially nothing had happened, and with enormous and constant effort, unto the end of their lives, the members of the Council could publicly pretend that they had learned nothing of consequence, and perhaps, somehow, by a mighty effort, believe it even in their hearts.

And yet the monstrous truth had been confirmed, and none knew it so well as the devoted sorcerers Baldon, Malachet, and Yuregias, who had seen all and learned all. They knew that the wonderful mind of Osthrakkias had triumphed again, and that he spoke of naught but horrendous reality. Knowing this in their hearts, realizing now that they, in their newfound unbelief, were living contaminants within the healthy body of Dyrezan, they did that which they must do, and which they—honor them for their bravery!—had always accepted as a dire possibility. They could not allow themselves to infect others, so they betook themselves to the Chamber of the Sacrificial Fire, and they bowed down, each of them, and made their peace with their Gods, and each of them, one at a time, stepped into the sacred and ever-burning Fire, there immolating themselves to the eternal glory of their names.

Not so easy, nor so willingly accepted, was the fate of Osthrakkias. If the three who had, so to speak, studied under him were lost causes, then as you can surely imagine he had absolutely no chance at all. Osthrakkias had to die, and there must be nothing about his end noble or poignant to excite the fancy or the reverence of the people: no ringing final speech, no dramatic poses. A battery of stern and powerful wizards gathered at his door, and they directed inward cruel spells that robbed him of his sorceric strength. Then armed men rushed into his chambers, and they dragged out that old man, he protesting and feebly struggling; yet they heard him not, for those grim-faced men had been ordered to stop their ears with wax, lest they hear what they should not; and they hauled him unceremoniously, very much against his will, to the highest rampart on the edge of the city overlooking the rim of the metropolis, where one could look out upon the emptiness far, far down to the distant surface of the earth below; and without formality or concern for the dignity of his last moments, they cast him from that precipice, and he plunged screaming to his death. When that had been done the pitiless wizards, who had stood at a remove during this operation, approached the rampart, and they as with one mind willed a gigantic ball of fire to appear, and spin among the clouds, and to dive down like a flaming meteor to the spot where the body had impacted, and there the fireball struck, obliterating all traces as it tore a smoldering crater in the ground. That was all. The masters of the city vouchsafed no public mourning for the great man, no eulogies, no condolences to the heirs; as a matter of policy he vanished as if he had never been, and in all the ages to come few would dare admit openly that such a man ever existed. Thus ended the life of Osthrakkias.

In this fashion was Dyrezan saved, and the dreams of the happy citizenry remained wholesome and sustaining, and so endured the magical city of the skies. While official remembrance of the deed was forever forbidden, the tale was long whispered, and somehow the story survived down to the day of Jacob Bleek, who records it in his poetic, yet detached and clinical manner. Bleek, ever the seeker of truth, professes to disparage the deed, doing so for reasons that, I can well believe, would not have impressed the elders of that olden world.

Those wise mages held Dyrezan so dear
That it drove them to a violent act
Virtue they derived from their gloomy fear
Crimes against mind they committed in fact.
Thus they conspired to uphold a false dream
Justified by their desire to survive
As it has been ever, so it would seem
Morality from need do men derive.
But as wizards to Truth dedicated
Should not reality they have embraced?
Honor they would not have denigrated
Had their city been forever erased.
Dyrezan is a trifling price to pay
For the triumph of mind; this I do say.
The men who ruled the great city of Dyrezan, disagreed.

Bleek tells us one more thing. Though remembrance of the event was sternly hushed, one of those wizards did that which expressed the prevailing wisdom of the age, and which was well understood by those of that day who knew or guessed what had been done for their sakes. He emblazoned above the portico of the Temple of Truth a bold inscription in words of fiery gold, where all of the devout and the studious could read them, and the inscription read: IN THE NAME OF WHATEVER GODS THERE BE, LET MEN DREAM IN PEACE.

The Dwellers in the Black Forest

Jacob Bleek, keen-minded student of obscure and mystic lore, sought the hidden house of Helvetius, that canny sorcerer with whom Bleek had crossed swords many years before. Helvetius came to a bad end on that occasion in Heidelberg, when he thought to best his younger competitor, yet before he strangely perished the older man had boasted much of the arcane marvels secreted in his other residence far from the city, prying eyes, and inconvenient questions. He bragged of scrolls stolen from ancient and exotic tombs, musty books handed down through countless generations in return for grisly fee; of magic, spells of revelation and power, hoarded by that wizard for his private benefit, wisely hidden from unimaginative authority, nor ever revealed to inquisitive colleague. He hinted also of a greatest treasure, a compilation of outrageous mysteries from a source lost to history, which he never would reveal. Through all the years of his journeys Jacob Bleek remembered, and when in the fullness of time he passed that way again he sought that house, which he hoped to find untenanted and unmolested.

Fortune ought to favor him, if the Helvetius of long ago spoke true. He had lived alone, having no family, making no friends, shunning neighbors. Smugly he had cackled of his devoted bond servants, who should obey him so long as he existed; but with Helvetius dead this age in the life of man his servants had surely since departed. A lonely house, therefore, unoccupied, with esoteric wonders doubtless cleverly concealed, made for Bleek a tantalizing attraction.

Locating it, however, gave him a devil of trouble. He guessed it lay somewhere across the big river in the depths of the Black Forest—supposed this, for Helvetius had at intervals absented himself into that gloomy fastness—but no map nor kindly direction marked the spot. Also, the old mage routinely took steps to ensure that his covetous fellows did not follow him to his retreat. Bleek knew well of this, too. Once he bribed a desperate and daring acolyte to stalk the skillfully furtive Helvetius to his lair. The next morn Bleek found the hired man on his doorstep, in three separate bags.

Of course now, eventually, Jacob Bleek found the house. The pale-faced scholar in his dark cloak and broad-brimmed hat traveled about the margins of the Black Forest, artfully inquiring in the rude villages that gingerly encroached upon that region, scarce trammeled since the bygone era when the bold legions of Rome foundered therein and met grim destiny. The villagers proved singularly unhelpful, averring that all the forest was unlucky, its remotest recesses positively haunted. He derived one clue from a timid burgher who whispered of a particular woodland path considered especially dangerous. No one, he said, no one in his wits that is, ever trod that trail by night, and its unpopularity carried over to such hours as the sunlight thinly trickled through the crowns of the densely clustered oaks. Bleek noted the area, focused there his search.

Success, via unexpected good luck, came to him in the form of an itinerant merchant, a Herr Katzmann, who fell in with Bleek in the tavern at Holgard. Herr Katzmann, who peddled trinkets of blown glass in pretty colors, fulminated at the necessities of business, which required him to risk a treacherous short-cut through the forest that he might attain his markets on the schedule demanded by regular customers. Bleek cared nought for the man's difficulties, treating him with short humor until, over his second stein, he said, "And if night fall with me still on that road, where am I to stay? I must then find lodgings as I can under the ghostly boughs, or worse still in that abandoned manor of stone, where it is death to go."

Bleek, suddenly the convivial sort, paid another round of ale, threw down a gold piece for a shared meal, and quizzed at length the seller Katzmann. "Aye, the house of a lord it may have been in its day, though be that twenty or a hundred years ago I cannot tell. It has seen better days, but it has a roof over it, and I avoid it only because the folk here-about call it cursed. I reckon they would know. What is it to you, sir?"

Bleek, without hesitation, concocted a complex lie to justify his interest, a tale involving lost patrimony, neglected holdings, opportunities for sale. Herr Katzmann perked up at the news. "On my own I would shun the place, but in company with a well-spoken gentleman such as yourself I could retain my courage. Do not terrors come to the solitary? It is so in story books. Master Bleek, I know the way. If you promise to stick by me, I will lead you to your goal."

The deal done, they drank a health, took rooms for the night, set out on the morn, Bleek on his pony with his few possessions, Herr

Katzmann trudging alongside his ass, heavily laden with a carefully packed trunk of trade goods. The forest swallowed them. Beyond Holgard they ventured into a region of gloom, of fat and untended trees never cut within living memory; spreading, leafy crowns that battled a timid sun; dank hangings of grayish moss. Dampness in the air beaded on leaves and bark, while a turgid creek trickled listlessly over stones and fallen branches by the wayside of the wretched road. That road inclined to shirk its duty to the travelers, conspiring rather to dwindle to scarce a sodden foot-path which would block a cart, so overgrown was it with pressing growth, meandering at whiles as if it debated toward which cardinal point it desired to lead them. Yet it continued, never quite fading away (though Jacob Bleek surmised that a few years more would seal this breach into the wilderness), in due course taking them to the verge of an expansive clearing.

At the approach Herr Katzmann gasped a choking cry, pointed into a particularly tangled thicket and said, "Something there moves, Master Bleek. I like not that." Bleek too having seen the vague signs of life, peered intently through the brush, made out little detail before the uncertain forms eluded vision. Said he that he styled them human, opining that Gypsies might use the forest to pass among their secretive camps. Herr Katzmann dolefully accepted this explanation, adding however, "I did not think to see another man or men here, nor am I cheered by the revelation. Dark woods lend themselves to dark deeds."

Bleek privately agreed with this estimate, which overall satisfied him, if the dark deeds be his own, nor did he fear passersby who scuttled off with such alacrity. Whatever the case, he cared not, for before them stood the house, surely the manse of Helvetius. Within a small, low-walled park it rose, two stories of weathered gray stone, dilapidated, unbeautiful but strong, its oak-shingled roof intact, a modest fortress against time and the elements, its door closed and windows shuttered. Bleek and his companion pushed aside the rusted iron gate, led their mounts through the vined wall into the enclosure, there to let them wander and freely graze on the weedy herbage once a yard.

The door to the house, oddly enough, was not fastened after all. It hung very slightly ajar, a curious sign on its heavy panels establishing to Bleek the identity of the former owner. Herr Katzmann instinctively recoiled in loathing from this inscribed image, but Bleek only laughed at the man's reaction—he knew well that sign, and what it conferred to the adept—shook the dirt of the journey from his black cloak and led the way into the building. Time had not stood still in that dusty, cobwebbed hall, nor within the musty, dank chambers beyond. All furnishings remained fairly intact, with little evidence of visitation since the final departure long ago of its mysterious denizen. That evidence consisted of scattered episodes of disorder, as if beasts of the forest had gotten loose indoors to browse and scratch at things. They beheld the worst mess in the kitchen, where shelves had been rifled, packages torn open and dispersed, a layer of litter left to congeal or rot on the tiled floor. That was not a wholesome place, although a few bottles of wine, of rare vintage, stood untouched in a closet. Better was the main living hall, a kind of den graced with decrepit furniture of once fine make, and a cavernous fireplace with logs stacked conveniently by. Herr Katzmann undertook to create there heat and light, and to prepare a meal from their carried resources. Jacob Bleek searched.

In that room he found nothing of note, save for a promising inscription in barbaric Latin over the mantel. On the wall panels of the corridors and lower rooms he spied occasional notations of the arcane, daubed spirals and starbursts and stylized eyes which hinted at sorceric wisdom without revealing any. A climb up disturbingly sagging stairs took him to the dead wizard's former bed chamber, then to a large store-room filled with dusty rubbish, antique objet d'art of peculiar and alarming cast, and an odd quantity of broken and splintered bones. These pitiful, yellowed items were obviously human, and while Bleek could conjecture certain unlawful reasons for their presence, it puzzled him that they should be so carelessly strewn. Whether plucked surreptitiously from the grave or snatched living from city street by night, proper experimentation by an accomplished mage would not leave behind the sordid remnants as refuse. Also, Bleek doubted the age of this osseous debris. The bones still attracted a dubious population of nasty scavenging insects. He pondered this for some time before he ventured on.

The final chamber of the upper floor, an octagonal room with a single round window which rose up a short walk-way into a small tower, gave him hopes for what he sought, for this was surely the magical chamber of the mighty Helvetius. Hideous carvings and painted scrawls in hieroglyphics festooned the walls; dusty apparatus of steel and crystal adorned the massive table; and many moldy books crammed the shelves. A lamp on a stand retained some moisture of fuel. Bleek lighted this, surveyed the literary morsels before him. A few bindings told much, ginger openings of others more. Here lay the secrets of Helvetius.

Better say, a selection of them, nor the most noteworthy. Cabalistic treatises, transcripts from the more virulent wings of Greek or Egyptian philosophy were well enough for the common wizard, but Helvetius had progressed beyond those at an early stage of his august career. There was more to uncover, the really appalling stuff that divided wolves from sheep. Even in his own house careful Helvetius did not take chances. Perhaps he forbade visitors, but there was his bygone staff of servants to consider, who must never be exposed to the wild profundity of his deepest arts. Bleek reasonably guessed that the real prizes remained hidden.

The crumbling shutters opened at the touch, the streaked glass pane with a shriek, and Jacob Bleek peered out the window across the neglected lawn to the impenetrable murk beyond the high wall smothered in unchecked growth. He felt a stirring of dismay as he again detected, now in failing light, furtive movement out there, just at the limit of vision, as if a numerous crew were on the move slowly circling the estate. He thought once more of Gypsies, wished for more thorough validation of that conclusion. It was passing strange that anybody should tarry in this neighborhood. He cautioned himself to maintain the security of the abode this night.

He rejoined Herr Katzmann, already eating his stew. Bleek ate sparingly. His companion said, "We thrive better than I expected. Walls of stone, a strong door I've locked with an iron bar, a warm fire and wine, lamps, candles in plenty; cozy we are, and up to now no ghosts to annoy us." He added jocularly, "I promise not to call them, if you do the same". Bleek averred that he did not expect visitation by ghosts. Herr Katzmann irritated him with constant small talk concerning the house, its lands, and what they meant to Bleek, who tossed off casual lies in few words while he brooded. A ghastly ululation interrupted their one-sided intercourse.

"What is that?" cried Herr Katzmann. "The souls of the damned?" Indeed those sounds were dreadful, that howling, wailing, and—yes—that growling. Those tones possessed an unpleasantly human quality, but insufficiently human, which rendered them that much more unpleasant. Bleek immediately advised checking the door and all ground floor windows. The merchant scampered to obey. Shortly they verified that they were sealed inside. Glances through the windows showed nothing. The outer noises soon subsided, but nerves stretched taut within.

"Master Bleek, who is out there? What do they want? They can't

45

be robbers, not in this lonely place, nor do real men, be they godly or knave, bark like the creatures that perish. I fear that the dead walk, craving our company." Bleek helped him to wine from the household stock, assured Herr Katzmann that spirits lay quiet there (thinking to himself that he should know, that his honed senses would warn him), yet admitting an uncertain peril lurked near. He recommended a wisely staggered schedule of watching and sleeping, each man standing guard in turn while the other rested. Herr Katzmann retorted, "My eyes are wide, my nerves unstrung. I stand this first watch. You sleep, if you can."

That is what Jacob Bleek did, but only after strictly admonishing Herr Katzmann to maintain his own wakefulness. Bleek did not know what went on out there. He hoped to complete his business by the morrow, and then get far away, that he need not deal with nebulous threats. So he lay himself down on a sofa before the fire, and in time he did sleep.

He got two hours for his efforts, if that. His companion waked him, in a fearful state. "I have heard them again," he moaned, "this time snuffling at the door, and the cries of our animals, too, in extremis. The saints preserve us! These fiends lust after our souls."

Bleek could not deny the seriousness of the situation, nor the foolishness of continued slumber. He rose, enjoined Herr Katzmann with resting if he might, resolved to investigate again from the windows, those on the second floor this time. He left his fellow man, who seemed in no mood for rest, to his own devices, scaled the stairs by candle and opened in turn the windows of the various rooms. If he sought minimal information, then what he saw might have cheered him; if edification, then he was doomed to disappointment. Beings of a sort there were out there, crouching near the house or flitting along the walls. They walked on two legs, but that was the extent he could discern of their humanity. The pony and the ass he did not see, unless those two dark, sprawled heaps indicated their sad lot. Bleek shut the windows after these sequential examinations, debated his next move. He wanted the secrets of Helvetius, his paramount goal. Disregarding the mounting danger, he repaired to the magical chamber, there to undertake a thorough hunt for arcane materials or clues to their location.

The weightiest matters might be concealed within covers of a nondescript tome, or mingled with magical wares, or secreted inside a hidden alcove. Jacob Bleek plumbed these several possibilities, and more, by light of the dying lamp, relying on the experience of his own

46

inventiveness to steer him to success. A minute brass stud on the floor beneath the big table yielded to the firm pressure of his boot. He heard a click behind him; a small section of shelving swung open. Inside the exposed dark cavity he spied a book; only the single one, but a hefty volume, immensely aged in appearance, bound in unusual leather. Bleek drew out the book, held it to the light. The unlettered binding felt dry, rough, not at all like conventional hide. He cracked it open to the first page, perused that inscribed there by a crabbed hand in age-old script. He muttered passages at random, including the bold heading, which read—so he hastily translated—*The Wisdom of Azamodias*. Jacob Bleek sighed, his breath rasping. He knew of this document by report, via mystic sources. It was an incredible find. He clasped in his hands the great secret. He had triumphed.

The voice called to him, "I did not prophecy that it would be you, Jacob Bleek, to disturb my rest." Bleek started, peered past the lamp at the shape which sat dimly at table. His hackles raised, Bleek sensed the intrusion of the arcane. He narrowed his eyes. Could it be? He demanded of this visitant its identity.

"Yes, it is I, Helvetius, whom you slew by a trick, when I thought to trick you to your destruction." To be sure it was he, goatish, harsh and cruel of face, exactly as he had been in life. "'Twas a pretty ploy, to send me down into hellish spheres while I teased you with my certain victory. It amazes me that we meet again.

"As are you, Master Bleek? Quite so, sir. I thought my secrets safe unto distant future eras, never dreaming that it would be you to defile my mental tomb. Let there be no mystery between us. A portion of my essence, resulting from decades of stern devotion, adhered to the weird substance of this book which holds the lore of our great antecedent Azamodias. I knew that its revelation to another brain, be it in a day or an eternity, would drag me forth from the pit. A brief meeting this shall be, yet one wholly agreeable to me. Your intellect, your imagination must recoil from the truths I have unwillingly learned beyond the pale of mortal body and stale reality.

"What want I of you? Nothing, my dear sir. My powers are lost to me. I do not threaten. Perhaps I do savor your discomfiture. Oh yes, I sense what goes on. For you these are trying moments. Danger approaches, of a species you do not as yet grasp. Those outside want in. Good Bleek, you ask me that? Surely you know them. I told you of old. They are my servants, loyal so long as I exist.

"You assumed, did you, that they dispersed with my passing? A foolish error, Bleek, mayhap as lethal as my own when last we

47

heroically contested. You should know by now that wizards never utterly perish. Something lingers, and fealty endures.

"I could not keep snoops about me, so I kept my servants low, twisting lightly their minds with my arts, and training them like beasts, that they might obey without comprehension. Brilliantly I succeeded. They descended the ladder of life, became somewhat less than man, while retaining more abilities than the creeping brutes of the wilderness. They dwell out there still, protecting, guarding. Nowadays they fend for themselves, acting according to rote. I commend to you the matter of diet. These dwellers of the forest, my dedicated servants, must eat, nor did I teach them to be choosy. Their instilled inclinations stood me in good stead when the unwelcome came calling."

A hideous scream tore up from the level beneath Bleek's feet. Helvetius crowed, "They have found egress at last. The old tunnel, I discern, which I had built for my own unobserved passage. Wisps of memory still motivate them. They are inside, Bleek. Pray to the Dark Gods. Take the book. Clutch it to your bosom, as they gnaw your flesh down to the bone!" Helvetius mocked with a polite nod, and vanished.

Jacob Bleek acted swiftly. He took down from the wall a pitch torch, enflamed it with the burning dregs of the lamp, sallied with that and the fateful book into the corridor, then down the stairs. Below he increasingly made out the frightful noise of snarling, snapping, feasting, and he steeled himself for what he must see, what he must do. He came to the door of the main lower chamber.

The fire had burned low. He saw mostly by torch light. There crowded the denizens of the forest, clad in pathetic and shredded rags, a dozen or more, engaged in the dismembering and devouring of the late Herr Katzmann. So much had Bleek been forewarned, or logic entailed, yet it was not this gruesome confirmation that staggered him. It was, rather, the aspect of the ravenous creatures that shocked.

Human they may once have been—they, or their fathers—but these dwellers in the Black Forest, these forsaken servants of Helvetius or their spawn, had deteriorated into things uncanny and unclean, repulsive shamblers with grotesquely manlike features protruding from unnaturally hairy faces. Their ruthless master had conjured strangely and well, creating for his cruel utility these nightmarish horrors, horrors that tarried abominably on Earth long after their prime necessity had ended. Now they turned from the red, sodden wreckage on the floor, their forms thin and wiry, hairy and befouled with gore; flexed their lips to show crimsoned fangs, and advanced.

48

Jacob Bleek bellowed in terrified rage and mortification, roared out a mystical curse that called upon the most vengeful demons, thrust at his attackers the blazing torch. They shrank back, barking like wolves at the flame, and he deduced their instilled or adopted dread of fire; recalled, too, that they had made no overt move by day. So it seemed to his generous hopes, but they did not flee, instead attempting to edge at him from the sides, the mark of savage cunning.

Beyond them he quickly noticed a yawning opening in the floor, where a trap had been raised near the fireplace; the tunnel of which Helvetius' shade spoke, through which they gained surprising access to Bleek's unfortunate traveling acquaintance. Wherever it led, that passage might have been on the Moon for the good it did him. The house's door, as well, was barred by the maddened, frothing monsters. Bleek backed up the stairs, reached the upper level. The creatures crept after him in a body, seething up the steps as a fleshy, furry mass.

He bought time by torching the frayed tapestries in the hall at the top of the stairs, dashed into the old bedroom, slamming the door behind, barring it, spun about to reconnoiter. If Bleek were to escape, he must do so by the window, a difficult drop to the ground, which thankfully should be soft. He scrutinized the means at hand, freed his fingers to tear thick strips from the bed clothes. These he wove together. His activity grew frantic as furious thudding commenced at the door. He feared their animal strength, feared too the stench of smoke which informed him that his carelessly set fire had spread. The creatures behind the thin panel howled in dismayed anger, but they kept after him with mindless determination. Smoke roiled in black puffs from beneath that door, choking him.

Bleek thrust open the window, gasping for air, played out the makeshift rope which he had tied to the bedstead. He cast the torch onto the bed, propelled himself onto the sill and, juggling as best he could the prize volume, started down. He heard the door crash open or break apart, and hardly had his head dipped below the outer sill than slashing claws raked his hat from his scalp. He let the book fall, and dangling by one hand reached into his cloak for his dagger to hack at those hideous fingers. They drew back, accompanied by grunts of pain. He slid down the rope as fast as safety would allow, and then some, landing hard.

He bounced, crawled to the book, scooped it up and sprang to his feet. His shadow wavered before him. A backward glance told him that the entire structure of the house had ignited. Bright flames shot from the roof, gushed out the bedroom window, began breaking out in other places. Bleek made for the darkness of the forest, where he might lie in concealment until the dawn. He reckoned that a reasonable plan, until the awkwardness of his position quickly came clear. The hungry creatures streamed from the burning building, repelled by the inferno, but once into the darkness beyond they came into their element again. Certain feral specimens spotted him, took up the pursuit. Bleek dived into a cluster of bushes, bit his lip while the hungry things milled about. Others joined them. They stooped, sniffing and snuffling and pawing at the dirt, then bounded up with a howl to rush directly at him. Bleek lunged away, making a mad dash toward the fiery, sparkling mass that marked the inevitable ruin of Helvetius' abode.

Thus wise Jacob Bleek spent the remainder of a harrowing night, weaving desperately between the glowing furnace of the disintegrating house, crouching under the wall where the creatures' dread of fire and distaste for light temporarily shielded him from attack, and the outer limits of the scrubby clearing, finding himself rapidly cornered whenever he made move to seek sanctuary under the benighted trees. Finally he gave up and squatted helplessly as near to the searing heat as life allowed. Even there the bolder of his adversaries attempted sporadic approach, animated by appetite and old habit to destroy he whom they might seize with claws and teeth. Bleek stolidly fended them with his dagger. In the meantime the house caved in, showering hurtful sparks, and toward dawn its protective light dwindled alarmingly. He attempted to employ his own esoteric skills against the foe, but his knowledge of peculiar lore applied to astral delvings or magical weapons against normal men. The indeterminate nature of the creatures baffled him. Nothing he could devise under such circumstances seemed to check their ferocity, much less put them down. When the early sun began to stab through the trees and flood the clearing, Bleek calculated that his life hung by a strand of minutes.

With the sun, though, his tormentors lost interest, or their bestial fears trumped their carnivorous desires. They melted back into the eternal shadows of the forest, leaving Bleek alone with the smoldering cinders and steaming piles of toppled stone. He survived, with his cloak singed, his recovered hat charred. He had the book, the choice secret of Helvetius.

Jacob Bleek vacated what was left of the premises with supreme haste. He did not relish the company of the dwellers in the Black Forest, be they sub-human creations or the mocking ghost of Helvetius. Even the thought of Herr Katzmann distressed him. Too

50

bad about him—and his customers who must brace themselves for sore disappointment—but in this magic-soaked ground even that poor fool's spirit might awaken to annoy. Surely Bleek must abscond on the instant, for menace lurked still, and many miles of wild and perilous terrain lay between him and safety. It would not do to be caught under these woods, on the lonely trail, another night. That would push luck a little too far.

On the other hand, this excursion had served him well. Should he escape, Jacob Bleek swore to raise a glass to dear old Helvetius, when he came to the first inn of his continuing journey.

The Advent of the Exterminators

Extermination Fleet Seven is currently warping into orbit around the designated planet, the world apparently styled "Earth" by its denizens. I have delivered the necessary commands. Scout ships already assume positions at strategic points above the globe, as well as in the vicinity of the single moon. Destruction Teams take up stations, quality control units even now finishing their check of all weaponry and instrumentation. With all systems in operational readiness, we are prepared for whatever transpires.

It was a simple matter to home in on the radio beams by which these beings unintentionally revealed their existence and location. Earlier doubts as to the likelihood of life thriving in this thinly scattered stellar sector proved groundless. Based on the transmission intercepts, the expedition was organized on the probability that we would face no more than Class Three intelligence and civilizational status. No signals that we detected during the voyage have served to alter this conclusion.

Preliminary reports are coming in from outlying areas. As previously determined, the other planets of this star system are lifeless, of no interest to us. It is with mild surprise that I now learn that this world's satellite is also unoccupied. It is a fairly large planetoid in its own right, and quite close to the mother planet, but all biological indicators read negative. That is good, if unexpected, for it will save a great deal of time and assure the result at one stroke. It appears that we will be able to focus the full efforts of our special action upon Earth.

***

Analysis completed. This Earth is an amazing world. The depth and richness of its biosphere, and the sheer size of its biomass, are staggering. Such a find comes along only once in a lifetime, and I am especially proud to be in charge, here, at this time, of such a project. All scouts have been called in, all information collated and double checked for accuracy. Despite the magnitude of the task before us, there will be no errors.

We confront a geologically active planet, with large, fertile

52

continental crusts and even larger, equally fecund oceans. The extent of the seas is inconceivable. I do not believe there is anything like it on record. For the purposes of giving rise to biological forms, this planet's structural development approaches 100% efficiency. In addition, its upper layers contain the complete range of atomic elements, and a bewildering variety of chemical and mineral combinations. This situation has clearly obtained for billions of years, and has well set the stage for the growth of the world's living systems.

Life has developed on Earth to an unprecedented degree. Every square inch of its surface swarms with animate entities, in every imaginable shape and size. It harbors a profusion of plant life, and legions of creeping things which feed upon it and each other. Some forms have taken to the air, and it is deduced that many kinds have burrowed deep into the soil, which is remarkably rich in places. Within the oceans, unique biotic environments in their own right, life thrives in abundance. The largest mobile types have been found in their depths. All in all, my experts estimate that millions of millions of species make their homes on this planet. Word has already spread, and there is much excitement among the crews. More than ever before, they are looking forward to this mission.

For the record, our final survey of this world's higher species accords with earlier expectations. The warm-blooded bipedal variety combines moderate mental faculties with impressive manual dexterity. Globally they seem loosely organized, but at the local level exhibit tightly knit social structures. Mechanical creation, architectural erection, and terrain alteration are concentrated in relatively limited areas, although spread across much of the globe. There are facets of interest in all this, but nothing out of the ordinary. These beings pose neither a threat, nor even a hindrance, to our upcoming operations.

Energy banks are fully charged and optimized. Stage One commences.

   ***

Our assault forces are in motion. Stage One is fully under way. Preliminary moves knocked out all orbiting satellites. At A-Hour strike units entered the atmosphere and proceeded to crush what passes on this planet for military resistance. Known targets were quickly dispatched; all sites which could be detected from space have been reduced to smoldering wreckage. Of course this galvanized the natives—who were already aware of our presence, judging from their ignored attempts to make radio contact—to unleash their defensive weaponry against us. Missiles rose into the air in enormous numbers, along with various sorts of armed, piloted craft. These we destroyed. Some fell back onto the surface, causing damage. Subsequently, lesser quantities would appear at intervals, all meeting the same fate, and in the process the launching sites have been precisely identified and obliterated.

Within the span of one revolution of this world, it appears that every form of weapon capable of long-range action has been eradicated. At the moment we are going after the absurdly large ground forces, which possess only limited aerial combat value, but which might constitute a nuisance factor. They are being atomically strafed. This will continue only until their organizations are broken. Some random smashing of cities is in progress, solely in areas of major military concentrations. For obvious reasons, we need not spend much time on those.

Assault forces will shortly return to the base ships. They will remain on temporary stand-by, merely as a precaution. Our casualties, as predicted, are nil.

***

Stage Two begins. The Destruction Teams have been unleashed. In their swarms they cruise the skies of Earth, spraying flame-gas into the upper atmosphere. This is approved regulations technique for oxygen-rich environments. The heavy gas rapidly descends and ignites on contact with the air. As it falls it reaches the layer of denser oxygen, where burning speeds up tremendously. Even minute quantities of flame-gas prove sufficient to set off a chain reaction of combustion, and we have more than enough to get the job done.

As I watch from my vantage point in orbit, I see vast arching draperies of red, yellow, and blue flame blazing into view and drifting toward the surface. Where those fantastic ribbons of writhing colors strike, spontaneous detonation of all combustible materials occurs. On the side of the planet facing the sun, great white and gray clouds boil up from the land masses. On the dark side, the lights of the cities are winking out, yet an orangish glow spreads. Through the telescope I can discern more detail where the smoke doesn't conceal. The cities are burning. Forests are crackling masses of fire. Agricultural regions smolder and blacken. Hour by hour the inferno creeps outward, or erupts in fresh territories.

Throughout this phase, no attempts at opposition have been reported, nor need any be expected as processing continues. I shall commend the assault units.

The ships are now returning to the fleet, but the Destruction

Teams are not quite finished. After servicing, their gas canisters will be exchanged in preparation for their next action. So far, so good. My experts tell me that 60% of the terrestrial surface is on fire or already charred, and more will go in due course. They also inform me that a possible one third of the macroscopic biological forms have perished. The oxygen level of the atmosphere has been reduced from approximately 21% to 12%, and may fall as low as 9% without a further spraying of flame-gas. A second treatment will not be necessary. The Teams may move on to their next task.

***

Stage Three: the Destruction Teams return to action. This time the sub-orbital wings are spraying poison gas. Not as impressive a spectacle, perhaps, but very sure. The wispy tendrils of vaporous yellow mist sink down through the air, diffusing in all directions. The gas settles and lingers in the low places, rendering avoidance strategies difficult. This powerful anti-biologent agency has a corrosive effect on the nervous systems and cellular structures of most carbon-based entities. The more highly organized the specimen, the more devastating the effect. A special formulation, of extreme toxicity, is being dumped in huge quantities into the oceans. This substance not only kills on contact, but also quickly transforms the H_2O into a substance incapable of sustaining the indigenous life.

By the time the gas has done its work, there should be very little left alive on this planet. If, for whatever reason, we were in a hurry, this latest action might be deemed sufficient, at least for now, by Headquarters. We are, however, on schedule, and I fully intend to complete the mission before we leave here.

It is with great regret that I must report one unfortunate incident. During the loading of the poison canisters one Team member, due to an accident, suffered slight damage to a tertiary appendage, likely the result of careless handling. Having read the medical report, I am confident that he will fully recover in time to fulfill his duties. I may deliver another lecture on safety issues. This minor procedural blemish in no way detracts from the luster of our achievement.

***

The Earth has turned four times since the poisoning began, as Stage Four begins. The robot investigation drones prowl the surface, searching for pockets of intelligent resistance hidden within the debris. Hunter squads follow in their wake, well shielded from the deadly environment, ready to pounce at the first sign of trouble. Nothing of an alarming nature has been discovered. Not a single native radio source continues transmitting. Traces of surviving organisms turn up periodically, including a handful of the sentient type, but not such as to interfere with the final phases of the operation. We approach the end.

***

With the completion of the robotic analysis comes Stage Five, the grand finale. It is a tense, awesome, and glorious moment. At my spoken command the massed batteries of Extermination Fleet Seven open up on the world below. Thousands of Planet Buster cannon blast in unison, sweeping the entire surface of the globe with their ferocious hail of explosive, highly radioactive projectiles. The Earth glimmers and twinkles like a tired, flickering red sun. Continents crumble; the seas boil. Fiery magma spouts from a million craters. Then an inky black shroud slowly covers all, somewhat illuminated by the raging holocaust beneath. The batteries continue to fire, and will do so for another revolution. By then the planetary crust will be thoroughly pulverized, right down to bedrock and beyond, hopelessly contaminated with long lasting radioactive materials. Nothing can survive this storm.

***

I officially announce the conclusion of Operation Earth. No more remains to be done. This has been a perfect, textbook procedure, the results everything I could desire. I commend all of those involved in this splendid undertaking, and trust that there will be personal rewards to spare for each participant. There should be warm satisfaction at Headquarters when I report. The facts are plain. This planet is dead, a smoking ball of fumes and wreckage. Within the range of certainty of our scientific instruments, I can state with confidence that all life, right down to the microbial level, is extinct. None of the sentient inhabitants managed to escape. The damage wrought upon the biosphere is such that little possibility exists of life ever regaining a foothold here. We have faithfully and diligently performed our duty.

We shall shortly return to base, perhaps for a deserved rest, or—more likely—to receive orders for a new assignment. I am in the process of issuing the standard statement, to the affect that Earth now possesses no value of any kind, and is of no further interest to us. It should not be approached in future. I formally declare this useless world off limits.

The Mud King

Captain Roeder, at the head of a company of battle-chewed German auxiliaries, had taken station outside Vyazma at the end of summer, performing banal occupation duty while the great Napoleon, leading his invincible legions, swept onward into the heart of Russia. That illustrious one, as Roeder understood matters, had proved victorious everywhere, had overthrown the enemy army and seized Moscow, where he tarried among the ruins of the burnt out capital while awaiting surrender offers from the defeated and helpless foe. Meanwhile, back in this trampled, blighted district, life must go on, with considerably less excitement perhaps, but with cares and concerns aplenty none the less. Though Roeder's soldiers did not march on, the weeks did, giving way to an increasingly blustery autumn. Bitterly cold nights mocked fair days, save when chill rains compounded misery. Indeed, misery became for Roeder and his depleted band the keynote of the campaign. They seemed forgotten by those tasked with maintaining the little force.

From authorized sources of provision they received no food; ever the advancing warrior's dilemma, the problem had reached by mid-October a stage of uncharacteristic crisis. The French in Vyazma looted everything for themselves, leaving nothing for their grudging, if faithful, allies. Supply trains no longer crawled up with sufficient regularity the long road from Kovno; washed out bridges and roving Cossacks saw to that. Orders came down from distant high places to subsist by forage, yet therein lay disturbing difficulties. For the better part of two months this land had been repeatedly raped of its resources, the major towns by the main highway utterly despoiled, the outlying villages eventually pillaged. The Russian peasants, mulishly obstinate from the start, had grown brutally obdurate when faced with famine induced by their hungry conquerors.

Now foraging patrols took on the appearance of major military operations, the natives fighting back, lurking in ambuscade, supported by nimble squadrons of half savage horsemen, both foes disinclined to grant quarter in a war that grew messier by bloody degrees. They took rare delight in capturing their opponents, torturing and slaying prisoners without mercy. Despite these obstacles, Roeder had kept his dwindling unit fed, if on paltry rations. They sacked the villages, punishing with noose and bullet those foolishly uncooperative, eking a bare living until a wide expanse of a long day's march had been rendered barren, irretrievably ravaged.

This morning Roeder and company broke camp from within the wreckage of yet another Russian village. He had ordered it demolished and burned after discovering there the bodies of three missing men. The locals had affixed them to trees with iron spikes through their eyes and hands. This grim finding fired the flames of retribution, but the perpetrators had absconded, eluding this time the firing squad, while the vicinity had already given up its digestible booty on previous expeditions. Now Captain Roeder said to Sergeant Helmholtz, after drawing up his thin ranks, "We must proceed farther, if we would eat this day. Yonder through the southern forest, if my information be true, lies the village of Istrekya, virgin territory, untouched as yet. There we may dine on other than rotten potatoes, and my horse craves fodder."

"It could be," replied that old soldier of Hesse, a veteran, like his master, of three campaigns. "If we find it. 'Tis a pity this map serves for naught more than the toilet." He folded that ragged parchment, replacing it in the worn leather case he carried in his pouch. "The roads don't match. Do we follow the trail, or cut through the woods?"

Roeder shuddered inwardly. Harshly he spoke, "Habitation requires access. In the forest we are lost; on the path, however winding, we make our way and know where we are. Thus we march. Now, Helmholtz, I discern inordinate grumbling among the men. What means this?"

"Spies and turncoats make mention of Istrekya," the sergeant reported. "An unwholesome place I gather, old with old ways, not very Christian, according to rumor. We've a superstitious lot on our hands. They hear tales."

"Balderdash."

"Probably. The folk about—those willing to talk—speak poorly of it. They shun the forest, or the village, or its denizens, or all three."

"Rubbish, I say," Roeder exclaimed. "I have still forty good men and more, suitably armed. In unison we need not fear peasants, and can bluff the Cossacks if necessary. There, I account for all hazards, excepting only starvation. We must eat. Pass the order."

Helmholtz told off the men for the march, encouraging them with kicks, curses, and vague promises of hearty meals. Roeder took the lead, he the only one horsed. The troops filed down the rutted, swampy road, too narrow for a military cart, where the forest enclosed them. They tramped rapidly for the first hour, steadily for the second, listlessly for the third. Dark birches walled them in, granting rare glimpses of leaden skies. They attained a sort of crossroads—as Sergeant Helmholtz observed, not marked on the map—where the road forked, the main route to the left, a barely passable trail to the right. No signpost explicated the spot, but two items of interest drew attention. One, a kind of totem, a log driven upright into the sodden ground, adorned at its level top with tattered eagle feathers and a crimson-painted skull; next to this a woman, of frightful age, withered and bent, black shrouded in finest peasant squalor. The scaly toes of her naked feet curled in the muck. Redolent of drab, her gimlet eyes surveyed the foreign band bright and unblinking. Captain Roeder called a halt.

Dismounting, he directed Helmholtz, who had acquired a smattering of the language—valuable man!—to interrogate the crone. This he did, at length, with fumbling intervals accompanied by many gestures. The Russian female responded with a dreadful voice, one supported too by gestures, copious and wild, punctuated by cackling laughter. As Helmholtz hesitantly reconstructed her statements, they ran rather thus:

The main road (as she styled it) curved back into regions known to the Germans, but in that direction, less than a league, a squadron of Cossacks lay in wait, ready to pounce from the forest. In order to avoid those hated predators, the secondary path must be chosen, but it led to Istrekya, her home village, where she was a personage of note, a seer and maker of potions. This, Roeder opined aloud, might translate as witch, a comment causing covert commotion among the ranks.

Said she, better they embrace the Cossack lances with their bosoms than venture into Istrekya. Hers was an old village, harkening unto olden ways, its folk holding on to elements of faith and showing fealty to powers predating the coming of the Rus. They rejected the outside world as it shunned or ignored them, asked for nothing nor wanted. Intruders would face implacable hostility, from the people and their lord.

Roeder quizzed her, through his interpreter, about this lord, with whom he hoped to treat. She spat a grotesque answer. By lord she referred, not to a titled nobleman, nor even a village elder, but to the

Mud King, who governed Istrekya and oversaw its affairs from his forbidden domicile beyond the world, far inside the Dark Kingdom. To him the folk paid homage, to him they sacrificed, and in return he granted protection from mundane afflictions, such as the sabers and muskets of the soldiers.

Mused Roeder, "We stumble into the midst of a nest of misbegotten primitives, refugees of the Dark Ages. The Mud King, I swear! The hag tells of a tribal deity, a quaint survival from antique times before civilization. Such stories we must expect, at the ends of the earth. Her mouthings intrigue. When peace comes to this land, scholars shall follow in our footsteps, that they may study such natives and record amusing anecdotes for learned posterity.

"Meanwhile," he said abruptly to Helmholtz, reverting to commanding tones, "practicalities beckon. Succor predicates on reaching Istrekya. There can we forage, take accommodations for the night. Tales fit for children shall not plague us, not while we rest with full bellies. Bring the crone. She may serve as hostage for the good will of her people."

It was not to be. Lo! the ancient woman had disappeared, with surprising fleetness of foot vanished into the forest, and the net of a cursory search among the nearby trees disclosed neither her person nor any trace of same. So, the march continued without her.

Designating two men as scouts, Captain Roeder sent them swiftly ahead, the rest advancing warily in single file on the terrible track. So closely did the trees press that a man could not outstretch his arms as he strode. The rain came, filtering through the boughs above, rain bitter and cold. The vocal ruminations among the ranks assumed frustrated and gloomy form. Roeder shouted them down, reminding them of largesse to come. Growling stomachs kept legs swinging in ragged tempo. At length the birches fell away, disclosing a clearing. They had arrived at Istrekya.

An unusual scene in these parts, in these times, this pristine village unscarred by war; a clump of crude huts, timber and wattle and thatch, grouped about the pitiful track that connected the site to the world, or more likely failed to do so. Swampy fields of late rye sprawled around the dwellings. A weedy mound, an oddity in this interminably level terrain, rose above and beyond the rooftops of the farthest structures. Captain Roeder's steady gaze immediately noted the absence of two common features. No church spire loomed from the village, a curious lack in a pious country; no human figure revealed itself there. The inhabitants had fled, or were in hiding.

Sergeant Helmholtz asked, "What became of our scouts?"

Roeder replied, "Cry for them. Call out to any in earshot." This Helmholtz did, without effect. Roeder added, "To business, then. A thorough search answers all. Tear the place apart, if we must." Their details formed, the men scattered in groups of five, searching for information and loot.

Within seconds shots rang out. Roeder galloped through the village, beheld a scattering of his men in combat stance, acrid smoke billowing. Cossacks! Those fell riders darted under the trees, only a handful, and one of their number stretched on the ground, a horse with an empty saddle racing away. One Russian turned, shouted back in good French, "You're welcome to it, madmen!" then disappeared after his fellows. Two stripped human forms, obviously corpses, lay askew in a trampled patch.

"Our scouts," concluded Roeder, a deduction subsequently confirmed. Burials were hastily arranged, words perfunctorily read. It was the nature of the times.

Helmholtz said to his commander, "They may return, with reinforcements."

"We will be gone by morning." The men were jittery, uneasy due to the trivial clash, or the isolation, or what not; Roeder reminded them of current necessities, useful work pending. Quickly they regained a semblance of proper spirit.

Indeed, this expedition paid off handsomely. The folk of Istrekya had apparently cleared out on the instant, removing nothing of importance in their flight. Most likely the Cossacks themselves had invaded this precinct for plunder, but now it all dropped into the laps of the Germans. The men charged into the huts, ransacking cabinets and chests, digging up unconcealed caches. Besides much grain and some bread they found dried meat and bags of potatoes and turnips. Water they had from a decrepit stone cistern, and more to drink as well. To Roeder's dismay and disgust his rapacious troops uncovered a stash of liquor in earthenware jugs. "Wine," cried the men. "Vodka," groaned Roeder after a sip; reprehensible stuff, which he forbade the men to touch, save in measured portions overseen by Helmholtz. He knew from experience, however, how far obedience carried in a case such as this. Any attempt to confiscate or destroy the dangerous drink would inspire a mutiny. The captain could only warn.

Throughout this phase, occupying the afternoon, officially deemed the "requisition of supplies," the soldiers often started, shot sharp glances, whirled about of a sudden, as if watched or dreading a presence. Other than nerves, or the after effects of drink, the cause was plain enough. A hunched, dark shape stood atop that little mound overlooking the village. Roeder, of course, had spied it at first approach. "A statue," he suggested then. Said Helmholtz, "Maybe a scarecrow." Maybe this or that, but the captain paid it no heed until one of his gangs scaled the mound to investigate the thing. Having tied up his mare, he then chose to march up the easy slope for himself. Not a statue, certainly, nothing possessing esthetic virtue; if a scarecrow or similar device, then surely a pathetic specimen. Helmholtz, trudging up to his side, put it simply, "The thing's a heap of mud."

True, thus far: jet black mud, crudely packed into the squat, bloated form of a man. Its shape reminded Roeder of Yuletide snowmen in the home country, except that this moist, clammy blob of a sculpture bore features less indicative of good cheer and happy occasions. From the ends of fat, stubby arms sprouted menacing claws derived from some animal, perhaps a bear. The remaining artistry— to employ a kind term—had been devoted to its head and face. The head was a squashed oval, with thorny sprigs taking the place of hair. The face grimaced back at its viewers with a disturbing suggestion of evil intent. The eyes were smooth, glossy, pea green stones akin to marbles, possibly polished, pushed into the mud; the nose an ugly fragment of yellowed beak torn from a large bird; the mouth only a double row of inlaid, discolored teeth, some of them broken and jagged, of various sizes. The ensemble produced a nasty impression. Helmholtz could not restrain himself from remarking that the teeth were indubitably human in origin.

"Strange tastes," Captain Roeder observed, with a shake of his head. "This reminds me how far we are from hearth and family."

There he would have left it, only certain mutterings among the men caught his ear. They referenced the old woman—the "witch"— her stupid chatter about the "Mud King," his reputed role in the life of Istrekya. This Roeder could not tolerate. "I hate the mud as do you," he declared, "but I have slogged through too much to fear it. By this act I dethrone the Mud King." And Roeder drew his ceremonial sword (a gift to him from King Jerome, brother of the Emperor), drove it repeatedly into the foul shape, then chopped and hacked at the thing until its arms fell off and its grisly head toppled. "I proclaim victory!" he jeered with a laugh.

Dusk flowed across the sullen sky, trickling darkly among the surrounding forest, drowning the huts of Istrekya in shadow. The company set up camp in the village. Within the perimeter of sentries the cooking fires flickered, pots of watery soup steamed. Joyfully sated bellies induced grateful sleepiness. The men laid claim to billets among the slovenly dwellings. Captain Roeder took the best, as was his right, but the choice caused him to brood on the relativity of man's desires. The biggest and most grandly accoutered hut was naught but a drafty shack, with few and inferior furnishings. Dirty rugs covered only part of the dirt floor. A peculiar clay stove belched more smoke than it radiated heat. The ghastly bed proved a haven for bugs rather than rest. Sergeant Helmholtz, as he had a thousand times before, laid out his personal camp site on the floor nearby, covering himself against the intensifying chill with his threadbare greatcoat.

The evening did come fast and cold. A light snow began drifting down from the darkness before the men had settled in. On the outskirts of Istrekya this day's losers in the lottery of duty haplessly circled, stamping feet and rubbing hands against the needles of frost. Quiet reigned for an uncertain spell. A man screamed.

Roeder came aware and active in a heartbeat, Helmholtz if anything more quickly. A torch lit, they dashed outside, the captain armed with pistol and sword. Pandemonium bubbled from the huts; barked orders drew an outsurge of tired, startled men. "Spread out," commanded Roeder, "and give us more light. Maintain the circle. Keeps comrades in sight to left and right."

Evidence they shortly discovered, in a puddle of clinging ooze, at the foot of the mound. As they feared, the fellow (it was Bulow from Cassel) had been done to death. During the course of his rounds someone had crept upon him and abused him to destruction. Roeder felt a deep dislike for the minutiae of the scene. Of course no bullet had inflicted that damage, yet Cossack lance or cutlass seemed also unlikely instruments. Spoken comments focused on the presumed frenzy of some animal. A bear—a wolf—an unknown beast of these unknown wilds?

An excitable private drew attention to marks in the snow. Just a dusting, but it revealed hints of obscure possibilities. Something had approached the victim, had descended from the mound, yet not on clearly delineated feet, either two or four. A slushy swath had been plowed to the location of the body, where the track terminated. If the source had continued from there, it must have retraced itself.

Then somebody would notice the vacancy at the top of the mound. Roeder climbed, found gone the decapitated pile of mud. He called down, "Our enemies toy with us. No relaxation this night, boys.

63

We stand under arms until dawn. Then we make haste. Until then, stay alert."

They surely did. Roeder demanded wood to fuel several constant fires. The men would not enter the forest, so they tore down a hut, expending all its combustible parts. Then they disassembled another. "Burn them all, if necessary," bawled Helmholtz. "We won't need them again for shelter."

Roeder consulted his watch. Midnight still an hour off, and dawn late at this season; fearing the results of weariness and inactivity, he proposed a sweep of the near environs with a reinforced squad. Twenty men he would lead, over the mound and into the fringes of the woods, to seek more signs of what assailed them. Helmholtz would maintain discipline among the remainder in the village.

Roeder drove his unwilling band along the track in the snow, realizing now that the sure path faltered at the summit. He cajoled them down the far side, to the edge of the trees, found nothing helpful. The men muttered, spouting idiotic notions. Their commander insisted on silence, while he endeavored to puzzle out matters. Some elementary clue, he guessed, eluded him.

So did one member of his team. Frightened ejaculations gave him to understand that a man had gone missing, without outcry or sound of any sort. Backtracking a few rods, the group examined meaningless marks in the snow. Yes, something had passed here, but what? The tracks, if such they were, commenced and terminated in limbo, as if a massive body had dropped down from the skies, stirring up a deal of mud in the process, progressed for a space, then either took wings or sank into the earth.

They made a show of hunting for Schmidt, the vanished man, calling out to him, accusing him of cowardice, begging him to show himself. An answer they received, but not one in accord with reasoned expectation. From the village, hidden behind the mound, arose an outburst of sound having nothing to do with the search.

Shrill screams, frenzied shouts—explosive oaths—gun shots, a cacophony of intolerable noise warning of impinging menace. Roeder steered his band around the mound, hugging the tree line that they might approach without making themselves easy targets. When the village came into view, they beheld chaos. Amidst the huts, few now standing, in the wavering glare of camp fire and torch, the men left in the rubble of Istrekya milled in most unsoldierly fashion, brandishing their muskets, firing them off haphazardly into the air or, seemingly, at shadows. Roeder charged into the mob, leading his group in skirmisher formation, strode up to Sergeant Helmholtz, who to his surprise appeared as discomfited and out of control as the rest.

"I demand an explanation."

Cried Helmholtz, "I have none, sir. It came at us from nowhere, was within the line before anybody spotted it."

"It?" repeated Roeder. "What, did a forest deer stampede the company? I imagined an attack by a regiment of regulars. What goes on?"

"More than I know, though I fear much." The captain had never before heard his aide's voice quiver with terror. "Suddenly it was there, standing in shadow. I didn't see it move, but then it wasn't there; it was elsewhere, then over there, then again..." He gulped a cold breath, exhaled a frosty cloud before adding, "It wasn't a man, sir, nor any of God's creatures."

Groaned a callow recruit, "The Mud King!"

"Malicious villagers," corrected Roeder, "inflamed by hate. Be someone here, without sanction? Repair the circle. Helmholtz—get a hold, man—restore the lines, locate the transgressors, capture or eradicate. Do it now."

Helmholtz, steadied by the presence of the officer, undertook the task. With order reestablished, he was shortly able to report further lugubrious tidings. No intruders found, one man hideously done to death, soaked in mud and gore; two more whisked away or fled. Roeder could scarcely credit what he heard. He doubted sanity: his own, that of Helmholtz, the men, Istrekya. Icy needles tingled in his spine, worked their way into his brain.

"We can not wait until morning," said he. "This place deals death in a manner beyond our strength. We march on the instant, immediate retreat. Close order, weapons cocked; give the order, Sergeant."

So in tight formation, according to the finest military drill and etiquette, Captain Roeder's little company drew together and marched on the double out of the wretched ruins of Istrekya. The yellow and crimson glow of the abandoned fires fell behind, the freezing dark forest closing around them as they tramped the narrow trail. Two men to the front bore torches to guide their feet. The thin snow crackled beneath their boots.

Retreat was seldom an option for the warriors of the Emperor's army, never a necessity, and after this night Roeder prayed that it would never again be. The night march continued the nightmare. The first assault came a quarter of an hour after departing Istrekya, when a black bulk crashed into the tail of the column. Panic, collapse of discipline, a mad scramble, and another man had gone as if evaporated. Whatever—whoever, Roeder doggedly insisted to himself—pursued them did not wait overlong before the next onslaught, came back to terrorize, contriving to appear without warning, barely glimpsed, seen only as flashing green eyes in a lumpish silhouette, one that could not convincingly pass as human or anything properly alive. Even Roeder felt forced to admit, from his single brief sighting, that either his eyes and mind played crazed tricks, or that (dare he believe it?) something inhumanly evil stalked abroad in a haunted land.

The final victim left his body, shredded by claws, chewed by teeth, soused in mire, crumpled at the base of the lurid skull post that marked the road fork to Istrekya. The poor fool broke ranks, raced into the murk shrieking of the Mud King, met fate, perhaps that which he most feared. By this time Roeder could not cobble together a better explanation.

So too, by this time, as the corpse was hauled out of the way to be dumped aside, the smothering blackness of night lessened, transforming into a somber gray. Men rejoiced as they welcomed the day, prayed that they had escaped from the deadly zone of Istrekya and its guardian.

The growing light disclosed, at a near remove among the trees, the abhorrent old crone of Istrekya, motioning toward them with bony fingers and hatefully gibbering. At his superior's less than eager command Helmholtz translated. Brokenly he whispered, "She hurls heathen curses, warns us not to set foot again within her lord's domain. What has passed, she vows, is nothing to what will be. The Mud King only rules here. Sir," he added doubtfully, "shall we seize her?"

"God, no," cried Roeder. "We who survive, let us speed to Vyazma with our skins."

Thus it proved. They returned to Vyazma without further incident, back to the mundane horrors they understood. Captain Roeder and his handful of men lived to experience new adventures, some of them quite noteworthy, all of them meticulously documented in the records he made over to headquarters before his military career came to an abrupt end with the conclusion of this campaign. His experiences in and about Istrekya, however, he chose to report partially—nay, it must be said, inaccurately—as it ran against his grain to submit claims of matters for which he could not rationally or sanely account. Of conventional death and destruction, the commonalities of the soldier's life, he could appreciate and boast... but how dress up in heroic prose the insidious madness of Istrekya?

A Curious Incident at the Office

I'm only able to tell this tale, it seems, because I wasn't there when the thing happened. Strange that it should be so, but I have no better explanation, for that or for much else. I was assistant manager over a small team of data processing professionals in a modest office on the sixth floor of the aging business tower, a nondescript operation of a sort commonplace in the semi-industrialized outskirts of most big cities. This particular outfit was located in Phoenix, Arizona, although I don't suppose that matters at all. Mr. Humphreys, my boss, also wasn't present at the critical moment (he tended to arrive late and stay late), but all of our employees were: the systems man Alf, the secretary Sheila, the processing clerks John, Morgan, Tammy, and Janet.

A road accident delayed my arrival, one in which I was not involved, but which inextricably snarled traffic for an hour. Not the first time, of course, nor did this especially concern me, for my crew were fair self-starters. I knew all would be humming nicely by the time Mr. Humphreys showed up. I was right, but that's one of the odd aspects of the matter, and to this day I still can't figure out why I was right. There's a lot I still don't get.

I rode the main elevator and breezed into the reception room to find Sheila absent from her desk, the boss' chamber empty. Alf wasn't in his techno-nightmare cubbyhole just beyond nor, I discovered, were the data processing stations occupied. This gave me a sinking feeling, of the proper, normal kind; I wondered idly if everybody had called in sick, or if I had slipped in time and come in on a Saturday by mistake. That latter wasn't so, else why had I fought swarming traffic, but it's funny I thought about a screw-up in time. Even then I thought it.

I passed down the aisle between the desks, past the coffee corner (where my people too often congregated) to the rear door opening onto another, seldom used segment of hall at the back of the building. The door stood ajar, a mumble of muted conversation filtering through. I pressed on to find out what has going on. There they were, some of them at least: Alf, Sheila, John, Morgan, also the elderly maintenance man Joseph, clustered before the old, creaky service

67

elevator underneath the round, antique wall clock. I strode forward.

"What's going on?" I asked, pleasantly and briskly, before gasping "Whoa!" for suddenly I noticed how the elevator doors gaped open and cavernous, nothing there but vacant shaft. I felt dizzy for a second just thinking about it, although I wasn't really that close, and a few warm bodies blocked the precipice. They turned towards me. Sheila was crying, the rest looking serious and woeful.

"It's terrible," Sheila exclaimed to me, "just terrible what happened to them." John nodded and said, "A great tragedy. I can't guess how it happened." Alf shook his head and sighed, "I don't understand things like this. Out of the blue they're taken away." Morgan, an older fellow, placed a hand on my shoulder, saying, "There was nothing we could do. It happened so fast."

"What happened?" I asked loudly. A dread surmise chilled me. "Where are Tammy and Janet?" Joseph grimaced and pointed down the elevator shaft. "There was nothing wrong with the mechanism," said he. "I check that stuff all the time." So I knew the worst. He added, "I don't accept responsibility. It's just one of those things."

I shoved him aside and, for no very good reason, peered downward. What I saw wasn't quite what I expected. Now this is one of the strange parts. I'd assumed from their talk and the minimal evidence before me that an elevator crash had occurred, or that a malfunction had led to the poor victims stepping off into space. It wasn't exactly that way. Tammy and Janet were down there, all right, but everything else was wrong. Let me describe it precisely as I saw it that moment. I didn't see evidence of an elevator wreck; in fact, I couldn't make out anything at the bottom of the shaft, which seemed to drop into impenetrable, Stygian darkness. One might have thought that the shaft didn't have a bottom, so opaque and mysterious was that void. The bodies of the women were there, approximately two floors down. They appeared intact, with no sign of lethal damage. I recognized them well enough: Janet lay face up, her features plainly visible and undistorted, her eyes closed as if sleeping. Most of Tammy's face was turned away from me, but I knew her, knew her pink dress, knew the shiny bracelet on her right wrist with the stylized fish symbol. She, too, seemed unharmed, yet dead, if you can follow that. I could account for them both without difficulty. I couldn't fathom the rest, how their bodies hung suspended in space, wrapped in a white, somewhat transparent, gauzy substance which adhered to the sides of the shaft and held them aloft. The stuff wasn't cloth, or paper, or plastic, or anything bought in the warehouse of sanity. It

68

looked a lot like an enormous mass of spider's web. The weird sight gave me the creeps right down to the core of my being.

I inquired after particulars. "I heard them shrieking," sobbed Sheila, "those awful screams, just for a second. I came running and found them like this." "That's the way it was," agreed Alf. "A couple of minutes past nine, as I was settling in. I heard Sheila's shout." I'd missed it by ten minutes. I thought then to check the current time, glanced at the wall clock overhead, noticed that it had stopped at 11:36. Obviously the device had failed the night before. My watch told me that only twenty minutes had passed since the disaster.

Morgan suggested that we do something. "We can't leave them down there," he observed. Joseph chimed in, "I'll notify the building manager. He'll take care of it." "It's a sad day for us all," said John. Tammy clucked her tongue and said, "It's pathetic how these things happen, don't you think?" I didn't know what to think. I felt confused, stuffy in the brain, strangely hot and cold. Tammy and Janet stood with us, staring into the shaft, appearing conventionally dismayed.

"But that's you down there," I said stupidly. John nodded vigorously, saying, "That was my impression." Janet chuckled nervously, replied, "It isn't. We're right here." "It's obviously you," I persisted, and Sheila backed me up. Tammy said, "There's a resemblance, if you look at them a certain way." At that moment I heard the booming voice of Mr. Humphreys calling from the office. "Wait right here," I advised, and left to brief him.

That I did, providing him with the barest facts, shorn of unusual details. He took it stolidly enough, offered to initiate official action. Meanwhile I noticed that the staff were settling into their standard routine, assuming their seats, ruffling papers. I thought their behavior odd. They were prone, at times, to seeking occasions for chatter quite less remarkable than this case. The level of oddity increased still more when I subsequently attempted to engage them in conversation, only to discover that certain notable recent events had disappeared from their memories. I didn't know what to think or say. It was as if nothing had happened. Suddenly I had no evidence whatsoever of tragedy. I returned to the service elevator, found it in fine running order, the wall clock keeping good time. I passed Joseph in the hall, he going about his duties, wholly unconcerned and oblivious. When I got back to the office Mr. Humphreys awaited me, asked me into his walled cubicle. "Maybe it's too early in the morning," said he, "or maybe my sense of humor isn't what it used to be, but I'm not amused. I don't get what

69

you're playing at. Drop the games and stick to business, all right?"

So I did, and the next hour and a half, despite an absence of untoward developments, was a most uncomfortable period for me, one of the worst of my life. I felt humiliated, naturally, for my boss thought I was being a silly jerk, but also I felt ill at ease, nagged by a sense of mounting tension, as if something improper was unfolding behind my back. Everything looked normal, but nothing felt so. Eleven o'clock stole around, and office chat picked up as the vital subject of lunch reared its traditional head. There was talk of sending out for Chinese. Tammy made a deprecatory comment about delivery charges, and in no time she and Janet were offering to slip out to pick up the hot food.

I casually overheard this, as well as the following exchange. John muttered, "Humphreys won't like it." "No problem," replied Tammy with a conspiratorial grin; "We'll sneak down the service elevator." "That's right," said Janet. "We'll be there and back in a minute, and he'll never know we're gone." The strange, unseemly tension welled up within me suddenly. I felt as if my head would explode. I examined my watch: 11:14. I thought of 11:36, and a terrible blanket of knowledge made to smother me. I knew that something was about to happen.

Tammy and Janet were out the rear door before I could blink. John was calling in the office order to the restaurant. I raced past him, caught up with the girls near the elevator. The wall clock read 11:16. I didn't know what to say, for I've always been lax about these minor office shenanigans. "Before you go," I fumbled, "I need the files on _____ and _____." I forget what those were, something supremely unimportant. Tammy and Janet frowned, glanced at one another, followed be back. "Also the papers from the _____ account," I added, something I invented on the spot.

They satisfied my requests as they might, then began edging towards the rear door again. I immediately advised attention to Janet's computer screen, which I claimed was emitting a warning message. She ungraciously verified that all was well. John whispered something about "having it delivered after all." Perhaps all was well. The time was 11:28.

Then Mr. Humphreys called me in for a routine matter. It took no time at all, but when I emerged the two ladies were nowhere in sight. "Where are they?" I demanded. Morgan looked at me blankly, then said nonchalantly, "They popped down to get a paper to read with their lunch." "Did they take the back way?" I shouted. On the instant we heard quick screams, followed by a dull, faraway thud. We charged into the rear corridor, me leading the pack.

The hands of the clock stood at 11:36. This time—the only time for all others present—there was no mystery. The doors of the elevator hung partly open, as if they had failed to close completely. I poked my head through and stared down. No, while it was very bad, it wasn't mysterious. The elevator had plummeted to the bottom of the shaft. I saw the obvious wreckage of the ancient box, the coils of greasy snapped cable, the human debris. Tammy and Janet had died in a tragic accident, and that was that. Who would have thought it?

Only Mr. Humphreys knew anything of the earlier event— actually, knew what I had said about it—and he later seemed more disturbed about me than he did of strange doings. I severed my connection with the company soon after, to his evident relief. I don't know what happened, or why the incident had more of an effect on me than on the rest. Label it a premonition, if you will, but understand there was more to it, some unreal factor I haven't grasped. I can't explain the things I saw and experienced that morning, especially the truly freakish details. I know they happened; I don't fantasize such unorthodox puzzles. Perhaps they occur more often than we realize, only most of us are seldom granted the dubious pleasure of bearing witness.

The Nasty Club

Horace Glifford was a quietly unhappy man, disappointed with his life and his hopes and his dreams, who held an unsatisfying job in a dead-end office, who possessed an uninspiring wife and a troublesome little three year-old girl, who had always expected more and gotten less; this man, Horace Glifford, perhaps rather commonplace in most respects, accustomed to deadly dull days which blurred one into another, dragging out into empty years, now tingled with unaccustomed excitement, for he was the recipient of a unique invitation from an unusual organization, a high-powered club for gentlemen of quality which, though obscure, sounded like the kind of outfit that was in a position to do him a great deal of good and turn his life around. Yes, he tingled.

Mr. Brentworth—the banking Brentworth, no less—had approached him (Horace still didn't understand how or why) and explained the matter to some degree. "A select, exclusive body," he revealed, "which searches out the right sort of man, incorporates him, and helps elevate him to his true level of status and accomplishment." It sounded pretty good. The details remained hazy. Horace gathered, from Mr. Brentworth's cautious hints and seemingly casual asides, that the club fostered the secret, unattainable desires of its members, a type of wild self-actualization scheme. Horace let the older gentleman know that the prospect interested him, thus a public meeting with the officers of the club had been arranged.

Now, on this dark, oppressive evening in one of the more ancient districts of town, Horace gamely mounted the steps to the door of the prestigious Restaurant Martinique. He hoped he had dressed appropriately. He had done the best he could, with his current wardrobe. It wasn't that simple to enter; he had to knock and identify himself to the doorman. That portentous fellow ushered him inside, into the cozy, dimly lighted, glamorous interior, and helpfully directed him past the handful of diners into a private room on the right.

Mr. Brentworth rose from an ornamental oak table, where he sat with two other impressive, well-tailored men, to welcome his guest.

"Join us, Horace. Sit here." Horace took the offered seat, across from the three, and his host resumed his seat, flanked by the other two.

"My friends," intoned Mr. Brentworth, "this is Horace Glifford, the young man of whom I've spoken. Horace, this is Mr. Jamison, advisor for the Bradford holdings"—he indicated the heavyset, stern-faced man on his left—"and this is Mr. Caldwell, chief counsel to the Gallagher Foundation"—the tall, thin, pleasantly smiling but hawk-nosed man on his right. "We shall represent to you, as well as report the substance of this meeting to, our organization, which we style the Nasty Club. Andre, we will be served now."

This he spoke to the waiter, who had suddenly appeared from nowhere over Horace's shoulder. Andre nodded amiably and silently departed.

"I trust that you appreciate," said Mr. Brentworth, "fine roast beef in a sweet, flaming Chateau Ormand sauce, accompanied by a relatively rare Moselle."

"I do," Horace replied. He squirmed, inwardly told himself to stop. "You call it the Nasty Club? That's the name of your group?"

"We are inclined to our in-house jokes," said Mr. Caldwell. "We amuse ourselves, but make no mistake, we take ourselves quite seriously."

"And that does happen to be the name of our club," put in Mr. Jamison, abruptly, "so why shouldn't we call it that?"

"Entirely correct," said Mr. Brentworth. "Yes, we are the Nasty Club, and we have intelligent and thoughtful reasons for so styling ourselves. All will be made plain to you. We are an unusual organization, with exceptionally specialized rules and strict requirements for entry. We have trained ourselves to locate and identify the sorts of men who might enhance our membership. We make the maximum use of knowledgeable, observant sources to spot our candidates. On the basis of information received, data analyzed personally by me, we are currently considering you."

"I'm flattered," Horace said. About time, he thought bitterly, that someone realized he wasn't just another mousy office employee, but a man with hot drives and cold ambitions. "Tell me more about the nature of your club. What I've heard sounds tantalizing, but—"

"Dinner, gentlemen." Andre wheeled a laden tray to the table, efficiently unloaded its contents, placed and poured, then left them as quickly as before. He shut a door behind him, granting the men absolute privacy. Horace began his meal, following the example of the others. They issued crisp comments concerning the highly esteemed quality of the cuisine, with side references to the marvelous Old World decor. Shortly Mr. Brentworth politely suggested that his colleague, Mr. Caldwell, do the honors.

"We of the Nasty Club," said the latter, "have determined than man can only achieve his true potential—as a man, as a creator, as a leader—by confronting, by sublimating, by overcoming his personal demons. We all contain within our individual minds secret fears, ultimate horrors which belong to each of us alone. In the normal way of the world, we retain these horrors within ourselves. To a great extent, we have been taught that we must do so. The dark thoughts which plague us are objects of shame, and we dare not reveal the grimmest depths of our fantasies to anyone, lest we face the certain scorn of our fellows. Such, at least, is the standard view. Therefore, we encapsulate whatever most causes us self-disgust or loathing; we wall off that portion of our minds, attempting to function by utilizing only the remainder of our brains, protected from the foul influence which festers beyond the wall. That method can work—of course it can—but it carries a cost, one which we are no longer willing to pay.

"We deduce, from the scientific, the psychological, and the moral realities of the human condition, that the mind must be truly liberated by embracing the worst within us, for by conquering it we raise ourselves to a higher, ultimately human level. Beasts, you see, flee from their terrors; we accept ours, and in accepting we learn to laugh at them. We defeat them by making them concrete."

"Do you follow all of this?" asked Mr. Jamison sourly.

"Of course he does," said Mr. Brentworth. "You grasp what we're driving at, don't you, Horace?"

"Yes, yes I do."

"I can assure you," continued Mr. Caldwell, "that we have found this technique most effective. We make, we do, we create, we move and shake in our chosen spheres, without any fear whatsoever, due to our triumph over the weaknesses with which society would burden us. The methodology, tried and tested, works. We have actually become everything that we can be."

"By facing your fears?" Horace asked.

"By acting upon them," corrected Mr. Jamison. "It's really very simple. You must identify that which you most dread—that action, open to you, which you consider most vile, the very thought of which chills you to the core—and undertake said action."

"An activity so grotesque," added Mr. Brentworth, "that, at this moment, you can't imagine yourself being able to live with; something within you, the very possibility of which you fear would torture you to madness. That you must do."

"Such is the basis of the Nasty Club," resumed Mr. Caldwell. "The accomplishment of such an action is the key requirement for membership. Having joined, naturally, all the benefits of the club—connections, support—become available to you in full. In practice, you will find that it really is a good deal. Not one of our members has ever complained. It is the opportunity of a lifetime."

"It sounds incredible," Horace muttered. He thought he understood what these men were trying to tell him; reading between the lines, it made some kind of sense. These guys were big shots, and the first principle of being a big shot stated that one could do whatever he pleased. They swapped wives and held orgies and gorged themselves and drank themselves silly. That was what their lives were all about. Liberation from convention, the abolition of confining rules for oneself, marked the most rarefied pinnacle of success. These men, so they were telling him, in so many words, lived up to that standard.

Of course they didn't quite explain it that way, he shrewdly noted. Oh no, they had to soothe their bedased consciences. He knew how they played the game. They would blather about the awfulness of the chosen action, maybe moan and weep about it, but what mattered was that they did it. What mattered to them was that he did it. Oh yes, he certainly had it figured out now. They couldn't fool him on a point like that. Not that they were really trying.

"It sounds good," Horace said. "I like it. I'm your man. I want to join, I really do."

"Capital!" cried Mr. Brentworth. "I knew you would see it our way."

"First, he has to put up or shut up," interjected Mr. Jamison. "Mere talk doesn't pay regular dividends."

"A similar point had occurred to me," agreed Mr. Caldwell.

"I'm game," Horace assured them. "I'm ready to get started. You must, however, clarify the terms for me. It's still not clear exactly what you expect."

"Only you can determine that," said Mr. Caldwell.

"Indeed," said Mr. Brentworth. "You, Horace, are the best judge of your own capacities."

"I just pick something really horrible—"

"That which is most horrible to you. Please understand us. You must stop thinking in terms of limitations or boundaries."

"Wow. So it can be anything, no matter how freaky. And you

75

gentlemen, for instance, have actually achieved this?"

"We certainly have," said Mr. Brentworth, with a note of righteousness in his voice. "Perhaps if we recount to you our personal stories, that will lay the matter bare before you. My friends, are you with me on this?" They were, and with that support Mr. Brentworth told his story.

"I am a banker. My profession, my life, is devoted to the sanctity of money, the validity of the contract, the honor of the financial deal. That is everything I live for, and no one does it better than I. Ever since I began my career, as a young clerk many years ago, the most shameful thought to ever defile my mind has been the notion of violating the sacred rules of high finance, of dishonoring trust. That I would almost rather die than do. Therefore, it logically follows that I must do exactly that—just once, in a big way—in order to trample that terror underfoot once and for all. I agreed to do that, forced myself kicking and screaming to do it, on the occasion of my joining the Nasty Club.

"There was a man, a good man, a pillar of the community, with a beautiful family and countless friends. He was my friend, the best friend I ever had. He had extensive financial dealings with me. He allowed me to handle all of his business affairs. He trusted me beyond mere confidence. He was absolutely right to do so. I honored him as I did no other man. This man I set out, with cold calculation and clear foresight, to ruin.

"I could fill a chapter with the details of my machinations. I began by transferring monies, earmarked for his most notable clients, into hidden accounts which could never be traced. I extracted sums of cash in his name—quite staggering quantities of cash—seeing to it that the sums were disbursed to disreputable social elements with whom he would never normally come into contact. I dropped his name in crude circles, fostering rumors concerning his mythical illicit activities. I made certain, as you will surely appreciate, that such scurrilous tales reached the ears of his wife and close associates.

"Nothing could be pinned on me. I did not ostensibly profit from any of these dealings. Clouds of suspicion gathered about him. Concerns grew, accusations flew, and before you could know it, formal charges had been filed. He denied everything, even stooped to claiming that he had been framed, but offered no coherent defense. I finished him. He did away with himself.

"Monstrous, I tell you, young man. It makes me queasy recalling the experience. In destroying him, I disgraced myself to myself. I spat in the face of my own personal code. Yet I am a better man for it. That is my story."

"In my current line of work," Horace mused, "there isn't much scope for—"

"Wholly irrelevant," snorted Mr. Jamison. "My excellent friend just happens to take his business that seriously, so it necessarily followed that he must dynamite his professional oaths. There is no room for confusion in that. My case was entirely different. Being a rather hedonistic, pleasure-loving fellow, my personal limitations are those of the flesh. I am most keen on matters of personal dignity. Being fastidious in my attire, I have an immutable horror of uncleanliness. That, we may assume, constitutes my Achilles' heel. Well now, sir, I ask of you, does that suggest possibilities? Could you, from that premise, deduce my final frontier of abject squalor and depravity?"

Horace didn't know if he could, and he feared that it might be impolite to overtly speculate. He said nothing.

"Then, sir, would you believe me," Mr. Jamison went on savagely, "if I told you that I have eaten a human corpse?"

This time there was no choice but to speak. "If you say so, then I accept your word."

"Very good. I do say so. I have done that. I will not weary you with long-winded exposition concerning the mechanisms of procurement. It suffices to relate that, in this world, anything can be had for the requisite sum, and a cadaver of the dear departed is no exception. I acquired a choice specimen. It was as awful as you can imagine, indeed considerably more. It was the body of a young man— about your age—who had apparently perished in an automobile accident or similar rending smash. The process of embalming had not begun, or had been dispensed with; I was most particular about that. I wished to auto-disgust, not poison myself. So, the flesh had been left to congeal, to decay, to decompose into putrid essences. I chose well, you see. On the brink I quailed. I thought of killing myself before indulging, I tell you truly, but I did not; I would not, for I must become the master of myself.

"I refrained from employing utensils. I tore into that rotting mess with my bare hands. Can you picture it? I hope you cannot. I always will. I scraped off the peeling flesh with my fingernails. I pulled out strands of disintegrating muscle tissue. Making a bowl of my hands, I scooped out the miasmic, stinking filth of the viscera. I raised these gobs of human slime to my mouth and I choked them down, I cupped the slushy liquor of decomposition and swilled it, quaffed it in great gulping mouthfuls. Oh, the singular agony of those moments of extreme revulsion! I will take second place to none in the category of frenzied self-abasement.

"That ghoul feast made me sick, literally as well as figuratively. For days I wallowed in darkness and despair. No man could ever recover his sanity, much less his self-respect, after such an extraordinary act. It is not possible! And yet I did it, and I am whole. I am a more complete human being."

"And you bask in the esteem of congenial companions who are proud of you," interjected Mr. Brentworth.

"I've never heard a story like that before," Horace mumbled, "not in my whole life. Mr. Jamison, that really did you a lot of good?"

"Beyond question. You will learn that we deal in facts, not suppositions."

"More roast beef, Horace?" asked Mr. Brentworth.

"No, no thank you."

"Allow me to refill your glass."

"I would appreciate it."

"I believe that I have a few facts of my own to relate," drawled Mr. Caldwell. "I might as well get my own story over with. It may not be as personally dramatic as Mr. Brentworth's, nor as original as Mr. Jamison's—it might strike you as stale and tedious, in this day and age—but it may prove useful by way of illustration.

"For me, the greatest good lies in the utmost respect for the inherent value of individual human life. I have devoted all of my years to the enhancement of that value. Furthermore, I am a religious man, deeply devout. Necessarily I have always refrained from condoning any action which would degrade or damage others. You may see where this is heading. Clearly, my challenge lay in visiting the evil of annihilation upon an individual, in such a starkly hideous manner as to prove me a madman or a fiend.

"This action I performed. Even now it is difficult to speak of it. The event haunts my dreams to this day. I kidnapped a young woman, about your age, perhaps; a beautiful young woman, and I carried her to a dark, secret place which I had previously chosen. There, in the most brutal fashion, I despoiled and defiled her, all the while making clear to her that she must abandon hope, that she was doomed. Her screams ring now in my ears. Through her I quenched every form of sadistic lust which my imagination could conceive and, it may be, invented a few. I relied to a considerable degree upon physical torture, but not for a moment did I ignore the psychological aspects of the situation. I behaved like a beast. There can be no argument as to the heinousness of my crime. It was despicable. In the end, with her shattered in mind and body, whimpering for mercy, I produced a large knife and began to carve, taunting her until she was dead. Thus endeth the lesson."

"You're making that up," Horace cried. "It didn't happen."

"I assure you that it did. Shameful, certainly, but exhilarating; the incident brought closure to my gnawing fears."

"It is unoriginal," said Mr. Jamison. "So many of our members have chosen that route. Still, so long as it serves the purpose—"

"And the purpose has been adequately explained," said Mr. Brentworth. "The methods, the procedures, take varied and manifold forms, but the goal is always the same. We have a large membership, Horace, including others who may be known to you by reputation. Mrs. Kowalski, for instance, who has been in the news lately. Yes, you have read of her: the dedicated head of the regional Anti-Abortion League. You must have some idea, from her public statements, how seriously she takes her good works. Perhaps you are not aware that, as a condition for membership in our organization, she chose to submit to an abortion herself. You hadn't heard that? I can't say that I'm surprised. I believe she still undergoes mental therapy, and yet she is a valued member, a great asset to our team. This year she is again arranging the Ladies' Tea. I hear that our female associates look forward to those occasions."

"It's incredible," Horace said.

"This is brass tacks time," said Mr. Jamison, "so let's get down to them. Horace, Mr. Brentworth has proposed your candidacy. He has his reasons, I'm sure, and we respect his acumen. We of the Nasty Club make up a marvelous team, and you would derive great benefits from belonging. In a very real sense, we offer you the world. In return we ask, all things considered, very little. Horace Glifford, are you interested?"

"I am," he replied breathlessly. "Please let me join. I want to be with you. I want to belong."

"A refreshing attitude," said Mr. Caldwell. "Then you know what you must do. You know it in your heart. Only you know what it is. Make that happen. Impress us with your choice, and you are in."

"Something—something especially nasty—that's the ticket?"

"Extremely nasty," said Mr. Brentworth. "I propose that we four meet back here a week from tonight, at the same hour, in order to evaluate your situation. I shall make the reservations. At that time, judgment will be rendered."

On the way home Horace thought about the elusively thrilling prospects held out before him by the gentlemen of the Nasty Club. He envied them, he wanted to be like them, and it didn't seem unreasonable that they should require a test of his resolve. To be a great and powerful man, a man who recognized no rules, marked the summit of his aspirations. What he wanted to be—what he knew he was capable of being—they were. Of course they dressed up their coldly rewarding philosophy in moral finery, just to make themselves sound good. That was the way of bigshots. Despite everything they said, Horace didn't doubt for a second that they committed those ugly actions because they felt like it, and because they thought they could get away with it. That was what it meant to be a top gun in this world. That's what it had always meant. Horace longed to behave accordingly.

At home, he avoided his wife, or allowed her to avoid him, so that he could think. He knew what he wanted to do. He had known from the moment the general subject arose. All his adult life a secret, brooding, occasionally frantic craving had gnawed at him. Of course he had never acted upon his fantasy—the penalties of exposure were horrific, especially these days—nor even mentioned it to a soul, but it had crossed his mind often, very often. It was exactly the sort of thing the club had in mind.

Horace didn't take action right away. He procrastinated, he fretted, he questioned, doubted, feared. He went about his regular business for days, wearing a mask of normality, while his overheated mind smoldered. It shouldn't be just any little girl. What if those he wished to impress deemed that passé? He imagined Mr. Jamison sneering at his lack of imagination. Yes, it must be his own daughter. That whiny brat ought to make herself useful for something. He pictured to himself the astounded look in her eyes as he approached with an evil grin, her squirming as he enfolded her (oddly, she never liked being touched by him), his affectionate cooing as he began to undress her; the struggle, his mounting brutality, her sobbing, inarticulate pleading, and then the blissful, long awaited moment of total carnal possession. Perspiration beaded his brow as he fashioned the scene. He thought about it, he thought about it some more, he thought about it again . . . and then he did it.

It was everything he expected it to be. He felt like a god. He was a god! Later, as he straightened his tie before setting out for the restaurant and his appointment with destiny, he noticed his wife and daughter together, through the open door to the living room, engaged in some form of conversation. The child seemed to be making statements, after her fashion, and the mother seemed to be responding. She glanced at him once, a furtive glance, as if she was beginning to understand, but couldn't make herself believe. Perhaps she would, soon enough. He supposed that he had left traces. He didn't care. Let the silly woman try to make trouble for him. What of it? Horace had progressed beyond fear. He had no need to fear. His friends in the Nasty Club would look out for him.

That night he strode through the door of the Restaurant Martinique like a victorious monarch on parade. His friends awaited him, Mr. Brentworth, Mr. Jamison, Mr. Caldwell; all fine fellows, men like himself. They greeted him agreeably. Dinner was served, a suitable repast for the occasion, Horace savoring every bite. Unlike the previous gathering, conversation did not flow until after the meal. He could scarcely contain himself, but it was pleasing anticipation which animated him. This time he felt no nervousness. As they would soon grant, he was one of them now.

At the right moment, Mr. Caldwell politely asked for particulars. Horace provided them. He told everything, in exquisite detail, dwelling on each juicy morsel of memory. He emphasized the lurid aspects—he knew they would appreciate that—he entertained them with fulsome descriptions of each blow, each barking demand, each thrust. As Horace spoke, flaming joy swelled his heart. He began to snicker as he recited the really disgusting bits. Once he laughed out loud. He could barely contain himself, experiencing difficulty in finishing his story, so great was his mirth and sense of self-satisfaction. Eventually he ran out of incident. He paused, breathing heavily, regarding his new colleagues with a smug, even arrogant grin.

Something untoward was happening, something Horace couldn't understand. Had his tale been too much, even for them? That would be a laugh—he might chide them for it later—but certainly right now he didn't expect this reaction. They glared at him as if he were some unclean species of insect creeping onto their spotless table. Their eyes bulged, their faces twisted as if in pain. What was going on?

"Have I made my point?" Horace asked, with shaken bravado. "Do you need to hear more?"

Mr. Jamison rose unsteadily from his seat, aiming his large finger like a gun to sneer, "You are a monster, sir!"

Mr. Caldwell shook his head wearily and muttered, "I cannot

believe that I have been sitting here listening to this."

Mr. Brentworth cast down his eyes at the table and sighed, "I do not know how I could have made such a mistake."

"I don't get it," Horace cried. "I did what you wanted me to do. That was as rotten of a thing as I could think of doing. It's what you wanted. It is!"

"You enjoyed it," snarled Mr. Jamison, his words dripping venom. "You actually enjoyed that atrocity. You did it only because *you wanted to do it.* You engaged in evil, because you are evil."

"My God," groaned Mr. Brentworth.

"Of course I did," Horace replied. "Isn't that what it's about; what it's really about? Sure it is. I knew all that nonsense about doing something I hated was just cover. I got that. We're all big boys— that's the point—and we all want to play our games as we please. All right, so this is mine. I'm the new king. Crown me!"

"You are an abhorrent brute," Mr. Brentworth cried. "You understand nothing. We meant everything that we told you."

"How can that be?" Horace wailed. "Those terrible stories, those sick things you did: you drove your friend to suicide, and you're a ghoul, and you're a sex murderer. You're proud of yourselves!"

"Far from the case, Mr. Glifford," said Mr. Brentworth evenly. "Never will I live down my shame, but I am a wiser man for accepting my burden."

"You lack acumen, Mr. Glifford," said Mr. Jamison, as he sat down heavily. "I loathe myself for what I did. Nausea still clogs my throat, but I endeavor to rise above such crudities."

"In your callousness, you fail to analyze, Mr. Glifford," said Mr. Caldwell coldly. "My deed seared a scar into my soul, but thereby strengthened my soul, and my earnest values sustain me always."

"While in you," declared Mr. Brentworth, "we behold a putrid man, rancid, corrupt to the core. Quite a contrast to what we all desired, I dare say."

"Amen," said Mr. Jamison, and Mr. Caldwell solemnly echoed him.

"You hypocrites!" Horace shouted. "I don't believe a word of it. You condemn me, only because you won't admit the truth about yourselves. You're a bunch of lying freaks!"

"Needless to say, I withdraw the nomination," said Mr. Brentworth.

"But what about me?" Horace's voice sounded falsetto in his own ears. "I could be in deep trouble. What is going to happen to me?"

"Your fate is of no importance. Please leave us. We find your presence exceedingly distasteful."

"As far as you are concerned," said Mr. Jamison, "this meeting of the Nasty Club has adjourned."

"We have further business to transact," said Mr. Caldwell, "so, if you would be so kind—"

Horace rose, swayed, gripped the table to steady himself. He staggered away, consumed by a red, blinding, destructive rage. How could they do this to him? How dare they look down on him, when all he did was follow his natural inclinations? He didn't have it wrong. That's the way it was done. For that they cast him into the darkness?

To hell with them. He stomped off, seeing nothing, out of the alcove and through the dining room. The doorman slammed the door behind him with a haughty crash. Maybe not—maybe it didn't happen that way—but to Horace's bruised ego it sure seemed like it.

The Saturday after the End of the World

It was the Saturday after the end of the world, by which I mean it was a Saturday, just like a whole bunch of others, but the world had already ended, only we didn't know it yet. We were just about to find out. I was stopping off at the usual convenience store that morning, having just gotten out from my night job, dropping in wearily as I often did before I went home to collapse, to pick up a loaf of bread and a package of sliced meat, maybe some soft drinks. I was running low on those. The fellow behind the counter was the usual Pakistani who managed the place, always there because he cut expenses on the hired help. There were a few rough looking customers, construction types I expect, and while I was standing in line some lady came in. That was all pretty normal, considering that the world had ended some time before. We didn't really know it had happened because nobody had come right out and said so, but there were plenty of signs that in retrospect, on that day, loomed large in the mind.

For weeks we'd been hearing about it, only it sounded so much like the typical drivel, if more intense. They spouted it in the sleazy tabloids, those rags that print anything for a buck, generating a craze of the week, then moving on to something else stupid and lurid. This time they hadn't moved on. "Space Aliens Taking Over the Earth!" screamed their crazy headlines. "Secret Bases Established!" "ET Infiltrators Replacing Humanity!" Pretty awful stuff, but we'd heard worse from the kook squads, the peddlers of conspiracies and pseudo-scientific rubbish. Wasn't this more of the same? Then it cropped up on chat shows, the daytime junk on TV, and then the radio talk channels, many of them spouting the "could it be" routine. At first they presented it with a grin, then with a nervous laugh, then in hushed tones, finally—I guess it was right around the end—with a trace of hysteria. Minor politicians got into the act. I'd heard snippets of this stuff, chuckled to myself, commented to my work buddies, but otherwise my life went on in the same tiresome grind it always had. It's a funny way to go through the end of the world.

The Pakistani manager had a TV muttering on a wall stand behind his head, tuned to one of those 24 hour news services, the kind that repeat thirty minutes of material all day and night. Some more fellows came in, youngish punks by the look of them. Then the special report came on. "News Alert!" followed by a burst of dramatic music, and "Special Announcement from the Vice-president of the United States!" Then his pudgy face appeared, and he spoke.

What he said was that it was all true: that we really had been covertly invaded by alien beings, creatures that had assumed the form of men and infiltrated all sectors of society, including the highest levels of government. They had even replaced the President, he said, and what we thought was that man was actually a vile enemy working to conquer and enslave us. He told us that, he told us a lot more, too, all of it horrible and unbelievable, yet it was the Vice-president saying it, and he sounded like he meant it. He screamed that the hour was late, that the take-over was practically complete, that our only hope was for all genuine human beings to rise up and fight. He shouted that; then the screen went dead, and on the instant pandemonium broke out in the store.

The young nasty guys pulled guns and began firing at some of the construction workers. A couple of those rugged men whipped out weapons too and went after their own. The manager turned around from where he'd been staring at the TV, shouted, "They're here!" The woman, way back in the store, shrieked, "It's the aliens!" and somebody snapped off a shot at her. I backed away from the bloody confusion, careened into the woman who was racing for the door. She and I tumbled out together, just as I glimpsed the manager going down, vanishing in a spray of red behind his counter.

Outside two creepy types who had been lounging there when I drove up were beating to death a teenaged couple with metal rods. They were right by my car. I hesitated; then the woman pleaded, "Come with me." She dove into her old Chevy and, as she was pulling out of her parking space, I lunged through the passenger door. She squealed out of the lot and away we went, zooming down the street.

Near sobbing, she said in an angry voice, "I knew it was true. I've seen it coming. Why didn't we take action when we could?" It was a mess on the road, plenty of cars pulled over with drivers in them, probably listening to their radios, others driving insanely fast, not all in the proper lanes. Once I thought I spied a dead guy on the curb. Black billows of smoke sprouted at distant points. I could hardly think, not about what I'd seen and heard, not about what I was doing now, speeding away from my place in a stranger's car. I flicked on the radio.

A female commentator was ranting about "disturbances," but before she could bring herself to mention a single concrete fact the radio went silent, or I should say converted to static. I punched buttons, checking channels; just dead squawking noise everywhere on the dial.

I said nothing as we drove into the country, past scattered farms, into a rather wooded region where we turned off and sped up a narrow rural lane. We twisted and turned along this for a mile or three, until we arrived at her house. She invited me in—demanded me in—and I went. There the woman directed me to the refrigerator to feed myself, while she plunked herself down in front of the TV and watched what there was to see.

Some stations were off the air, others went off during the day, while still others that had been off came back on. Her cable system kept going, with a two hour break, all day, returning after the hiatus with a new message. I was drawn in by the rapid developments, the news in the making. The channels initially reported horrid crimes, riots, wild-eyed speeches prophesying doom and screaming for mass action. Later reports, from stations that came on or returned to the air, counseled calm, urged citizens to stay home, referred to troublesome elements that were being quickly suppressed. I didn't hear the VP again that day, but the President showed up, to assure us all that the episode of unnecessary public panic, fueled by the foolish statement of his mentally disturbed subordinate, was passing, would soon die down. All would be well shortly, he said.

There I was, in that old, creaky house in the middle of nowhere, on that unusual Saturday, and there I stayed, with my new companion. Let me say something about her. This was no desperately hopeful romantic interlude. The mistress of the home I made my own was a Mrs. Gladys Hooper, a middle-aged widow who until then lived alone (save for her nervous poodle) on the proceeds of her late Jonathan's estate. She was frumpy, overweight, sad-faced, perpetually miserable, probably had been before all this started. All she did was watch TV and smoke cigarettes, smoked like a chimney all the time. She had a pile of cartons stashed away, along with a big cupboard full of survival rations, mainly canned stuff. Having, I gathered, always been a denizen of Kooksville, she had taken this business seriously from the earliest reports weeks before, and had prepared for the worst. I suppose I should have been grateful for her forethought, only I was still too mixed up to figure things rightly. I still wonder if I have.

My views shifted from one moment to the next, influenced by the weird communications reaching us from out there, affected by her

86

emotional state, which ever swung between frighteningly quiet, brittle calm and noisy periods of chaotic psychosis. I endeavored to wrestle with the evidence as I knew it, struggled to make sense of what had happened. Could I rationalize events? I tried hard. What had I witnessed, what had I heard? My personal experience might suggest a botched robbery, perhaps an uprising of gang violence, coincidentally corresponding to some worse than average political zaniness. The current crop of leaders didn't impress me, so I could, with effort, imagine the VP and others popping off, running at the mouth like I'd known many a good citizen to do. If this was more of the same, then maybe matters would sort themselves out and life would clank along in its good old meaningless fashion, which was all I hoped for.

But I wasn't entirely buying that, not that Saturday, and not since. I stayed. Gladys foamed at the mouth when I broached the subject of leaving. "I can't face them alone!" she whined. She was a bad influence, to be sure. There was more, though; the barrage of garbage pouring out of her TVs and radios got under my skin, unsettled me, caused me to doubt reason and sanity. I'd never been a determined consumer of that crap, preferring to pick up tidbits along the road of life, knowing enough to fit in and sound "with it," not needing all the details. In her isolated house I was exposed to the wide world, and what I learned wasn't sweet. Television shows had suffered considerable deterioration from when I was a kid. It was all noise and lights and video trickery, with what spewed out of mouths of the endless stream of talking heads sounding bizarre at the best of times. The times weren't always the best. Before Saturday turned to Sunday the cumulative patterns and indications of subtle change chilled me, fostered the conviction or delusion that something had occurred, an alteration that could not be undone. It gave me the creeps to think that the world had been ending all this time, and that I'd only realized now, when it was a done deal.

By that night every station and channel was oozing a soothing syrup, seemingly operating in tandem to assure us that we need fear nothing, exactly as if they all read from the same script. That wasn't natural, it wasn't show biz, it didn't reassure or convince. By that night the commentators and news readers who had been yanked from the tube were back, most telling such a different story that I couldn't connect the earlier persona to the later. That gave me the creeps, thinking they'd been duplicated and replaced. What became of the originals? Gladys harbored really filthy ideas on that score, drawn from tales published in the more despicable scandal sheets before the trouble . . . or before the world ended.

Many breaking developments of that day were never mentioned again. I thought they liked to talk every story to death. Not any more; they put a lot behind as if it had never been. And those TV faces behaved strangely, too. I had the feeling now that they were speaking on two tracks, one the ostensible, for my benefit, the other a kind of code, delivered to somebody else. They paused oddly at certain words and glanced meaningfully at the camera when there wasn't need. It was spooky. Spookier still when, as happened occasionally during those weeks, a TV chatterbox would suddenly go berserk, crying out against what one termed "the menace," and on each such occasion the screen would go blank, to come back on without that commentator. He might return in a few days, but if he did he didn't explain himself or try to reveal anything again. I brooded about those instances. The Vice-president, incidentally, turned up again, to apologize for the fuss he'd caused. I brooded about him, too.

As I've surely already made clear, that Saturday came and went, so I can say that I lived for a while after I learned about the end of the world. If my worst imaginings were right, if the tales repeated by Gladys were accurate, the aliens had triumphed completely, seized everything, were now engaged in hunting down and eliminating or replacing anyone who might oppose them. It was their world, not ours, the few of us who possibly still lurked and skulked and hid among the invading swarms. Were all the survivors as inert and scatterbrained as Gladys and I? The only way to find out was to go out, and despite fleeting inclinations I couldn't bring myself to do that. I remained in the house, biding my time, waiting for something, not knowing what it might be, dreading what it might be. Gladys mentally rotted in front of the TV, smoking mechanically, sometimes with the tears running unnoticed, unwiped down her broad face. I sat around, munching crackers and nibbling potted meat, washing down such savory meals with water, soda pop, the infrequent beer. The beer went fast, I had to conserve it, but it still didn't last. Everything kept working though, the electricity, the water, the TV cable. It was all running, as if the world still existed, which it didn't.

I picked up the truth, convinced myself of the ultimate horror, sitting there in that house and paying attention to the data that streamed in. It was real, all right. Once in a while the TV pap slipped up and made a telling mistake, let out what should have been hidden longer. If it was error, that is; in time maybe the new masters felt more sure of themselves, didn't bother so to mind Ps and Qs. One smiling digital face would say to the other, out of the blue, "We just about have them all," or "We'll get back to that when disguise is unnecessary," or "The time for pretense passes rapidly." Why would they talk that way? Why the sneaky references to "private channels," for those "in the know?" Why the sneers at those "who still haven't learned?" And images in news stories presented curious scenes, like the spidery towers of shiny metal and sparkling glass that began to appear in the background of many shots. What were those things? I'd seen some before the Saturday, wondered idly, knew too little to understand or even question. The radio (the channels had come back on before that awful day was out) was worse. There the hosts would ramble on for hours, dropping so many oblique allusions to "the new order" or "the final stages of mopping up" that they terrorized me. At times somebody would call in to the program, begging for information about what was really going on—"for God's sake"—only to be met with nasty laughs.

Other types of TV programming provided clues. During those weeks the broadcast dramas and comedies grew so wretched, unfeeling, and false that Gladys, the soap addict, gave up on them in disgust. I caught a snatch of a gardening show, of all things, in which the winsome hostess broke off her desultory chatter for a public service message: "The meteorites have landed safely, and the snakes have been recovered and secured." I didn't want to watch any more.

And once, just once, I heard over the radio what I definitely wasn't meant to hear. Turning the dial, as I infrequently did, on my companion's old box set, I picked up an extremely faint channel on which an amateurish announcer implored help "for our people," and described in graphic detail air strikes against Omaha. That there might continue to be disorders in this country I could accept, but fire bombing, unreported by any major outlet? It was too much to contemplate. I never received that station again.

I thought to make plans for the future. The food wouldn't last much longer, we needed fresh supplies, I quailed at the notion of going into town for them. Gladys was oblivious to the problem, while I was merely ignorant. I spun schemes for hunting in the forests and farming the lonely glades. There were ways to do that, if only I could learn them. With luck I could live a long life here, if it absolutely had to be.

There came a morning. It was a Saturday—I kept track, of that and other items, just to keep myself balanced—several Saturdays after *the* Saturday. Call it a Saturday after the Saturday after the end of the world. There's a date for you. Gladys let the dog out to do his business, she careful not to set so much as a foot out on the porch. We'd dwelt in there like prisoners, which I guess we were. We heard the noise of an engine. A pickup truck came around the bend, a truck with an opaque windshield, directly into view a hundred yards away, halted. Buffy—that's the pooch, of course—yapped frantically and lit out for it. The truck cranked, started up, backed out of sight, with the dog chasing. Gladys broke. She wailed the creature's name and burst through the screen door, dashing madly across the leaf-littered lawn. She disappeared, too.

That was this morning, one more Saturday morning, and it's about time to wrap up my tale. I give myself some credit: I made it a ways past the end, and at least I go down understanding, which is more than most of the human race got. Gladys never came back. She won't. There are shapes moving among the oaks at the edge of the yard, human shapes mainly, although I glimpsed a couple of things that didn't quite agree with me. They're out there, closing in, and I don't think they plan to throw a net over me, as I might once have believed. I think they're going to replace me, or kill me, or eat me, or all of the above. That's really what they're going to do.

I know this is for real, and I'm about to be sick thinking of what's coming, but something inside still doesn't want to buy it. I say to myself again and again, "It can't be, it can't be. Things like this don't happen."

Notes on a Clinical Case

(Written in the hand of Doctor Ashton Oxbury)

I prepare this statement in a rush, for I may not have occasion for a formal paper; other, pressing matters, I believe, will shortly occupy my time. The technical details, therefore, must be found among my professional papers. It is necessary that I preface this explanatory account with a brief history of my recent patient, Mr. Harrold Lemmurs.

Lemmurs came to public attention as the sole survivor of the Caulfield coal mine explosion last year. That April 18th the resultant cave-in killed five outright, trapped two, Lemmurs and Wallis Tomlinson. Imprisoned in a chamber eight hundred feet beneath the surface, they fortunately possessed a telephone connection to the outside world, allowing them to signal their continued existence; possessed that, tanks of oxygen, and a modicum of water, but very little else. Attempts to quickly reach the trapped men failed. The communication link expired on the fifth day. A surer method of plumbing the depths afforded scant chance of rescue, for it took over three weeks to approach that subterranean position. This heroic, seemingly futile endeavor was reported day by day in the various media.

They found Lemmurs alive, Tomlinson dead. The press hailed this much of an achievement, celebrating technical ingenuity and manly determination, until certain ancillary facts leaked out. Tomlinson's purloined autopsy report disgraced the front page of a lowly tabloid, and speculation grew rank. The crude incisions, the missing portions, suggestive marks on bones: had Lemmurs any comment? After several days incommunicado he admitted, through a spokesman, the unpleasant truth. He had prolonged his life until rescue by feasting on the corpse of Wallis Tomlinson.

He claimed that his fellow miner perished naturally, nor was evidence to the contrary presented, so this grotesque development did not become then a concern of the police, merely a sour final note to an otherwise rousing tale. Early this year, however, I was called in by the authorities on what had since become the Lemmurs case. Following his ordeal the man had lain low as best he could, striving to avoid the understandably embarrassing limelight. Then his story broke afresh. Now, as a result of his subsequent actions, he stood accused of abominable crimes, the desecration of the dead and at least one murder, falling under suspicion of more instances of the latter.

His counsel asked me to interview him, develop a formal presentation concerning his state of mind, catalogue any factors which might bear on the question of legal guilt or innocence. They paid me well, up front. I thought my task the usual one of formulating a standard insanity defense. I am pretty sure that I was wrong about that.

The defendant faced major logical hurdles. Known instances of what I termed "necessity cannibalism" never led to a proclivity along those lines, yet the lawyers of Lemmurs wished me to determine just that, nor could I wonder why. Within two weeks of his release from the mine, as established by his ambiguous confession, Lemmurs commenced haunting the repositories of the dead—hospitals, funeral homes, mausolea—sneaking or breaking in, absconding with dietary flesh. These gruesome events became known, tighter security obtained, and Lemmurs was, as he put it, "forced" into new channels of carnal acquisition. He proved nonspecific on this point, but the police filled in the gaps as they claimed the evidence dictated. Thus commenced his sporadic murder spree, undertaken solely for dubious nourishment. Fingerprints tied him to one mutilated victim, while informed supposition placed him at the scene of four more ghastly killings. What was found in Lemmurs' freezer seemed to clinch the case.

Harrold Lemmurs presented himself to me as a regular, unassuming citizen, a normal guy who, after a very bad time, inexplicably went off the deep end. He could not explain himself. If I may anticipate, his wife and colleagues too, as much as they had lately come to loath him, all expressed to me their amazement at the monster into which he transformed, a metamorphosis of personality lacking any foreshadowing in his previous life. I recorded everything they told me, without granting it great credence. Anyway, I first conversed with the accused, and to the extent that I took him at face value formulated a similar opinion. His childhood and early life lacked bizarre episodes. I uncovered no traces of suppressed cruelty, unnatural lusts, peculiar interests. What little reading material he absorbed was of the tamest, most puerile sort, his movie-going unexceptional. His mental condition? Well, I had not known him before, nor had he ever experienced psychoanalysis. I knew him as I met him, avowedly a changed man.

Lemmurs spoke much of the insidious cravings that overpowered him after the mine catastrophe. He dated their manifestation to the initial moment when, with utter distaste and horror, he forced himself to swallow that first mouthful of Tomlinson. I recall the manner in which he described it. My files are at the office, so I do not have the transcription before me, but I remember his statement—the gist—in my own words: "The mental agony gave way to ecstasy, as the sublime nectar slid down my throat." He said something like that. Also: "It was as if my life truly began then. Previous existence seemed empty, the future ripe with possibility." In so many words, this he told me. He proved, in addition, much more forthcoming about his extremely altered behavior following rescue. While struggling to maintain a normal front, early on in his reintroduction to the world Lemmurs began obsessively plotting to gain access to the objects of his awakening culinary tastes. When opportunities for morbid theft deserted him, he shamelessly and without hesitation turned to more dire mechanisms of satisfaction.

The murders (He admitted them all, and a couple overlooked) meant nothing to him. He chose his victims at random, hunger his sole guide. He wished to eat forbidden morsels. He felt it his right— it must be so!—the viands counted for more than life, honor, and reputation. He must eat, and he must eat *that*. The killings, he insisted, entailed only from lack of recourse.

What should I do with this material? Any decent prosecutor could make hash of him on the stand. At this stage in my investigation I best served knowledge by collating the statements of Lemmurs with other data. It was then that I interviewed those who knew him best, to no useful purpose, then that I consulted his medical records, seeking something, anything, that might provide a clue.

I think I found one. I am eager to expound, but professionalism reins in my ardor, nor do I have time now for a complete delineation of my theory. The evidence is still equivocal, I know—further tests are required, extensive study which I may not be able to pursue—yet I can not wait. I must set down a glimpse of it here, lest my full summation of findings be delayed or prevented.

His public defenders saw to it that Lemmurs received the full battery of medical tests. The medical men poked and probed, tapped and scrutinized his several fluids. The genetic tests bore strange fruit.

Lemmurs possesses an uncommon gene; not strictly rare, in no way isolated in the population at large, but thinly spread. This hitherto unexplained gene, a recessive trait, falls at the K2 position in the human DNA sequence, is considered inactive, and has not heretofore been linked to any behavior or physical trait.

I think I can do so. Noting this minor oddity, I checked the city's hospital databases, detected the mysterious gene in many subjects, none of whom (I then learned) exhibited freakish tendencies. Imagine my amusement when I located the inactive K2 gene in my own chart! As I said, uncommon, not rare. Perhaps one per cent of the populace, judging from my preliminary search, owns and transmits this gene. It appears to have no function; yet in Lemmurs, the tests established, the gene had been activated. With what result?

An incredible idea came to me, the mere beginning of a hypothesis. Suppose there were a cannibalism gene? In the dim past of our race that abhorrent practice was widespread, well nigh universal. Perhaps it had been genetically fostered and controlled. Modern research, after all, is discovering a genetic basis for practically everything. Why not this? In lost ages, maybe, the gene constituted a regular part of the human code. It became recessive, maybe, long ago, dwindled in proportion, grew less of a force in the affairs of homo *sapiens*. At length laws or taboo forced it underground, so to speak. Like many known genes, it "switched off", stopped expressing itself. With certain lusts totally denied, the bearer of the gene might live his entire life without exhibiting peculiar tendencies. The gene, however, survived, borne by heredity, descending with our species, lying dormant... until such time as, in lurid or tragic circumstances, an outside stimulus operated to activate the gene, said stimulus consisting of the ingestion of human proteins. This, I deduced, might instantaneously instigate an irrepressible craving.

Faced with this possibility, I re-examined the historical data. Modern material offered me still nothing, or approached the matter with such priggish reticence as to allow for big doubt, but ancient and medieval sources provided obscure hints which fueled my theory. I investigated the scholastic literature discussing certain dubious Biblical tales, including that of the "night monsters" haunting fallen Babylon; uncovered new meaning in the conflicting reports of the shocking disgrace of St. Beneficio; I came to terms, unlike most historians, with the repulsive saga of Sawney Bean and his depraved family. I could see how it could be—the data could be made to fit without great effort—and the sum total of musty lore and up-to-date genetics readily explained the hideous actions of Harrold Lemmurs. For those cursed with the K2 gene, a single taste of forbidden fruit did the trick.

I wanted proof. The strength of the logical argument convinced me, but I could not leave it there. Without hard supporting evidence my grand thoughts remained pretty words, readily dismissed. How to test the hypothesis? I required, of course, a confirming case, an experiment in diet. Simple, clear-cut, excruciatingly difficult to arrange. A subject bearing the moribund K2 gene must be led to eat what he would not choose to eat.

For what it is worth, I admit to getting carried away by the notion. Naturally the convenient fact that I myself possessed the suspect gene occurred to me. Once it did, the spectacular idea fastened upon me with sharp fangs. Presenting myself to the authorities, with fair honesty, as a member of Lemmurs' defense team, I demanded access to the police evidence. They freely allowed me to enter the sealed freezer at county hospital where were stored, in preparation for trial, the unmentionable items removed by detectives from Lemmurs' home freezer. When I left there no one dreamed, could bring themselves to imagine, that I had subtracted from that store of remains.

I learned what I wanted to know. Just one confirming case, I realize, but the results are so dramatic, the consequences so profound, that in my mind all debate has ceased. I had to steel myself to do it. That seems ludicrous now! I smuggled the stuff to my quarters, thawed it, baked it lightly—I dreaded over-charring of the amino acids, which conceivably could weaken the test—laid the finished product before me, and then I did that. I disbelieved my actions, even as I raised hand to mouth.

I know all. Nevertheless, I do not intend publication of this document, unless my future circumstances require it. Perhaps my findings may aid Lemmurs, perhaps not; I do not care, for it is my needs that matter now, not his. This is my private revelation. Everything has changed for me. I shed the strait-jacket of phony existence. I know what I do now, what I will do tomorrow and the next day, so long as I can, however I can accomplish it.

I ate the meat. I must have more.

One Day, Complete With Aliens

Vince decided, subsequently, that he was glad it happened on one of his off days, but at first he didn't see it that way, no indeed. Then it galled him, for work was bearing down-- it was one of those seasons when the common drudgery of retail grew painful and fierce, like an infuriated viper hissing and striking at his numbed brain-- and his private life had gone to pieces again, what with that business with Jenny finally falling through-- not due, certainly, to any fault of his own-- so he was under pressure already, looking forward to nothing more than a couple of days of peace and quiet. That morning he watched a bit of TV, until the blurred emissions from the deteriorating set infiltrated his skull and made his brains begin to leak, then walked down from his dingy one-room apartment in the heart of town to the corner market in order to purchase an armload of cheap goods to replenish his failing larder. Returning an hour later with the white bread and plastic-cased sandwich meat and potato chips and root beer in a single paper sack, Vince re-entered the old apartment building, a relic of former generations when it functioned as a fine house in a real neighborhood, tramped up the creaky wooden stairs to the second floor, fumbled for his key at the door, which unexpectedly swung open at a touch before he could commence the ritual of unlocking.

In the short space of an hour so much had changed. His small combo room, with its adjoining kitchenette and impossibly cramped bathroom, had served him as a refuge, however squalid, a haven where he could relax in private among his grubby but treasured possessions. Now it was largely empty. A quick glance of a survey established that all of his personal belongings had disappeared, the only recognizable items remaining being the few sticks of junky furniture grudgingly provided under the heading of "furnished room". Nor was his sacred privacy maintained. In place of the varied accouterments of his life, he was granted the presence of two fresh objects, a duo of well dressed men.

"What's going on here?" Vince demanded. "Where's my stuff? Who are you? What's going on?"

The two men wore matching suits, jackets, ties, slacks, polished shoes. Their suits were neutral gray, their ties vibrant and loudly red, their shoes gleaming black. Their hair was brown, combed to the left, their features bland but firm. They greatly resembled one another. Vince imagined they could be brothers.

One said, "Allow us to introduce ourselves. We are agents of the Federal Government." After confirming Vince's identity he gave their names, but these, too, were strikingly similar-- Smith and Smitz, or Schmidt and Smith, something like that-- in the heat of the moment Vince didn't adequately connect the information to the faces, so he shortly lapsed into denoting them as Mr. One and Mr. Two.

Mr. One continued, "I'm glad we caught you before it was too late."

"Caught?" Vince repeated. "Am I under arrest?"

"Oh no," replied Mr. Two, "nothing like that." Even their pleasant, well modulated voices tended to blend. He went on, "To the contrary, we're here to help you."

"Somebody stole my stuff?"

"Hardly," said Mr. One. "We arranged for its removal to safe quarters, and we hope to do the same for you. You see, sir, you are in great danger."

"I don't understand."

"Of course not. You're a citizen; it isn't your place to understand. That's our job. Shall we make ourselves comfortable before we begin?"

"Let's," Vince replied gruffly. The intruders took seats at the scarred wooden table, missing its ratty cloth covering, easing themselves onto the two stiff-backed wooden chairs from which the soiled cushions had vanished. Their host dumped himself, ostentatiously frowning, onto the now naked mattress of the noisy-springed bed.

Mr. Two lightly smiled, leaned forward slightly, commenced. "It's like this, Vince. Via our sources and contacts we have detected a threat aimed at your personal welfare and existence. You see, aliens from outer space have targeted you for destruction. Indeed, we have reason to believe that you are in great and pressing danger of elimination. Confronted by this immediate peril, we quickly took steps leading to your relocation and safety. We considered your effects as well, which could be used to trace you, and have conveyed them to an unspecified place of storage. Now we may concentrate entirely on you."

Faced with this, Vince could only find it in himself to ask, "So, that's the explanation, is it?"

Mr. One said, in somber tones with serious frown attached, "Sir, this is not a matter to be treated lightly. Death stalks you. These invaders will stop at nothing to get at you, and if they do the consequences will be unpleasant; I may go so far as to describe them as horrific. We are ready to take you now. We will send you far away from here, concealing all evidence of your movement; a new name shall be bestowed upon you, while all traces of your former existence shall be erased. That, we believe, may be sufficient."

"For the time being," added Mr. Two. "Later, more severe measures may prove necessary."

"But it's crazy," Vince retorted. "I've never heard of these aliens. I don't know anything about them. Why should they care about me?"

"They are enemies of the human race, sworn to our annihilation. Do not imagine yourself exempt."

"I mean, why me in particular?" Vince persisted. "I've done nothing, know nothing. It doesn't make sense for them to pick me out of the crowd."

"They're aliens," declared Mr. One. "Their minds work differently from ours, operating according to standards wholly detached from those of our space-time continuum. Our incredibly efficient methods of data collection reveal their proximate aims, unfortunately entirely divorced from the sinister, inhuman logic underlying them. These creatures want you. They will get you, unless we act fast."

He rose briskly, Mr. Two following in an identical trajectory. He said, "We must report officially on our meeting. Sir, we shall return precisely on the hour. Be prepared to accompany us then." Vince commenced to expostulate warmly, but the two men, with all courtesy, excused themselves and departed, muttering to one another of a certain form (a jumble of arcane letters and numbers) which must be filed and entered at headquarters. They left.

After a lingering period of blank stasis Vince stormed downstairs to accost his crabby old landlady Mrs. Scithers, whom he found in the open office (which doubled as her rooms) fussing with the frayed cord of a vacuum cleaner. He demanded to know why she allowed strange men to enter his apartment and remove his private property without consulting him first.

"You weren't around," she replied, more intent on her tired machine than him, "and it was government business." She got the vacuum going. It roared an aggravating, staccato howl. Mrs. Scithers turned her hard, lined face to him, pushed back a thin lock of dishwater gray and cried over the noise, "I don't interfere with that stuff. It don't matter to me what you've done."

"They told you I did something?"

"They told me nothing. I didn't ask. I don't interfere. They got jobs to do, that's all. It's none of my business. You take it up with them."

Vince would not listen to her galling whine further. He headed back to his room with a thunder cloud in his brain, arrived to remember that there was absolutely nothing for him there save for the bag of lousy food, still resting on the kitchen counter where he dumped it, put it away in the rumbling antique of a refrigerator, then sulked downstairs again and out into the open air of the hectic street.

He didn't know what to do with himself. He scarcely understood what he was expected to do, much less what he should. He wanted to complain to somebody about the unfairness of this intrusion into his busy life, but beyond his unhelpful landlady he could conjure up no relevant authorities. He feared that the story was not such as to fire the police with sympathy. They would dismiss him as insane, or refuse jurisdiction over this presumably high level affair. His sole dealings with them in the past had been via the medium of traffic tickets (these before his third-hand crud-mobile puked out its transmission), and those one-sided experiences had not inclined him toward further communications.

Vince, pondering developments, wandered the circumscribed avenues of his existence. Absently he paced north, then west, south, then east, heeding neither the tumultuous lanes of shops, bars, offices, nor the animate, mangy, furtively hostile figures that thronged them. Cars whizzed past, one honking long and loudly when he stepped dangerously from the sidewalk. He thought of the strange tale of menace and warning the men had carried to him. It gave him the creeps, in a dry, dusty fashion, like sour news read in the papers, unappealing yet oddly impersonal, so utterly disconnected from his typical grim concerns, which still bulked infuriatingly large. There were bills to pay, silly conflicts on the job, aggravating romantic crises, and-- oh yes-- space aliens wished to kill him. What a dirty trick that was.

It could make a fellow morbid. Barring a lunatic practical joke, he guessed they were out there, among the herd that choked him, watching and waiting for their opportunity. They must be invisible, or disguised, or hidden, otherwise he could have figured out the problem for himself. Did one require others to bear witness to such matters?

If genuine, he thought there should be signs he could discern from his milieu.

Did others take an inordinate interest in him? That might constitute unsettling evidence. Vince cursed himself for his former lack of attention to his surroundings (a lack born of extreme distaste), swore to remedy the lack. He set out to notice. He looked at things. He studied objects: the fire hydrant, that radio tower looming over the boxy office block, the illegally parked cab. Did terror lurk in these? Anything could hide in a hydrant-- who knew what went on in there-- but it was hard to feel it. What of the people? Were they what they seemed? There were in the city, surely, a plethora of overt menaces; any one of these desperate types might stick a knife in him. As he strode he observed. When one passerby glanced at him, he stared back. The young, hard-faced woman wrinkled her nose at him and turned away with a sneer. The scroungy street worker held his stare, grinned to his equally wretched associate. Was there something in that? He kept trying. Vince didn't gain much from most of these trials, only there were vague instances (of course he doubted them) when he sensed a lingering interest, as if his silent quizzing disturbed a subtle game centered on him. The frumpy old man, balding with thick glasses, who ran the corner convenience store; say now, there was a possibility. It suddenly occurred to Vince that this guy, in previous wanderings, had done more than casually acknowledge him with his glazed eyes, but rather had scrutinized him as if suspecting criminal intent, or perhaps for more nefarious reasons.

Vince locked gazes with him now. The man's eyes did not waver. He stood in the gloom of his open doorway across the street, a sad, sagging sack of a man, his face nondescript, his eyes-- think about this-- his eyes cold and dark as marbles. Vince occasionally traded with him. He'd been in the man's close presence. He recollected obscurities of emotion, layers of masked meaning in simple statements. He'd thought that the way of the city. Was it always? Was it this time?

He dodged into traffic, slipped between sluggish vehicles, narrowed the gap. Vince reached the curb. He planted his feet firmly on concrete, beheld the man. That one seemed to recede into the doorway, wreathed in sliding shadows, but still Vince saw him clearly. Visually they dueled, motionless, tension mounting. Vince tingled with mysterious, assured expectation.

It happened. What he saw then was as objectively real, as prosaically certain, as the wind-twirled litter in the gutter. The man's head burst into flame. It exploded into leaping tongues of yellow and

100

red fire, with black smoke that foamed and boiled, and when the flames died and the smoke dissipated Vince looked upon a grotesquely altered visage. It horrified; it sickened; it reeked of the loathsomely alien.

From the man's overly tight collar protruded a yellowish-gray lump of flesh, a massy nodule of clammy, spoiled dough shaped by flabby talons into the crazed caricature of a face. A hairless, lopsided dome of a skull overhung three gleaming eyes sunk into an upward pointing triangle of deep sockets. Noseless slits of nostrils spread wide about the thin, lipless mouth. The mouth fell open, chinless, gaping to reveal a fine, serried array of close, minute, needle-like teeth, from which dripped thick, pearly ichor.

Vince shrieked, broke contact, spun away and fled in mindless panic. He did not plan his course. He left the scene as fast as his legs would carry him, inconsiderate of those he thrust aside in his career. He ran until he could not gasp enough oxygen, until the breath honked like a maddened goose from the back of his tortured throat.

He returned to awareness in an alley which he recognized as connecting to a cross street near his block. Wheezing, he stumbled amidst debris to the exit, made his way forlornly in the accustomed direction out of habit. He didn't know where to go. Obviously there was something after all to this day's peculiar revelations. Menace did lurk-- perhaps it was focused upon him-- maybe the furtive horrors were so sure of him that they now disdained concealment. Instead they chose to toy with him, before they struck.

Vince emerged into his street, saw his building up the way. Near at hand he spied something else. Before that big slabby warehouse he noticed a heap. Elements of the heap drew him as had, rather differently, the freakish-headed alien. What was that junk piled before the open door? It was his belongings, that's what, many of them anyway, jumbled carelessly, thoughtlessly discarded. He approached angrily. He could see that several items were stacked just within, but the remainder lay on the walk, as if those in the process of conveying the tatters of his life had grown bored or punched the clock for the day in midstream. That's government for you, he thought.

He sat down wearily, hunched against the wall by a slatted wooden box from which the contents sloppily spilled. He realized what they were: treasures formerly buried in his shunned closet. These were the comic books and Sci-Fi magazines of his boyhood, retained when so many other mementos of the years had been banished to the trash dump. Vince had wondered what became of them. He poked through the scattered selection. Oh yes, this was all the good stuff, survivals of wide-eyed innocence. He especially longed for-- here it was!-- the long sought after "Mars" edition of *Impossible Tales*, which he hadn't managed to unearth in fifteen years. Every story therein dealt with imaginative aspects of the creepy Red Planet, a place he'd dreamed to be formidably exotic in those days.

Maybe it really was, wholly unlike the drab orb that modern mechanized blandness allowed. Feeling hopelessly at loose ends, Vince sat and read, and in the reading he was happy.

Presently two men swung round the warehouse, advanced on him. He sprang to his feet, fists clenched, prepared to deal with annoying agents or tentacled invaders, saw that it was only his good buddies Biff and Lennie. They hailed him, dashed forward grinning. Biff said heartily, "We were looking for you, thought you'd join us for dinner," while Lennie grinned, surveyed the odd scene, asked, "What's up, pal?"

Vince gave them a wan smile, shrugged and replied, "I'm the victim of attempted robbery. As you can see, they didn't get far with the goods. Say, will you help me move this stuff back?"

"Sure!" they chimed, and the trio scooped up armfuls of stuff, lugged it across and up the avenue, into the apartment building to his rooms. They repeated this chore five times before they got it all. Mrs. Scithers grumbled at the noisy activity, the repeated pounding of heavy feet on creaky wooden stairs, muttered about the quality of her tenants, but she refrained from interference. Lennie said, "You never know what you're worth until you have to haul it." Then they went out to eat.

Vince returned home alone, after a satisfying meal spiced with delectable conversation. Dusk darkened the streets. He unlocked his door, breezed in to find the government men lying in wait for him; if standing stiffly at attention could be called lying.

Mr. One said, "This is unpardonable behavior, sir." Mr. Two said, "We expect better from United States citizens." Mr. One observed, with a tinge of heat, "You undid hours of regulation labor. This must be reported."

Vince replied, his voice escalating in volume as he spoke, "You can get out of my room, out of my life, out of my memory. I've had enough."

"But you are in great danger!"

"I guess."

"The aliens are making their final preparations!"

"I accept that."

"There is not a moment to lose!"

"I've already lost too many today," announced Vince. "Listen, guys, I thank you for your concern, and I suppose you mean well, but you're both royal pains, and I want you out, now. My life is difficult enough as it is. There are so many threats these days, I can't keep track of them. Something, I know, is going to get me sooner or later, and your aliens simply don't rate any higher than the rest. That's funny: being stalked by monsters ought to count as a big deal, but it just doesn't, not any more than lots more I can think of. Maybe I'll feel differently tomorrow. This moment, I don't feel like worrying about it."

Vince saw them out, nodding politely at their formulaic protests. He shut the door, locked and bolted it. Vaguely hungry again, he made himself a bologna sandwich, opened the potato chips, hunched himself comfortably onto the threadbare couch with his old copy of *Impossible Tales*. He laughed and grinned and sipped root beer as he read. He felt at peace, for a little while.

Nightmares in the Castle Titana

So Jacob Bleek, seeker after strange knowledge, grim and obsessive student of arts arcane and uncanny, came out of the desolate southern hills late that afternoon into the shallow valley split by its ribbon of green in the bottom lands, and down to this glad sight he ventured, there to water his horse and slake his own thirst in the thinly trickling brook which ran so low that he subsequently rode easily over the exposed stones. On the far side he entered a dense wood, riding up a neglected path that chance sent him, one which led presently to a decrepit foot bridge across a minor tributary, and beyond this he approached the village set amidst its slender mantle of grain and turnip fields. Alongside a muddy irrigation ditch he encountered the first peasants, swarthy men united by mops of lank black hair and wary black eyes who greeted him deferentially, for despite the wear and stains of hard travel Bleek possessed the proud demeanor and brazen assurance of the gentleman. He fixed them with a stony stare from under his broad-brimmed hat, his dark cloak flapping in the stiff breeze, asked them if this place were Gromengatz. They allowed that it was. He asked further the way to the Castle Titana, and to this they reacted oddly. "Do not go there," they advised him. "Good sir, Titana is an evil place, shunned by decent men. Nor does the Count welcome visitors. He will not receive you. Accept instead our hospitality, meager though it must be."

Jacob Bleek briefly disputed one of these points, averring that Count Tharaspas himself had called for him by special messenger. At this the village folk refrained from comment, merely indicating by abrupt words and gestures the direction he should take. Other gestures they also produced, superstitious signs of protection which wrung from the traveler a smirking grin. Bleek spurred his horse among and past the crude huts and cottages of stone and thatch, up the gentle slope by way of a disused wagon track toward the harsh ridges to the north, wondering again that Count Tharaspas should come to know of him, that a courier in hire of that worthy should reach him while Bleek amazed or scandalized the nobles of Buda and Pest with his occult prowess. The gloomy scholar leapt with alacrity at the promise of fine accommodations and unspecified rare insights, for his curious skills and objectionable views had begun to pall on his Magyar hosts, whom he feared entertained notions of handing him to the aggressively watchful church authorities. Knowing their blinkered outlook on matters ultra-mundane, their penchant for teasing guests with marvelous instruments of interrogation, he thought it high time to leave in any case. The Count's mysterious charge determined his route, not the journey itself.

This journey neared its end as the chill wind of evening blew. Bleek urged his slathering beast, burdened by his weight and that of his leather bags of unique books and exotic materials, over the spine of a sharp, bouldered ridge to behold, atop the next steep rise, the interesting outlines of the Castle Titana. Interesting, for it resembled no conventional man-made burg, but rather protruded from the rugged landscape as kin to the prominent natural crags and spires surrounding it. It rose gray, angular, a mass of broad slabs of limestone and granite tapering toward the top, a faux hill blank save for scattered window slits and the fortified oaken gate in the circled wall. Toward this Bleek rode, passing on rattling planks the dry moat, an obsolescent defense where, apparently, fear commanded.

Bleek hailed the inmates. A bearded face appeared at a port next the gate, demanded his business. This stated, the massy door creaked inward. With suitable cringing and protests of devotion servants saw to the needs of his animal and conveyed Bleek into the courtyard, a squalid space belying the rustic comfort of the keep within. Thence they led him through corridors and chambers bedecked with antique furnishings to the meeting with his new host.

That eminence sprang from his couch before the smoldering fire, greeted him warmly and eagerly. "I am Gregor of Titana, Count Tharaspas. I bid you make this your home, Master Bleek, so long as our convivial association endures. Much we must discuss. Your needs, however, are my priority." Rang the Count for immediate refreshment, with the further statement that family dinner beckoned. "Rest and relax in our company. Big matters shall weigh upon us soon enough."

Indeed, scarcely had the weary Bleek quaffed a tankard than a fawning liegeman and house maids whisked him into the dining hall, an over-large room ringed with sooty portraits and the mounted stuffed heads of hunted beasts, where gathered the great folk of the family Tharaspas. At the long table sat they, only Gregor the Count, his lady Lutetia, grown daughter Drusilla, and younger brother Pavil.

105

The servants, all peasant stock of the local type, seriously outnumbered them. The lords and ladies of Titana were goodly to the eye and ear, being obviously of high-born blood and educated or mannered in their speech. Countess Lutetia, once of Ravenna, combined courtesy and grace with well preserved beauty; Drusilla, though oddly withdrawn, radiated the natural charms of youth; Pavil, coolly polite, was disinclined to conversation, somewhat abrupt when he spoke, and then only of inconsequential matters. The master of Titana impressed with his physique, a well formed man, tall and strong, with power and hardness in his hawkish features and intense gray eyes. The repast, laid out the length of the satin-covered table, more than satisfied the guest, an additional helping of the roast replenishing his tired body, leaving his mind to be sated.

At what he thought the right moment Bleek broached the subject—still obscure—which brought him there. He studied blandly the reactions to his vague words. The women lowered their gaze and grew more pensive, while the brother twitched instinctively, a disgusted shake of the head, a fleeting grimace. Tharaspas, with haughty nonchalance, suggested withholding discussion until later, in his private chamber.

Later came. Framed by walls of hoary books and stashes of crumbling scrolls the Count sat at his massive desk, with his guest before him in a comfortable chair with one small crystal goblet in hand, and commenced. Said he, "I heard of you from Kronnberg. Does that surprise you? My informant praised your acumen, Master Bleek. I face an intricate problem, one demanding lofty skills and knowledge for its resolution. You may help me, in return for munificent reward.

"My family are old. I possess records dating back to shortly after the Romans abandoned this kingdom which they styled a province. My lineage exalts in tales of greatness; though not what we once were, we hoard and husband much of that heritage. Scant details linger in documents produced by scribes during the Age of Darkness, yet I know a fearless ancestor, a score of generations ago, raised this my peculiarly designed castle upon the blasted ruins of a heathen temple of sinister renown. It is about the devotees of that temple I would now speak.

"Attend patiently, Bleek, and hear this tale of olden history, that you shall understand my dilemma. Those ancient ones who throve when civilization fled this land constituted a particularly despicable sect, the Sons of Xenophor, dedicated to gods possibly false, surely unpopular. They practiced repellent rites, indulged unnatural cravings, amassed amazing wisdom. They knew the secrets of the elder philosophers, and more; so much more. They might have been rulers of a new empire, had not their ways disgusted and terrified the citizenry hereabouts.

"My ancestor—like me, a Gregor—at the instigation of the priests, in a fit of stupid righteousness surprised them by a trick and slew them all. He set men to gouge a great hole in the swamp that hugs the cliffs behind this location, into that ordered their corpses cast and forever covered with muck, where insects might chew them to bare bones. He basked in the acclaim of the common scum who lavished honors upon him for destroying that nest of evil, until among the wreckage of the temple he detected evidence of what those lurid thinkers had conceived. That Gregor had bested the Sons and destroyed them by feigning sympathy to their cause; after they were gone, fired by genuine curiosity, he delved into their partly burned papyri, realized somewhat their glorious aspirations. Subsequently he established Titana on the site, connecting its lower vaults with what remained of theirs. And he studied the tantalizing fragments of lore left by his predecessors.

"His new-found zeal has descended, skipping a generation now and again, to me. I desire to learn the mysteries of the Sons of Xenophor, to imbibe their magic, to stride the planes and soar the spheres beyond the mundane. That I might know as did they, I have taught myself, as best I could, from books and correspondence, the ways of mages and sorcerers, but in these I do not excel. I lack their knack, or that searing elemental substance that burns within the born magician.

"In the stating I thereby disclose to you the cause of your presence. Your fame flows warily, Bleek, in the right channels. Boasts of your abilities precede you. I think we can conjure our way to a reckoning with destiny. Name your price; what of Earth I can deliver will be yours, if you open the unseen gate to me.

"What is that? Ah, Bleek, it matters little in this fairer era of ours what the Sons did to inflame such revulsion. So many stories, many doubtless absurd, and the strangest claim of all... but you would hear it? Make of it what you will. The pious scribblers from that time of night equated the Sons of Xenophor with the tribe condemned by Grecians of old as Anthropophagi. Yes, Bleek, if legend or slander be true, they subsisted as devourers of human flesh."

Appointed a spacious room of his own, in such wise began Jacob Bleek's sojourn among the denizens of the Castle Titana. The passing

107

of the days found him closeted with moldy books, his few prized possessions and the expansive library of Tharaspas, several volumes of which might reveal unto him useful insights and indicative revelations. His host especially wished to discover a means of communicating with the departed spirits of those who had long ago rotted in the marshy pit behind the castle, that he might question them and wring from them their olden keys to wonders. As they cooperated in this intellectual task Bleek learned that the Count had, months before, inspired by his illustrious ancestors, attempted spells of this sort on his own, with dubious results. One formulation, drawn from a sorely tattered partial manuscript of the great sorcerer Azamodias, had appeared to promise much, in that it claimed to raise shades from the gulfs beyond the veil and hold them in thrall, yet in the end it neither produced ostensible ghosts nor opened a path to their materially disintegrated minds. On reflection, Bleek discerned the flaw, in that the lord of Titana sought to raise those whose power in life vastly exceeded his own, and were unlikely to submit to commands fomented by a lesser adept. From this point, therefore, Bleek labored.

The passing of nights brought to Bleek's tired, restless mind nightmares insidious and terrifying. A masterful dreamer, he knew how to turn the images of slumber to advantage, only these fell dreams behaved as if directed upon him from without rather than within, in that he could not structure and focus them to his bidding. They impinged, struck his psyche as physical blows, which puzzled; nay, alarmed.

At the end of their first interview Count Tharaspas had asked if he were sensitive to the outer influences. "I am," confessed Gregor, "at whiles suspecting subtle entities about me, seeking admittance to my cognizance. Fortunately none of my people possess that heightened awareness, but I fear some of the village folk do. In recent weeks a deputation from Gromengatz pestered me with ludicrous fears. Rubbish, all of it, but I suppose they feel morbid stirrings too."

Bleek avowed that he was, indeed, open to whispers seeping through the ethereal barrier, that said ability meant much in his trade. During those early days he toured the castle, including those lower vaults which were actually relics of the demolished temple, unfortunately containing nothing from the old days, the largely forgotten catacombs empty or given over to tombs of the Tharaspas line. He explored the castle's environs, including the reeking swamp which had in ages past swallowed the Sons of Xenophor. Bleek bathed in the atmosphere of these places, oft detecting signatures of non-material forces at play. He ventured into Gromengatz as well, there to quiz the village elders. They told of disturbing moonlight visions, which news Bleek pondered deeply; and in the village he also felt unseen presences.

Wearing and sobering were those nightmares that Bleek deduced were fostered or enhanced by his unique sensitivity. They paraded through his unconscious mind as vile snippets from a pageantry ripped from the pages of obscure history. He gazed upon scenes of a rude time, when amidst intriguingly familiar terrain there stood a squat, octagonal building of unpolished granite surmounted by a low copper dome. Intricate designs chased into the stone and metal surfaces portrayed images obscene and bestial. Black-cloaked forms filed into the yawning entrance, its double oaken doors thrown back. Two of the forms carried a shrouded, elongated burden that feebly struggled.

Within the domed structure (dare he believe, the temple?), he beheld, then or on a similar occasion, a shocking rite of slashing death, punctuated by shrill screams; of hacking dismemberment, replete with gouts of spurting crimson; of base, fiery culinary practices followed by frenzied feasting. Then chanting, in language—a species of corrupt Latin—almost foreign to him, weird motions of geometrical precision, and a definite response to the rite as something black and shapeless intruded into the torch-lit chamber.

More dreams: again torches, only this time without, as a mob of rough men crudely armed lapped at the walls, shouting in rage and hysteria; a mob headed by smug-visaged priests and one other, a large man in armor riding an armored horse, sword cleaving the air over his head. They stormed the pestilential citadel. Bleek saw flames, heaps of the slain, walls crashing asunder. Another vision showed Bleek the great bloodied knight unhorsed, a single bedraggled priest, and a seriously reduced company straggling away from the collapsed, blazing ruin.

A few fragments more, glimpses without context torn from lost years: the last devotee of the temple, sinking under a tempest of flailing knives and clubs, cursing "Gregor," thundering at the last about "transference of energies;" the noble knight, now gray of head, leafing gingerly through scorched documents, the light of mania or something else in his eyes; and solitary shapes, darkly robed, spied by moonlight in the vicinity of a well recognized castle.

This final dream image, at least, Bleek could relate to his local wanderings, for on certain evenings he had glimpsed, on the cliffs above the funereal swamp, lone, motionless figures in black, who he imagined observed him keenly as did he them. He knew not who they were. Never did they tarry long; vanishing when approached, they came and went in the blink of an eye as mortal man could not. Bleek debated with himself possibilities, recalling with special fervor the failed experiment of Tharaspas months before. It surely had not opened a door, yet might have cracked it ajar.

As he wrestled with his complex studies and harrowing nocturnal torments Jacob Bleek attracted the inhabitants of the Castle Titana. Drawn, perhaps, by his easy air of assured wisdom, they conveyed to him their cautions and their dreads. Said the good wife Lutetia, "Give my husband strength to turn aside from the ugly thoughts that plague all his days. Guide him back to the righteous path." Recommended the meek Drusilla, "Beg my father to abandon the shadows for the sunlight, for there lies life and health. What blessing flowers in the morbid gardens where he treads?" Snarled the increasingly angry Pavil, "Amuse my brother no longer by encouraging his crazy antics. If you do, he walks the road to perdition, and I must take stern measures for the family welfare." Even the servants trooped to Bleek with their cares and worries. "God save us all," cried they, "if them walk as shouldn't, as the master would have, and as some tell tales already do. If they should come, what would they want, what would they have of us?" As time passed, however, he heard less from the help, for they began to bolt and desert that fearful abode.

The breakthrough came during the span of the fourth week, when the full moon nudged Gemini, and the dusk spread an ominous sickly green pall over the wind-sculpted ridges and jagged hills, and Bleek's disjointed lines of evidentiary notes and warped, non-Euclidean schemata united to reveal an untrammeled avenue into regions of cosmic potency unrelated to contemporary life or the living. By this time, wholly aware of his milieu, Bleek realized that his nightmares, no matter how they disordered his spirits, served as guides across a psychic landscape, propelling him unerringly toward a goal which was his should he so choose. He informed Count Tharaspas of his success, predicted quick developments. That worthy crowed his delight, exclaiming, "At last I approach the far peak my kindred longed to scale! With the powers of the Sons of Xenophor at my beck, I shall reign supreme over the kingdom; nay, over all the firmament. Forswear diversion, Master Bleek; initiate contact without delay." Bleek did not tell him of the latest visitations in sleep, when shadowy forms akin to robed men had accosted him to promise rare and exotic boons in exchange for heavy fee. They whispered into his brain of the need to "balance the scales," of the requirement to "satisfy the urges," of the unstated bounty due "the supreme Lord of All Things." With as much knowledge pouring in from nightmares as from literary rumination, Bleek struggled to explicate the distressingly unspecified terms, yet with so much being offered he shrugged at hazard, determined to proceed.

On a soon and subsequent night Jacob Bleek made magic for his anxious host Count Tharaspas. All who dwelt within the Castle Titana knew this moment loomed, and they reacted after their natural lights. The ladies of the great house adjourned to their bedchambers to smother their terrors in prayer. The last servants, save Panto the redoubtable, bearded gate keeper, found occasion to abjure their fealty and flee into parts unknown, carrying with them stray gossip and rumor that dampened the simple folk of Gromengatz with uncomprehending dread. Brother Pavil, by degrees more obstinate and rebellious in his humors, finally erupted in heated accusations, drew knife on the household's objectionable guest and made to kill him. The Count, with the dutiful gate keeper to second him, drove his brother into a barred vault deep below the living quarters, one void of ancestral bones; locked him in securely, dismissing his frantic protests.

In the private study of Count Tharaspas made Bleek the magic, simmering wildly colored solutions of precious, painstakingly gathered materials that bubbled thickly, producing a remarkable stench likened by the Count with a merry sneer to that of unfresh graves. Bleek smiled inwardly, for his host's impression deviated little from the actuality. His eminence served as collaborator in this rite, laying out the written formulae and intoning in husky syllables on cue the unintelligible chants that Bleek first solemnly and precisely thundered. As the double recitation continued the foul broth in the pot boiled above what the modest fire beneath could explain; a misty black cloud suffused throughout the room, a rancid fog entirely divorced from the thin steam wafting from the noxious brew.

Bleek enunciated three times the terrible name *Xenophor*, and Gregor, Count of Tharaspas, cried out in delirious joy. Something happened. The conjuration chamber receded from view, another scene superimposing itself upon their gaze. What was it? A dark scene, yes, but illuminated by moonlight; yes, they recognized the cliffs, the murk of the marsh at their feet, the blunt planes of the castle. What meant this baleful frieze? Yet all was not still. Stirrings in the mire, the steaming of putrid gases, as several rounded shapes protruded. Further they rose, slowly, haltingly unfolding themselves until the

111

artfully inspired eye could grasp what it saw.

Tharaspas quailed at this vision of things seen at a mystical remove. "They rise, Bleek," he hoarsely bellowed, "they rise from the swamp, the Sons; their animate bodies, more than bones, if scarce clothed in flesh. What means this? I would pick their brains, not regale their corpses at table."

The curious drama rolled on. The incredible train crept from the marsh, hatefully thin limbs jerking, like spiders in their relentless motion. Tharaspas, his voice made hollow with uncertainty and dismay, barked, "See, they mount the slope! Come they hither! Tell me, Bleek, tell me at once, how this factors in our program? Why do they lurch like driven automata toward my castle? Must I peer into their dead eyes ere they speak?"

Bleek thought how like his nightmares this ghastly procession seemed. A dream-like telescoping of time hastened events. The things, a score and more of them, clustered under the castle walls. They waved loathsomely skinny arms. The heavy gate toppled to the paving with a wooden thud. The gruesome gathering surged inside the court, ravaged mouths agape to reveal gleaming teeth. Tharaspas groaned, an animal noise, lunged forward to upset the conjuring pot. The vision vanished on the instant.

"Sooth me, Bleek," rasped the Count, "calm my mind. By canceling the image, deny I the spell? Again the Sons steep in the swamp?" Bleek uttered no word, merely shook his head slowly. The countenance of this Gregor grew ugly, hostile. "I sense betrayal. I know why they come; your damned arts convey their desires as well as their filthy images. It is revenge they seek, revenge for olden wrongs, and the satiation of greedy, unhallowed lust! You have called up those monstrous cannibals against me. This you knew, spiteful knave, and for this you die!" He whipped out a dagger, but just then a hideous scream of pain and death from the forecourt rent the night. Bleek recognized, even in extremis, the lingering cries of Panto the gate keeper, and of course the Count had no doubts whatsoever. He broke and ran unceremoniously from the chamber.

Came to fruition that night the unspeakable culmination of deeds done in dusty centuries, when nightmares assumed the mocking mantle of life and darkness fell eternally over the Castle Titana and the house of Tharaspas. Fate toyed with and gibed at the castle inmates, taking them in turn according to no plan, but in an orgy of freakish violence. Panto went first, not believing, despite all previous signs, what could be happening, what it was that groped and grabbed and,

112

once dragged down, shredded him. A plea to God choked in his throat as grimy fingers tore it out.

Countess Lutetia lived up to her position and standing in this world, prior to her departure from it. From her chamber window, where she huddled with Drusilla, she beheld the insurgence of implacable horror, gave thought not for herself, but for her only daughter. She took hold of the young girl, hustled her through to the other side of the keep, muttering endearments in a strange calm, contrived to barely squeeze her sobbing offspring through a narrow window and lower her to the ground below. "Run, my child," she shrieked, "and look not back!" Thus, incredibly, against all odds, Drusilla survived that night, never to see her home or folk again. Perhaps, despite cruel memories, she found contentment elsewhere. The selfless virtues of the mother deserved reward other than that received. Maybe the next world fairly ordered her account, as this one did not. She could not leave by the window herself, must fly from the room and seek haven through chancy corridors, running straight into the reaching arms of things best unfaced! In her memory one may forbear dwelling upon the foul minutiae of her end.

Poor Pavil, of course, locked in his dungeon, never had a chance. Lutetia would have saved him if she could, a sentiment, as it happened, of no practical significance. Four of the horrors discovered him trapped in his cell. Pavil looked, screamed pious inanities and pressed against the back wall of the chamber, away from groping fingers, overturning his single oil lamp in the process. A robust and beefy man, he could never pass the rusty iron bars, but those others, heedless of damage to their dead flesh, were not so nice in their concerns. They thrust themselves against, they squirmed through those bars, sloughing off slimy skin and unnaturally stretching dry joints as they greedily advanced. Once inside, in that terrible dark, they made short work of Pavil.

Gregor, Count Tharaspas, lord of the Castle Titana, made a diverse showing prior to his demise. By turns cowardly and brave, in his terror he gave no thought to the welfare of his people and the menace that overwhelmed them, sought only his own safety. His crazed dash through the keep led him in feverish haste, via unstudied habit, to a secret door that opened upon the courtyard at an unlikely vantage, getting him that far with mere glimpses of the fiends that stalked in and contaminated his halls. Armed now with the sword of his fathers he attempted a race for the gate, recoiling from the sodden mess that represented the miserable culmination of Panto. Unerringly,

113

drawn by insights unfathomable to mortal man, his pursuers closed in and swarmed over him. A lesser man, a true coward, would have surrendered to fright and pitifully acquiesced in destruction when brought so hopelessly to bay. Not so Tharaspas, though clear sight of his foes understandably staggered him. Evil souls awakened, driven by ancient hate and abhorrent hunger, urged those impossibly mobile corpses forward to block and encompass him. They knew nothing of soldier's tactics, advanced without plan save for the feral craving for unholy ingestion.

Gregor fought them, under the steady beams of the moon and the wavering of scattered wall torches. A stream of barbaric oaths, punctuated by manic laughter, issued from his frothing lips as his sword sang, as grubby hands fell from frayed wrists leaking rancid ichor, as stinking guts uncoiled from gaping stomach wounds. A blank-eyed head spun from spewing neck, severed by a single mighty swipe of steel. Briefly he dreamed of freedom... but then the point of his blade caught in a cloven breastbone, and endeavoring to recover Tharaspas unbalanced, while bony, questing fingers clamped upon his virile frame, driving him to the ground, smearing his face in sweaty grit. Then he felt the teeth, the champing, rending teeth biting, biting deep into neck, back, limbs, into his skull. Tharaspas shrieked, flopped and floundered, still clung to waning, agonized life as the monstrosities— even their more intact fragments—systematically devoured him.

Jacob Bleek, student of enigmatic arts, his formulations largely responsible for this night's festivities, kept his head, so to speak, that he might keep his head. Gaining the court unmolested, he wisely realized that those few extra paces to the broken gate guaranteed a bitter death, so he mounted the creaking steps to the wall parapet, from where he pensively observed the extermination of his host. When the long dead ones had completed wreaking their vengeance upon the folk of Titana they trampled over human pulp with bare, withered feet, shambling into a loose cluster at the foot of the stairs, there to pause expectantly. Bleek eyed them with dread, and (ever his way) with cold calculation. After intense deliberation with himself he descended the steps to confront the Sons of Xenophor.

From amidst their ragged ranks one lurched forward, matted in gore, swathed in tattered remnants of blood-soaked raiment that suggested special authority. A worm writhed in one soiled, oily eye set deep in a fleshless socket. The corroded jaws, spitting nauseous gobbets, worked in spasmodic rhythm. In a parody of human speech, such to make the hearer visibly cringe, the thing said, "Jacob Bleek, you spoke to us across the black void, as did the despised house of Tharaspas before, yet while they succeeded only in disturbing our rest and attracting like flies our spirits, you promised to unite dead minds with moldering bodies into a useful whole, that we might labor again within this material realm. You did not ask of our purpose; rather, you demanded for yourself the keys to our wisdom." This was entirely the truth. Early on Bleek had deduced the weakness in the scheme of the late Gregor, and of those of his house who came before, their earnest and amateurish attempts to treat with ghosts. Bleek guessed that the correct answer, however dangerous, required sparking the mire-submerged corpuscles of the hatefully carnivorous Sons with renewed vibrancy, that they might walk again, act with will, even speak, and thereby transmit their learning to the living. This the itinerant scholar had achieved, hopefully reserving to himself a share of the sordid spoils. He received now his answer from the Sons of Xenophor.

"Jacob Bleek, our accumulated lore, the mainspring of our boundless capabilities, falls into your hand for the taking. Your mind pleases us, and He whom we cherish. Great Xenophor, He of the Thousand Eyes, master of the red-fanged gods, creator and destroyer of all within this petty cosmos, imparts His majestic gifts to the chosen who bow in obedience to serve Him. You must become as we were when we ruled the land. Pledge your soul to Xenophor; partake of the sacred rites; indulge in the warm, quivering flesh of your lesser brethren, that the substance of your brain fulminate and wax mighty amidst the spheres and chambers of celestial dimensions untrodden by puny minds. You need not delay; the feckless peasants of Gromengatz shall make suitable prey. Do this, and the universe belongs to you."

The nightmarish throng stirred, muttering horribly a wheezy chant from their pest-ravaged throats. Bleek, smiled, nodded, threw out his arms as if to embrace their spokesman, stepped forward, then dodged suddenly and in a flash dashed through the gate which had been vacated during the weird speech. A croaking cry of mingled travesties of voices arose behind him as he scurried with leaping strides to a nearby tree where his horse waited tied, saddle bags packed, straining against its leash in animal terror. This the cunningly cautious Bleek had arranged that evening, he being one to anticipate and prepare for all eventualities. Slipping the cord he mounted, yanked about the steed's head and galloped into the gloom, quickly outdistancing his awkward, if determined, pursuers. In the years to come he occasionally gave thought to how they fared on the living Earth, and how the living fared among them.

It could not be. Jacob Bleek, alas, conjured in vain. Coldly might he entertain paying abominable fees in return for rich reward, but he could not abide such allies. The Sons of Xenophor asked too much of him. His soul might seem a small price, yet speculation warned he might have need of it in future; and as for the other, well, there were limits after all. He disdained stooping to the basest of their demands. As contemptible as he deemed his fellow men—fools they, to be wantonly cajoled and gulled—he would not lower himself by eating them. At this his stomach churned. Though casting aside all else of peculiar value, Jacob Bleek must retain his good opinion of himself.

A Critique of Vorchek's *Holobiologia*

In this latest edition of "Weird Case Files" we consider the curious new book, just published by Starfire Press, entitled *Holobiologia: Unlocking the Ultimate Secrets of Life*. This largish volume, by one Anton Vorchek, Professor of something-or-other, purports to be the latest entry in the "life, the universe, and everything" contest, and seems to be making quite a splash in certain fringe circles. The book has not yet received wide distribution but, if it should do so, may excite the fantasies of die-hard true believers everywhere. As always, this is a pity, for despite some more than usually imaginative elements, Vorchek's work is merely another contribution to the pseudoscientific literature of the supernatural.

First it must be noted that, by even stooping to review this work, we violate our standard policy of not paying attention to strange claims without possessing adequate background data. Vorchek, and for that matter, Starfire Press, are quite unknown to us. The latter, to the best of our knowledge, has never previously published anything. Its personnel, and the location of its offices, remain obscure. The distinct possibility exists that Starfire is one of those "home presses", operating for the sole purpose of putting out this book, in which case it may well be the brainchild of the author himself. If so, he has done a fairly good job of printing, but we learn little more from this deduction, for Vorchek, as of this writing, remains a complete man of mystery. Frankly, we are not convinced that there is such a fellow; the name may be a pseudonym. On the title page, and in the introduction, he identifies himself as a professor—omitting, however, his actual profession—but otherwise provides no personal information of any kind. After considerable checking, we may state with near certainty that the name of Vorchek appears in no recent academic listings; is associated with no prior publications; and all attempts to make contact with him have been fruitless.

Secondly, it should be pointed out that *Holobiologia*, on the question of style, is a terrible book. This volume clearly received no quality editing, boasting weak grammar and hopeless structure.

Vorchek rejects the tried and true formula of stating a claim, amassing evidence for it, and then presenting his conclusion. Instead, what we find is argumentative chaos, with data scattered willy-nilly throughout the four hundred closely written pages, conclusions preceding data, claims separated from argument by many chapters, and odd anecdotes distributed randomly. In short, the book is a mess. In this critique we will do our best to sort the material, create order where it is not originally found, and explicate the grandiose and bizarre views of this remarkable man.

Thesis

Vorchek argues that all systems of human thought, including the scientific and religious, have missed the boat when it comes to understanding the nature of life and consciousness. Although he gives passing credit to all, he rejects the "fragmentary approach" which fails to "realize a coherent theory" covering all known facts. The basic facts in question, he assures us, are: the existence of self-perpetuating organic forms; the impossibility of such forms in a purely material universe; the ubiquity of consciousness in all living things; and the necessity for a higher mind underlying life. Some of this sounds drearily familiar to students of the weird. If one presumes, however, that Vorchek is just another creationist on the rampage, presume again. He actually has very little to say that they want to hear, and nowhere in the text does one find evidence that he is the orthodox religious type. He passes himself off as a true scholar. On the other hand, he has no use for what he styles the Darwinian "dead dust hypothesis." Our budding biologist (he may be, for all we know) tells us that evolutionary theory explains only the form, not the substance, of life and mind. Complex, willful action is invariably a sign of a higher, thinking mentality.

The substance of life is far different from what we have supposed. Living creatures are not specific, concrete entities connected only by descent, but rather tiles in an unseen mosaic, organic shadows cast by an overarching being of infinite possibility. In all their variety they are products of "mind/energy templates," which must be seen as deliberate conceptions of the "Ultimate One." More will be said about him later. What matters here is that life, these template images, are embedded within a "cosmic matrix" superseding the universe as we know it, especially in relation to time. At the cosmic level, there are no temporal bounds; in a very real, though untraditional sense, the consciousness of living forms inherently possesses immortality.

118

While this is the least of his findings, Vorchek claims to have conducted experiments which prove the underlying intelligence of all living things, even at the microbial level. In a long, involved passage he describes chemical tests performed upon "living material"—ranging from dogs to bacteria—tests which reveal "mental components" in all cases. The same tests, performed upon dead specimens, yield similar but more diffuse results. (1) We must consider ourselves enlightened.

Communication with the Dead

At this point *Holobiologia* begins to get very strange. With consciousness disconnected from matter, it logically follows that it survives the death of the physical body. If mind lives on, there might be a way of contacting it and learning a thing or two about the future state. This Vorchek claims to have done. Being a clever fellow, he doesn't try to palm us off with a medium or any séance nonsense. This is science in action, after all, and the methods employed must be appropriate. Instead of making do with old fashioned mechanisms, Vorchek developed a new technique which, he says, can read the lingering consciousness in dead organisms as a camera fitted with the right filter can detect fading phosphorescence. In addition to a complicated electrical apparatus, the nature of which we are not competent to judge—nor to understand—he writes of a radioactive "plutonial solution" injected into dead tissue in order to excite the "latent mentalism." What makes this attempt interesting is that, for the first time, Vorchek acknowledges that he has experimented with a human corpse.

Where did he get it? He doesn't say. Was he legally authorized to acquire it? No comment. He admits that the body, of a young male, is "alarmingly fresh," which conjures up sinister ideas. Whatever the source, it is upon this single case (presuming that any of this really happened) that he derives some of his most unique conclusions.

Once again, we must point out that Vorchek does not follow the standard rules of mystical story-telling. Professional spiritualists, a class of people singularly weak in originality, will not be pleased by his claims. While their profitable beliefs, however tiresome, offer lachrymose comfort to the living, this author's findings are merely outrageous. He has spoken to the dead; he has received responses; and these responses, in the tale they have to tell of the afterlife, are simply horrifying.

Vorchek paints a picture of the scene: a small chamber, the walls crowded with hardware, a single burning light bulb dangling from the ceiling, and below that a lab table bearing the body, extensively betubed and wired to the instruments. The experiment begins with the irradiation of the dead man. Constant checking of needle fluctuations in graphs, the wavering of oscilloscope readings . . . and then the first sign of mysterious, impossible life. The indications mount in intensity and then, without warning, from a connected microphone: speech!

At first haltingly, then with greater ease, a conversation of sorts ensues. Vorchek has transcribed the fun bits, such as the following.

Vorchek: Where are you now? Are you aware of your surroundings, your body?

X: Absolute awareness of infinite nothingness.

Vorchek: Do you retain your identity? Do you know your name?

X: All is remembered. I was ____, now I am nothing.

Vorchek: But you speak. You still exist.

X: Only the living exist. Only they hope and dream and love. I can only hate.

Vorchek: Hate? Whom do you hate?

X: The living. All who live, who still have possibilities.

Vorchek: You had a wife, children, friends I presume; surely you do not hate them.

X: Hatred for all. My only satisfaction lies in knowing that one day they will all become like me.

It is not a pretty picture that Vorchek paints of the future state, based on his experiment and other source materials. (2) The dead seem to continue as a kind of psychic residue, awareness without real life, sustained only by a cancerous envy of the living. In general they are inert, incapable of volitional action. At times, however, their rage may take on such concrete form as to render them able to lash out at the living, including at those once their nearest and dearest. Vorchek believes that "the more substantial" cases of historic hauntings may be explained in such terms. Visitations may come to persons or places to which the residue clings most closely. In all these anecdotal reports, he points out, the effects eventually fade.

So, apparently, do the living dead fade. The recorded conversations reveal a gradual lessening or disintegration of the surviving personality over a period which appears to have lasted some weeks. Vorchek thinks that his specimen was a man of weak will, with insufficient mental energy to last long without organic support. Others may continue longer-- even much longer, with more of the persona intact-- but in the end all (barring a freakish exception, discussed

120

below) will dwindle into nothingness. This energy, which the author considers the scientific basis of the soul, is reabsorbed back into the cosmic matrix from which it originally came, and at that point, as a rule, the trappings of individuality vanish with it.

Here we reproduce a telling item from one of the final transcripts:

Vorchek: Can you still hear me?

X: Very faintly. All is going away.

Vorchek: You are going away? Where are you going?

X: Fragments breaking off—consciousness crumbling—enormous power drawing me down into it. Cannot maintain contact much longer.

Vorchek: What is the source of the power?

X: Blinding light within total darkness—the sightless Eye which observes all, coming near—no escape. What it sees, ceases to be.

Vorchek: Tell me what is happening to you. Describe the sensation.

X: No words, no images. Something out there, and within, and of me, some thing of burning cold, feeding on me.

Vorchek: What do you feel?

X: Terror.

Vorchek's theories identify him as a most artless pseudoscientist. He ignores the first · requirement of becoming a successful, thoroughgoing crank, that one write in such a manner as to pleased one's chosen audience. They should always be told what they want to hear—that's how one rakes in the big bucks—yet surely he falls short. Our friends out on the lunatic fringe may cheer his arguments in favor of post-death survival, and the annoying reiteration of the claim that such matters possess a scientific basis (for they all crave that, however much they may deny it), but otherwise Vorchek must disappoint. The survival he postulates is limited, ephemeral, and unpleasant. The true believers desire comforting tidings of their upcoming lives after death: reunion with loved ones, communion with God, a fitting and eternal reward for lives well spent. *Holobiologia* provides nothing of the kind. (3)

The Fate of the Dead

What eventually becomes of organic vitality, of consciousness; or, if we must employ the term, the soul? Vorchek has already indicated that the final fate is not one to which we can look forward with great relish. Indeed, at various points in the text he elaborates this theme, with conclusions truly disturbing.

Consciousness dissipates over a period following death, a process of absorption into this "matrix" of which he frequently speaks. The next boon he grants the reader is the claim that this process is a *volitional* act, not on the part of the individual, obviously, but rather at the behest of the universe itself. At first it appears that Vorchek refers to the operation of some hitherto unknown natural law, an inherent aspect of the material cosmos. That turns out not to be the case. We suppose that did not sound impressive enough, so he chooses to push the envelope one step further. There is a supernatural—or, as he clumsily styles it, a "hypernormal"—mind at work making these things happen.

Vorchek's subject, or victim, makes reference to something "feeding on me." Vorchek, treating this as a literal statement, expands upon it. A greater power lords over the universe, one which depends for its sustenance upon the mental energies of once living creatures. Man, unfortunately, constitutes no exception to this rule. One may imagine this being harvesting the dead, extracting what is essential in them—i.e., the non-material—making use of that essence for its own purposes. If the eating of souls be not a flat statement of fact, it is yet an adequate analogy to what is taking place.

This then, is the long sought meaning of life: we are all, from microbe to man, members or parts of a crop, possessing only utilitarian value, a value not defined by us. Vorchek carries this thinking to the limit by deducing that we are sown, and considers it a given that we are reaped, by a creature of unimaginable vastness, one which may dominate the universe; one which may comprise the hypernormal totality of the universe. Heady stuff, if not particularly edifying. One wonders what the crystal gazers will think of it all. Can they incorporate these "truths" into their own blandly optimistic weltgeist? (4)

Overall, *Holobiologia* tells us that the living (by which Vorchek means the dualistic mind-body combination) are immune to the direct machinations of this cosmic being. It has no interest in us until the combination naturally breaks apart. Vorchek makes a nasty comparison to the eating habits of vultures, or the actions of putrefactive bacteria. He does allude, at first in passing, later with greater urgency, to rare cases, which will be relevant shortly, in which living beings may be threatened by this awesome force. This grim possibility arises only among the sentient, meaning man (although he casually allows for the existence of other, extraterrestrial, intelligent types). Those individuals of superior mental clarity and awareness— those smart enough to achieve an understanding of the true nature of the universe, and our place within it—may actually draw the attention of this entity unto themselves, always with fearful consequences. The best minds throughout history, scientists and thinkers who seek truth too far, live at constant risk of gaining this shattering knowledge, thereby allowing themselves to be *discovered*. Vorchek interprets, or reinterprets, many famous and traditional cases of disappearance in this light. (5) By collating these stories, and viewing them through the lens of certain disturbingly consistent myths from various points of the globe, he finds that these chosen unfortunates have been directly translated to the post-death stage, without any subsequent degeneration of consciousness. They really do "live" forever, but trapped like flies in amber, contained for eternities without end within the mystical substance of their hypernormal tormentor, in a state of all knowledge, and permanent shrieking madness. There is no heaven in Vorchek's twisted world view, but there is very definitely a hell.

The Master of the Universe

The infernal being posited by Vorchek bears all the hallmarks of a devil, but by any impartial standard must be considered the true god of the universe. Judging from its treatment of the living and the dead, Vorchek deduces that it exists for its own purposes, with no anthropomorphic regard for its subjects or victims. To such an entity, we are nothing but foodstuffs and playthings. It follows that all conventionalized religions have missed the point of the deity, have compounded wishing and hoping into a sweet intellectual syrup tolerable to uninformed minds. Vorchek is scarcely the first to say so, but he attempts to take his case beyond deduction. He offers what he calls data.

He gathers his answers mainly from ancient myths, those marvelous Rorschach tests of the dedicated pseudoscientist. Whether it be ancient astronauts or creationist mumbo-jumbo, these curious old tales from man's youth offer something for everyone. We should have known that Vorchek would reduce himself to this level. He has surveyed the "relevant literature," interpreted it to the breaking point, and (who would have guessed?) found exactly the sort of primitive story he set out to find.

Vorchek bases his arguments upon a widespread and ominous cycle of myth which has, at its foundation, the belief in an amoral, conscienceless creator being—the real, ultimate "God"—Who made the cosmos at the beginning of time and has ruled it, after His fashion, ever since. Given the magnitude of His works and actions, He is considered omnipotent and thoughtlessly, almost casually omniscient: He can do anything, but serves only His own ends, whatever they may be; He knows everything, but often has little or no interest in the day to day management of the universe He devised. His intervention, when it rarely occurs, is necessarily spectacular and grotesque. This spooky legend, naturally, has never garnered the support of the masses, yet has cropped up throughout human history in surprising times and places. Wherever it has arisen, and by whatever name He has been styled, His cult followers have disdained hopeful prayer to their God; the results are not good. More commonly they have prayed out of fear, deep from the heart, that He let them alone.

Our Professor has accomplished yeomen work in collating the history of this morbid idea. Furthermore, we must grant that he appears to be correct when he discerns linkages among the cases which he extracts from the works of various scholars, both modern and antique. Other, superior thinkers, have already drawn attention to this pattern. Thus we are told of the obscure Egyptian notion of "the lidless eye that cannot but see," first mentioned in verified documents of the 22cd Dynasty; "the Eternal Seer in Darkness" who troubles the dead, from the 3rd Century B.C. *The Thoughts of Heratakos*; Labian's late Classical Neo-Platonic maunderings on "the All Knowledge Which Knows All;" and the medieval *Visions* of Antigon, with their "eyes swimming in sight." More recent authors provide additional data, oddly gathered from widely separated regions of the globe. Much is made of "the glowering eye in the highest tower" which Chard and Bromhead, in their volumes of Chinese studies, connect to a frightful body of esoteric lore with deep roots in that country's past. Obermeyer, the Polynesian expert, in his *South Seas Tales* writes of the great Inyora, "the forbidden creator," who "strides haughtily through the dreams of the dead." Barrent regales us with the atrocious Bantu fable of "The Talking Eyes in the Box" from his *Sub-Saharan Travels*. Of course Vorchek, being Vorchek, also drags in Bleek at this point, as well as Henreid's *Unbound Truths*, a trashy Theosophist tome which, surely by coincidence, refers to an omniscient Law Giver who "sees from within and without," "who judges, but cares not."

It is Stromberg who, in his *Survivals from Prehistory*, first alludes to the awesome name Xenophor. (6) He cites Indian legends about this horrendous being, "the thousand eyes that see everything and nothing;" the "creator Who rages at His creation;" "the insatiable Eater of the Dead, never satisfied." This is the fullest statement of the myth which Vorchek makes his own. The parallels once again are impressive; often, in their precision, astounding. All very nice, but are we to conclude, with Vorchek, that this mass of so-called evidence—the myths, the talks with the dead, the speculations about cosmic fabrics and matrices—add up to a coherent whole? The myths are but imaginative stories, the rest only fragments, logically broken, leading nowhere. Even setting aside the issue of honesty (we have to take the author's word about a great deal), we need not accept his fabulous claims. He has not solved the mysteries of life and death. He has not begun to do so. Vorchek has simply spun another wonder tale for the benefit of the true believers . . . in this instance, we suggest, believers of a particularly deranged state of mind.

The Last of Vorchek?

Shall we learn more in the future at the feet of the brilliant Professor Anton Vorchek? If the final chapter of *Holobiologia* is to be taken seriously, perhaps not. He argues (friends and faithful readers, he prepared us, so we should have been ready for this) that the all-seeing eye, or eyes, of Xenophor are upon him, and that there may be no escape from that baleful gaze. He has drawn attention to himself—he has discovered too much—he has been located, and retribution swiftly approaches. Ominous portents gather. He writes of a series of dreams which have begun to plague him, dreams in which he senses a malevolent force closing in on him. Now *there* is evidence. He assures us that evil strangers "of foreign aspect" have accosted him on the street, and have made mention of a certain horrible name. He predicts the immediate appearance on earth of strange radiances from the farthest corners of the universe, a sure sign that He is coming. (7) "Even I," he cries, "cannot imagine the awfulness of the fate which may await me."

Professor, that is too bad, really. To where should we send flowers?

What we have here, probably, are the makings of a publicity stunt. Vorchek's nonappearance among the living, and his non-responsiveness to letters, become clear. (8) He has been taken away, at least until book sales flag. We wish him luck, and trust he isn't really trapped, screaming, forever in the clutches of his cosmic bogeyman. Vorchek is an imaginative fellow, and *Holobiologia* an entertaining read in its way, so when he returns from his flying saucer ride, or wherever he is, we hope he will be in a position to provide us with an update.

(1) Vorchek cites the work of Dr. Leslie Harrison in support of his claims. Harrison is a well-known pathologist and reputable scientist and, in fact, has conducted experiments which resemble those of Vorchek. Our author doesn't inform his readers, however, that Harrison has repudiated his own study, stating that his results are "ridiculously fantastical" and "unworthy of sane belief." (see *The Journal of Theoretical Pathology*, XI:73) Vorchek ill serves himself by citing Harrison.

(2) He cites as authorities various folk beliefs, including the morbid afterlife tales of the ancient Greeks, Hebrews, and other pre-Christian peoples. Also, he relies heavily upon the infamous *Collected Wisdom* of Jacob Bleek, a gathering of mystical notes written by the man-- regarded by some as a ground breaking amateur scientist-- best known as a self-proclaimed dark sorcerer. These peculiar ramblings do supplement Vorchek's theses in dramatic fashion. We are supposed to assume, of course, that the recent author did not crib his ideas from the old. Well, maybe. Bleek's works have been taken seriously by scholars who really ought to know better. We will not fall into that trap here.

(3) Let us not fall into the error of granting him too much credit for this. It's hard to figure out what kind of game Vorchek is playing, and we confess ourselves unable to get a handle on his motives. His argument is a public relations disaster—exactly what one might expect if he were an honest researcher, presenting genuine discoveries which the uninformed reject on emotional grounds (the history of true science is replete which such sad episodes)—but we know this cannot be so in this case. We must conclude that the Professor is either too clever by half, or a remarkably stupid man.

(4) According to Vorchek, at least one group already has. He cites Isaac Blanchard's semi-anthropological study on *The Cult of Blug, the Destroyer*, whose worshippers deliberately sacrifice themselves to that dread god out of a shared sense of nihilistic unworthiness. Blug annihilates the corpus and psyche only of the acolytes who come to him seeking mystical eradication, on the grounds that they possess no inherent value. They cease to be, they cease ever to have been. Blanchard describes rituals which are unspeakable in their foulness. Since he actually joined the cult in the end, and has since dropped off the radar screen, we are scarcely in a position to consider him a credible

or unbiased witness. This illustrates yet again Vorchek's substandard and scatter-shot method of sourcing his claims.

(5) His hair-raising retelling of the old and well known Hebrew tale of Elijah will especially outrage the orthodox.

(6) Bleek, who makes much use of the term, apparently follows Stromberg; not for a moment will we accept that it works the other way around. It would help if we could pin Bleek down in time. Everything about him seems to be a mystery, even his dates of birth and death.

(7) An astronomical colleague of ours, Dr. John Kelly, humorously notes that the flaring of the quasar NGC-1232 amply fits the bill. Six months ago, for the first time in known history, such a distant and mysterious celestial object was actually, for a brief period, visible to the naked eye. It would indeed be a fine joke on us all if Vorchek penned his worrisome words just before that sighting occurred.

(8) As of the final editing of this review, he still has not come forth.

Critical Information

Harold Blake knew that things weren't right, had sensed this for quite some time before the blow fell, yet it still managed to take him completely by surprise.

For starters, there was this business of the strange trio of men in bowler hats. They had been following him for months; at least, that was the only way he could explain to himself their numerous appearances, ludicrous though the explanation seemed to be. Still, it was difficult to escape the conclusion. Months before, Blake had casually noticed those curious men, dressed in long black coats and cloaks, with their odd black hats, lounging in his vicinity. He thought nothing of them at the time, nor did he do so when they appeared again a week or so later. It might be some new style—there were so many of those coming and going—and it didn't occur to him then that they were the same three men. Eventually, as the sightings multiplied, he was forced to admit, with concern gradually superseding annoyance, their continuous identity. They never actually appeared to pay him any attention, but it finally crossed his mind that they were ostentatiously avoiding the appearance of doing so. It was a puzzle, which grew to disturb him in its quiet, inexplicable fashion. He had reached the point of mentioning it to his wife one night over the dinner table, but the kids were acting up, she had other matters in mind, and the moment passed without serious discussion.

Then, of course, there were the killings. It had become increasingly difficult to shun that subject. Men of his acquaintance were dropping like flies, the victims of terrible murders. It didn't shock him that tragic death should impact everyday life, but it unnerved him to think that it should affect his own. Lately, very much against his will, Blake had begun to ask himself if the deaths were somehow connected to him. Obviously a ridiculous notion, though the developing pattern of the murders inspired the direst thoughts. How many men could claim to know three victims of violent homicide, all killed within a short span? He guessed that such things happened by chance, but the idea didn't entirely satisfy.

First went Trelawney, the therapist. Some years back, during a time of marital disorders, Blake had attended several sessions with the man. They had talked much, and solved little, though the spousal situation had contrived to stabilize on its own. That had constituted the sum of their association, and Blake had thought no more of the fellow until six weeks ago, when he had read in the evening newspaper of Trelawney's ugly demise. The man had been found in a ditch, beaten to death, wallet and money still on his person; killer or killers unknown. It sounded like random brutality or the working out of a grudge. No further significant details were forthcoming in subsequent editions.

The second victim was Marston, whose grisly end a month ago hit closer to home. Blake had worked regularly with the man in the insurance office, and while they were not really close, they had chummed together on numerous occasions. One morning Marston hadn't shown up for work, an unusual omission for such a reliable guy, and that night the paper had told Blake why. His colleague's car had been found abandoned, and later in the day his mutilated body had been discovered in a vacant lot in the wrong section of town. The police contacted Blake about this case, as they consulted everyone who knew the man, searching for leads. Naturally Blake could tell them nothing. He gathered that robbery wasn't involved in the crime. This event touched him considerably, but no more than one would expect. His wife thought it was just awful. The office buzzed with horror and speculation for days.

It was the third murder which truly contributed to Blake's feeling of personal dismay, giving birth to his sensation of formless, creeping fear. Beddows was genuinely his friend, his oldest friend; they went back to high school together, their close association having continued throughout the years, through all the vicissitudes of college, marriages and jobs. Beddows was somebody who really mattered to Blake, and his old friend's horrific slaughter two weeks ago had been a shattering experience. He had apparently been taken from his home in the dead of night—although no one had heard anything, without evidence of forced entry or struggle—to be disgustingly butchered. The police recovered the scattered pieces of his dismembered corpse from a marshy ravine just outside town. They concluded that foul play was involved, but otherwise had very little to say. In the course of their rounds the authorities quizzed Blake, which made good sense, but led to nothing. They seemed rather surprised to be talking to him again so soon, as part of another murder investigation. It surprised his wife as well, who had something to say about bad luck and signs of the times. It more than surprised Blake; it gave rise to strange ideas in his brain, crazy ideas which he fought against without thinking too clearly about them. He felt comparatively happier when he didn't speculate about possible links between these crimes.

So, Blake already had things on his mind, but that didn't do him any good, and as it happened fate befell him without any clear warning. As he strode down the street this morning on the way to his office he approached a seemingly deserted intersection. Suddenly the three men in bowler hats crowded close; a gloved hand slapped a caustically scented handkerchief over his mouth and nose . . . and when he awoke, with a slight headache and an empty feeling in the pit of his stomach, he found himself in a dimly lighted stone chamber, strapped tightly into an unpadded metal seat, surrounded by the three mysterious men, who were clearly ready for business.

They looked much alike; they might have been brothers. One sat at a small desk in the corner, fiddling with writing materials like an officious clerk. Another stood attentively to one side, as motionless as a statue, holding a thick sheaf of papers in a manila folder. The third, a taller fellow wearing rimless spectacles, stood before Blake, in front of a draped section of wall. The bound man, his seat somewhat akin to a dentist's chair, could see only that portion of the room ahead of him, the large headrest preventing him from looking behind where the door must be. He could crane his neck sufficiently to discern the single naked light bulb burning overhead.

"Let us commence the interrogation," said the tall man in a hollow voice. He cleared his throat and asked, "You are Harold Blake?"

"Who are you people?' cried Blake, straining against his bonds. The atmosphere in this dreadful room was warm and clammy, bearing a smell of stale water. He spied a mop and bucket propped against the wall. If they had cleaned out the place recently, they had done a pretty poor job. It was still remarkably dirty. "Why have you taken me prisoner? What do you want of me? Why am I here?"

"You will know these things," replied the tall man. "First, however, I must clarify one important matter. It is my role in this scenario to ask the questions, and yours to answer them. Please do not forget that again."

"What's this all about?" Blake wailed.

"So be it; you insist on a demonstration." The tall man produced from beneath his cloak a short wooden staff from a leather strap on his belt, passed around Blake beyond his line of sight. Without warning the prisoner felt a crushing blow to the top of his head. He screamed, reeled and shook, then hung limply in pain. The tall man reappeared, tucking away his staff. "I trust that will not prove necessary again. The next time, if it come, will be much worse. Now, the point made, I shall continue."

Blake said nothing, but looked up warily.

"Excellent. I repeat: you are Harold Blake?" Blake nodded. "Answer, please; we expect verbal responses." The captive offered the appropriate monosyllable. "You live at so-and-so, your telephone number is so-and-so, you are employed at such-and-such?" The tall man ran through a series of questions pertaining to basic identity, and as he asked, and Blake gave a "yes" each time, the clerk scribbled with his pen on a long form. "That satisfies the prerequisites. My friends, do we all agree that this is our Harold Blake?" The other two men nodded curtly. The speaker smiled and said, "Let's get to it.

"Harold Blake, we require information, critical information which only you can provide. You've got it, we want it, we shall have it. It's that simple. You can make it difficult for yourself, in which case the consequences will be exceedingly unpleasant to you, but that will not alter the final outcome. We will acquire the information we seek, even if our methods must cost you your life."

"I'll tell you anything," Blake groaned. "Just ask me, I'll cooperate. Don't hurt me again. I'll tell you anything you want."

"Wonderful. That is a sound attitude on your part and, based on our recent experience, a refreshing one. The other sources we've contacted, concerning your case, have not been so forthcoming. I refer, as you're surely aware, to Messrs. Trelawney, Marston, and Beddows, whom we've had occasion to interview in this very room. They proved most obstinate, to their ultimate detriment."

"You're the murderers!" shrieked Blake. "Oh God, I knew something was going on. You killed them in cold blood. Why?"

"'Why' connotes a question," observed the tall man. "You have been warned."

The prisoner, struggled with his thoughts, then tried again. "There's nothing I can tell you worthy of murder. I don't understand why you're doing this."

"What you do or don't understand is a triviality on both the cosmic and the personal scales. It suffices that you possess the information we want. We attempted to acquire the data without intruding directly upon your life, our preferred method, but that scheme unaccountably failed. Therefore, we've had to go straight to

131

the prime source: you. Does that elucidate?"

"It doesn't."

"No matter," snapped the interrogator. "All you need know at this juncture—and you should consider this much a boon—is that we've been collecting all relevant material pertinent to your case since day one, since your actual birth. We maintain meticulous records on you, derived from documents, questioning of associates, systematic observation of your activities and behavior, etc. We know much, we're learning more, we see almost everything. There's little about you we don't know."

"But what's the point—" Blake caught himself as his captors tensed. "I'm not important. I don't get the point of your surveillance of me."

"You need not. It makes no difference to us, whatsoever, whether you 'get' it. We know. That's good enough for us, and for your sake it had better be good enough for you.

"So that you don't doubt our competence, I'll oblige you to the extent of throwing out a few salient facts relating to the life of one Harold Blake." The speaker extended a hand; the statue moved suddenly, removing a paper from the folder and handing it to his partner. "Born 12-8-58, in Beaverton. First attended school at Cadwallader Elementary." He reached for and received another sheet. "Your father gave you a football for your sixth birthday, which you lost at age twelve (on 3-17-71, to be precise), while playing with friends in the vacant lot behind your apartment. As a teenager, you used to hide with other boys in an abandoned shack on the banks of Thatcher Creek, there to peruse pornographic magazines. You attended your high school graduation wearing a ridiculous, cheap brown tuxedo with brown ruffles, which drew a cutting comment from your date, a Miss Emily Shaw; we have her remarks on tape. Let me see . . ." He scanned another paper given him by his otherwise motionless assistant. "You completed your formal education at Carmichael College on 7-1-82. You married your present wife on 5-13-92, shortly after receiving what you called a 'big promotion' at the office, where you're still employed. On 9-24-97, at a card party held with your next-door neighbors, the Morgans, you were overheard to opine that—"

"Stop!" screamed Blake. "Enough. I don't want to hear any more of this. It's incredible, but I'm convinced. You really have been tracking me my entire life. Some of that you could learn from records, but how you could find out the rest beats me. I wouldn't think it possible."

"It is quite possible. We possess the desire, the means, and the determination. There is much more here in your personal file, but I grow weary of delay. I'm here to gather information, not to present it." The tall man adjusted his spectacles, motioned for yet another form. "Yes, this is it. Mr. Blake, we've gone to all this trouble to discuss a certain lacunae in your file. There is a gap we must fill. If we achieve our ends, we will release you, and trouble you no more. That's a good deal, wouldn't you say?"

"The very best," Blake agreed. "Thank you, yes. Tell me what you want to know, I beg of you."

"That's what we want to hear," said the tall man. "Now, my question concerns an event at the school picnic which you attended, in the company of your mother, at the Fanbury Farm on the eleventh of May, nineteen hundred and sixty-nine. You, of course, recall the gathering of which I speak."

"I do not," moaned the prisoner. "What are you talking about? What does this have to do with anything?" As the staff was drawn forth Blake squeaked, "I mean, I don't remember it, that's all, I'm not asking anything! I simply don't recall!"

"You disappoint me—"

"I'm cooperating, really I am. Please, please refresh my memory. That was a long time ago."

"This occurred when you were eight years old. Surely you haven't blanked that day from your mind? We would consider that a suspicious development." The questioner ran his long, thin index finger down the page. "Picnic, Fanbury, end of semester treat, chaperoned by parents and teachers, the entire grade level present; hamburgers, hotdogs, potato salad, Cole slaw, chips and ice cream provided at tables in the meadow, horse rides offered by the property owner, a Cecil Fanbury. Mr. Blake, do you still feign ignorance of that day?"

"No," Blake replied, not caring to dispute the implied accusation. "I do remember it now; the picnic at the farm, the horses. I don't think I ever knew the name of the place. Yes, I know what you're talking about now."

"It's good of you to confess that much. Let me inform you that one of our operatives was on the scene that day. He took notes. He snapped photographs. So that you accept without further obfuscation, I show you this." The man with the folder handed the speaker a card, which the latter flashed before Blake's eyes. "Dare you deny the evidence?"

So astounded was Blake that he would have fallen to the floor if he hadn't been tied to his chair. He was looking at a clear, crisp black and white picture of himself as a young boy, a picture taken at a medium remove, but allowing no possibility of error. That was him, and what he could see of the background—other children, adults in the dress of that period, the food-laden tables and the pastoral setting—brought that long ago day vividly before his mind.

"That's me, all right, and that's the picnic."

"I'm so happy," chortled the tall man, as he discarded the photo, "that you're willing to grant that much. You see, we had our man there, tasked to observe and report everything you did that day; a sound fellow, with a fine record up to that point, the product of our strictest training. Naturally we expected a full accounting of your activities at the picnic. However, something went wrong—something highly irregular—an occurrence for which we'd made no provision. You got away from him; there was a certain lapse in his observations, and he missed a few minutes. Once he detected the mistake he naturally took action, to no avail. He paid for his lapse, paid most severely. In fact, he died screaming. A pity, perhaps, but it is our way.

"We attempted to rectify the matter through indirect means, for we've always been leery of directly invading the life of our subject: you. There has been any amount of debatable, even worthless, speculation and theorizing. Try as we might, it seems, we have been unable to close the gap to our satisfaction. It logically follows, therefore, that you must close it for us."

"I will if I can," Blake said eagerly.

"You will, or else. I come to the critical point. At exactly 10:17 A.M. You walked into the woods at the south end of the picnic field, accompanied by your classmate Wendy Hamilton. The two of you emerged from the woods and separately rejoined the party at 10:21. Tell me," demanded the tall man, his voice rising to a shout, "what happened during that interval?"

"I don't know!" Blake shouted back. He giggled despite himself. "It's ridiculous. You must be insane, all of you. You don't really care about that."

"I assure you we do."

"But why? What's the justification? What does it matter?"

This time the staff leaped into view and lashed out, catching Blake on the jaw. He groaned helplessly. "You've been warned," snarled the inquisitor. "Don't hold back. Resistance at this stage may prove instantly fatal. I urge you not to forget what happened to your

134

uncooperative friends, who also held back on us.

"We've wasted enough time trying to extract this information. My patience is not unlimited; however, I'll have you know that our modus operandi is based upon the influential theories of Professor Anton Vorchek, as reported in his small but seminal early paper, 'Psychological Analysis By Means of Integrated Hermeneutics.'" The speaker was handed a tattered, dog-eared copy of a slim paperback, which he waved wildly in the air. The bland cover was torn and stained; the title and that curious name could be discerned. "You are, I presume, familiar with this work?"

"I've never heard of it. I'll bet no one has."

"Don't be a wise guy. Years ago Vorchek unlocked the secret of delving into the deepest psychological mysteries of the human persona, by means of total evidentiary saturation; generating comprehensive data on every aspect of the target's life: actions, activities, modes of behavior, expressed thought patterns, turns of speech; and bringing all this particularized, day to day knowledge in order to genuinely explain the meaning of the target, to actually know a fellow human being down to his most minute essence. Vorchek outlines the powerful predictive properties of his theory, when his preconditions are met. It's all right here, page by page, in black and white, laying out everything we need. There are no conceivable limits, if the requisite knowledge has been acquired.

"We have experienced some successes in your case, yet experienced difficulties as well. You still surprise us, on rare occasions, and it has become plain that we lack, up to this point in your life, evidential totality. We have narrowed the problem sector down to this single event. We must fill the sequence, and only you, it seems, can help us." The tall man took one step forward. "Or, do you disagree with that conclusion? Perhaps, you might argue, we should have continued interviewing others? Maybe we should put your wife and your children to the question?"

So saying, he strode forthwith to the drapes behind him, seized a hanging cord and drew back the curtains. "Behold!" The prisoner saw before him another room, separated from this one by a wide glass pane, and in that room the three bound and gagged forms of his family, strapped to chairs like his own. Blake cried out in horror. The tall man chuckled evilly and said, "Now choose. Cooperate, or we begin on them. We will interrogate them one at a time, and should they fail us, we will still come back to you. Your position is hopeless. Choose."

Blake called to his family, who did not respond. "It's a two-way mirror," his tormentor pointed out, "of exceptional thickness. They cannot see or hear you. They don't know you're here, yet their fate rests in your hands."

"I'll talk," Blake said desperately. "What I know, you'll know. It's been so long since I've thought about that day—it's so unimportant—I never dreamed—give me a moment—"

"Your remaining moments dwindle."

"Nothing strange happened."

"Don't characterize," snapped the tall man. "Report."

"All right," Blake temporized, "I'm thinking. Okay, it was like this." He noted, with a heightened sense of horror (if that be possible), that the clerk was taking down every word he spoke, and that a hitherto concealed tape recorder whirred nearby. "Yes, yes, this is it. I saw a couple of rabbits run into the woods, and I said that we should go for a closer look. We went—wait a minute—actually, I said that to Johnny Forsythe, a pal of mine, but he wasn't interested, so he wouldn't come."

"We know all that. We have notes on Forsythe. Get to the point."

"Sure, sure; I'm just remembering how it came about. Wendy overhead our conversation. That girl had a talent for butting in. She insisted on going with me."

"We have copious records on this aspect," said the tall man coldly. "Tell us what we don't know."

"We entered the woods. We didn't see the rabbits. She got bored, and we came back. We split up upon emerging, and I didn't talk to her again that day."

"Yes, we know. Details, please; describe everything that occurred behind the tree line."

Blake talked. He delved into his stubborn memory and resurrected the few simple, childish words which had passed between he and Wendy during those uneventful minutes. He strained and recalled little gestures, facial expressions, wisps of thought which had passed into and out of his mind, all of it signifying nothing, yet so murderously vital to these maniacs. In desperation he relived each inconsequential detail, covering it so thoroughly that it was as if he had stepped back in time. As he spoke the clerk's pen raced, moving in perfect conformity to his words. When Blake had told every silly thing he could think of, and every thing that could be prompted out of him, he stopped, sagging wearily into his chair, terrified by the finality of the moment and of what might come.

The tall man stood musing for a tense, somber spell, then nodded, casually saying, "Very good, Mr. Blake." He snapped his fingers. He stepped behind the prisoner while the other two men gathered up their materials and passed out of sight. Blake heard a door opening as he felt his bonds loosening.

"Remain seated for a reasonable period," spoke the voice from behind. "We shall trouble you no more." Footsteps, then the sound of the door closing, and Blake realized that he was alone.

He raised himself shortly from the chair, staggered out of the room, and made his way into the adjoining compartment where he liberated his wife and children. She had much to say, and demanded many explanations, but neither then nor later could he satisfy her with a coherent account of the strange business. Blake subsequently undertook such actions as would be expected after such an ordeal, all to no effect. The perpetrators could not be traced. He never learned any more about the weird trio, who they were or why they were fascinated by him and had plagued him so. Up to the present he has never seen them again, although he remains convinced that they are out there close by, watching him, observing, recording, analyzing his every move.

Much later he sought a copy of Vorchek's "Psychological Analysis," hoping that within its pages he might find clues to the meaning of his harrowing experience. It was quite difficult to find; no bookstore carried it, no standard reference listed it, but he eventually tracked down and borrowed a copy via inter-library loan. Though a short work, it was extremely technical and convoluted in its language, a hard slog to read. He couldn't make any sense out of it, and finally gave up the effort as not worth the bother.

A White Mountains Mystery

When Professor Anton Vorchek ventured into the frigid White Mountains of Arizona that harsh January, he did so neither to uncover evidence in support of supernatural strangeness, nor to seek resolution in a case of ancient tragedy. On the contrary, despite a proclivity for scientific or semi-scientific arcana, conventional academic concerns had directed him to Show Low, site of a regional conference pertaining to matters of local geological interest, where he expected to spend a few days based in a well heated hotel fondly discussing the picayune data esteemed by the handful of exorbitantly educated attendees. It was the mild earthquake of the sixth, centered on the picturesque hamlet of Greer and radiating from there along hitherto unsuspected fault lines, which drew Vorchek from his cozy debates and plunged him into the murk of a sinister mystery.

As for the subsequent, possibly related criminal investigation, Vorchek had absolutely nothing to do with that, refusing to volunteer such pertinent information as he may have possessed, since it lacked any prosaic value to the inquiring authorities. Indeed, they never guessed his most germane role in the affair, which suited him. The books remain open on that one, though Vorchek quietly professes to have settled, to his satisfaction, the rather more lurid elements of the curious business that the police quite naturally ignored or failed to detect.

Professor Vorchek drove over to nearby Greer early on the morning of the tenth, after bracing himself with a hot breakfast, traveling in his tired old van down the ice-glazed lane heading south from the highway between expanses of frosted conifers and frozen meadows. Recent snow lay thick on the pretty landscape, with patches of slippery ice on the road surface, the negotiation of which required intense concentration, a circumstance deterring any of his colleagues who might have cared from an immediate visit. Vorchek, as usual in such instances, was quick off the mark. Also Greer as a destination, a place where he had previously vacationed, formed a beckoning lure, so he set out once his basic duties in Show Low had been concluded.

In Greer he found a scene of picture postcard perfection, a quaint hamlet thriving off tourism, consisting chiefly of cabins and lodges at the bottom of a valley watered by the Little Colorado River; imagery especially beautiful at this time of year, with the really remarkable snowfall, heavy even for this high elevation of over eight thousand feet, converting the otherwise verdant terrain into a kind of fairy land. Vorchek relished the excuse to see this, while looking forward to spending a couple of days analyzing the seismic after-effects of the earthquake with the instruments he brought with him.

That quake, an entirely minor one producing no reported damage, nevertheless intrigued him because detection devices (readily available at the conference) revealed waves of vibration emanating from a point source in Greer, this a scientific oddity, and spreading straight and focused as arrows in flight—another peculiarity—to three notable geographical points in the area: Greens Peak, a lofty cinder cone to the north-west; Escudilla Mountain, an extinct volcano to the east; and Mount Baldy, a still greater volcano to the south, topping out at over eleven thousand feet. That trio of impressive locales doubly attracted a scholar of Vorchek's broad intellectual inclinations, both for their geological significance, and because all three comprised elements in the age-old lore of the local Indians.

To the White Mountain Apaches, the tall summits of those massifs traditionally possessed loci of otherworldly power, fountains of spiritual energy from which flowed the boons and dooms of their antique gods. Recorded legend and ritual songs made much of the strange insights into cosmic wonders derived in olden times from those places, of the supreme beings whose mystical lands lay in extraordinary planes of existence approachable only via those peaks.

Vorchek knew quite a lot about that as well, which tells something important about the man as a researcher. During the course of a long career his esoteric intellectual tastes had drawn him in widely different directions, some not entirely favored by his peers. This eclecticism surely helps explain how he got so deeply involved in this unusual Greer matter, which must now be told.

He intended to reside for the duration of his short stay where he had stopped before, at the historic Devon Lodge, oldest and reputedly best of several in the little town, only when Vorchek carefully pulled into the snowbound parking lot off of the single paved road he found the place closed, shut up, the front door padlocked. Surprised and nonplussed, he continued his drive a short distance, made arrangements at a lesser but still most attractive competitor. Having

139

gotten situated, he took his time about commencing operations. They were not difficult, but it was incredibly cold in Greer, and the haze-masked sun refused to serve, and despite multiple layers of clothing Vorchek felt sluggish and tired beyond his years.

He came armed with computer-developed graphs, print-outs which showed in great accuracy the courses of the shock waves that had lately shot out from the vicinity. These graphs were of such large scale that the professor could track the pinpoint source of the quake by trudging up the ice-slick street and noting landmarks; at first the high ridges overlooking the village, then certain key structures. His chilling hike led straight back to the forsaken Devon Lodge. The quake's origin had sprung directly from the heart of the locked building.

In the interests of getting to the point it is well that for Professor Vorchek events began to happen swiftly. He had not been there long in frustration, losing his battle against the cold as he casually admired the fancy wooden façade of the wonderful old lodge, when another man halted there, exiting from a hefty pickup to pleasantly accost him. Vorchek introduced himself, briefly explained his business in a few simple sentences, allowed that he had hoped to get inside to precisely locate a spot of scientific importance.

"I'm Andy," announced the other, extending a firm hand; a big fellow with a friendly smile wreathed in full beard, dressed like a mountain man. "Andy Devon, pleased to meet you. I own the Devon Lodge, me and the wife." The smile twitched to a frown as he added, "It's currently out of season for us."

"I did not expect that," replied Vorchek, in his well-modulated, slightly accented speech. "I should have thought, sir, that the nearby ski slopes would keep you full of customers."

"So they should," agreed Andy with a deepening frown, "but we've had problems this last month, and a couple of days ago our troubles shut us down. It's not fair; when I think of how much work we've put into this place... Everybody left, including our best annual regulars. I can't keep the lodge open on spec, so—"

Vorchek nodded knowingly. "So the earthquake hit you hard?"

Andy shook his head vigorously. "Not a bit of it. Some broken glass—the neighbors didn't get that much—anyway, nothing for worry there. Say, what kind of professor are you? Do you only tackle earthquakes, is that it?"

Vorchek grinned. "I 'tackle' many disparate topics, sir, when there is true knowledge to be gleaned."

"Oh yeah?" The stout, rough-looking fellow stared down at his enormous boots, stamped snow as he seemed to debate within himself. Raising his eyes again to his companion, he beat gloved hands together and asked, "What do you know about ghosts?"

Vorchek's eyes widened behind gimlet spectacles. "A thing or two, I dare say. They may, at rare whiles, connote entertaining items of investigation. However," he added, with an ostentatious shiver, "as a subject of discussion under these conditions . . ." This broad hint led shortly to his appearance as guest in Andy's warm, cozy cabin home in the pine woods across the frozen river.

Shorn of repetition and a host's digressions Andy, supported by his wife, explained his current circumstances thus: "It began just a tad over a month ago, right after the big celebration. That's when the hauntings started. We—Wendy and I—didn't pick up on it ourselves at first, but we heard from the paying customers. Little sights and sounds, moving shadows of nothing and noises like somebody creeping around, but nobody there when you open a door. That tickled me. In these goofy times a ghost can be great for business. I imagined us starring in one of those silly TV shows; you know, the kind with grubby characters running around in the dark wearing green lights, spooking themselves."

"I never thought we needed that business," opined Wendy, a raw-boned convivial sort, as she poured more hot chocolate for all.

"Well, turned out you were right, honey. Professor, something about these episodes didn't sit pretty with the clientele. They complained more than they bragged. Still, it wasn't hurting us in the wallet until the night of the earthquake."

Vorchek interjected, "Excuse me, sir, but I require clarification of data. Scientific analysis advances through the study of patterns. Do I discern one forming? You alluded to untoward events instigated by or correlated with a celebration. Something connected to Christmas?"

"Oh, not at all, Professor. Last month we celebrated the one hundredth anniversary of the lodge's founding. We had a big to-do, right there, kind of a second grand opening, that same night. Boy, were we busy. Everybody in town showed up."

"So, patterns. One hundred years, you say, exactly, and then with the quake came more?"

"Yes, a month later, actually shy a couple of days."

Vorchek sniffed. "Really? Sounds like a lunar cycle. Patterns; what happened then?"

"The ghost ran wild," exclaimed Wendy.

Andy filled in the details. "No one could miss it now. Shrieks in the night, more like animal howling, or somebody dying bad; and gobbledygook chatter, hateful foreign stuff coming out of the air. We heard it, but that wasn't the worst. People were touched in their beds, and had room doors open on them—locked doors, they swore—along with those terrible sounds. It didn't take long before folks were clearing out. Some said they saw something, more than shadows: a walking dead man, like a mummy, all dried up, coming after them. They didn't stick long. In two days we had to close down, couldn't even pay for the heat.

"That's where we stand now. Twiddling our thumbs at home won't work. I mean to give it a few days, then open up again, hope it's over and done with. Unless you have a better idea?"

Vorchek grinned, sipped his steaming cocoa. "At present I have no ideas, only more questions. Let me make clear to both of you that I reject, in the main, all popular presentations of the supernatural. They invariably prove bogus, however profitable. The instigation of genuine haunting, if valid, must be extremely rare. What sets it off? Death is the usual claim, an insufficient one, for armies of the dead do not prowl battlefields, nor do ghosts disturb our teeming modern murder sites. If a location be haunted, then an intense psychic force must operate there. The key question is why?

"In your case patterns emerge. I ask of you the obvious: what, of a dire nature, happened a century ago?"

Shaking of heads, a reply in unison, "Nothing."

"Inadequate," said Vorchek. "Tell me how the Devon Lodge came to be."

"There's nothing to it," said Andy with a shrug. "My great- great-grandfather—"

"Ah?"

"Yes, we've kept the lodge in the family all this time. My ancestor Andrew Devon—I'm named after him—"

"Ah."

"Andrew was a colorful character, a typical type of those days. Pioneer times lasted longer in Arizona, especially in isolated territory like the White Mountains. Really, the lodge was the beginning of civilization hereabouts. Old Man Andrew, as the lady at the town museum calls him, was a reformed outlaw who turned sharp businessman. He built the lodge on the cheap, advertised from Albuquerque to Las Vegas, made big money for himself and put Greer on the map. That's about it."

"There must be more," pressed Vorchek, absently fondling his short, manicured beard. "Give me data on the erection of the lodge."

Andy squinted, nervously ran fingers through his bushy facial hair as he went on. "Not much to tell. Andrew hired workmen from the Apache reservation—the border is only a few miles from here, in fact they own the ski resort—ran them like slaves, I believe paid them more in booze than coin, then chased them off at gunpoint when they finished. After that it was standard tourist practice. The lodge was a lot smaller then, just the central part. It's been added to a bunch since."

Vorchek nodded. Shortly he observed, "The quake radiated from that central portion. Patterns indeed, but to what significance? Did anything like a local newspaper exist at the time?"

"Not in Greer," Wendy replied with certainty. "Not a chance. Springerville and McNair, I guess, were the closest."

"I see. I can check those." Vorchek pondered. "As a stab in the dark, the Apache connection pricks my curiosity. Does history, or legend for that matter, record any disturbing events associated with the Indian presence at the lodge, at that time?"

Host and hostess looked blank. Andy drawled, "I don't recall any such. The old man, as I've said, didn't exactly behave himself. It's fair to say he cheated the workmen. Their big chief got into the act, came here himself to demand proper compensation for his folks, swapped sharp words with Andrew. Threats flew back and forth, as I've heard it. Nothing came of that, though. Great plus Grand Dad paid him off, so goes the story, and the chief went home happy. He went away, at any rate, nor returned for more trouble. Professor, I don't believe there's more to it than that."

"Then there is nothing," Vorchek declared, "in which case your problem stems from little more than collective hysteria." He raised a hand to silence protests. "I shall investigate, by your leave. Patterns deserve study, regardless of outcome. Mr. and Mrs. Devon, thank you both for your hospitality. This much I require of you . . ."

Professor Anton Vorchek indulged his whims by scrutinizing every scrap of evidence which might conceivably bear on the conundrum. His first step, which consumed all of the following day, was to conclude the geological exploration which had brought him to Greer. The timing and proximity of that quake indicated a pertinence, likely spurious, which held him temporarily to his original plan. Armed with a borrowed key he entered the Devon Lodge that freezing morning, before the late sun rose, toured the interior by flashlight. Having devoted scant minutes to reveling in the splendid architecture and furnishings, he got to work with his portable instruments, the readings from which, detecting the merest hints of after-shocks, enabled him to locate the exact source of the quake. It had radiated from beneath the polished antique floorboards of a cramped, oblong storage room adjoining the highly rated house restaurant.

During his sojourn within that establishment Vorchek acknowledged a profound sense of disquiet, a nagging feeling of mounting distress which increasingly inflamed his normally controlled emotions. It annoyed him to admit that he felt fear. Twice, out of the corner of his eye, he imagined a disturbing dark shape standing near, one that vanished when he gazed directly at it. Once, while stooping to read a swinging needle in an illuminated panel, he distinctly felt coarse fingertips brush the nape of his neck, accompanied by guttural muttering, and his reaction made him feel foolish. Of course nothing was there.

The few sunlit hours available at that time of year he spent in slow and careful drives to the mountains Baldy, Escudilla, and Greens Peak. The former two he approached as closely as he could by van on fair dirt roads. The latter mountain received most attention, for Vorchek forced himself to undertake the horrendous drive to the very top, bouncing and skidding on the icy service road, hardly more than a jeep trail, which linked the world to the forest of television and radio towers on the snowy, windswept summit. In each case he attempted to verify the original supposition that the shock waves had, one might say, "beamed" directly at those peaks. Baldy and Escudilla required estimation, but for Greens Vorchek, shuffling about in the miserable cold, could determine with precision. His seismic recordings placed the still faintly vibrating terminus spot beneath the loftiest point, right under the fire tower.

Which meant what? When he dined with the Devons that evening he remained enigmatic, claiming nothing to report.

His second day of pleasurable labors involved more staid and sedentary scholarly pursuits. This day he hit the books, so to speak, seeking out thought-provoking lore relating to the founding of the Devon Lodge. Delving beyond popular accounts spun for tourists, he sought that information on the past which tends to linger forgotten or disregarded in dusty files or the memories of aging natives. He did examine the sparse available newspaper reports of a century before, and spoke at length with Gladys Hobson, elderly volunteer custodian at the Butterfly Museum, repository of collected data on Greer's pioneer period. With her thick glasses pushed up into her graying hair, she regaled him for over two hours, taking her time about focusing on his specific questions.

"Old Man Andrew?" she laughed at last, after Vorchek had repeatedly broached the name. "There was a mean cuss. Hard to believe he's related to our sweet Andy. Nothing but an outlaw made good, that Devon, rustler and thief turned honest citizen—hah!—only because he saved his loot. Why, he's the guy who shot Billy Powers up on Escudilla Mountain, they say in an argument over stolen cattle. That was way before he skedaddled for Greer, though. He was smart enough when he came here to put on airs, a false front that tricked folks. A sorry sort like him should have gone out hard, but he died in his bed years later, laughing at the world I bet. It's not fair, but he got away with it.

"You want to know about the Indians at the lodge? Typical Devon meanness, for sure. He rustled them up like stolen cattle to do his heavy lifting, then dumped them like hoof and mouth rejects, unpaid, once they'd raised the since famous lodge. There's passages in the Butler diary that tell what happened next. A hot-shot Apache chief—Tonkeyana they called him—came up from the reservation to collect what was owed. Shoot no, Old Man Andrew didn't pay off nor bribe. He boasted of running off Tonkeyana, putting a scare into him. That's all he said, I suppose all he did. Whatever Devon did, the Apache chief never came back."

That evening, the beneficiary of another home-cooked meal courtesy of the Devons, Vorchek allowed that his studies made headway.

On the third day he drove down to Whiteriver, the administrative seat of the Fort Apache Reservation, home of the White Mountain Apaches. There he consulted records, spoke with equally eager and loquacious Indian counterparts of Mrs. Hobson. Before he drove back to Greer that afternoon he had learned much, filling in details of events a hundred years gone, uncovering information which added suggestive twists to the old tale of the founding of Devon Lodge.

"I begin to deduce a glimmer of actuality," declared Professor Vorchek. Over another fine hot repast he explained to the Devons, as simply as he was capable, what he had found out. "Everywhere I turned the Apache connection loomed. I hypothesized that as the unitary element. The anecdote relating to this Tonkeyana bulked large in my mind. In Whiteriver I derived dissonant, corrective data. An ominous note emerged, which we may provisionally postulate bears on your troubles.

"Tonkeyana was indeed an eminent worthy among the Apaches, but not a chief, though certainly a council elder of high standing. Rather, he was a *shaman*—a medicine man—reputed a magician wise and powerful, even dangerous. His own people granted him fearful respect, dreading to anger him, calling on him and his alleged supernatural abilities only out of necessity.

"This matter of the cheated workmen apparently inflamed passions on the reservation. A delegation of those men dared approach Tonkeyana to beg for succor at his hands. He agreed, journeyed here to confront your ancestor, insisted on recompense. Reading between the lines of olden reports, we may assume that the shaman's insistence would not constitute a pleasing experience for the receiver."

"I guess not," agreed Wendy, "but where does that get us? Old Man Andrew didn't back down."

Andy put in, "He sure didn't. Based on this version of the tale, whatever threats the medicine man made, Andrew refused to buckle. He ran off Tonkeyana, probably at gunpoint, given what we know about him."

"Ah, but did he?" Vorchek responded, flourishing a finger in the air. "We may choose to wonder just how the Mr. Devon of yore would react to this kind of threat. Tonkeyana, you see, dealt in curses, the laying of malicious charms upon his victims. A hot-blooded—not to say, hot-headed—man such as your ancestor might conclude that 'running off' was insufficient. He might seek a permanent resolution."

Andy said, "I don't get you."

"Do not you?" Vorchek motioned for a refill of his wine glass. "My research in Whiteriver bore surprising fruit. The voice of history states that Tonkeyana never returned to his people."

The remainder of this conversation may be skipped, for it led directly to activities lending themselves to detailed description. The following day found Professor Vorchek and Andy Devon within the confines of the lodge, this time armed with a different assortment of instruments: digging tools.

"The secret lies beneath these boards," Vorchek declared, "the explanation, sir, for your ills, at this spot from which the earthquake originated. I urge you to accept my theory on faith, until our labors confirm or refute."

Andy, an obviously unhappy man, nodded. "All right, I guess we tear it up." This they did, engaging in crude excavation of the floor of the aforementioned store room, chopping with an ax and prying with a crowbar until their efforts revealed bare dirt. The lodge's owner had turned the electricity back on, so with plenty of light they had no difficulty performing or observing. During this task both men confessed to a sense as of unwholesome company close by, and were glad that the dangling overhead bulb banished all shadows.

The brisk employment of two shovels soon quarried a hole from which an unpleasantly musty odor, tinged with the bitterly acrid, welled up to assail the nose. The smell escalated to a gagging stench. They shortly began to uncover a largish, elongated object. The shovels cast aside, Vorchek descended into the hole with a spade, which he used gingerly, carefully scraping away earth. He continued methodically, steeling his nerves against the breathless whispering that caused Andy to start and glance round wildly. Before long they could not doubt the grisly nature of what they had exhumed.

Andy guessed much straight away. "My God!" he cried, sweating profusely despite not having activated the heater. "The maniac—my own kin, too—he never learned. Even then, murder was his solution." Vorchek nodded in agreement, for this discovery, to his mind, narrowed the possibilities down to one.

They beheld a horribly rotted corpse, with the bones showing through darkened parchment skin and shreds of coarse, multi-colored cloth, the limbs bound and drawn together with dried leather thongs. Empty eye sockets stared above high cheek bones from which the flesh had peeled back, ragged teeth grinning from gaping jaws. The human remains lay on their side, exposing the wide, unnatural cavity in the posterior of the skull.

"It had to be," Vorchek murmured solemnly as he climbed out of the pit. "The facial structure, remnants of robes of office; yes, it fits." He sighed. "Granting the admissibility of a supernatural cause, once I knew that an Apache sorcerer was involved, all the data lined up in an orderly sequence. The hauntings commenced one hundred years after the fateful encounter. One lunar cycle later came the quake, emanating from here, strangely radiating only to three holy Apache sites, the mountains, places of legendary power. Tonkeyana was long gone, of course—assassinated, I deduce, when his back was turned—but his curse continued, delayed perhaps by his destruction but not canceled, for the curse could only be lifted in life. Your ancestor's hasty crime may have saved himself—an outrageous miscarriage of justice—but he has made your situation most problematic."

"Me?" Andy blurted. "What about me?" Shuddering, he indicated the horror below. "This has nothing to do with me."

"I am afraid that it does," rejoined Vorchek. "Were Tonkeyana alive, he might agree with you—that we cannot know—but he is most evidently deceased, and what is done—in a case of this sort—cannot be undone. The shaman clearly laid a curse on Andrew Devon. After a century the arcane cycles of time and magic have come round, and the curse blazes forth once more, to meet... Andrew Devon. You, sir."

"It's not fair!" shrilled Andy. "I've done nothing. This awfulness isn't part of me. It's something old, that should have been buried and forgotten."

Vorchek allowed himself a morbid chuckle. "So it was, sir. Unfortunately, that counts for naught."

Andy shook with anger. "Well, I don't buy it, anyway. It's nonsense, that's all, a lot of hooey. I'm not going to let this wreck my life."

"It will produce more complications," Vorchek pointed out, "at the very least. We must inform the police of our finding."

They did that, of course, and quite a nine day wonder it was, of enormous popular interest, once the authorities established that they were dealing with an extremely cold case, a matter of ancient history. Vorchek readily bowed out at that juncture; the police cared not, and by then Andy was glad to see him leave. The academic's advice nettled so.

Andy declared—possibly convinced himself—that with the offending corpse removed, and returned with full honors to its people, that his troubles were over. In the Greer newspaper, and several trade sheets, he announced the forthcoming reopening of the Devon Lodge. He routinely delivered as his opinion that the place ought to be free of terror, maybe with just enough of a lingering ghost, in approved contemporary style, to be attractive to guests. Wendy made no comment on this.

Events proved Andy wrong. His plans did not quite come to fruition as intended. On the night before the first new visitors were to arrive, while he made his solitary rounds within the building to ensure that all was prepared, a mysterious fire broke out. Its point of origin could not be determined; fire department investigators stated that blazes seemed to spring up throughout the structure simultaneously. They declared the lodge a total loss. Some postulated that the slight tremor of that evening (another quake difficult to explicate on geological grounds), which ran up and over the highest peaks from Whiteriver, could have factored in the disaster. Regardless, they did find that Andy had not perished from flames or smoke. Rather, a ceiling beam had plunged with great force, smashing his skull, killing him instantly.

Professor Anton Vorchek, on hearing the news, pronounced with an air of resignation, "Do we expect fairness in this world? Surely we seek it, consider it our due, yet what hope have we when the evil past arises to sully the innocent present? Do not count on textbook justice in a scenario defiled by theft, murder, black magic, and disembodied revenge. The first Andrew, a double-dyed scoundrel, got off scot-free, while the second paid the price. What happened to the recently late Mr. Devon was not fair. It may have been unavoidable. It is certainly a shame."

Peril in the Red Zone

The narrow road ran straight across the plain, through territory covered with desert scrub and dotted by fewer and fewer houses, until it came to the base of the low, broad hill, where the pavement ended. From there a rugged dirt road mounted the hill and wound its lazy way to the flat summit. At the top loomed an old, two-story wooden house, of goodly size but dismal aspect. The expansive yard differed little from the surrounding terrain. One might have suspected abandonment, yet the numerous windows were intact, nor had the whitewash yet degraded to utter gray.

The red sports coupe growled to a halt. The driver's side door opened and a girl got out, bracing herself against the winter wind which whipped the hilltop. From this vantage she noticed the murky skyline of Phoenix far to the south-east. The rest of the sky was brilliantly clear. She stared at the house for a minute, then looked all around her, then examined a slip of paper which she removed from her purse. With a shrug she replaced the slip, slammed the car door, and made her way across the yard to the front door of the house. There a brass knocker of unusual design caught her eye—a knocker fashioned in the likeness of a Mayan sun god—a repellent, leering visage which did not invite use. It might be considered a minor test of determination. The girl hesitated, then gingerly knocked.

The curtain over a nearby window fluttered, and immediately thereafter the door creaked open. A dark figure stood within the shadowed interior. A cultivated masculine voice, with just the slightest hint of the foreign in its tones, asked, "What is your business?"

"I'm looking for," the girl began; "that is—I need to speak with—are you Professor Anton Vorchek?"

"I am Vorchek." The door rasped wider. "Enter." The figure stepped aside.

The girl strode into the dark hallway. The door closed behind her. Through the deep gloom she could barely make out her host preceding her down the hall. They entered a large room, also dimly illuminated only by the feeble rays which penetrated the heavy curtains. The man stooped, fussed with something that clinked. A match flared, and then an oil-burning storm lamp flickered into soft yellow radiance.

The warm glow revealed what might have been styled a living room, boasting a cavernous, empty fireplace, a floor graced with thick Persian carpets and occupied by large, comfortable antique furniture, and with impressively Impressionistic paintings adorning the paneled walls, where those walls were not concealed by shelves and cases overflowing with books. The books were mainly old and worn, and those with legible titles indicated various abstruse or peculiar topics. The man straightened up.

"Professor Vorchek, at your service," said he with a bow. "Now, my dear, tell me your name, and how I may serve you."

"Thank you," replied the girl, as he motioned her to the sofa. He remained standing. Vorchek appeared to her an interesting figure: a tall, thin, angular gentleman, dressed in a stained white smock, with dark hair turned iron-gray at the temples, and a hawk-face in which the sharp nose predominated. The thin lips of his harsh mouth pursed primly above the strong chin, which sported a small, neat beard also flecked with gray. Piercing black eyes loomed inquisitively behind round wire-framed lenses. "I've come about my father," she continued. "I have to talk to you about what's happened to him."

"The question of identity still eludes me," reminded Vorchek, but he did so with a charming smile, for he found this girl also an interesting figure. Young, comely, very finely formed, with small, soft features on a face peeking out from under a great mass of golden hair; quite unlike the other visitors whom he irregularly received. Her appearance denoted quality, her manners suggested breeding, and her attire; well, that indicated daring. This girl, as he found when she handed him her expensive designer jacket, was dressed to kill. There was not much to her china-blue dress, but what there was made him feel good to be alive. The fishnet hose and the high, tight-fitting black boots curiously complemented the dress; the whole ensemble oddly complemented her abundant natural charms. Gold jewelry of fancy make ornamented her slim neck, her white arms, her wrists and her earlobes. She was obviously accustomed to pleasing someone, if it be only herself.

"I refer to my father," she said, "Doctor Walter Delaney, whom I think you know."

"I know of him," said Vorchek. "Walter Delaney, the physicist. Yes, I've heard something about him. As I recall, I ran into him at the big conference at the Lowell Observatory some years ago."

"That is correct. He told me about that."

"And in conversation he mentioned something more: a daughter. You are, I take it, Theresa Delaney?"

"The one and only," she admitted. "Wow, so you remember that."

"I remember everything," declared Vorchek. "It is the secret of my success, such as it is. My memory never lets me down, nor does it ever leave me alone. I knew of your existence. If your father had told me of your loveliness, Miss Delaney, perhaps I would have made haste to make your acquaintance."

"You're too kind," Theresa said, with a blushing smile. Then she recovered her sober demeanor and added, "Right now I've got problems. My father, you see. Do you mind if I smoke?"

"Please yourself." The girl produced a short, black onyx holder into which she fitted a cigarette. As she puffed it alight Vorchek mused congenially. "Up to the time of the Observatory conference—a convention on applied physics—I read several papers published by your father. Dr. Delaney had a knack in those days for converting scientific principles into financial success. He was working out of Flagstaff, had his own research institute associated with the university there; a good school, with considerable monetary backing for a scientist who produces the goods. That gadget he designed for the space program—some sort of remote television or camera eye—made him a wealthy man. It pleases me when a colleague gets ahead in the world. I can see that you have benefited from his gain, most charmingly so. However, I haven't read anything of his since those days."

"That's because he hasn't published since."

"Indeed?" Vorchek nodded. "At the conference he referred to a new theory of extra-dimensional travel, the possibility of penetrating into other realms of existence. I found it most fascinating, although I disputed the efficacy of his views. I regret to say that we had quite an argument over it."

"That's right," cried Theresa, waving her cigarette holder in the air like a baton. "Father was pretty bitter about it, too. I'm sorry to tell you that he had some harsh things to say about you afterward. On the other hand, he often noted that you were the only man who understood what he was talking about. That was a great deal more credit than he was ever willing to grant anyone else."

"To that extent, he honored me. I understood him. Furthermore,

I could accept his basic ideas. The concept of the reality of other dimensions, other planes in time and space, is sound enough. It is, in theory, possible to imagine spanning such gulfs, with the requisite knowledge. I did not believe that such a process would yield the immediate practical rewards that he envisioned. From his silence over the years, I presume that he has come to see it my way. Is that the problem? Does he want my help?"

"I don't know what he wants, Professor," Theresa said grimly. "That's the point. My father has disappeared."

Vorchek offered her a drink, an offer she accepted with gratitude. He left her for a moment, to return with a decanter of brandy and two glasses. He poured a large one for her, a small one for himself. Theresa downed hers in a gulp. He refilled her glass, then sat opposite her in a plush chair. "Tell me about it, Miss Delaney.."

"My father pursued his extra-dimensional studies," she began. "In fact, that subject became his life's work. I was just a child when he started, and I knew nothing of physics—still don't, much that is— but I picked up a thing or two along the way. First he had to establish the existence of these other unseen regions—"

"That is the easy part," Vorchek broke in. "No competent authority today would question the principle. The idea has always fascinated me, although my research has followed a different path. Dr. Delaney utilized the methods of cutting-edge physics, while I have devoted much effort to analyzing the claims embedded within ancient folklore. I remember thinking at the time how familiar some of your father's claims were, though I knew of them mainly from old texts, rather than recent experiments."

"I guess," Theresa said absently. "Anyway, he assured me that he was staking out new territory, and judging from his colleague's comments—public and private—I never had reason to doubt him on that score."

"They weren't as supportive as they could have been? Believe me, my dear, I recognize the type, far better than your father ever could." Vorchek lit a strangely angled pipe and leaned back in his chair, puffing. "There are limits to conventional thought, which may only be overcome by extreme dedication to one's goal. So, your father persevered?"

"He certainly did. I could tell you the matter became a mania, except that wouldn't be fair to him. He knew what he was doing, he knew what he wanted, and he suspected that his goal was attainable. Then, last year he commenced construction of the machine."

"Ah!" Vorchek exhaled heavily. "So he did take that route. Most intriguing. Describe to me the machine."

To the extent that I can, I will. Father called it a 'dimensional transport device.' DTD, for short. It's hard to describe: it's a room, and a machine. The room he called a 'dimensional chamber.' It's a shielded alcove in his laboratory, the space within which the entrance to other dimensions can be brought about. As he explained it, anything within the chamber could be projected far away in space and time, or simply elsewhere, to places where space and time aren't relevant. Does that make sense to you?"

"Oh, yes. Do go on." Despite the girl's gravity of presentation, Vorchek positively beamed.

"All right. In the beginning he put objects into the chamber and sent them away. They vanished; I can tell you that much. After experimenting at that level for a while, he designed the DTD. The DTD is the mobile machine, a kind of capsule which he fabricated according to his own secret blueprints. This is what he thought would make his name.

"As you must realize, there wasn't any practical value to simply sending off items into thin air. For there to be any value to the experiment, he had to be able to get the stuff back. Travel had to be both ways. So, he built the DTD, which could be projected into the other dimensions, but which, if he was correct, could home onto a preset signal and return to its starting point in our dimensions."

"And he tested that?"

"For weeks, Professor, he did nothing but test it."

"Did it work, girl?"

"Don't get excited, Professor. I'm telling you. Yes, it worked. It passed every test he devised for it, verifying every one of his hypotheses. My father handled it by the book—by the numbers—and made sure everything functioned perfectly.

"He began with small items, books, gloves, knickknacks. He sent them away, he brought them back. With each test he reset the coordinates, which were intended to transmit the items to different places. I'm afraid I know nothing about how he determined that. On every occasion but one, the objects came back intact. That one time, a plastic water jug returned exhibiting signs of heat damage. The DTD was scorched as well, though still operating fine. Father crossed those coordinates off a list. Once he'd established that the capsule worked, he sent an instrument through the dimensions. This was based on another design of his for the space program. It took air samples, measuring density, gaseous composition, and the like. He tried that half a dozen times before he got an atmospheric reading which approximated that of the Earth."

"So far, so good," observed Vorchek. "Dr. Delaney was obviously aware of the risks inherent in entering these mysterious realms. There was always the chance that conditions on the other end would be utterly non-terrestrial. He wished to be sure of his ground before he grew too ambitious with his tests."

"That was his way."

"What came next? Some sort of live demonstration, I presume."

"You are right, Professor. Father next experimented with animals, in order to verify conditions on the other side, and to make certain that living organisms could survive the process of transmission. He used a rat, a canary, and a rabbit. Each passed through, both ways, with no ill effects at all."

"How rapidly did transmission occur?"

"It could be any length of time," Theresa replied, as she lit another cigarette. "In the first experiments with any objects or creatures, he sent them and brought them back almost simultaneously. Then he would leave them in the other dimensions for longer periods, up to several hours. As far as I know it never made a difference."

"How spacious is the DTD?" asked Vorchek abruptly.

"There's plenty of room inside," said the girl. "Its capacity is somewhat like the interior of a car. It was built to allow one to travel comfortably, accompanied by a fair quantity of gear and supplies."

"I suppose I see where this is leading."

"I guess you do." Misery mounted in Theresa's voice. "All along the plan was to send through a man. After the animal tests checked out, my father began preparing to undertake the journey himself. He'd convinced himself that he'd ruled out the possibility of danger. 'I'm going to take a little trip,' he said, 'and I'll go for a little stroll on the other side. Then I'll come back to you.' That was the idea. I argued with him. I suggested he seek volunteers, bring others into the business. He would have to do that sooner or later anyway. Father wasn't interested. Ever since my mother died, many years ago—she was a physicist, too—he tended to work alone, until a project was in the final stages. Then, when he was satisfied that his task was complete, he would hand it off to others. In this case, he wanted to make the first human trip himself, and then demand a high price for his knowledge."

"That practice had served him well in the past."

"It didn't this time. I offered to go in his place, so that he could operate the controls on this end, but he wouldn't hear of it. Instead, he taught me to run the controls."

"That is excellent news," cried Vorchek. "You can operate the instruments?"

"Well, some of them."

"Tell me the rest, Miss Delaney."

"The day came. He had gathered together his supplies—food, water, spare clothing, and scientific materials—and placed them in the capsule. As I told you, he intended to be gone no time at all, but he wasn't convinced that time would pass at the same rate on the other end; he'd experimented by sending a clock through, but that didn't satisfy him. He hedged his bets by taking two weeks' worth of supplies. He made me promise not to try and bring him back until that period had passed."

"He wouldn't set the device for automatic return," noted Vorchek, "because he might not be in it at the time."

"Exactly. Then, he climbed into the DTD and locked the door. I activated the sending controls. I pressed the buttons, I turned the dials with my own hands. I sent him away into the void. The DTD vanished, carrying him with it. That was the last time I ever saw him. He went, and he hasn't come back."

Theresa paused, as if out of breath, emotions agitating her lovely face. "That was three weeks ago. Father didn't return immediately. Days passed, with no sign of him. After a week I couldn't stand it any longer. I activated the return controls."

Vorchek shook his head in dismay. "Was that wise? Given what you have told me, such precipitate action on your part might have increased the risk to Dr. Delaney. If he were exploring at that moment—"

"It may have been foolish, Professor," she said, nodding wearily, "and you can claim I panicked, but he had assured me so that he would make only a quick trip. I imagined him hurt, unable to operate the machine on his end, and . . . and not able to communicate with me. I had to do something. I brought back the DTD. He wasn't in it, but it wasn't empty. Virtually all of his gear, and most of the food and drink, were still inside."

"That is bad."

"I thought so, but, believe me, I didn't leave it at that. Since the coordinates were still set, I sent the capsule back out, waiting another day before reversing the process again. It reappeared. Careful

156

examination showed that nothing inside had been touched in the meantime."

"I see. No question, something went wrong. What did you do then?"

"Nothing sensible, at first. I called the police. What a stupid thing to do! I guess I did it because I thought I ought to do so. What could I expect from them? They treated it as a missing persons case, asked a lot of dopey questions about his friends and associates. I doubt they accepted much of my story. It's a wonder they didn't arrest me. After that, I contacted some of his colleagues at the university, those who would know something of his work. They weren't any more helpful than the police. None of them believed his theory was sound. The general consensus was that he must have burned himself up somehow during transmission, which was ridiculous."

"The fools," muttered Vorchek, with real feeling.

"I won't argue that point," Theresa exclaimed, with considerable feeling herself. "Through my father, I'm accustomed to a different kind of scientific attitude. Well, their rebuff left me at loose ends. I had nowhere to turn. I thought about hopping into the capsule and chasing after him myself—maybe I should have—but what if that went wrong? What good would I do him? And, to confess, the thing scares me. I needed to talk to somebody who could understand. Then a distant memory came to my aid, and I thought of you."

"A wise thought it was, my dear. I do not shun the daring idea, or reject brilliance. There is much to learn from Dr. Delaney's theories."

"It was awfully hard tracking you down," she added. "I heard you were located in Phoenix, so I sent a message to your university. Receiving no reply, I flew down here. I found your office on campus, but also discovered that you hardly ever use it. Nobody had seen you in ages, and—well, they said things about you—and they didn't know when you would be back. Some of them thought you might be out of the country. I got your address, such as it is, rented a car and drove out here. I wasn't sure I had the right place."

"But you found me after all," said Vorchek jovially. "I entertain few visitors here, and as a rule that is the way I prefer it. For the record, my connection to the university is tenuous. I regret to say that they do not have much use for me. I maintain an office there, which I seldom occupy, and occasionally teach special classes, of my own devising, for special students. Most of my work is performed right here. I have a laboratory, of sorts, in back, although it can not possibly rival the magnificence of your father's. My research does take me away at times, but at the moment, rest assured, I am free, and eager to help you."

"You are? That's thrilling. I need help; my father needs help. He's in trouble. There's got to be a way to get him back, and I want somebody with me who knows what he's doing."

"You have found him."

"Have I?" Theresa eyed him critically. At your university—the things they said about you—I didn't expect that. Resolving this terrible business is so important to me. It means everything. I've got to tell you: your colleagues dismiss you as some kind of kook. They told me not to waste time dealing with you. They said you talk crazy and act crazier, and that your ideas are a joke. They said you weren't even a real professional, but just a scientific hanger-on. Professor Vorchek, what kind of man are you?"

He chuckled. "Yes, I do believe they said those things, and perhaps a deal more. It is fortunate that not all of my fellows feel that way, but far too many do. Miss Delaney, I have devoted most of my life to the study of the unknown, the unsuspected, and the unimaginable. It is my passion, rather than my vocation. In pursuit of weird and esoteric knowledge, I have rubbed shoulders with pseudoscientific cranks and perhaps, sadly, some of their reputation has rubbed off on me. No one is more distressed by that than I. I assert to you, however, that I am a keen and loyal follower of the scientific method, and that nothing matters to me more than the truth. If it is the truth you seek, then Professor Vorchek is your man."

"And what kind of professor are you?"

"I am a professor of everything. I do have a propensity toward dabbling, but at the moment, my dear, I consider myself the world's leading expert on the subject of discovering what has happened to your father. I have a general knowledge of the issues, the capacity to understand the science involved, and I appreciate the company of a beautiful girl. Therefore, this case offers me everything I desire, and I promise you my full support and the complete exercise of my brain. Now let's get down to business, girl, make our plans, and get this show on the road."

II.

Five days had passed. Theresa had flown back to Flagstaff immediately after the conversation described. To her amazement and annoyance, Professor Vorchek had not accompanied her. He refused to fly—ever—instead choosing to come on later, creeping up into

Arizona's frigid high country in his tired old van. Having arranged accommodations in town, within easy walking distance, he changed into his best suit and dress hat, then proceeded directly to the sprawling NAU campus, where a large, modern building housed the Delaney Institute. Joined by the girl, who still attired herself like a model in a risqué fashion magazine, he spent some time there, discussing the situation with the staff, who scarcely knew what to make of him. He and Theresa then quickly traveled to their final stop: a smaller, low, oblong structure in the snowy pine woods overlooking frozen Lake Mary, which constituted the missing Dr. Delaney's private preserve. There the missing man had performed his seminal or secret work, bringing to fruition projects not yet ready for revelation.

This well-heated building consisted of an office, a machine workshop, and an expansive laboratory, also a bedroom and bathroom, for its owner was known to inhabit the place when duties pressed. There was another room, The Room, the dimensional transference chamber itself. It was a lead-lined compartment, big enough to walk around in but not much more, surrounded on two sides by computer banks and batteries of controls. One entered the chamber through a complicated hatch which could be hermetically sealed. Vorchek admired the exquisite engineering of the advanced machinery, the construction of which had been personally supervised by Dr. Delaney, who himself bore the exorbitant costs. He had spent a fortune on that room, certain that he would earn it back many times over.

Within the chamber stood the DTD. It was a rather cone-shaped capsule, blunted at the top, mounted on a chassis of several tiny wheels to facilitate movement. Its door contained an observation port. The capacious interior was mainly composed of another sealed chamber, which Theresa had emptied of the personal effects and other movables belonging to the lost scientist. It contained only its essentials: a seat with straps, an overhead light, and a conveniently situated set of controls.

Vorchek examined everything, asking Theresa to show him how to operate the key instruments. The result of this initial phase gratified him. "I think I have gotten the hang of the basics now," he said. "I could not have built this, but I understand it. Our great task, now, is to determine what went wrong."

One point had puzzled him on the day of their meeting, and continued to do so. "Your father was—is, excuse me—an expert on advanced communications; yet, I gather, he made no provisions for testing communication across the dimensions. That is a surprising oversight on the part of Dr. Delaney. I would expect that idea to naturally occur to him."

"He did think of it," the girl replied. Vorchek noted that she seemed startled or distressed by the subject. He wondered why. "Early on he sent through his space camera, which also possesses radio capabilities. He got nothing from it. When Father departed, he took with him a special radio which he had designed for the occasion. He hoped to establish a long distance link. I'm not in a position to know if it worked."

"He did not communicate?"

Still she seemed uncomfortable, even sullen. "The radio came back with everything else, still packaged. I can tell you for a fact that he never communicated with that."

"You did not mention this before."

"That isn't what matters to me, Professor," she said warmly.

Despite reservations, Vorchek did not press the issue. "Of course not," said he. "Let us move on. It is necessary that I learn everything about the experiments that Dr. Delaney knew. I require his daily notes, all of them. Bring them to my hotel when you have them ready."

Theresa came to him around noon the next day, bearing an armload of fat manila folders. Vorchek took her out to lunch at a restaurant of her choosing, where she demanded to know what he intended doing to retrieve her father. He patiently explained that he refused to take action until he had mastered the problem.

"My going off half-cocked will serve neither you nor your father," chided Vorchek. "You were right to come to me, rather than rush off, chasing blindly after him. Grant me the same forbearance. I must study. Then I will act.

"All in good time, my dear. Pass the marmalade."

For the next three days and nights, Vorchek read the notes. He did not see Theresa. She telephoned him frequently; he fobbed her off. In his mind's eye, through the tersely written story revealed in the papers, he saw the incredible experiment of Dr. Delaney develop. Vorchek was there when the missing man inaugurated the first test, sending through a book, which a marginal annotation reported to be an unhelpful volume entitled *Raising Modern Girls*. "It might as well make itself useful," the author had wryly added. Vorchek was there when the book came back, undamaged. There followed the other items, anything within reach, each test punctuated by instrument readings and calibrations. The animal studies commenced. The notes revealed the glee of the researcher as he verified that living organisms could survive the journey, returning intact and in fine health.

Before Dr. Delaney utilized live creatures, he had already narrowed down his coordinates to one promising set. His instrument probe (really a clever contraption) had provided him with information and samples of the conditions in that mysterious world, place, whatever and wherever it might be. Atmosphere checked out: oxygen thin but breathable, the air containing no obvious poisons. Temperature readings were unremarkable, those of a balmy spring day in Vorchek's country, which might be a little warm for some. The professor was pleased to find that his lost colleague had tested for background radiation. The results were rather higher than they need be, and there were oddities on the graph, sporadic jumps of the needle, but nothing of a serious nature. A human explorer could cross over and remain for an extended period without necessitating any extraordinary precautions.

It all sounded very good, and yet Dr. Delaney, having made the passage, never came back. The solution to the mystery would not be found in his notes.

On the third morning Vorchek called Theresa at home. "I've learned everything I can from reading," he announced. "The time has come for me to conduct my own trials. Meet me at the laboratory in one hour."

As Vorchek had predicted, his admission to the secured complex, without the girl's blessing, would have been difficult, if not impossible. The others disapproved of him, didn't want him there, and might have been inclined to resistance. Her word carried weight, however, and he supposed that, in her company, he would have no trouble. Theresa awaited him on the covered porch, dressed extravagantly as always, though her long thick coat concealed her brazen charms until they were within doors. Vorchek deduced that she must be extremely popular in her circles, but she seemed to think nothing of it.

"The police called me last night," she informed him. She shook her head. "They're still searching for leads."

"Forget the authorities," advised Vorchek. "We are the authorities in this affair. Is everything ready?"

"The Institute will supply all the power we need. The rest is up to us."

Vorchek commenced by repeating the initial experiment, sending through an object to the set coordinates. He did not doubt the result— was fairly sure what would happen—yet it paid to guarantee that the priceless machinery still operated according to specifications. Theresa produced a clay flowerpot and, placing it within the DTD, sealed the chamber door. Vorchek adjusted the dials, as per her instructions, then pressed a button. He heard sounds from the machinery, the hum of data processing, following by a whirring from the chamber, a noise like a gust of wind. The operation ceased of its own accord. Theresa opened the door. The capsule and the pot were gone.

"Let's bring it back," said Vorchek presently. Theresa slammed the hatch. He reversed dials, activated the power. Another sound of a gust, and shortly he saw with his own eyes that the capsule had returned with its meaningless cargo, just as he had seen it before.

"Apparent we can not blame a mechanical fault," said the professor.

"I could have told you that," Theresa snapped. "I'm the one who brought it back before. The process works perfectly."

"I have gotten as far as I have in this world," sagely replied Vorchek, "by not taking anybody's word for anything. Any machine can fail, no matter how sound its construction. We must cover all the bases. I require an animal subject."

"This is old news," Theresa persisted. "Father and I did that. What more is there to learn from such tests?"

"You established that living organisms can make the trip safely. Then your father took the jump, and you misplaced him. It may not have been so safe then, Miss Delaney, and it may not be so safe now. Let us investigate conditions at the present time."

This they did. Theresa placed a box containing a laboratory rat, along with food and water, into the capsule, which they sent on its way. They retired from the scene for the afternoon, ate dinner—where Vorchek vainly attempted to prop up the girl's drooping spirits—then returned as evening gathered. By this time Vorchek understood the controls as well as his hostess. Their subject came back to them, as hale and as cheerful as a rat ever is.

"A superb result," crowed Vorchek, after the intrepid animal had been returned to its cage. "We gain ground. Our knowledge advances."

"I don't see that, Professor. It's just more time wasting."

"Not at all, my dear. Consider what we previously knew, consider the facts that we have gained, and correlate them. We can be reasonably certain that Dr. Delaney completed the outward voyage without incident; correct?"

"Obviously."

"Something happened to him, however. We must conclude that whatever occurred did so after he reached the other end. Danger, of a sort, met him there. We have not the slightest clue what that might be. For all we knew, it could be a danger still lying in wait for any living thing which goes through. As a result of further examination, especially this last, we can provisionally dismiss that possibility. What goes through to that dimensional point, comes back alive and unmolested. That is vital knowledge!" exclaimed Vorchek. "We move forward. In fact, I am tempted to say that we have learned as much as we can from this end."

"So what do we do now?" Theresa asked excitedly.

"We do nothing tonight," said Vorchek crushingly.

"What do you mean?"

"We rest, and meet back here first thing in the morning." His voice had changed, from its characteristically mellow, polite tone to one harsh and stern. "Before you sleep I want you to think very carefully. Try to remember everything that happened when your father vanished. If there is something that you have failed to tell me, recall it and brief me tomorrow. We will proceed when I am convinced that I possess all the pertinent facts."

"I don't know what you're driving at," Theresa said coldly, but there was a furtive look in her eyes, and her voice quivered. She hesitated, stared down at her shiny high heels, then added lamely, "No idea at all."

"If that be so, then it is of no importance," said Vorchek crisply. "Harken to my words, girl. Give the matter thought, before you see me again."

The next day, sequestered in the laboratory, Vorchek skimmed notes at a desk while Theresa stood nearby, maintaining an obstinate silence. He had said nothing about further steps. She lit a cigarette and smoked it, then began working on another, marking time. He pretended not to notice the mounting tension. Finally, in exasperation, she broke her silence.

"I'm ready to proceed."

"Then start talking," responded Vorchek, in an offhand manner.

"About what?"

"I do not know. You do, so you must broach the subject. There is something you refuse to tell me. If I may hazard a guess (quite contrary to my nature!), then I conjecture that it involves communication with your father."

Theresa gasped. "How did you know that?"

"There were signs," said Vorchek. He tossed aside the notes, which he had memorized. "The subject bothered you, and I could not infer the rationale. There had to be an explanation, and I have to know what it is. I am capable of assuming great risks, but I must know where we stand. Miss Delaney, before I play another hand, lay all your cards on the table."

She collapsed into a chair across from him. "I've nothing to conceal," she began, her voice faltering. "I don't mean to hide anything from you. That would be silly; you know how important this is to me. In the beginning I withheld one fact, because I didn't know you, I needed your help, and I didn't think you would believe me."

"You should have realized by now that I will accept any verifiable claim."

"Maybe," Theresa replied, in a manner that might indicate agreement. "I still haven't entirely figured you out. Having kept quiet, it was hard for me to bring it up later. You still won't believe it, and I'm tired of not being believed. I'm afraid that speaking out will slow you down."

"An inaccurate conclusion on your part," announced Vorchek. "So much for preliminaries. Now tell me."

"I did hear from my father," blurted Theresa. "That's why I brought back the capsule early."

"For the love of God, girl!" cried Vorchek, almost in a scream. He leaped up, then recovered his composure and resumed his seat. "How could you not inform me of that? I will have you know, that I have been working on the assumption that Dr. Delaney is dead, and that our task is not to rescue him, but rather to recover his remains and learn of his fate. If I had known of this before, it is possible that my actions would have been different. Probably not, but I would have retained that knowledge in the forefront of my mind. All right, Miss Delaney, you have confirmed my suspicions. Explicate, please."

She nodded, blinking back tears. She accepted his proffered handkerchief and said, "It was that night, after he had been out there for a week. I slept here, you see, in the next room, because I wanted to be close by when he returned. During the day I regularly checked the instruments, making sure everything was up to snuff. Anyway, I was here, only a few feet away from the chamber, sound asleep. That's when it happened.

"I heard his voice. It was Father, speaking to me as I lay in bed. I'd barely woken up, and I continued to lie there, listening to him speak. It was his voice, clear as day, talking rapidly, without a pause, directly to me. I sprang out of bed, turned on the light and spoke to him, but he wasn't there, and the voice had stopped."

"You describe a dream," groused Vorchek.

"I'm not!" Theresa shot back. "See, I knew you would say that. It wasn't a dream. Hear me out, buster. You wanted the story; this is it.

"I did feel like I was going out of my mind. It's not only that he wasn't there; it's what he said, and how he said it. The voice belonged to him, but the words and intonation were strange. It sounded like quick, stream of consciousness chatter. He would say something— present an idea or thought—break off, then start on another, which might have no connection with what preceded it. I heard random, jumbled statements, without any real attempt at conversation.

"Mind you, Father spoke directly to me. He called me by name, several times, and even used a pet name for me that nobody else in the whole world knows (and which I won't tell you, ever). He was talking at me, though, rather than with me. In certain passages he spoke so fast that it came out as gibberish.

"I dream once in a while. I know what mine are like. This wasn't one of them. I had truly heard his voice. I ran into the lab—not there either—checked the chamber; nothing. He hadn't returned, but he spoke to me! How could that be? I thought of the radio link, from which I'd never received a transmission. It was set up so that any contact would be recorded on tape. I ran the tape. It was empty."

She paused for breath. "So I decided to reverse the controls and bring back the capsule. You know how that went. It returned, but he didn't. I realized immediately what a bone-head mistake I'd made. Now he was cut off from home. I sent the capsule back to him, and waited.

"He didn't come of his own accord. Night turned into day, and still nothing happened. I asked myself if I could have been wrong about what I heard. I couldn't. That afternoon I passed out from exhaustion. Just before sundown something woke me with a start.

"It was his voice again, just like before. As I came to full wakefulness I could hear him, still talking fast, even ranting, but sounding a bit more like himself. This time I lay there, motionless, listening to his words, until they began to fade away. When I could no longer hear him I got up. I did pretty much the same things again, only this time, having brought back the DTD, I held on to it. It's horrible, but I refused to send it out again.

"Here's the final point that blew me away. I wouldn't take the

165

chance on hearing his voice again, by myself. Most of what he said to me was weird, and some of it was vile. He was trying to talk me into joining him, to pass through the dimensions and meet him on the other end, before he returned. There was a phrase that he used several times: 'You must come to me in the Red Zone.' Then he would gabble that term. He made all kinds of promises as to how wonderful it would be there, with him.

"Some of his inducements were sickening. They were of a frankly sexual nature, presented in a manner that my father would never employ with me. He spouted a lot of noise about peace, and happiness, and contentment. It was like he was using every argument in the book, that might appeal to any sort of human being, to get me to the other side. Well, despite my concern, I was terrified. It was Father, but it wasn't. Something was wrong—I had to do something right away—only I couldn't stand to hear that voice again. I decided not to send the capsule back until I'd sought help, had someone with me. That's where you came in.

"I stuck around another day, but I didn't hear him anymore. I guessed that retaining the capsule had broken the link, whatever it was. When you and I tested the device, I dreaded hearing the voice, and yet I sort of hoped you'd hear it too. That hasn't happened, obviously. It must require a certain state of consciousness."

Vorchek slammed both palms onto the desktop and said with decision, "It requires you to be asleep and dreaming."

"No! I tell you, no!" Theresa rose and poked a finger at his face. "It happened, just the way I described it. Give me credit for knowing what's real and what isn't. I can't explain it, true; that's what you're here for!"

"I have explained it."

"Then try again."

"So, must we play games?" sneered Vorchek. "Very well, let fanciful imagination drive reality from the stage. Consider the following. Dr. Delaney has entered a dimensional state—a pleasant one, I trust—where it is possible to transmit thought at a distance. Something in the nature of that dimension also amplifies the thoughts. As a result, his thoughts can actually bridge the dimensional barrier. However, their wavelength is such that they can not be detected against the turbulent background of an active mind, nor within the quiescent recesses of a fully sleeping brain. Ergo, you are capable of reading them only in a condition of semi-consciousness, when the mind approaches awareness, yet is not blinded by sensory input. In short, you heard him when you were half awake, or half asleep, whichever you prefer.

"As for the strangeness of the voice, the things said to you: bear in mind that we never, in the normal course of events, really hear the unfiltered thoughts of another mind. We do not know what pure, direct thought sounds like. It may differ markedly from audible speech. Like it or not, what you heard may be the way your father's mind operates. On the other hand, it may be a sign of a mind in stress or under duress. Regardless, one might predict that he would come across sounding rather bizarre."

"An incredible analysis, Professor!" Theresa cried. "I think you've got it. Just like that, you explained everything."

"I've explained nothing," said Vorchek dismissively. "I spouted billows of perfumed hot air. In the absence of sufficient data, all I can do is spin tall tales. I require much more evidence before I reach even tentative conclusions. That evidence can be gathered only on the other side. The time has come. I shall learn what has become of your father. If I am to tear off the veil which masks the mystery, I must follow Dr. Delaney into the unknown."

"I'm coming with you," Theresa said flatly.

"You are not. Until I learn more, the mystery remains to be penetrated. The perils are unknown, and theoretically immense. You stay here."

"Until my father is found," Theresa pointed out, "I am in charge of the apparatus. You can't touch a single switch without my say-so. That you don't get, unless I come along."

"Then you shall accompany me," said Vorchek, after a fretful pause, "under my strict orders. Accept or reject."

"It's a deal." They shook hands on it.

There was something still on Vorchek's mind. "Miss Delaney, this reference to the 'Red Zone' confounds me. Does that term have any special significance for you? Or, did it mean anything to you in context?"

"No, Professor, nothing at all."

III.

They spent the rest of the day in preparation and making plans. Vorchek collected scientific gear. He especially desired instruments which could measure radiation or read various forms of energy. As he pointed out, acquiring information on the spot should constitute their first goal; they had to know, quickly, what sort of world or realm they had entered. Such knowledge might prove invaluable later on. He also gathered a sufficient quantity of camping gear. There was no telling how long they would have to stay, although he did not intend to remain long enough to establish than a makeshift camp. The assumption of a few days, at most, sounded right to him. Anything further would require more carrying capacity than the DTD possessed, which must have been a factor for Dr. Delaney as well. Theresa purchased food and drink, mainly imperishables, although a few items went into a small ice chest. She observed that they seemed to be embarking upon an extended picnic. She also complained about Vorchek's severe strictures concerning her wardrobe. At his insistence she limited herself to a couple of utilitarian outfits, ensembles of blouses and skirts which looked to him like suitable attire for an African safari. Vorchek emphasized comfortable walking shoes; no high heels on this expedition. Theresa produced the necessary clothing, from what her companion presumed was a well-stocked closet. Despite his requirements, she still somehow managed to come across to him as a self-conscious, fashionable young lady.

Although Theresa argued about it, Vorchek demanded that they both get a good night's sleep. He did so, she tried her best, and so the morning came.

They stowed the gear in the capsule, which now seemed problematically cramped. Vorchek would "drive," so the only seat belonged to him. Theresa would sit on the floor, between bundles; an awkward situation, to be sure, but they had no evidence that the dimensional transmission itself was dangerous. They and their belongings ought to arrive safely. The fun would begin on the other end.

They checked the relevant machinery in the laboratory, the chamber, and the capsule. All systems ready, it was time to go. Vorchek felt the bigness of the moment. He adjusted his hat, which he normally wore on formal occasions. He also patted his jacket pocket, which concealed a small pistol. He did not intend leaving anything to chance.

"I am ready when you are," said he. They proceeded into the chamber. He shut the door behind them. Theresa, outfitted as if to hunt big game, entered the capsule and squeezed herself into a corner. Vorchek followed, sealing the hatch and situating himself at the controls. From where he sat he could see out of the view plate, which revealed a bare gray wall. Once more he silently fingered the knobs, dials, and buttons, which he now knew by touch.

168

"Here we go," said Vorchek. He cranked up the power dial. The sound of a low, reverberating hum filled the machine. Beyond the chamber, barely audible, could be heard the chattering of computer banks. He pressed the green start button, the background hum changed to a thin whine, and then the gray wall beyond the thick glass faded to absolute black.

They felt no definite sense of motion. Theresa described a feeling somewhat akin to that of an elevator ascending, but if real, it lasted only moments. Considerable time passed.

"Transference is not instantaneous," noted Vorchek. He divided his attention between the controls and the view plate. The former revealed nothing amiss. A meter ticked off the relative "distance" which they traveled. The indicator moved imperceptibly, like the minute hand of a watch. Eventually he began to detect fleeting flashes of radiance from outside, flashes which came and went too fast for him to make out detail. He told Theresa about them, for she could see nothing from her vantage. He removed his glasses and massaged his eyes.

"Difficult to spot, yet they hurt," said he.

"There's no reason why I can't stand up and see for myself," the girl said, doing so. "It's like flying through a storm cloud, with lightning far away."

Vorchek joined her. "Except for that flickering, it is as if we are flying through nothing."

"It's taking a long time."

"We are about half way now."

The indicator crept to the right. As it approached the end Vorchek took note of the time. "Not quite an hour, all told."

They resumed their stations. The flickering stopped, the darkness became total once more, and then—Vorchek distinctly felt this as well—they experienced a curious sensation, as of an elevator suddenly dropping. They braced themselves as the meter ran out. All of the power dials swung to zero. Vorchek turned a knob which shut off the controls.

"That, Miss Delaney, is all there is to it," said he. "We have arrived."

Both leaped up to crowd the view plate. Although still extremely dark outside, there was something to be seen; they were someplace. Through the glass they saw a rough, rocky surface, fairly level up close, sloping upward farther away. The minimal light, appearing to come from the left, was scarcely brighter than the interior light which dimly leaked out onto the landscape.

"We're on another world," Theresa breathed.

"Something like that," replied her companion. "Let us assume nothing. Indisputably, we are elsewhere."

"Unless my eyes are playing tricks, there's something on that mound, just over there." She pointed. "Right there."

"I see it. The flashlight, if you please." Producing the device from a bag, Theresa handed it to him. Vorchek focused the beam in the direction indicated. "How about that, my dear. Your father must possess a romantic streak."

They saw, hanging limply around a short pole inserted into crumbly rock, a small American flag. Not a breath of wind stirred it.

"Father has been here!" the girl cried.

"He certainly has," agreed Vorchek, "although we had no cause to doubt that. The coordinates were most precise. Still, I am happy to receive immediate confirmation on such a central issue. We need not waste time and mental effort wondering. Instead, we may get down to business. Stand back, my dear."

Vorchek slowly rotated the wheel which opened the hatch. He cracked an inch-wide gap, thrust his nose into it. "The air seems all right; a little thin, as expected. We have nothing to fear in that quarter." He cranked the door open all the way. "If you will pardon my manners, I shall go first."

Vorchek, flashlight in hand, exited the capsule, with Theresa right behind him. They set foot upon the surface. At first darkness was the most notable feature. As they grew accustomed to the dim luminosity, they began to discern the chief aspects of this new realm. They and the capsule stood on an uneven plain, which rose gradually before them, descended slightly behind. It was mainly bare rock, dull black in coloration, with patches of weathered material which might be styled soil or sand. Vorchek used his pocket knife to scratch at the rock. Incredibly hard, it resembled basalt, and he speculated that it had been formed by vulcanism. Nothing moved out there, nothing grew. Except for their ability to breathe, they could have been on the moon. Beyond the flag mound, which was not more than fifty yards away, the basaltic terrain began to steeply rise, and farther that way loomed jagged peaks of large hills or low mountains, barely visible. In other directions the surface tended to drop down, but it appeared that they were ringed in the distance by mountains, many of them rounded, humped shapes, others poking into the inky sky as rocky spires. It was a grim, desolate landscape, lifeless, perhaps always so. As far as they

170

could see there was no trace of native living things, nor any evidence to suggest that such things had passed.

They walked to the mound and examined the flag. They found no notation of any kind, nor other artifacts. The object testified to the previous presence of Dr. Delaney, perhaps to his excitement over his achievement, but nothing else. Theresa stroked the flag, then they walked away.

"There does not appear to be much here," said Vorchek, "of any practical interest. I see nothing that would have led your father far afield."

"Or addled his mind," Theresa replied.

"Well, we know nothing, as of yet, except that he arrived safely, left the craft, and made his mark for those who would follow. So far, so good, for him. More may be revealed to us soon, if that be the dawning of the sun, rather than the sunset."

Vorchek indicated the only visible source of natural illumination, the faint reddish glow emanating from the horizon. It was this which had allowed them initially to see anything at all. Save for this, they must make do with the light they brought with them.

The more he considered this, the stranger it seemed. He cast his gaze above, into what he thought of as the night sky, and grew puzzled. The thin air appeared perfectly clear. He detected no hint of weather patterns, of fog or overcast conditions. Such formations, surely, would have reflected the feeble ruddy glow. Nothing of the kind occurred. He viewed a clear sky, totally black, as if he gazed into the fathomless depths of outer space. Unless his senses deceived, he could not be mistaken. There were no stars up there.

He brought this to Theresa's attention. "At the moment, I can not explain it. Perhaps a simple answer will develop later. If we are seeing straight, it is a peculiar finding. We may need to frequently remind ourselves that this is not Earth—certainly not of our time— nor planet with which we are familiar. We may not be within our own universe, as we conventionally understand it. Travel through or into another dimension may take us beyond the known, beyond the imaginable."

"It didn't take much imagination to create this place," Theresa observed wryly. "The artist had just one color in his palette, and he made the most of it. If there was more red over there, and some fires burning, I'd think we'd died and ended up in hell."

"Surely you have another destination in store, my dear. Regardless, if day is coming, we may feel differently. I grant you, current conditions look woefully bleak. They chill the soul. Dr. Delaney deserved a more rewarding terminus to his voyage."

Musing, Vorchek surveyed the scene. "Perhaps we landed in a volcanic wilderness. We can not see more than a square mile of what may be a gigantic world. Much will be learned as we advance. That should wait, however. I suggest that we make camp, then discuss the next steps in our campaign."

Vorchek ordered the girl to prepare them something to eat. While she dragged out those supplies, he erected a tent. Neither activity took long. Theresa made plain ham sandwiches, which she served with crackers and cheese. They sat on towels spread over flat rocks. She poured water into paper cups.

"I did bring a bottle of wine," said Vorchek, "in honor of our historic journey. I recommend it to you; an excellent vintage, a Fournelle '83."

She handed him the cup of water. "Celebrations can wait, Professor, until we've found my father alive and gotten him back home in one piece."

They ate in silence. Presently Vorchek, affectedly clearing his throat, hesitantly embarked upon a subject weighing on his mind. "Miss Delaney, we must not entertain sentimental expectations. Your father has been missing for some considerable time. He disappeared with few supplies, and it does not seem likely that he could live off the land here. Whatever happened to him was sufficient to prevent him from returning to his machine and rejoining you. That could have been almost anything. As I see it, our task is to search for a man who is incapable of helping himself. We should mark out, in our minds, a grid over the terrain, and search each square for clues. That may lead to the answer. There are cliffs and gullies out there, where he may have fallen or become trapped. That is my current analysis of the problem before us.

"I say to you, hope for the best, but prepare for the worst. Foolish optimism will cause you greater grief in the end."

"You think he's dead?" Theresa asked acidly.

"I suspect it, as must you as well."

"I don't. I know better. I heard from him."

"So you say," acknowledged Vorchek. "I have made known my preliminary views on that issue. I relish the possibility of discovering my error. For that, I hope. Nevertheless, his chances are slim."

"You are wrong." Theresa lit a cigarette and threw away the match. The sputtering flame arced into the gloom and vanished. "I know what I know. He's here, he's alive—in trouble, but alive—and I must find him. I can't rest until I do."

"So be it." Vorchek tried to sound more cheerful. "If he is out there, anywhere within reach, we will find him. I promise to leave no stone unturned."

"Thank you for that."

In reality, he had never anticipated rescuing the missing man. Recovering the body, now; that could happen, with plenty of luck. Vorchek had been drawn into the matter in order to please a beautiful girl, and to satisfy his scientific cravings. Exposure to Dr. Delaney's notes and apparatus had thrilled him. He foresaw gaining fabulous knowledge here, too. If he came away with vastly more data about the universe and its marvels, he would count the expedition a complete success. It might not be appropriate, however, to present this viewpoint to the girl. It occurred to him that she could, conceivably, take it the wrong way. That would make it much harder for them to get along, and it would not entirely distress him if they got along very well indeed.

Vorchek now brought out his instruments, set them up around the capsule and activated them. The machines ticked, purred, beeped. On a note pad he recorded his observations, calling them out aloud for his companion's edification.

"So far, nothing with which we need concern ourselves. Radiation levels as expected—interesting spikes—bursts of gamma rays, but not a serious matter. We will not have to return for our lead-lined suits. Over here—" he indicated a meter—"I get curiously directional energy readings. I can not tell what they mean, but they seem to be associated with the light. Excited photons, I would say, although that would suggest amplification. A better explanation may appear. I will check frequently." He yawned.

"Rest may serve at this juncture," stated Vorchek. "If we plan to go exploring, we should be at our physical peaks. I think of catching a short nap. It is a habit of mine; nay, a routine, which I feel the need to indulge at present."

"I'm not sleepy."

"Relaxation will do, if you can manage that. The tent will suit me. Of course you may stay in the capsule, if you like. You will be marginally safer there. On the other hand—" he grinned—"the tent is spacious, and will accommodate us both."

"I'm on to that ploy," Theresa said, but she smiled as she shook her head. "I hear it all the time."

"That does not surprise me one bit. I would be astonished if you told me otherwise. In all seriousness, one of us should always remain awake and alert for the duration of our stay. We do not know what to expect, nor what may come at us without warning. I will be eager and vigorous after my nap, and then you may have your turn, if you prefer. For the present, consider yourself assigned to guard duty. Take what photographs you can, if you want to keep yourself usefully busy." With that being said, Vorchek busied himself with personal tasks, then entered the tent.

No time seemed to have passed. Vorchek might have dozed briefly before he felt himself shaken to awareness. Theresa was bending over him.

"It's getting lighter now," she informed him. "The sun is coming up."

Fully alert, Vorchek rose to a crouch and stooped through the tent flap. It was still quite dark, no more than deep dusk at home, but he could instantly tell that something had changed. The reddish glow on the horizon had intensified, and by its reflected light he discerned more stark detail.

"How long has the change been noticeable?" asked he.

"Only a few minutes," Theresa replied. "I wasn't paying attention, but it seemed to happen all at once. I thought we should get ready to explore."

"That makes sense." Vorchek sniffed the air. "My goodness; what is that odor?"

"I knew I smelled something strange," his companion cried. "I believe it came up about the same time. Is it significant, Professor?"

"Not to me." He sniffed again, and rolled saliva around his tongue. He spat. "I can not place it. There is a change in the chemical composition of the air. Perhaps it is a substance in the rocks, reacting to photons, or a component of the atmosphere doing the same. Then again, it might be out-gassing of some sort. I trust that we do not experience any freakish weather effects."

"The place seems so changeless."

"Nothing is forever," said Vorchek. "Unless it be the dawning, which was in progress when we arrived, and is developing at a glacial pace. The rising of the sun leads me to infer that we reside upon a planet, as they are known in our dimension. Would you infer anything else, Miss Delaney?"

"Very slow rotation."

"Excellent, girl. I am inclined to agree. At this rate the sun should

174

be up any minute now."

That did not happen. The glow, which had deepened to bright crimson, remained, and the unknown odor persisted, yet the sun did not emerge. Vorchek grew increasingly puzzled by the lack of the predicted event.

"Something is not right. I miss a crucial point." He keenly scanned that patch of horizon. Then he nodded and waved his index finger in the air. "Suitably equipped—" he tapped his glasses—"I possess superb eyesight. I begin to see, but it is so far away. I can clear up this. Fetch the binoculars."

"At once, sir!" Theresa said smartly. In a moment she had fished them from the capsule and handed them over. Vorchek raised them to his eyes and devoted a long minute to studying the mysterious luminosity.

"Yes," said he, "now I understand, or am coming to understand. My preliminary conclusion was inaccurate. It is so easy to make the mistake of assuming normality of conditions. In our universe we take for granted the existence of globular worlds with suns, which appear to rise due to planetary rotation. Yet we are in a different sort of place. The same rule may apply, but we cannot count on it. Certainly this phenomenon provides no such evidence. You know, I could postulate the existence, in this dimension, of an endless land mass, extending to infinity in one plane. I do not state it as fact, but would it not be wonderful?"

"Whatever are you talking about?" Theresa cried.

Vorchek chuckled. "Forgive me, my dear. I am getting far too ahead of myself. Forget my speculations, and let us concentrate on what can be learned at the moment. Here; take the binoculars and observe for yourself."

As the girl stared through the instrument, he continued to pontificate. "That is not the sun, or a sun, of any kind. Look carefully at the line of the horizon. It is easy to spot against the glow, if you are looking for it. See the crags, those spires, lighted on our side, rising before the background darkness? The actual horizon over there is as purely black as it is anywhere else. The luminosity appears to be radiating from the crust, coming from below, rather than beyond. Now, look just this side of the band of redness. You can detect another dark outline, somewhat closer to us, of broken terrain.

"We are looking into a titanic fissure or gorge, a vast rent in the surface, from which the illumination pours. My first thought is that we have been most fortunate. If we were out of sight of that fissure,

175

we would have no natural light at all. For what I know, there may be no heavenly source in this realm. A curious notion, I say."

"I see it as you do," Theresa said. "It resembles a volcanic vent."

"In certain respects, it does. That could be out-gassing, which would explain the odor, perhaps. Somehow, though, I do not think that is the entire answer."

"I hope it isn't about to erupt."

"It has not been doing so," said Vorchek. "None of these formations are fresh. They seem utterly primeval. I am fairly sure that we need not fear lava. Other perils may introduce themselves in time. I am afraid that I will find out for myself when I pay that place a visit, which I propose to do at the earliest opportunity."

"Is that really necessary?" Theresa asked. "Let's not get distracted from our mission."

"No distraction, I assure you. If we are to discover the fate of your father, I must go there."

"Professor, what do you mean?"

"It is simple, my dear Miss Delaney. I am surprised that you do not see it. We have identified a peculiar region in this dimension which emits light the color of blood. It may be too early for geographical assignations, but if you had to grant that region a name, might not you call it the Red Zone?"

IV.

The most direct route led them downhill, then into a ravine or cleft which gaped at the bottom of the slope. Of course Theresa insisted on coming along, and there was nothing Vorchek could do to prevent her. They packed food in their bags, and he brought the first aid kit in case they injured themselves on the rocks. The girl opined that it might come in handy for her father as well. Vorchek held the flashlight. Although he had spare batteries, he chose to use the light only when they were cut off from direct sight of what both now referred to as the Red Zone.

Off they went across country, through terrain which only cooperated by degrees with their design, marking their path with ripped pieces of white towel. Their initial route led in the proper direction for a time, then began to veer away between steep rock walls, beneath which they could see little. They climbed the slope, continued onto a flattish mound affording a fair view of the goal, then down into another jagged crack in the sterile crust. This route eventually led them smack against a blank wall of primordial stone. Retracing their steps, they attempted a fresh avenue of approach, were balked again, tried another, won through a few hundred more yards. They advanced, but it took time. Theresa complained.

"We are getting there," responded Vorchek. "Be confident, and keep your eyes on the Red Zone."

They had to navigate by sight, for a standard compass proved useless. This world contained no magnetic field, or the one it had did not function according to known laws. Before they left the capsule Vorchek had taken final readings from the other instruments. Background radiation still held stable, but the mysterious energy readings—the interesting ones—were going through the roof. Something was happening out there. Vorchek wanted to learn what it was. Theresa, naturally, had different matters in mind.

"So I was right," she observed as they marched.

"It seems so," replied her companion.

"My father is alive."

"Given our current state of knowledge, that is my tentative conclusion," agreed Vorchek. "He is, or has been. I can not explain it, but it appears likely."

"He did speak to me."

"The discovery of the Red Zone supports your curious account. Its existence would be too much of a coincidence, otherwise. At the moment, I can conceive no other source for that information but Dr. Delaney. Somehow, he communicated. I wish he had done so again. I trust he is still in a position to do so."

"Of course he is," Theresa cried. "He's out there, Professor, and he needs me."

"He is out there. It has been many days since you heard his words."

"Conditions haven't been right," the girl opined vaguely.

"It may not be long before we find out. He suggested that he was in the Zone. If so, we shall reach him shortly. I regret not being able to bring the energy meter. Further readings could be useful. I should have chosen a less cumbersome device."

"To hell with that," Theresa said.

When they did surmount a rise, it seemed to Vorchek that the strange reddish glow had intensified at a rate which could not be entirely due to their approach. At this nearer remove the cold radiance shone above a larger swath of landscape, but it seemed to have acquired a greater intrinsic brilliance as well. Furthermore, it no longer looked entirely homogeneous. The glow had developed minute

177

pulsations across portions of its expanse, with rays of enhanced power shooting up like searchlights. Vorchek could not avoid speculating as to the cause of the increasing display. He kept all hypotheses to himself, but wondered if the aerial events were connected with his and Theresa's approach. He entertained himself by trying to deduce the answer from the paltry evidence available to him.

Dropping back down into darkness—having placed a cloth marker—they advanced by aid of the flashlight, when suddenly the girl stopped short. "Can you hear it?" she asked.

"I hear nothing," replied Vorchek. "What do you mean?"

"Listen!" She held up a hand to command silence. They stood motionless for long moments, she earnestly straining for concentration, he watching her, mystified.

"I hear nothing," repeated Vorchek.

"I hear it plainly now," Theresa said. "It's like—it is—whispering. I'm telling you, Professor, I hear a voice!"

"Identify it."

"I can't, yet. It's just mumbling, but there's no mistake. You must be deaf!"

"I am not. Tell me more."

She turned in place, cocked both ears in turn. "I'm not sure where it's coming from; maybe down there, around the bend. Let's see." She raced into the gloom within the ravine, temporarily disappearing from his sight.

"Miss Delaney!" Vorchek caught up with her quickly, for she had halted again, looking about helplessly. "We will have no more of that. Never must we be separated."

"Of course not. Sorry, Professor, but—"

"I still can not hear it. Are you certain?"

"No doubt. It's someone muttering under his breath. I'm not sure if I recognize the voice, but it could be. Don't you think it has to be?"

"Is this," pressed Vorchek, "anything like your experience back on Earth?"

"Very like. This is how it started, both times. Oh, Professor, it's got to be him. Father is calling to me again!"

"Then I tell you for a fact that Dr. Delaney is not communicating via normal speech. Otherwise, I could share the moment with you. It may be (I only spin ideas, mind you) that due to your genetic connection with him, you are better able than I to derive information from this unknown medium of transference. It may be a species of mental, rather than aural linkage. Has that possibility suggested itself to you?"

Theresa gaped at him, eyes wide. "I'll take your word for it, if you take mine that it's happening. Let's go on."

They did. Presently they emerged upon a broad shelf of slick, glassy rock. The blaze of the Red Zone encompassed the totality of their vision. From this point they could see that the radiance flared up from a narrow, roughly linear gorge of immense size, backed by a sheer, towering cliff which reflected and scattered the crimson light. They had no further need of the flashlight. Here the terrain shone as bright as day.

Here, more than ever before, Vorchek sensed the magnitude of the force which they confronted. This was not merely the shining of light, but the surging of limitless power from deep within the rent crust. The color of the Red Zone did not radiate; it boiled upward, thrusting itself solidly into the sky and against exposed surfaces. He imagined that he could feel the pressure of that force, against which he must strain to hold his balance. It was like a subtly persistent wind, though nothing objectively stirred the dead air. Without realizing it he leaned into it, as if to avoid losing his footing. The girl seemed similarly affected, but she reacted by reaching out toward the source of the disturbance, as if to embrace something.

"It's Father, all right," she said at last. "I know the voice now, I can make out the words. Professor, he's speaking to me again. He's talking directly to me."

Vorchek marked the spot. "Keep moving, Miss Delaney. Tell me what he is saying to you."

"It's like before. He's asking me to join him. He wants me to be with him in the Red Zone. He's telling me I don't have far to go. He's—oh, he's making promises—he's saying weird stuff. Why is Father doing that?"

"I do not know why Dr. Delaney would do so."

"I don't get it. Now he's asking about you. He wants to know who you are. He has questions about you; about your mind."

"Does he, indeed? I shall satisfy him."

"Professor," Theresa cried, "why can't you hear him?"

"I hear something." So he did. As they progressed across the wide shelf, which proved to be a broad plateau, he began to detect a faint, insistent sound, like a furtive noise heard over the rustling of leaves in a forest. What he heard was not speech, however. It resembled, to his ears (or mind, he thought), a squeaky twittering, more

179

accurately, the discordant hum of a colony of insects. Vorchek did not wholly approve of the sound. "I am picking up something, my dear, but you still have the advantage. What else does he ask you about me?"

"He wonders if you are worthy material. He offers to let you join as well."

"Fascinating. I look forward to justifying my worth." He seized the girl by the arm as she stumbled. "Keep your eyes on the ground, or you will hurt yourself."

"We must hurry!"

"No!" Vorchek spun her around and held her by both arms. "We must not rush into anything. This situation is novel, and dangerous. Do you understand?"

"He's waiting."

"Your father will, with paternal devotion, wait another minute. Does he still talk to you?"

"Yes. His words are crazy, some of them, but he can't mean all of it. If I can only talk back to him—"

"Talk to me," demanded Vorchek. "Focus on me. Can you blot him out, concentrate on what I say to you?"

"Of course. Don't be silly."

"That is far from my intention. Listen to me, young lady. You must keep your mind clear, and free of unusual influence. Do not allow yourself to be overcome by promises and pleas reaching you out of the air. We face a mystery. First and foremost, we must solve it. The resolution will better serve your father than blind acceptance of superficial indications."

"What are you babbling about, Professor?"

"Make note of the voice. Keep track of what it says. Under no circumstances, however, should you obey it. Obey me. Got it?"

"I hear you," Theresa said sullenly.

"You keep hearing me," ordered Vorchek. "Do not forget that I am in charge. We shall now proceed. You stay behind me. If I think you are going to take off on your own, I will knock you down with my fist."

"Professor!"

"I mean it."

They went forward, Vorchek in the lead, Theresa close behind him. His steady pace reined in her impatience. They were now well within the Red Zone. It was a region of fountaining scarlet hues which soared into the sky, offset only by painfully black shadows. The patches of darkness wavered with the seething of the luminosity;

180

otherwise, only the travelers moved on that open terrain. As they advanced, they slowed.

That was Vorchek's doing. Now he could hear more. The insistent buzzing in his mind gave way to an oppressive, disturbing sound reminiscent of mumbled human speech. This, he knew, was what the girl had been hearing at intervals since her father had vanished. The voice did not please Vorchek. He cared for it less once he was able to decipher individual words. He could tell that the voice was speaking to him.

"—not much farther. Grandeur on the cosmic scale awaits you. You want knowledge? I have it. You want power? It is mine to give. Anton Vorchek, do you desire riches? Is it women that you crave? Come to me. Your dreams are here. Allow me to describe them. Harken to my words. This will be yours—"

The voice ran on, whispering to his brain a rambling, repellently graphic account of the vulgar joys he would find within the Zone. It sounded like the fevered ravings of a madman, the unbridled fantasies of a degenerate. In the context of this place, in the context of the reputed source, it made no sense. It was horrible, but Vorchek—a man not given to self-delusion—knew how much some of these offers attracted him.

They were not entirely tailor-made for him, however. The speaker utilized the shotgun approach, attempting to cover all the bases. The voice left out no possibility for encouragement. Calling him by name, yet it seemed at the moment, at any rate, to offer generic wonders.

He tried to respond silently to it, in his thoughts, without effect. The mélange of discordant words and jumbled phrases did not even break stride. It did not converse; it broadcast. It wearied his mind, without enlightening it.

Vorchek shrugged off the voice. He could still hear it, getting louder now, but he would pay it no heed. Let the voice rant, until such time as he could derive genuine answers from it.

Theresa began to lag behind, a surprise to him. "Miss Delaney," prompted Vorchek, "how do you fare?"

"I could use a lie down," she said heavily.

"You are not going to get one. Keep your mind active, but ignore the voice. Do not allow it inside you."

"It's just talking."

"It may be more than that," cautioned Vorchek. "Do not let it wear you down. It occurs to me that such is the intent."

"Why would Father do that?"

"An excellent question. You may have your answer quickly. I am beginning to think—" Vorchek broke off with an uncharacteristic oath. "Stop where you are!"

Theresa froze. Vorchek paced forward a few more yards. They had attained a point very near the lip of the great fissure from which the fiery redness belched forth. Here there were no shadows, only a uniformly bloody color. He could see partly into the rocky chasm; an impression of limitless depth. Beyond the enormous gash soared the sheer far wall, a straight precipice hundreds of feet high. Close at hand, on the very edge, loomed a long, rounded boulder which seemed to teeter over emptiness.

Atop the boulder stood the figure of a man.

V.

The strange inner voice stopped, the silence coming like a thunderclap. After a pause, the figure spoke. "Welcome to the Red Zone. Welcome to both of you."

"Father!" Theresa cried, her voice joyous but faint.

"It is an honor to meet you again," said Vorchek, his voice strong and reserved. "It has been a long time, but I do recognize you. You are Doctor Walter Delaney?"

"That is so, Anton Vorchek. Professor Vorchek, as you style yourself. I recall our meeting at the conference, long ago. Long ago, in another place and time; I remember it well. Yes, I know who you are. It was good of you to come."

"Father, are you all right?" Theresa asked. "What are you doing out here? How have you been living?" She made as if to move toward him.

"Don't!" snapped Vorchek, seizing her by the arm. He had no trouble restraining her. She seemed weak. As he held her she sank to her knees. He settled her into a sitting position, then rose. "Before we do anything, let us find out where we stand."

"I must go to him—"

"I wish to embrace my darling daughter," Dr. Delaney said. "You have no cause to hold her back from me."

"That remains to be seen," replied Vorchek. "There is much we must learn."

"And learn you shall. You have entered the realm of total knowledge."

By the fantastic red light Vorchek could see the figure in sharp detail. It certainly looked like their man. A balding fellow, with

182

gleaming eyes set within pleasantly bland features, Dr. Delaney was casually dressed, as if for an outdoors jaunt. His light jacket hung open, revealing a buttoned shirt loose at the collar. He wore sneakers, and he lacked a belt. He had with him no gear of any sort, and nothing bulged in his pockets. He might have just stepped away from his campsite, which was odd because, based on Vorchek's information (derived from Theresa's statements), the man had brought no such equipment out here with him. No supplies, no food or water to speak of, and yet the man appeared hale and hearty.

Vorchek noticed something else even more strange. When Dr. Delaney spoke, his mouth moved, but his words did not quite fit the movement of his lips. The words came out clearly—their reverberation surprisingly loud—but Vorchek felt as if he were watching a poorly dubbed foreign film. Motion and sound were correlated, yet not properly mated. It crossed his mind that the physical manifestation of speech was merely a matter of form, perhaps a case of convention, rather than necessity.

Indeed, now that he pondered the point, Vorchek was not convinced that Dr. Delaney's voice emanated from that mouth. Like the somewhat similar voice they had been hearing, it possessed no firm sense of directionality. Vorchek allowed for the possibility that what he was hearing still entered his mind without passing through the medium of his ears. If so, this was truly food for thought.

"Bring us up to date, Doctor," said Vorchek. "As you must be aware, we have been extremely worried about you. Theresa has been frantic."

"She's a good girl," Dr. Delaney said. "I appreciate the concern. There was no need, of course, as you will shortly find out for yourselves. Now, as you refuse to come to me, I shall join you." With that the figure effortlessly climbed down from the boulder and stood before them. Vorchek stepped back slightly. Delaney smiled what should have been a disarming smile. In Vorchek's case, it did not serve the purpose.

"Father, I was worried," Theresa muttered listlessly. "I didn't know what had happened to you." Dr. Delaney did not even glance at the girl. His bright eyes, which could only appear red under the circumstances, bored into the Professor.

"We both were," added Vorchek. "I did not expect to find you alive. It seems a miracle that you have survived. I would like to know how you did it."

"Surely such matters," Delaney replied, "are of no relevance now."

"Humor us," urged Vorchek. "Tell us your story."

"Very well," Delaney agreed, and he began to tell them, speaking in that weird manner of his, with the mouth flapping randomly, the words coming from elsewhere. "I broke through the dimensional barrier precisely as planned, as you have since done. I took notes, implemented procedures, did everything I ought to do, everything that once seemed important to me. I found myself in this wonderful, mysterious place. When I came through and emerged from the DTD, I found myself in an utterly dark world, without any source of light other than what I brought with me. I learned that I had reached a solid surface, as predicted, but at first little else. That condition of ignorance didn't last long, however. Soon I discovered the Red Zone; or shall I say, that it discovered me?

"Instrument readings warned me that something was happening out there. Then the glow began to spread from the horizon. That drew my attention. In time I realized that a great power was surging up from within the crust. Without delay I set out to investigate. I knew, you see, that I was supposed to do so.

"Thus I came to the Zone. It was waiting for me, calling to me. The Zone drew me in. The Zone taught me. The Zone augmented me. Much time passed, I presume. I've paid no attention to that. I didn't need to any longer, not within the Zone. Here I found everything I'd always desired, everything I'd ever imagined, and much that I hadn't. The cosmic totality that is the Zone lay revealed to me, and since that period I have lacked for nothing which is vital to my being. In other words, I've been in no danger. Survival isn't an issue. I have existed happily with an absence of risk. I hope that clarifies my position."

"It does not," said Vorchek vehemently. "You say a great deal, but you do not communicate. You take too much for granted. Let us take this a step at a time. First things first: where are we? Is this a planet?"

"This entire dimension constitutes what I call a unitary universe," Delaney explained. "It exists, as surely as does our universe, that vast space of worlds and suns and galaxies, but without, as a rule, any connection whatsoever. Think of parallel universes, taking very different forms, operating according to different laws. There is sufficient similarity to allow us to enter this universe and live, but that's about all.

"The world on which we presently stand is a planet, a round orb

184

of the type you know. However, it is the only native material object existing within this universe, which is otherwise a limitless void. Think of it! A whole universe of nothingness, and this one world, the sum of all this dimension's possibilities and development. This planet has no sun, no satellites, no companions in space. It is all there is, has been, will be!"

"That does not make sense," said Vorchek. "Where did the planet come from? How did it form? What natural processes were involved?"

"Where did it come from?" Delaney chuckled, as if at the question of a moronic student. "Where does anything come from, if you follow its existence back to creation, to ultimate origins? There is no point in rationalizing its reality in terms of natural processes. Here, even more so than in that other universe, the processes are inconceivable. The planet has always been, since this universe was formed. It simply is."

"And what of the Zone?"

"The Red Zone is pure, coherent energy, the font of practically all power in this dimension. Other than residual radiation in the rocks, and stray particles in the void, the Red Zone is all."

"Come on, Delaney," snapped Vorchek, "that is quite enough with the mumbo-jumbo. Give it to me straight. Are we talking about a gas, or radioactive material, plasma; what?"

"I told you, Professor. It's pure energy, this universe's entire complement of energy, confined to a relatively small space."

"Which resides in this canyon?"

"No, Professor. It constitutes the seething core of this world. It can't be fully bound by any solid substance. It breaks through at any weak point in the crust. There are several such vents."

Vorchek, instead of replying, took a moment to attend to Theresa, who had recovered somewhat and was staggering to her feet. "Something made me feel woozy," she said.

"How are you feeling now, Miss Delaney?"

"Very tired."

"What is wrong with her?" asked Vorchek.

"Nothing is wrong," Delaney assured him. "The girl has felt the full effect of the Zone. It takes some getting used to at first."

"I am sure of that," murmured Vorchek. "Once more, about the Zone: you speak of it almost as if it were a living thing. Is it mindless energy, or entity?"

"Again, Professor, your question falls short. It's difficult to

185

answer adequately. By terrestrial standards, there's no life in this dimension. By the standards which pertain here, the Red Zone is the ultimate essence. It reacts to our presence. It observes, it knows, it calculates, it acts. It acts according to its nature."

"Intelligently?"

"I bow to your prosaic conceptions," and he did physically bow. "Every universe must contain Mind. Mind is an essential component of reality, a fundamental of any universal structure, the inevitable concentration of higher energy states. It may take various forms. In your plane, intelligence tends to present itself in a weakened, fragmentary aspect, without cohesion or unitary purpose. There, Mind clashes with Mind. Here, where all universal energy is focused and tightly bound, Mind must necessarily emerge as the single dominant facet of reality."

"If you say so," said Vorchek. "So, you made contact with it?"

"It spoke to me. It offered me many things."

"I just bet it did. You came, and it took you."

"It accepted me," corrected Dr. Delaney. "We became one. I joined, and in the process have grown. My mind has overridden the feeble limitations of inanimate matter. I've seen the infinite, have plumbed the hitherto dark abysses of cosmic knowledge. I've learned all things, as will you."

"We will see about that," said Vorchek. "I am in no hurry to dive in. You did not return to Earth as planned. Why did not you?"

"There's no need. Earth, a minute fragment of that universe, offers me nothing. What can I have there: money, fame? Those are inconsequential. They count for nothing. Only the Zone is real and meaningful. Here the cosmic truth has triumphed, and I have become part of it. No questing mind can ask for more."

"I heard your voice, Father," Theresa said. "You called to me, from here. At times I could even hear you on Earth. You spoke, and you offered . . . well, strange things. I didn't understand. I still don't. Why did you say those things?"

Vorchek nodded. "Those were some rather crass, materialistic benefits you dangled before us. How does that square with your cosmic Nirvana?"

Delaney shrugged. "In reaching out to your brains, I had to frame the rewards in terms that your untrained minds could grasp. What awaits you both is actually far greater than anything I've told you. Even now you haven't conceptualized the gains. You can only know the reality when you have been admitted."

186

"How about coming back with us to Earth," suggested Vorchek, "where we can all be comfortable, and you can take your time and tell us all about it there?"

"Yes, Father," Theresa pleaded, "come with us right now."

"You know quite well," Delaney said to Vorchek, "that's not possible. There is no other place. For me there is only here. Although you haven't accepted it yet, only here exists for you, too. There's no point in leaving . . . and the Red Zone doesn't desire it."

"You can not leave," said Vorchek crisply. "What is it: mind control, or mind replacement? Are you the man, Walter Delaney?"

"You see me, Anton, you hear me."

"Professor Vorchek to you. Your response is insufficient. Can I touch you?" Without waiting for the answer Vorchek lunged forward and seized Delaney. Just as quickly he let go and backed away. "No dice, Doctor, no deal. Miss Delaney and I are clearing out of here. Come with us if you can."

"We'll take you with us, Father," Theresa said. "Professor, there's something wrong with him."

"There certainly is. You have no idea."

"This place has affected his mind."

"And much more than that," added Vorchek. "I fear it is hopeless. However, you and I still have a chance."

"We can't go without him!"

"You can't go anywhere," Delaney said. "We won't let you."

"We?" prompted Vorchek.

"We of the Zone. There have been other visitors through time. The lucky ones have remained. We are all here, within the Zone, and we've all decided that you shall stay."

"Come, Miss Delaney." Vorchek began pulling the girl away.

"Not without Father," she cried, fighting him.

"Listen to her, Anton," sounded that voice, with no pretense of lip movement. "I might obliterate you where you stand. Such a tragic waste of mental energy that would be. Submit, and experience joy forever!"

"Theresa," said Vorchek earnestly, "we must save ourselves. If you are trapped here, what can you do for him? Come with me!"

He urged her away from the figure of her father, and this time, as if in another daze, she acquiesced. She stumbled forward, then ran, pressed by her companion. Vorchek glanced back once as he hurried her along. Delaney stood where they had left him, by the boulder, motionless, staring after them.

"Mental energy is the key," muttered Vorchek to himself. Of course, I understand it now. A universal, sentient energy form, which can only accrete more energy and build itself by absorbing that from travelers who enter its domain. A fascinating system, closed but not entirely sealed."

"I don't get it," Theresa said timidly. "There's only Father—"

"Hurry on, girl," insisted Vorchek. Then, to himself, "Which way now? Look there; one of our markers. Down into that ravine, past the rocks, and to the right, if memory serves me. Let us get down there."

"Father is following. He wants to come."

"So he follows." Vorchek glanced back, saw the figure of Delaney advancing, moving at a measured pace, yet appearing to cover ground at a disturbing rate. "How long will he do so? Is there a break point? I wonder if he need retain that shape. It has occurred to me that his form may appear ahead of us, unexpectedly. That would be a troublesome finding. There is much to learn, but these conditions do not allow it."

They descended into the cleft, leaving behind the plain by the grand gorge from which the awesome redness shot forth. It was not so dark down there as before. The ominous luminosity continued to intensify, now uncovering details of terrain which ordinary terrestrial light could never have revealed. Vorchek realized that the Zone was now exerting its full power, around and over and against them.

During the outward journey he had made little note of the distances involved, expecting or hoping to have much greater leisure time for calculations later. Now Vorchek found himself in a disquieting position: he knew the way back—so long as the cloth markers served—but he possessed only the haziest notions of how far they had to go. He knew that he wanted to regain the capsule at the earliest moment, and not chiefly for his own sake.

Theresa was suffering. He could tell that she was under pressure, more so than her emotional conflict justified. As they marched on she drooped; her steps slowed, she looked behind them more and more. She seemed to be responding to stimuli that he did not feel. Presently, as they emerged into a higher field of rubbled terrain, she made clear her difficulty.

"Father calls," she told him, halting abruptly. "He's speaking to me again. He wants me with him. I can't go on."

"You have no choice, Miss Delaney. It is impossible to remain here." He pushed her forward. She resisted, seriously this time, obstinately. Breaking free of his grasp, she leaped away from him.

"But I hear him," she cried. "Father is lonely. Oh, Professor, how could I have allowed you to take me away? I won't abandon him."

"There is no one to abandon," said Vorchek. He held her fast. "That is the fact you must accept. Face it, before it is too late. Dr. Delaney is dead. He died shortly after arrival here."

"You're crazy!" Theresa shrieked. "He's here, now, begging me for help. Let me pass; I must return to him."

"You will not!" shouted Vorchek. Strangely, he felt that he had to shout, although he heard nothing but silence. He guessed at the crescendo of pounding confusion in her mind. "The Zone is breaking into your brain," he continued, "as it did your father's. He arrived with his mind fully open, eager to understand. He could not defend himself against the psychic assault, or would not, and it ganged up on him and annihilated his persona. The Zone absorbed that, to use as it would, to lure others to it. It devours the energy of life, as it eats all energy. It created a puppet of Dr. Delaney. That is what calls to you. Give in to it, and the force will devour you as well. Reject it; close your mind."

"You lie. Release me. Let me go to him!"

He realized that Theresa's will-power had completely deteriorated, rendering her frighteningly vulnerable. She was succumbing to the mental attack. Vorchek swung his fist. The blow connected with her chin. Her head rocked back with a terrible snapping sound, and she collapsed in a heap at his feet. He picked her up, slung her over his shoulder and trudged forward, reminding himself to apologize later.

Then he began to hear the faint buzzing and humming of sonic waves which never reached his hearing. He soldiered on, hauling his limp burden through the desolate, red-litten landscape, assailed by intensifying powers. As he staggered over a bleak ridge he detected the beginnings of articulate words. They grew more comprehensible as he fought to ignore them.

"Why do you resist?" asked the voice of Dr. Delaney. "You puzzle me, Anton, truly you do. How can you resist?"

"Because I came prepared," replied Vorchek aloud. "I wished to learn, but I expected danger, nor was I ready to blindly accept. I had formed barriers against you before I knew what you were. I will not allow you in."

"You can't keep me out forever."

"I can repel you long enough."

"You handled the girl neatly," said the voice, with—perhaps—a trace of a chuckle. "You closed her mind by turning it off. Otherwise

189

she would already be mine. However, that won't last. She still emits energy, and her awareness will return. When it does, I'll be waiting. What will you do then: beat her to death?"

"I am getting her out of your unholy dimension," said Vorchek through gritted teeth, "with her consciousness intact. Once back on Earth, I will destroy the machine. With the gate closed, she will be safe from your influence."

"Too late. She awakens."

He could see, in the remote distance, the mound with the little flag, and the tent, and the capsule. The scene, formerly so dark, blazed with one dreadful color. Not so far now, but Vorchek suddenly saw something more dead ahead, something that had not been visible a moment before. Standing before him, without warning, there patiently waited the figure of a man. Vorchek knew that figure.

Theresa stirred. Setting her gently down, he approached the false Dr. Delaney alone. "So you assume shape again," observed Vorchek. "More than projection; a kind of crystallization of the energy waves, I presume. Marvelous, but do not get any ideas. I can deal with you physically, I think, and I have this." Vorchek produced the pistol.

The pseudo-Delaney shook his head sadly. "I trust that you don't expect me to fear that crude mechanical device," he said. "Try it, if that will make you happy. Consider it a foolish but amusing experiment."

"I must." Vorchek fired. The gun roared, Delaney's frame jerked back, but he remained standing, laughing quietly. As the echoes died Vorchek heard Theresa's querulous voice behind him.

"What was that? Professor . . . Father!" She was on her feet within seconds. Vorchek turned to her.

"How do you feel, Miss Delaney?"

"Lousy, thanks to you." As she rubbed her bruised chin she realized the situation. "What are you doing with that gun? Don't threaten my father!"

Vorchek pocketed the pistol and drew close. "Quite right, my dear," said he, in a stage whisper, "but we must act immediately if we are to get your father home. Is not that your desire?"

"Of course it is, but force isn't necessary!"

"He refuses to come!" thundered Vorchek, "so we must take him. You will help me."

Theresa considered, nodded. "Whatever it takes, Professor."

"Let's go." They advanced on Delaney. "You hear that, Doctor?" cried Vorchek, with mocking cheerfulness. "Your daughter and I are taking you back to Earth."

"I shall stay here," Delaney replied, "within the wonder of the Red Zone, as shall you. Theresa will join me. She will obey her father."

"You can not fight both of us. What will you do? Perhaps you can disappear like a ghost. Will you do that? As soon as you do, the scales fall from her eyes. Try any strange tricks and your illusion is forever smashed!"

They seized Dr. Delaney. Theresa gasped, as Vorchek knew she would. She felt, as he had at the rim of the gorge, the hot, vibrating, inhuman force coursing through that manlike form. She held on, however, and the two of them drove Delaney forward, pushing him to the capsule. He protested, he promised; he argued, he struggled, but they ignored him; Vorchek because he knew the truth, Theresa because she did not. They ran him inside the cramped space, pressed him into a corner. Vorchek shut the door and assumed the control seat. Within seconds, before Theresa could even settle herself, they were off on the return journey through the dimensions. Power on, the humming of machinery, the push of a button, and it was done.

Flickering light followed momentary darkness outside. The image of Delaney pleaded with his erstwhile daughter all the way, to no avail. He did not bother tempting Vorchek further, that being clearly hopeless. The girl tried to quiet their prisoner, but he kept talking, inexhaustibly talking all the way, his voice growing fainter, his statements becoming disjointed. The mouth of the entity ceased to move, but the words droned for a long while.

They arrived. Vorchek sprang from his chair and threw open the door; then, with his companion's aid, pulled out their passenger and propelled him into the chamber. Vorchek was amazed that the human shape had lasted so long, but as it turned out, that was as far as the false Dr. Delaney got.

Before their eyes, without any more argument, without any more ado, the thing that pretended to be Delaney went entirely to pieces. At first its edges shimmered, appeared to ooze like cold honey. Theresa choked, staggered backwards. As she screamed its proportions distorted and diffused, like a heavy gas released from a container. Minute glimmering particles flew away from it, and suddenly everything let go all at once. The shape vanished, radiating in all directions in a million almost microscopic bits, and then it just was not there anymore. It had vaporized without a trace. Theresa crumpled to the floor, sobbing.

"I knew it could not be long," mused Vorchek as he surveyed the pathetic scene within that sterile metal room. "Divorced from the Red Zone, there could be no power to hold it together, or allow it to do harm. It had to be quite safe to bring it back with us . . . and this was the only way."

He drew the girl off the floor and, holding her tightly, walked her out of that sad place. He had much work to do, and would not tarry more than private matters required. Theresa, he supposed, would soon be busy as well. Once she had collected herself, memorial arrangements were in order. There must be appropriate remembrances and quiet dedications to the dearly departed Dr. Delaney.

The Seal of Jacob Bleek

"I received today a remarkable communication," said Professor Anton Vorchek, researcher into arcane or overlooked aspects of science and history, "from a Mr. Alfonse Lorient, a gentleman unknown to me styling himself a dealer in unusual antiques. He wishes to buy an item from my collection which, so he says, he recently learned has passed into my hands. He claims willingness to pay a princely sum. This business puzzles and intrigues me. Here is the letter, my dear. Read it for yourself, and make of it what you will." The professor tossed the missive to his companion, Theresa Delaney, who had just arrived at his bidding. She was young, beautiful, dressed to the nines (in some frothy scarlet outfit, a stunning and expensive combination of skirt, blouse, hat, boots, scarf, tasteful but dazzling jewelry) and, as it seemed, bored. She had driven from the city of Phoenix, at his command, far out to the desert hill where stood his lonely old house, which also served as his research library and laboratory, in order to be present at a matter, he had hinted, of urgency.

This letter didn't cut it. Theresa dropped herself gracefully into a plush chair, whipped off her hat so that her golden hair tumbled out, lit a cigarette, perused the short document, threw it on the table. "So what?" she said. "Sell if you like, don't as you please. You're not hurting for money again, are you?" Theresa was extraordinarily wealthy, it must be understand, and she often imagined that Vorchek lived on the verge of poverty.

"I assure you, no," said he, in his crisp, precise, slightly accented voice. "Recent grants from the Anthropology Institute meet my needs, and that last check from Applied Physics should keep me jolly for months to come. I wear this dirty smock, Miss Delaney, because I have been employed in my laboratory. If you will excuse me, however, I will take leave to change into formal attire, for our visitor arrives shortly, having traveled all the way, so he says, from Peru."

That was news. While Vorchek was absent the doorbell rang. Theresa answered, to find before her a short, dark man of uncertain extraction who announced himself as Alfonse Lorient and requested admittance as per appointment. The girl attempted to engage the taciturn fellow in desultory small talk, with little success, until the professor returned. In all his glory Vorchek could give Theresa a run for her money. A tall, lean figure of a man, in his fine suit, gleaming black shoes, natty tie, and with his graying temples and clipped, rakish beard, he looked a formidable fellow, the man in charge, which was exactly the impression he strove now to create.

The professor extended a firm hand. "Sit down, Mr. Lorient," he said warmly. "Will you take coffee, tea, or perhaps wine? Miss Delaney, bring a bottle and goblets." All present soon made themselves comfortable. Vorchek wasted no time. "Your offer interests me. To begin, how did you become aware of an artifact which you believe I have?"

The visitor, who sat in his chair at a remove from his hosts on the sofa across the coffee table, frowned, seemed ill at ease. In a halting fashion, and with a definite foreign inflection, he said, "I expected a private meeting, sir." Vorchek assured him that Theresa was his assistant, privy to all of his affairs, and by nature discrete. "Very well, then," replied Lorient. "To answer you, I've had profitable contacts in the past with Termigant, the dealer from whom you acquired the object. When I heard, through my regular sources, that he had purchased the item, I sought him out right away. Thus I learned that he had already sold."

"Ah, yes," nodded Vorchek. "Termigant is a good man. I have not heard from him lately. I trust he is getting along."

"I found him most cooperative." Lorient smiled.

"That is good. Now, I would know why you are so keen on this piece. It is only a nondescript metal fragment, after all. I cannot make much of it myself; something to do with this Bleek fellow, I gather, from way back."

Lorient leaned back in his seat. "You are correct, Professor, on all points. The object counts for little in and of itself. It's a fragment of a larger whole, an embossed seal of considerable size designed by Jacob Bleek, the historian or chronicler of centuries past. He designed it with his own hands, incorporating bits of lore that were valuable to him in his work, matters pertaining to odd beliefs of his time or former ages. The seal, originally about the size of a notebook, was broken up after his death, and the pieces scattered. I have managed, with much diligence, to reassemble all of the parts but one.

"The completed seal of Jacob Bleek is an item of some historical value to scholars. The Lima Museum of Archeology has expressed to

194

me their great interest in adding the seal to their collection. They've offered to pay me for that service, and their promises are most generous. I must, therefore, acquire the missing piece. Since I expect to profit, I'm willing to pass on a portion of my largesse. I will pay you well, if you have what I want. May I see the fragment?" Lorient leaned forward intently.

"I keep new materials elsewhere," said Vorchek, "but I made a rubbing—a poor one, I must admit—which may serve for the moment. Look at this." He produced from his coat pocket a folded sheet of paper, handed it across the table. Lorient eagerly opened it, studied long and quietly the smudgy markings in blue ink on the sheet.

He frowned, his lips moving silently. Then he smiled and said agreeably, "I can't make out all of the detail I would have wished, but this is undoubtedly a copy of what I desire. The name of Bleek came through legibly, and the appearance of this other word—the meaningless syllables beginning with 'X'—is as predicted. I'm pleased. I must see the original."

Vorchek stated, with a disarming air of regret, that he was leaving town for the week, but that if his guest would make an appointment then the professor could soon display the item. With that they got down to business. Price was discussed, arrangements bruited. When everything had been said that could be said, Lorient left, promising to call in a week. After seeing him to the door Vorchek called for coffee. "What do you think, Miss Delaney?" he asked shortly.

Theresa threw up her hands and cried, "Take the money."

Vorchek chuckled. "That seems the proper solution." He grew sober, absently jiggling his coffee cup. "Now, I want you to hear a few facts of pertinence which Mr. Lorient left out or obscured. For starters, it is vaguely misleading to describe Jacob Bleek as an historian. He was, long ago, a philosopher of fearsome repute, an intellectual who, in his pre-scientific age, is thought to have unlocked many amazing secrets of nature and supernature. By the lights of his day he was considered a wizard, a sorcerer with a penchant for the most arcane and deplorable aspects of magical knowledge. He sought, from all the annals of history, forbidden lore of a kind that terrified his contemporaries; studied it, collated it, brought it together in one grandiose work meant to embody the greatest mysteries and marvels of the ages. There are stories of his power and prowess, of his control over strange forces, which are simply incredible, yet the testimonies support one another in a surprising fashion. Much of his work has been lost, but what remains bears out his impressive and disagreeable reputation. His writings have long been sought by scholars of the esoteric, such as myself, and by others keen to apply his knowledge for their own purposes. In the covert world of magical delvings there is quite a traffic in scraps and tidbits of Bleek.

"You heard our visitor claim that he learned of my purchase through Termigant, a respectable dealer in unusual curios. That intrigues me much, for two reasons of unequal weight. One: Mr. Termigant is famed for being a closed-mouthed fellow, not one to reveal confidential details of transactions to outside parties. It sounds odd to me that he would have spoken so freely to Mr. Lorient, when it would be customary to refer the matter first to me. I find that strange; however, I deduced the source when Mr. Lorient contacted me, so I immediately telephoned to Mr. Termigant's shop to demand an explanation. I hinted otherwise to our visitor, of course. Anyway, this leads to the second point: Mr. Termigant is dead. He was killed two weeks ago, murdered in fact, and the evidence (which I derive from the police report) suggests that he did not die easily or quickly. All signs indicate that he was tortured to death."

"My goodness," exclaimed Theresa, "that's terrible. Do you think this Lorient guy is involved?"

"It crosses my mind. I have no way of knowing, at present."

"But why would he—or anybody else—do it? What've you got that's so important?"

"That is a good question," said Vorchek. "Miss Delaney, fetch me a cookie from the jar on the shelf." The girl looked askance, shrugged, walked to the earthenware pot, removed the lid, fished inside. Then she rolled her eyes, extracting something from the jar that was surely not a sweet. "That, my dear," continued the professor, "is the current focus of interest. I did not want Lorient to get his hands on it, nor leave it in an obvious place in case he harbored ill intentions. Behold a veritable relic of the dark mage Jacob Bleek."

What Theresa held in her hand was a flat, triangular chunk of grayish-black metal, rather rough on two sides as if broken from a larger mass; somewhat bigger than her palm, and about half an inch thick, heavily inscribed with tiny letters in bas relief that covered all of one surface. Most of the letters were recognizable to a writer of English, though there was Greek mixed in, as well as a number of mysterious symbols which meant nothing to the girl, and the majority of the actual words conveyed no information to her mind. She returned to the sofa and sat by Vorchek. "It's gibberish," she said, "just a jumble of letters, with this queer stuff thrown in. There's one

196

word I can read—B-l-e-e-k—which must be the name of the spooky man, but I can't figure out the rest."

"It is code," explained Vorchek, "one of Jacob Bleek's devising, and a tricky problem, I can tell you, for an amateur cryptographer. I have been working on it. The author did not trouble to conceal his name, and there is this other term, the X word of which Lorient spoke, which should be read as given, but the rest is intended to be hidden from the prying of uneducated minds. As you can see it is only a fragment, a lower corner of what is possibly a square or rectangular whole."

"Fair enough, but I still don't get it. You think people are willing to kill for this. Is Bleek trivia really that valuable?"

"Not for the material, certainly, in this case. It is composed of an unusual alloy of lead and aluminum, the latter once a costly metal, but with no intrinsic value now. That is not gold, nor do I expect jewels inside the piece."

"Maybe it's a treasure map," Theresa said brightly.

"I doubt it," said Vorchek. "Bleek's writings generally fall into two categories: compilations of bizarre historical anecdotes, and carefully delineated statements which purport to be descriptions of intricate magical spells. From what I have deduced thus far, this seems to be a portion of the latter."

"And that's worth money, is it?" asked his companion. She handed the thing to the professor. "That's worth killing for?"

"It might be, to some," he observed, "especially if it works. Whatever Bleek placed on that seal, it was something he wanted to last, something he strove to render permanent. That could be a crucial datum. I wish I had managed to decode the message before Lorient showed up; I might have a better idea already what kind of man he is. Still, it is a big world, full of information, and I have ways of learning. For starters, I possess an excellent private secretary who occasionally works wonders, when her interest is stimulated."

"What do you want me to do?"

"Thank you, my dear. Please perform for me the following task—
"

Four days later they met for lunch at the Calico Cat. Vorchek ordered a soufflé, Theresa a peppered tilapia. She said, between bites, "Here's the dope. There isn't a Lima Museum of Archeology in Peru. There's a Lima Anthropology Institute, but they've never heard of Alfonse Lorient. The name Jacob Bleek didn't register with them either, by the way."

"Tiresomely typical, that," observed the professor; "Bleek is too unorthodox a reference point for conventional wisdom, therefore he recedes into undeserved obscurity."

"If you say so. Well, Lorient tends to recede, too. I couldn't match up his name or claimed profession in all of Peru. You know, I don't think he's a Peruvian after all."

"I never believed he was. So you conclude that the name is spurious?"

"It may not be phony," Theresa said, "if that's what you mean. I came up with an Alfonse Lorient operating out of various parts of the world, with no fixed address, but cropping up here and there, involved in numerous activities. I have him buying ancient papyrus scrolls out of Istanbul eighteen months ago; putting up money for an Egyptian excavation this time last year; purchasing old manuscripts at a New York auction just six months ago." She removed a typed sheet from the notebook at her elbow. "Here's a list of his reported acquisitions. We have a *Fourth Book of Artocris*, sold as is, a damaged copy of *The Insights of Maltheus*, and a 'fine condition' *Critique of Azamodias*, 'complete with diagrams,' it says. Does any of that ring a bell with you?"

"It does, rather," muttered Vorchek, "too many bells."

"And that's not all," announced the girl merrily. "Lorient—this Lorient, anyway—is connected, in a somewhat vague capacity (apparently no official title), with the Visions of Peace outfit in San Francisco. They're a private charity with New Age leanings working off of a handful of big donations from flaky international bigwigs. They do good deeds for sad folks, the usual stuff—as far as I can tell they're on the up and up that way—but I did learn something thrilling about them as well. Their cash outlay for publicly proclaimed projects constitutes a dwindling fraction of their publicly received grants, and since they're private they don't have to declare everything, which probably makes the ratio worse. How about that?"

Vorchek shrugged. "That is interesting, but scarcely ominous. I have read stories of such organizations suffering from absurdly high overhead—"

"Not like this one," Theresa said crushingly. "There isn't any known accounting for where most of the money goes. The contributors don't care—they get their write-offs—and these Visions characters do as they please with the income."

"So you suspect—"

"It's a front," she concluded. "It has to be. They're spending the money on something else, something they don't report, and Lorient is right in the thick of it. He must be our man."

"I agree," said Vorchek. "Furthermore, I deduce that Visions of Peace is funding his purchases, along with other activities. Yes, it is he. Those manuscripts you listed are famous and rare magical tomes, all of them very old and very costly, when they are not treated as priceless. Now he wants the complete seal of no less than Jacob Bleek, reputed to be the supreme wizard of the ages. It all fits nicely."

"He might be a collector," mused Theresa, "of the crazy variety. We've run across those before."

"Crazy enough to commit murder? Remember Mr. Termigant. I suspect Lorient of that." Vorchek paused, fondled his beard. "No, he is more, much more, I am afraid. I say to you that Alfonse Lorient is a cultist, a seeker after dangerous knowledge, engaged on a mammoth project with unknown designs. We have run across those before, too, the silly sort that is, but I suspect more in this case. There is too much money involved; I sense too much long term planning. I must find out what kind of cultist he is."

"What do we do now?"

"We wait. Lorient calls me in three days."

Alfonse Lorient did telephone on schedule, in order to confirm his appointment. Vorchek casually informed him that a further meeting was no longer necessary, since he had decided against parting with the artifact. Lorient politely urged reconsideration; Vorchek refused. Lorient remonstrated, insinuating the possibility of repercussions. The professor pled a prior engagement and broke the connection.

Two days later untoward developments ensued. While Vorchek conducted a lengthy evening seminar, on "Seminal Occult Influences among the Southwestern Yotapai Tribe," his house and college offices were raided by unknown intruders. In both cases nothing was stolen, although the resultant disorder and even damage were serious. His locked collection cases and file cabinets had been rifled extensively, as if would be thieves had sought something in particular without success. The professor guessed what that was.

Next day, in his laboratory, Vorchek brought Theresa up to date on events, with the object of contention before them on a table strewn with various artifacts, tools, and papers. "I left it in the cookie jar," he said, "where, as I expected, they never looked. Poe remains a remarkable educator in the art of deception. The system of "The

Purloined Letter" truly works, and so, it appears, does that of "The Gold Bug." I have deciphered my fragment of the seal. Few sentences are complete, and several words at the line of breakage cannot be reconstructed, but we may glean the gist of the substance, and form ideas as to the overall meaning." He had written it out like so:

"—marshal the forces which revolve in the outer . . .

"—and through their baleful power seek He who lurks and watches . . .

"—three times aloud the unspeakable name of Great Xenophor of the Million Eyes, and . . .

"—cast the formulated powder into searing fire stoked in pure iron, and make the forbidden passes described in the Seventh Illumination and denounced by Aza(modias?) . . .

"—it is done, if all should have been performed rightly and sanely. Lastly, keep the fourth level safeguards of the Rhexellites firmly at command, and haply an audience shall be achieved . . .

"—wisdom of old be true, then power and glory at His feet are assured. My test, though constrained by caution, verifies the efficacy of the spell. Knowledge triumphs, and the barriers of nature are overthrown and trampled . . .

"—unblinking eyes have gazed upon me, yet I live. Gather thoughtfully the materials, and know the words by heart, and the motions of hand and body that unlock unseen doors, and one may pass through and commune with He who rules and governs all things in time and space. So writes Jacob Bleek."

Said Vorchek, "Most entertaining, is it not?"

"I suppose," Theresa replied, turning the sheet this way and that as if looking for more. "So this is what all the shouting is about. Professor, I'll let you in on a little secret: I can't make heads or tails of it. What I'm reading won't justify money, murder, and robbery."

"It will not on its own. Joined to the rest of the seal, much would become clear which is still mysterious or debatable." Vorchek paused to light his pipe, puffed while he marshaled his thoughts. He took up a pencil and began checking references on the scrawled document. "We can learn a deal from this. The bulk of the text constitutes a magical formula, instructions for the attainment of a mystical goal. It incorporates special words, substances, and motions. All together, they cause a change in the natural state, one which renders possible communication with a power from outside, by which I mean beyond the conventional realm known to man. The spell opens a crack in the space-time continuum, as I would put it, allowing egress or regress into another plane or dimension. In that plane resides a force, an entity of note, which one might, for dubious reasons, wish to contact. Such communication is dangerous—there is that reference to safeguards—either because the cosmic powers are difficult to contain, or because the entity of choice is strong and willful; perhaps all are factors. The intended goal, apparently, is an accretion of personal might and knowledge and possibility beyond the norm. What one wants can be had, if the risk be deemed worthwhile. That is how I read it."

"But what of these weird words?" asked Theresa. "Do you derive anything from those?"

"Too much," Vorchek said darkly. "The inclusion of each term is fascinating by itself, and taken together they suggest awesome notions. 'Rhexellites' is the traditional name of a lost race, thought by some to have existed long prior to the dawn of accepted history, who once mastered the fundamental secrets of the supernatural and built a globe-spanning empire on that basis. Their best minds are said to have been brilliant, courageous, and reckless. Legend states that their empire disintegrated due to some unbelievable catastrophe."

"That doesn't sound promising," observed the girl.

"It makes me think. Now, I reconstructed this term 'Azamodias'', but I am sure my footing is sound. You are already familiar with that word."

"Lorient bought a manuscript about that guy," she recalled. "Yeah, it's falling into place. Professor, what about this other?"

"I saved the best for last," said he. "Xenophor"—he unconsciously lowered his voice as he pronounced the word—"is a cultic figure obscurely referenced in texts and myths dating from all times and cropping up in furtive tales from widely scattered locations about the earth. He is proclaimed the ultimate deity, the 'Lord of All Things,' He who made all and knows all. He is the engine of the cosmos, both creator and destroyer, as He pleases. He observes His universe with His 'Million Eyes,' missing nothing, caring for nothing save as it amuses Him. He has seldom been considered a God worth contacting; quite the contrary, scholars of old who mention Him tend to advise avoiding His gaze at all costs, for the consequences of His attention can be severe, unimaginably so.

"A Xenophor cult exists, however, has since time immemorial. There have always been the insane and the narrowly wise who thought they could treat with Him on an equal footing, often to their regret, and there are those others, the lesser minds, who see in Him the true

God, wish to bow down before Him, demand that others do the same. These are the cultists, still with us, still active, still pretty frightening."

"Wow!" said Theresa. "I don't like them at all. Lorient must be one of them."

"I fear so," Vorchek sighed. "These creatures turn up on occasion, make trouble, commit vulgar crimes, get themselves suppressed. It happens that way. This seems something more than a simple festering of religious mania. I get the distinct impression that they have now organized for a great task, one which requires a vast amount of scholarly knowledge. It could be that the Visions of Peace people are the current center of the cult. That provides them with a firm base for operating in what passes these days for regular society. Regardless, they have been piecing together the necessary information. The seal of Jacob Bleek is the last required link in the intellectual chain. Once they have that in complete form, they can proceed."

"Proceed to do what, exactly?"

"I do not know," replied the professor. "They would beckon to Xenophor; that is the purpose of Bleek's spell. They desire to converse with Him, likely for no decent or wholesome reason. To what end I cannot say, but I suspect it will not be healthy for the rest of us."

Vorchek urged his companion to investigate more thoroughly the Visions of Peace, find out who provided the money, who actually ran the organization. Theresa agreed—it sounded like creepy fun to her—and before the day was out had caught a jet to San Francisco. She contacted him later that day to report her arrival and choice of accommodations (the most expensive in town, as he had already deduced), promising to deliver a preliminary report on the morrow. This she did the following night, recounting her researches in a text message.

"Dear Professor:

"Visions of Peace is certainly a wacko bunch, the members being mainly bohemian types and foreigners. The first are wild and crazy, spouting the usual sort of 'cosmic oneness' crap you're always sneering at. The second are quiet and mysterious, reminding me of Mr. Lorient, and I get the feeling they're the ones really in charge or running things. Their establishment is a big old building, very impressive, in a run down area on Water Street, not so impressive. They have all kinds of flaky exhibits that promise a lot, but don't say anything. Swarms of people come and go, most of them no more than tourists, who are fed the standard line of bull. I asked some pointed questions, dropped a few names and phrases, and got a real earful.

"They were cagey, not giving away much, but they revealed enough when I mentioned, among other things, the names Jacob Bleek and Xenophor. They seemed to hold the former in high regard, as a kind of prophet or really brainy guy with all the answers. My reference to that weird word made them go quiet and mysterious, but they took me aside and unloaded about a coming reign of the 'Great One,' who would reward the 'anointed' with everything they asked for. They said the dominance of the elect over the world was coming soon, and all true believers would benefit. They hinted I might be choice material for their outfit. Isn't that a laugh? I picked up some worthless brochures, nothing to interest you; however, I'll bet I get the real goods before long. Stay tuned.

"Theresa D."

Vorchek wished that she had not charged in so boldly, and he wondered fretfully at the nature and number of the specific allusions she had made to them, but he hoped for the best, looking forward to more useful detail when next he heard from her. Instead, he received a telephone call that morning, in which a hushed but possibly recognizable male voice hissed, "We have the girl, Vorchek. If you want to see her alive again you will deliver the seal to us. Stand by for instructions." The connection broke off.

Vorchek regretted this development, which seemed to bode ill for his charming companion. He contacted her hotel, learning, predictably, that she was out. Then he got in touch with a metallurgist he knew, a fellow employed by a major mining company who gave lectures about artistic metalworking on the side. Vorchek called in a favor, made a deal with him for a certain assignment. The man agreed to undertake the task without delay.

Vorchek received a second call, for which he was prepared. The voice ordered him to instigate convoluted arrangements which, in sum, would result in the seal being shipped to a generic location in San Francisco. Upon safe receipt, Theresa would be released unharmed. "Not so fast, Lorient," said the professor. "I want to hear from the girl, know that she is alive and well. Put her on the line." The familiar voice—of course it was Lorient, though he would not acknowledge the fact—demurred, pleading the necessity for caution. He did offer, however, to mail express a recorded message from the captive, which would contain statements confirming her current existence. Vorchek acquiesced with an air of concession, while in fact the offer pleased him perfectly.

Next day he received a cassette tape, hand delivered by courier, which contained the following statement, clearly in Theresa's voice:

"Dear Professor Anton Vorchek:

"All is well with me, under the circumstances, although as you have no doubt deduced Iran into a modicum of trouble in San Francisco. I am not currently altogether at liberty, nor will I be until the package is received as arranged. Please do exactly as you are told, and then I will see you soon, and all will be well.

"It is Theresa Delaney who speaks to you."

This message pleased him mightily, not only because it verified Theresa's continued sojourn among the living, but because of the amount of precise information that it conveyed. This may seem strange, but it was so, as a result of a curious addition to the girl's education which he had once pressed upon her. Vorchek, though he had dedicated his life to the study of strange matters, had never been taken in by the fashionable pseudosciences and odd popular beliefs which so thrilled the masses. It had always been his goal to separate the true from the false, utilizing the tested traditional standards of science. He had once delivered unto his companion a lengthy disquisition on the topic of mind reading, in the course of which he illustrated to her a common method of fakery employed by mentalist acts composed of dual operatives (the assistant who received the information normally, and the "psychic" who supposedly plucked the knowledge from the aether). The subject had so amused her that he had received her full cooperation in an experiment to derive their own private form of trick, which they had used to astound her credulous friends.

This tried and true technique, known throughout the ages, utilized a language code to convey secret information, which could be passed from one member of the act to another, a transmission unsuspected by the intended patsy. Certain words possessed double meanings, while variations in vocal intonation indicated still more verbal concepts. Such a code could be as complex as memory allowed, since intensive memorization was the only stumbling block. If a secret be known by one, it would be quickly known to the other. This system Vorchek had taught, and he had found Theresa an excellent study. She had learned and, as he now knew, she had remembered.

The use of his full name and title in the address immediately alerted him that she was speaking in code, as he would have guessed anyway from some of the curious pronunciations, word choices, and verbal inflections she employed. The near duplication at beginning and end—"All is well" and "all will be well"—told him that the message was genuine and above board on her part, which indicated to him that it was truly spoken in response to his request, rather than a subterfuge arranged at a prior period by Lorient and his cohorts. "San Francisco" was a base geographical point, reasonably inserted, while her tone explained that she was no longer there. "Altogether," unnecessarily inserted, connoted the direction of "south" (or "down," as context would dictate), while the tones of that word and "package" indicated "miles" and "twenty" respectively. "Circumstances," so spoken, suggested anything from "bowl" to "hollow" or even "valley." The final statement, incorporating her name, indicated extreme, perhaps immediate, danger to her, although it also indicated that she was presently unharmed.

So Vorchek analyzed, and so he read the covert bits and pieces of the message. The girl had done well, though she laid on the intonations and odd pauses in a heavy-handed manner; astute native speakers of English might have caught on, but since the tape had been passed to him, he presumed that their secret was safe. As he reconstructed the message, Theresa was telling him that she had been spirited away to a location approximately twenty miles south of the city, to a valley or bowl-shaped region, and that though she still lived and was in health, she existed in a state of dire peril.

Vorchek's metallurgist friend came through for him. Without delay the professor prepared a padded mailing box, inserted the desired contents, wrapped it, addressed it, and sent it on its way by overnight post. Then he dressed for travel, putting on his best broad-brimmed hat, finagled a quick flight to San Francisco on the private jet of yet another acquaintance, and within the hour was on his way.

Upon arrival he hired a car and proceeded directly to the Visions of Peace headquarters, to discover the building closed and abandoned. He surreptitiously broke in, finding the place practically a vacant shell, with virtually all documents and other private matters removed. A heap of charred debris on the floor of the central hall indicated a great burning of papers. Learning nothing there, Vorchek examined the shreds of evidence that remained—posters on the walls, announcements tacked to a bulletin board—then drove south in a hurry.

He was no fool—in fact, Vorchek was supremely clever—and he already had some idea where he was going, beyond the general instructions slipped to him by his captive assistant. Perusal of maps granted him knowledge of a Bonita Valley some thirty minutes' drive southeast of San Francisco, about fifteen miles inward from the coast, a natural feature of which hasty thinking jogged his memory: Bonita Valley was a special sort of terrain, a shallow, bowl-shaped hollow in the landscape not carved by the action of ancient ice or running water, but rather theorized, by many geologists, to be the result of a primordial meteorite impact. The relic of this Permian event was now a land of forested circular ridges encompassing a grassy depression some few miles in extent, with a charming lake in the center, now the focus of resorts and vacation getaways. Vorchek had still more with which to work, for one poster in the desolate Visions of Peace hall alluded to a retreat operated there by that outfit. There was no mention of it being used at present, but by collating the evidence at hand Vorchek felt convinced that Theresa had been taken there. Furthermore, Bonita Valley struck him as an interesting place for the cultists of Xenophor to congregate at this time, when their plans were coming to fruition: a place with extraterrestrial connections, which might thrill those seeking contact with a mythical being not of this earth.

In good time Vorchek sped through suburban sprawl, whipped by patchy farmland, then crested a wooded ridge from which he beheld the valley. It was indeed a pretty sight, with its fringe of leafy green, its orchards and meadows, the sparkling Lake Bonita, but Vorchek had not come for sight-seeing. He stopped at a gas station, inquired for directions to the Visions of Peace retreat. That was no secret—he was told it lay at the end of the road which swept round the lake—nor, if his source be any guide, was it considered a place in any way remarkable. The locals, it seemed, were accustomed to odd visitors from the nearby big city, judging them a positive boon to the economy. He was also informed, much to his logical satisfaction, that an enormous number of such visitors had arrived during the previous forty-eight hours.

He proceeded at a good clip around the lake, passing lodges and cabins, until he finally drove up short at a closed gate and small guard house. A simple sign on a pole read "Visions of Peace". Vorchek pulled off the road and observed, from a safe distance, in the waning afternoon light. He saw what appeared an expansive fenced property, extending from the lake shore to the gentle slopes of the upper ridges. Scattered trees graced a pleasant meadow, in the midst of which was situated a large, drab, functional building which must be a communal hall, surrounded by a number of smaller prefabricated structures and a flock of white tents which must constitute temporary dwellings. Many people were wandering about within the broad enclosure. He saw nothing overtly alarming in the scene.

Yet Professor Vorchek knew that he had come to a place of great evil. The cultists had developed plans of action which, however imperfectly known, boded ill for anyone not of like mind. Even should they release the girl, he realized, safety would prove elusive until they were defeated. He had ideas on that subject—had already set in motion his own counter-plan—but he was at a loss what to do now. The conventional response at this point should be to call in the police, yet he feared the girl's instant death should the authorities clumsily intrude. One immediate solution suggested itself, a tricky, chancy scheme which nevertheless appealed to his forthright nature. If it failed, his efforts at rescue would count for nothing. Nevertheless, it was a real chance, and he could not resist it. Vorchek cranked the engine and drove up to the gate.

He identified himself. "I don't know you," barked the guard. "You're not on the list."

"I am here to meet with Alfonse Lorient," Vorchek replied casually.

"You know him?" The surly fellow hesitated, then placed a call from his wall phone. "Go on in," he said, emerging from his box to push the swinging gate aside.

Vorchek cruised at a slow, even rate along the graded gravel road to the main building, where a herd of other vehicles were grouped in a large dirt lot. He squeezed his car into one of the few remaining spaces, and by the time he had stepped out no less than the man himself appeared from a doorway and approached, flanked by two burly goons as dark and seemingly foreign as he.

"Professor Vorchek," said Lorient warily, "you amaze me. It is incredible that you tracked me so fast. I did not think to see you again. Your presence here mystifies me, for you must realize that you have entered a lethal situation. Why did you come?"

"I am not afraid," said Vorchek. "You have no reason to harm me, or the girl. Where is she?"

"Where is the item of our transaction?"

"In transit. You may expect it tomorrow, with the first post."

"Very good. Men, watch him. Professor, come inside."

Vorchek followed Lorient, the thugs followed the professor. They entered a building very different from the forgotten headquarters

207

in San Francisco. No fine furniture here, no classy fittings or ornamentation, no absurd posters, only crude wooden walls decorated with strangely abstract paintings splashed primitively on the panels, images of spirals and star bursts and—an ever-present motif—a myriad of staring eyes. Slovenly types came and went, mainly young men and women of various nationalities or races, saying nothing, appearing busy and earnest.

Lorient turned and held up a hand, signifying halt. "You know, of course, that the arrival of any more unexpected visitors—say, visitors with badges and guns—will mean only your quick end, and the tragic demise of the girl?"

"Of course. No one comes after me. It would be ridiculous to risk that. They could have no understanding of what is happening here, nor could their efforts affect the outcome."

"It is well that you see that, Professor. I have nothing more to say to you now. We may speak further tomorrow, before the main event. Men, take him to her. See that they are fed."

The tough-looking pair led Vorchek down a narrow corridor with creaking wooden floor, stopped at a bolted door, which they opened. They thrust him inside the room, dimly lighted by a single lamp, slammed the door. Vorchek collected himself, doffed his hat and said suavely, "Miss Delaney, it is a pleasure to see you again."

Theresa sprang from where she had been sitting, brooding, on a crude cot, wrapped herself around her mentor. "Oh, Professor," she cried, "I am so happy to see you. I knew you'd save me from this band of lunatics. Did you receive my message? Did you figure it out? Wasn't that clever of me? I knew you'd get it. So, what's the plan? Did you sneak in the back way? Who else is coming? Did you arrange a big operation with the Army, Air Force, and Marines? How soon do they arrive?" She patted his coat pockets. "I'll bet you're wearing an arsenal of concealed weapons. I'll take a flame thrower if you've got one. Nothing is too horrid for these creeps. Well, tell me, tell me!"

As gently as he could, Vorchek explained the situation to her. Theresa blanched, grimaced, rolled her eyes and stamped her foot. She looked lovely even when she did these things, but it did not serve to tell her so, for she was furious. "Professor, you are a ninny. You let me down in my moment of peril. I wanted you here to get me out, not for a fact-finding expedition. Now they've got us both, and nobody knows we're here, and they can do whatever they like, which means we're doomed. Thank you, thank you very much. Have you a light?"

She flopped onto the cot, puffing her cigarette. Vorchek sat in a ratty chair facing her and said, "My dear, the situation is not as gloomy as you suppose. I have set in motion a scheme of my own, although nothing of the sort you call for. I tell you frankly that we remain in great danger, and will do so for approximately twenty-four hours, but if we survive for that span, then we stand a fair chance of leaving here alive and growing to a contented old age. The next day is critical—until tomorrow night, I think—but if they do not kill us out of hand in the meantime, our distressing position should resolve itself. Have patience, child. I am quite eager to observe the unfolding of the final chapter in this story."

"You would relish your own death," Theresa screeched, "if you had the chance to study it while it happened. I'm not that way."

"I know, but be patient. I have planted a kernel in Lorient's mind, a seed which may bear fruit. He wants to boast, I think, and I made clear that I grant him the opportunity. In order to make use of that I believe he will keep me alive for a period. If he desires my willing audience, he will naturally refrain from harsh measures against you. All is well, you see, and we may experience together amazing events."

This scarcely mollified Theresa, but she was a chipper sort, and there was not much she could do about it, and besides, she really did have faith in the professor. She showed him their accommodations, spartan but mercifully including a functional bathroom. Dinner came at last, of a quality hardly worth waiting for, yet providing enough calories to get them by. After a great deal of quiet talk they made their beds, Theresa on the cot, Vorchek on the floor with a blanket.

They stayed trapped in the room for hours after waking, feeling the sluggish passing of every minute. Then two new goons appears. Lorient had sent for them, they must come at once. Theresa feared immediate termination of her life processes, while Vorchek mused silently. As it happened, they were taken to a commodious suite on the second floor where Lorient awaited them alone. He invited them to a private breakfast, which was served so soon as they seated themselves at the big oak table and the guards assumed their positions outside the door. Vorchek and the girl ate as if famished. Lorient ate sparingly, watching them with amusement.

Presently he said, "I hope you are both well, and as happy as circumstances permit? Very good. Professor Vorchek, you are an intelligent man, a learned man, one who knows a thing or two of outré matters, although not nearly enough, I can assure you. Nevertheless it seems a pity to destroy your magnificent brain before you have the opportunity to witness the miracle of the ages which will transpire tonight. In a sense, both you and I have lived for that moment, though for wildly different reasons. Mine are obvious enough—I crave the ultimate becoming with my Lord—but while the future, I am afraid, holds an ugly fate in store for you, you must certainly crave the prospect of the astounding revelations which shall shortly spew from the boundless cosmos.

"Throughout time, Professor, we devoted acolytes of Great Xenophor have labored behind the scenes of history for one goal: the introduction of the physical reign of our Master upon this world. This is His world, as all the worlds are His, but we, His devoted possessions, crave His material Lordship over us. Always we've sought the key which unlocks the barriers that separate us from His presence. We knew that such a key must exist, for Xenophor, He of the Million Eyes, is the Creator God, is everywhere and always, seeing all, knowing all. His holy substance pervades His creation, which He fashioned for His pleasure; He is here, in every speck of matter and force, and we are here, therefore it must be possible for us to reach Him. It was only necessary for those who believed and worshipped, to learn the secret way.

"You may ask, Professor, what do we gain by contacting Him? Mighty Xenophor cares nothing for His temporarily animated trinkets. He doesn't stoop to caring that we live or die. We exist merely as elements of His eternal, cosmic Plan, the vast tale He chooses to tell. We are as naught to Him, true, but He is everything to us. We are gripped by the unshakable faith that He expects us to scale the impossible heights, upon which we have ever gazed with longing, and attain that pinnacle where we may prostrate ourselves before Him. I tell you that soon the earth will form that pinnacle. He will come, in His actual substance, and through us He will rule.

"How do we achieve this? One does not speak with the Most High by radio or registered mail. The materialities of our age, the sciences, avail us not. It is, instead, through olden, forgotten means, hallowed by time, that we must endeavor. The ancients knew; they delved into the illimitable aspects of magic, surer guides to knowledge when wielded by the proper brains, and they initiated the process of intellectual accrual which has led us to this moment. There were numerous superior minds that gleaned a portion of the answer. Reckless Artocris, most brilliant of the Classical mages, guessed a part, though his clumsiness led him to grief; noble Azamodias, that redoubtable scholar of the icy north, discovered the gate, but his stupid skittishness forbade him from attempting the final step; so it fell to Jacob Bleek, he of the perfectly cold and logical mind, to sweep away the ignorance of the eons and reveal the way. Bleek learned the secret, and for callous reasons of his own—not out of kindness to us, I may add, for in his day he laughed at us and opposed our designs—he sought to preserve the secret for all time. Thus what we call his Seal of Revelation came into being, a jewel for which we have quested throughout the centuries. At some point in history it was broken up, the fragments scattered. We tracked them down, one by one, utilizing bribery, theft, torture, and murder, until we possessed all but one critical piece. That piece, Vorchek, you have delivered into our hands.

"Yes, Professor, it has arrived! Your package is here, the contents verified by experts. Many of my comrades were impatient; they wished to proceed with our undertakings months ago, working with what we had, which seemed to them sufficient. I counseled patience, and a good thing, too. Your apparently trivial fragment contains two small but critical elements not referenced elsewhere in the seal. A rather unusual magical solution devised by Maltheus the Wise, we learn, must be heated in a container of unadulterated iron. We had wondered what to do with that substance, the preparation of which had been clinically described. Furthermore, the passes of the Seventh Illumination must be employed at that juncture. We knew of them from our documents, of course, but never realized their application. Now we know. We know all, and we are ready.

"Tonight we act. A handful of hours will see the deed done. You will be here, Professor, to observe, so be content. Your intelligence has won you a further pittance of life. The girl may remain as well, though I have no need of her; were she a believer, though, she might make a fitting sacrifice to Him. I suppose you and your delightful companion will shrivel into screaming madness when those million unwinking eyes glare down upon you and wrench your souls away, but then you surely knew that a certain amount of unpleasantness awaited you. Meanwhile, consider yourselves at liberty within the compound. If you approach within one hundred yards of the fence or the lake, Vorchek, you will be shot down like a dog, and as for the girl, well... I am too polite a fellow to tell you in detail what my stout lads will do to her." And he laughed.

Afterward Vorchek and Theresa strolled about the chaos of the Visions of Peace retreat, taking care to heed their host's cautionary warning. The place hummed like a beehive with frantic activity. Many people came and went with great rapidity, looking harassed and important, dispatching messages or obscure announcements. Many others, hundreds or even thousands, milled about unceasingly, breaking up into spontaneous groups to discuss arcane points of mystical lore or burst into weird chanting and strange, uncouth prayers. Most of those present, save for those radiating official airs, were shabbily dressed, unwashed, or otherwise bizarre in appearance or manners Said Theresa, "It's the biggest collection of freaks I've ever seen. I can't stand it here."

Vorchek was ebullient, leading her cheerfully about as if on a sightseeing excursion. "No harsh thoughts, I beg of you, Miss Delaney. Why, it is a fine day, the scenery is entrancing, God is in his heaven and all is right with the world, eh? What more could we ask for at present?"

"Not to be murdered, for one thing. I'll never forgive you, Professor, if I get killed here. I'll bet these loonies are digging our graves right now."

"They have too much else on their minds. You heard the kind words of Mr. Lorient. He grants us a reprieve until the great coming, when I presume that we, along with a few billion other unbelievers, will be erased. Until then, we live, and must be happy with our lot. We shall have a marvelous view of the festivities." Vorchek indicated a big wooden amphitheater, consisting of tiers of long benches, which had been erected within a dell up against a steep slope of the wooded hills. "I presume the ceremony will take place there."

"Is it actually going to happen?" Theresa shook her head in despairing wonderment. "Are things like this really real?"

"They are. It is a strange world, sometimes unbearably so. Much of the strangeness is just foolishness, but a great deal reeks of monstrous validity. This is one such occasion. Lorient and his cohorts are willing, and more importantly able, to unleash a fiendish horror upon our planet, and a great time of trial is approaching which, if they have their way, will mean the end of everything, extinction for most, the destruction of reason and sanity for all. There is no point in fretting about that, however. Besides, my dear, you forget that Lorient is not the only fellow hereabouts with cunning ideas. There is my plan to consider . . ."

"I've seen no evidence of your plan!" cried the girl. "I don't even know what it is. It had better involve a bunch of tanks and missiles, otherwise we're cooked."

"It does not, and we are not. Ye of little faith, think not the old man a fool. My arrangements advance splendidly. I know this, for the

212

news comes from the best possible source, Lorient himself. He told us as much, though you did not attend." Theresa, all excitement and glee, pressed him for particulars, but Vorchek chuckled and would say no more. He seemed thoroughly serene and in his element, but his attitude infuriated Theresa, who tried to impress upon him the seriousness of the situation.

All too soon the dreaded evening came. The thronging masses discarded their common attire—some of them nonchalantly stripping to the buff—and donned white robes of homemade appearance. They surged through the gathering gloom to the amphitheater, carrying torches and flashlights. The first arrivals, the lucky ones, grabbed seats on the benches, from which they gained a good view of the wooden platform or dais at the center of the semi-circle. The rest kept coming, however, and they had to pile up on the turf beneath the bench supports or settle themselves on nearby slopes, where their lights twinkled and glistened. Vorchek insisted on pushing to the front, though he and Theresa were too late for a seat. "It is for the best," he observed. "When it is time to move, we must move quickly." A ring of tough men held them and the other standees at a perimeter some distance from the dais.

Alfonse Lorient appeared, wearing a white robe of professional make, flanked by six other believers similarly dressed and bearing implements, books, packages and a big iron kettle carried by two men. Lorient spied Vorchek, brusquely directed his fellows onto the platform, strode over to his captive and smirked. "All is in readiness, Professor. I imagine your sojourn among us has not been too painful?"

"We have been fed again, for which we are grateful." Theresa snorted at this. "We do not suffer," Vorchek continued, "and yet, nevertheless, I am prey to grave forebodings. I think you should forego this particular experiment. I fear that no one will derive benefit from it, including yourself. Why not leave it best alone?"

"Do you wish," laughed Lorient, "to trying arguing me out of the culmination of an ancient dream? I have no time, Professor, otherwise I would treat myself by listening. I can enjoy a good joke. I go now. Watch, believe, and fear. That is all there is left to you." He turned and pushed through the crowd.

He mounted the steps to the dais, checked the preparations. His assistants had kindled a fire beneath the kettle. Lorient raised his eyes to the skies. The sun had died, the countless stars blazed. He nodded, faced and addressed the muttering masses, who grew silent on the instant. "Tonight," he shouted, "we shall speak to Great Xenophor, and He shall cast His inescapable, multifold gaze upon us, and we shall know ecstasy in His sight. If He deigns, He shall speak with us in return, and open to us the gates of ultimate power and eternal glory. The faith of our fathers, lovingly maintained these innumerable generations, comes to fruition at this time and place. Great is He, damned are our foes. So it shall always be henceforth. The ceremony commences."

Lorient took from the hands of the man on his left a fair sized object in brown paper, shredded with his fingers the wrappings, held aloft the contents. The crowd roared. Vorchek immediately knew the rectangular object for what it was. "The complete Seal of Jacob Bleek," he sighed. "They have joined together the pieces. What I would give for a closer look at that."

The man to Lorient's right unwrapped a smaller package, holding it carefully in the cup of his palms, and cast the powdery contents into the reddening pot. A flash of flame dazzled all eyes, and a cloud of dense, bright smoke boiled up. Then began a curious sort of pageantry on that stage. Lorient's six companions started to dance, writhing and twisting and waving their arms and fingers. They did so according to what appeared to Vorchek's learned eye a practiced, well-honed ritual, every move of every man, however odd, connecting to and dove-tailing with the moves before and after. Hands darted and knifed the air, fingers groped at emptiness, feet shuffled in peculiar rhythm. They commenced a low chant to themselves, scarcely audible from a remove, something formulaic and foreign. At a certain high note one dancer (a woman, Vorchek noticed, the only one on the dais) dropped her robe and stood naked. She plunged her arms deep into the simmering kettle, cried out in an unplaceable tongue, and then drew forth her steaming stumps. Theresa gasped, while other onlookers expressed joyous awe. Lorient removed a dagger from his robes and rammed it into the mutilated woman's breast. She collapsed onto the platform, motionless, while the chanting rose to a yet higher pitch.

Lorient waved aloft the bloody knife and bellowed, "I pronounce the secret, sacred words of the Seal," and he spoke three sentences, strings of inconceivably alien compound words which Theresa could not follow at all, and which even Vorchek had difficulty grasping. "One portion derives from a spell of Maltheus," he whispered to the girl, "but the rest is meaningless to me. That seal must contain esoteric knowledge of an incredibly advanced order. I could pen an entire treatise on those words alone. Will I ever have the opportunity?" Theresa stared at him as if he had lost his mind.

And Lorient roared in a voice like thunder, "Xenophor, Xenophor, Xenophor!" at which the throng went wild, rising from their seats and stamping furiously, or pressing frantically against the perimeter guards. Vorchek placed his lips to Theresa's ear, raising his voice so that she could hear over the din, "This is the moment, Miss Delaney. It is best that we be gone. They will not pay attention to us now." He seized her around the shoulders and propelled her through the maddening crowd.

Theresa froze and pointed up into the blackness of night. "Professor, look!"

"Yes, I know. I really should study this, but it is my duty to save your life. Keep moving." She did, and they both hurried through the crowd, into the empty meadow lands leading to the main hall. From here they could look back upon the gleaming, stampeding mob. Theresa cried out again.

"Oh, look now, Professor!"

"Remember Lot's wife," he snapped, though he could not resist the urge to quick glances himself. Something was happening up there in the dark, starry sky. A hole had opened in the blackness, a curious irregular hole blacker than the aerial background, which gave an illusion of utter emptiness, an intruding void from beyond the natural darkness. Now something appeared to emerge from that gaping maw in the heavens, a hint of formless nebulosity which grew in intensity and transformed itself into a seething, bubbling mass of green luminescence. It glittered, swirled, and frothed; hints of definite form took shape, many tiny forms, resembling a swarm of bees.

"Inside," commanded Vorchek as they reached the building. "This is as far as we get. It had better be good enough." In he shoved Theresa, pausing once more for a backward glance before he took cover. He saw the amphitheater with its eager hordes, their flickering, stabbing lights, Lorient gesticulating on the dais, and he saw the thing in the sky, an evilly glimmering, ever shifting, kaleidoscopic cloud of baleful, staring eyes, from which luridly glowing, smoky streamers were descending like tendrils toward the focus of human activity. Then he dashed inside and dived for the floor, carrying Theresa down with him.

Came a flash of red, penetrating light—a roar from the crowd, a cacophony of horribly different timbre from what had gone before— a reverberating crash reminiscent of a sonic boom—a shuddering of the earth! Vorchek held the girl beneath him as the walls buckled, things toppled and broke, glass smashed. Then frightful silence reigned supreme. Vorchek took his time about rising. Ordering caution, he crept on hands and knees to a shattered window and peeked outside.

"What do you see?" whispered Theresa, though her voice sounded unnaturally loud.

"Nothing to speak of," replied the professor. "There is nothing happening at the amphitheater. It is not there anymore." At that Theresa got up to see for herself. After an eyeful Vorchek discoursed on prudence and suggested that they clear out. They left the building, which had lost part of its roof, detoured around the wreckage and made for his hired car, still parked where he had left it. It functioned, though somewhat the worse for wear. "There will be the devil to pay with the rental company," said he.

"I'm good for it," said Theresa.

The amphitheater was indeed gone, along with all those people who had clustered in the vicinity. There remained in that clearing beneath the gloomy slopes of Bonita valley only a circular charred space where all trace of organic life had vanished utterly. Even the fertile soil had gone in part, with banks of blasted bedrock protruding from the ground. The ceremony to Xenophor was over.

Much later, in the pleasant surroundings of her fashionable apartment, Theresa invited Professor Vorchek to tea. As he puffed on his pipe he waxed voluble concerning recent events. "These stories in the papers," he exclaimed; "so much they get wrong, and the uneducated questions they ask! It is well that we remain anonymous during this nine day wonder. Given the caliber of the reporting, I would hesitate to risk offering anything resembling the truth. The powers that be would never forgive me. Still, I can not complain. All things considered, my plan worked beautifully. The menace of the Xenophor cult is smashed for the moment, and we live to tell about it... or not tell, as we choose. Such is life."

"I'm sick of hearing about your plan," Theresa retorted, "especially since I haven't really heard anything about it. It looks to me like dumb luck saw us through, and nothing more. You were supposed to rescue me, but didn't; you should have stopped the ceremony, but didn't; and I thought you'd beat up the bad guys, but didn't. If it was up to you they'd have gotten away with it. Some plan!"

"Miss Delaney," said Vorchek in mock sorrow, a sly grin breaking through as he spoke, "some wounds never heal. I may not survive your poor esteem, therefore I must endeavor to change it. I told you

I had a plan, and I meant it. I had worked out all of the details before ever you saw me again, and developments proceeded pretty much as predicted, save on two points. I did not know for certain that the end of the affair would constitute so grandiose a catastrophe, although even there I realized a range of probabilities. Also, and far more important to me, the marvelous seal of Jacob Bleek was lost along with all else, which truly is a disaster for science. There should have been something I could do to salvage it."

"I couldn't care less," cried Theresa, "about the seal, or Jacob Bleek, or any of those old weird guys."

"Forbidden, thoughts, child! You sneer at the mystic masters of yesteryear. I will not hear your words." He grinned again. "Your safety was paramount, you know. I could only hope that Lorient spared you until I arrived, but once past that hurdle I felt myself on firm foundations. The ceremony would proceed, once the cultists had what they wanted, and it was logical that we would live until it was complete, for they had no reason to kill us then. They thought Xenophor would handle that distasteful business for them when he exterminated the unbelievers."

"It was a crazy risk."

"Yet necessary," said Vorchek. "I had to know, to see it for myself. Knowledge is my life. I learn or I perish. I accomplished one, avoided the other. I desired to know whether the great spell contained in Bleek's seal possessed genuine efficacy. To a sufficient degree, I do know now. I am happy."

"You wouldn't be so happy," Theresa pointed out, "if the spell had worked the way the cultists wanted. Yet you gave them the last piece of the puzzle they needed. That was horribly dangerous, Professor."

"I did not give it to them."

"You did! I heard Lorient, remember? I know."

"Not at all," replied Vorchek, and he laughed heartily, easily. "There was one more feature to my plan. Of course I could not allow the cultists of Xenophor to succeed. Had He run rampant in our world, He might have acted exactly as they wished; a problematic proposition at best—the true believers are ever too reliant on their faith—but an awesome consideration. I, therefore, employed a subterfuge. I did not hand over the fragment. I mailed to Lorient a magnificent reproduction fashioned by an expert metallurgist. A perfect copy—quite good enough to fool those people—save in one small detail. I removed from the engraved text the reference to 'the

217

fourth level safeguards of the Rhexellites.' I have studied this, you see, and knew those antique spells to be formulations of unimaginable power, perhaps the only safeguards which could render congress with Xenophor survivable. Lorient and his gang did not recognize the necessity, and in their ignorance went ahead without any protection at all." The professor paused, then added soberly, "They tried and failed, to their horrific and, I fear, eternal cost. Xenophor is a grim God, I am told, with strange humors, and it may be that He amuses Himself still with the souls of His acolytes."

The God in the Machine

Just when everything seemed to be going right, everything went completely wrong. The experiment had been designed with care, the parameters judiciously fixed, the predicted results apparently in hand. We had impeccably calculated our equations, and there were few of us who doubted that the desired outcome would be attained. Of course morose old Gerald Steen, my learned but disputatious colleague, doubted and questioned and griped, but I'd never known him happy about anything, in his work or his personal life, the latter being a total mess. The rest of us at Applied Physics Processing, however (those of us who counted), confidently expecting victory over the unknown, were nonplused and chagrined when fresh mystery arose.

At heart it was a simple test of theory, which I, Kevin Phelps, had arranged and managed to completion at the behest of APP. Theoretical physics had carried man's knowledge, in a few short decades, beyond (or below) the atom, into the realm of the subatomic particle. Physicists had delved into the nucleus of the atom, broken it into its constituent parts, then dived deeper to break up those parts, the building blocks of reality. Dalton long ago thought the atom indivisible, but his heirs presented us with the proton, neutron, and electron, and those who came after peered closer and observed the quarks and superstrings and other fragments of existence which come together to create all that we see and feel in this material universe. What, if anything, lay beyond that infinitely microscopic level? There was a grand question for a team of dedicated and reputation-hungry scientists. We were sure that we had not yet touched bottom, that another infinitesimal layer of the space-time fabric remained to be observed and described. In our huge ultra-modern, state of the art laboratory we had all the necessary apparatus at our command, all the required cash, and we had an idea which made sense according to ironclad theory and equation. We couldn't lose.

This is what should have happened. The hypothesis of Feinberg and Kimoso deduced the existence of a basal non-particulate state, a substratum of ultra-dimensional energy in which the higher known

219

particles swam like fish in the sea, drawing their substance, their structure, their reality, from that cosmic stream. We applied physicists at APP proposed to bombard a sample of pure plutonium with high intensity lasers, excite its atoms, smash their cohesion, knock them apart into individual strings, and then continue on to what no one had accomplished before, the rending of the strings themselves. If our working theory were correct, the latent, all encompassing power of the unobservable substratum should operate to reconstruct the strings according to a precisely defined formula. This chemical process we could measure, and if events developed within a certain range of probability, we would be fairly on our way to achieving our goal. We would have established the secret power hidden far beneath the atom and, incidentally, just might have conceived a method for tapping it, a factor of enormous import to practical scientists in the hire of a commercial corporation. The possibilities were dizzying.

Only it didn't happen the way we expected. As I said, everything went wrong. We cranked up the accelerator to full blast, burning to thin vapor that incredibly dense lump of plutonium, and we kept at it until there wasn't a single intact atom within the vacuum chamber; we isolated the fragments and boiled them with the lasers until there was nothing tangible surviving in there, neither matter nor organized energy; then, when all readings hit zero—when the meters told us that we had generated an utter emptiness—we switched off the beams and waited breathlessly for a sign. We predicted one of two things: no reaction whatsoever, or a feeble but indicative increase in energy release, a by-product of the process by which the strings were recreated and recombined. The latter result would constitute victory.

We got neither prediction, not the good, not the bad. We got something startling and frustrating and costly: an immense power surge that shattered the vacuum chamber, wrecking the extremely costly accelerator and blowing all our theories and equations to bits. Every needle in the banks of connected meters suddenly shot off the dials, and before we knew it we had a big problem on our hands, for the surge poured unbidden into our massive controlling computer, searing its circuits and rendering it expensively inoperative. The laboratory filled with smoke, electrical arcing, puffs of flame, and chaos. Then all of our machines shut down with a crashing silence, and we were left, gasping, to pick up the pieces and figure out what had caused the catastrophe.

"And now for your next trick," Steen sneered at me. "I hope you've been saving your lunch money." Of course I was in no way responsible for the disaster, as I was quick to point out—I had worked out the operating parameters to perfection, as always—but it was my show, and his snide suggestion rankled. Everything did at that moment. Fortunately the others present were more inclined to offer useful aid than gloating comment. I directed the immediate recovery procedures, saw to it that the dangerous equipment failures were addressed, hovered over the minor technicians as they damped the smoldering flames and suppressed the crackling electrical systems by turning off the remaining power. It was a sad mess, but we got it under control without further financial loss.

Then I had to report to J.D. Cunningham, the big boss. He wasn't a physicist, more an inventor, and a good one, too, but he knew the basics, and expected to be kept informed, especially in circumstances like these. His office was located at the top of the administration building at the far end of the APP complex. "Find out what happened," he said upon hearing the preliminary details. "Fix it, introduce new safeguards, try it again and make it work." That's what I wanted to hear, what I expected and needed from that no nonsense fellow. I intended to get down to business without delay.

Upon my return to the laboratory I found fresh trouble awaiting, and this was where matters began to get really weird. Despite my impression from the initial damage survey, it turned out that the central computer, that marvelous technological behemoth which occupied one whole wall of the main laboratory, hadn't fully shut down after all. It seemed to be in good running order, in fact, which should have been wonderful news, except for two things: one, I had examined it myself, and had made sure of my observations on its burnt out condition; two, the power was off by my command, so the beast should have been quiet even if in fine fettle. Output from consoles and meters, however, clearly proved that major internal activity was ongoing. It couldn't be—it wasn't possible—but there it was, and no mistake. With the help of Martin Bremmer, my intern assistant, I peeked and pried into every panel and cranny, but couldn't shake the conclusion that the machine was running on its own, from sourceless power.

Mystery on top of mystery! "If we can bottle this," quipped Martin, "then we'll all be billionaires." To which I responded, "Not if we first blow up the lab every time." It gave me a headache even to think about it. Our job was to explain as well as to achieve, and I, among others, wasn't having much luck. The first result had been unexpected, the second inconceivable.

And it got worse, much worse, before the night was over. I called

221

for our handyman Mirrhatta to recalibrate a sensor. He had been there earlier, in the thick of things, but now I couldn't find him, and when I asked around I learned that he'd suddenly thrown down his tools, taken off and run out of the lab. That was childish behavior, and quite uncharacteristic; he was a somber fellow, but supremely dedicated. I sent someone to look for him in his workshop. The someone returned shortly to inform me that Mirrhatta was dead, apparently by his own hand.

At the head of a small party I looked into his shop and found him there, as described. What a grim sight he was lying sprawled face up over his desk. The indications were clear enough: he had drunk concentrated cleaning fluid, a highly corrosive solution used to strip and sterilize electrical wiring, straight from the can still clutched in a clenched hand. It was powerful stuff—I splashed a drop of it on my arm once, and it was already hurting before I applied the soap and water—so I could imagine the agony he suffered before he died. At least he went quickly, or must have, and yet I was disturbed anew, for reasons beyond the obvious. Even at the time it struck me that the look on his dead, contorted face was wholly improper. It should have revealed only the aftermath of searing pain, and that was there, but there was something else around the mouth and in those staring eyes, a look of peace, of contentment; of joy. He died that way, and yet I could believe that Mirrhatta was happy when he went!

There came one more shock before that cavalcade of tragedies concluded. A few hours later, after the local authorities of the law had come and gone, and we had finally derived some order from the mess and could think of hitting the sack at last, another horror struck. Shortly before dawn, as we subsequently pieced together the facts, our nuclear chemist Jamison, a decent enough guy, though usually quiet and withdrawn, suddenly grew garrulous, even belligerent, stomped out of the lab laughing loudly to himself, then ascended to the third floor, the office level, where a number of witnesses reported him singing at the top of his voice. There he broke into an emergency exit, made his way onto the flat roof and without further ado pitched himself down to the hard pavement below. He died by the time anyone got to him. He was a bloody mess, naturally, but I thought, when I viewed the body, that he seemed pretty chipper about it. The sight of his smiling face gave me a queasy feeling.

It would be a while longer before I took to my bed, despite being already dog tired. Cunningham had to be briefed once more, to bring him up to date on our festivities. I did that, and he mused for a bit, ordering everyone home for the day, promising immediate action, a complete investigation. By then I couldn't have cared less, although certainly nothing had been resolved by that time. The computer continued to misbehave unexplainably, and our people were killing themselves over it. I went home and slept, an enervating sleep which didn't refresh, although it might have had I been left alone until I got my fill. The boss called me around four that afternoon, to inform me that he was contacting outside help. "We have a puzzle on our hands," he pointed out, "of a sort we aren't equipped to handle. There's too much about this business that's mysterious, that doesn't make sense. I need a man who can put together pieces when they don't seem to fit. I've heard of this Vorchek character—a Professor Vorchek, one of your colleagues—who might be able to aid us. I hear he's a whiz at unusual scientific matters, the sort of man who can step in and tie knots when everybody else is at loose ends. I sent a dispatch to him, telling him about the experiment and the computer glitch, referring him to you, making mention of a hefty fee. Look out for him." Fine, if that was what Cunningham wanted. I thought it too soon to panic myself, but I had to admit that I didn't have any idea in hell as to what was happening just then.

Come the next morning a select team, consisting of myself, Martin, Steen, and a couple of high-powered technicians went to work on the computer again, attempting to download all stored data before, as I feared, we lost it altogether. No dice; the machine wasn't giving up any of its secrets, although it continued to chirp and whine merrily, as if something gargantuan was going on inside. Steen was particularly keen on tapping into storage. His was the only cheerful countenance around that day, and he truly applied himself to the work, as if he thought himself facing a worthy challenge at last. I hadn't wanted him around then, when I had so much on my mind. Frankly, I simply didn't like the guy, but he insisted, and he did know his stuff, so what could I say?

"I tell you, Phelps," he said, as we crowded at a terminal, striving without success to input, "this is big, really big. We've got to break into that machine. It's all there, inside, waiting for us, and all we have to do is unleash it. Maybe you screwed up, but this is a bonanza, and I want it. I want it all." "I don't know what you're yapping about," I shot back. "We have a technical problem of an unforeseen nature, the life's blood of science. We will establish what went wrong which lead to this unfortunate state of affairs, then return to first beginnings and start again. Next time, suitably prepared and forearmed, we will succeed. It's as simple as that." He raised up, leaned back against the wall and said, with a note of wonder in his voice, "You really think so, don't you?" "Of course. There's nothing else." Steen grinned wolfishly, as if enjoying a private joke at my expense. "Well, well, we'll see. I have grander hopes."

We didn't see anything that day. I received a message, one prepared and sent by a "T. Delaney", from the offices of Professor Anton Vorchek. The stationery heading told me nothing about him, though there was an odd symbol next to his name which resembled Red Indian art, a complicated image of a grotesque face or ceremonial mask. The body of the letter read as follows:

Dear Doctor Phelps,
The professor is a very busy man, with a lot on his plate, but he might be willing to solve your problem for you, as requested by your superior. The money is acceptable. Professor Vorchek says you are to describe in full detail the nature of the problem, if you are capable of doing so. He expects an immediate reply.

That was all, but it considerably irked me, both the amateurishness of the tone and its domineering manner. Who in hell was this Vorchek anyway? I took a break from my fruitless labors to look him up in the *Guide to the International Physicists Association*, without success. A perusal of listings for degreed professionals of any kind turned up nothing either. A catalogue of working professors gave me what I wanted, without pleasing me one whit. So he was Vorchek, Anton, visiting professor at a minor private college in Phoenix, Arizona. No statement of credentials, which mystified me, but a list of published papers, which mystified me more. I supposed that there was a place for such academic masterpieces as "Yotapai Legends of the Third Advent," "Psychic Responses Among a Test Group to Pictorial Presentations of the Demon Astrodemus," or "Mystical Realities Deduced From the Seventh Book of Artocris," among others, but I couldn't see it myself, and I sure didn't see what any of this had to do with me. One item did briefly fascinate, "Second Level Energy Disturbances In the Vicinity of Cathedral Rock," but it sounded like rot. Taking his publications as a whole I gathered he was some kind of esoteric social scientist, which marked him as a pretty useless specimen at the present moment. Okay by me if I never heard from him again, but Cunningham insisted that I cooperate, so I sent in response the full scientific particulars of our recent travails, describing fully and accurately the procedures of the experiment, as well as the specific inglorious results obtained. I explained about the computer as best I could. I felt silly recounting that part, for I knew it didn't make much sense, but I left out the dreadful personal responses to the failure among our staff. Whatever Vorchek was intended to provide, those sad deaths weren't relevant.

I came in the next morning to find Steen already working at the computer, still trying to tap its contents and discover the secret of its automatic operation. I quickly learned, to my surprise (for he hadn't let on his intentions), that he had been up all night hacking at it. He claimed to be on to something, although he couldn't back up the claim with satisfactory evidence. "This is marvelous," he cried, full of life and vigor, though he looked shabby and worn. "It's as if the machine has fabricated for itself a new language, a binary-style code with its own inherent logic. I think I can crack it—I know I can—given enough time." "You mean," I asked, "that the computer language has become garbled, but can be reconstructed?" "Have it your way," he sighed. "I'll figure it out. I will read this."

That morning there occurred the third death involving APP personnel, this one especially freakish. An administrative clerk I'd never met or heard of, a long-term female employee called Maggie who, so I was told over the grapevine, had recently experienced a divorce and suffered from other personal difficulties such as debilitating obesity, did the deed. She killed herself in the strangest way, an incredible act of self-brutalization. Absenting herself from her station and slipping into an empty break room, she downed most of a pot of coffee, raided the larder of doughnuts, then thrust her right hand into the garbage disposal in the sink, with her left hand flicking the switch. In an amazing display of sheer willpower she held her hand inside the rotating choppers, without a scream or any outcry at all, until her hand was reduced to a raw stump and she bled to death. It was all over by the time the next peckish employee walked in.

The legal authorities duly swept in again, this time sternly recommending that we shut down operations and evacuate the complex while they endeavored to get a grip on the alarming situation. Cunningham went along with that as far as unessential employees were concerned, maybe having thought of it himself, for as he told me, "We need a cooling off period. Our people are getting too worked up, taking everything too hard." So they were, I guessed, although I couldn't imagine why. I'd heard, somewhere along the way, that tragedies come in groups, or in threes, and what was happening fit the bill, though the latest case, not involving our core team, seemed more bad luck of timing than anything else. I doubted that this Maggie gave a damn about experimental difficulties; perhaps, being on the edge for other reasons, the earlier deaths pushed her over? I heard lots of talk like that.

I received a second Vorchek missive, prepared again by the irritating T. Delaney:

Dear Doctor Phelps,

The professor is intrigued by, but hardly impressed with, your account. He tells me that it wasn't necessary to describe your dopey experiment at such length, having heard all about that from Mr. Cunningham. He is delighted by your computer trouble, though.

The professor, whose time is valuable, expects more information from you concerning corollary consequences. Please send, soonest, everything you know about bizarre behavior arising among APP employees or others in the area since the mishap. He desires a full catalogue of crimes, murders, suicides, and psychotic mania. Only then can he take action to clear up the mess you've made.

The nerve of that person! Who was T. Delaney to write to me like that? Yet this fresh request shook me. The professor asked about suicides, although I'd avoided mentioning them, and I didn't think Cunningham had either. Perhaps this Vorchek had heard something in the news, but the way he phrased the request (or demand) suggested otherwise. He was fishing for data, yet had somehow managed to put his finger, as illogical as it seemed, precisely on our sore point. It might be coincidence, yet it created the illusion that he knew something. With a heavy heart, thinking ill of Vorchek, T. Delaney, and the wide world, I transmitted everything I'd learned about the three deaths.

The response to my last narrative arrived fast, before an hour passed. This time it was just the short and messianic sentence, "The professor says, 'I AM COMING.'" Bully for him; I now imagined that he intended to deluge us with psychological tests, to find out if any more of us were contemplating self-homicide. Come to think of it, that didn't sound such a bad idea. There was, it transpired, plenty of destructive nuttiness among our folks. This Vorchek might do some good, although I couldn't help but brood more—it was my job, after all—about our wayward computer. There was nothing a man like him could do about that.

It wasn't just a stimulating puzzle. Until we got the machine back on line, functioning as we dictated, then we at the lab were out of commission, unless we bit the bullet and purchased a brand new instrument. Computers of that caliber weren't a dime a dozen; the Pentagon would bust its budget ordering a dozen, and just one was a gigantic expense for us. We had every incentive to struggle round the clock to fix it, and if we hadn't seen it that way, Cunningham would have chided us, possibly by waving termination papers in our faces.

I didn't, however, know what to do. It kept coming back to that, and no matter how I or anybody else strained our brains we didn't advance. Martin was a jewel, as ever, always quick with the clever suggestion which might pass muster—often had in the past—but which got us nowhere now. Steen was Steen, a heavy, awkward, grouchy fellow, competent but uninspired, doing nothing for me despite his current enthusiasm. I needed him for fundamental calculations, at which (I granted) he excelled, but it was virtually impossible to tear him away from the consoles. His whole life seemed glued to the terminals, from which he watched and noted the workings of that contrary electronic brain.

Vorchek arrived. My first intimation of visitation occurred when I went in early to work, to find an astoundingly beautiful girl, a dazzling, blue-eyed blonde in her twenties, ambling casually about the littered accelerator room, handling delicate gadgets and fingering buttons. She was provocatively attired in a short, low-cut crimson dress with a broad-brimmed hat to match, fishnet hose and tall, high-heeled black boots. Such a vision was entirely out of place there, as was unauthorized entry, but she was a sight for sore eyes, and I paused before I determined on rounding upon her. Scarcely had I begun a brusque comment before she laconically introduced herself. "I'm Theresa Delaney," she stated, "Professor Vorchek's private secretary." So this was my epistolary nemesis. "The professor is talking to the big man right now," she added, "but he'll show up momentarily. He sent me on ahead. Where is this Phelps character, anyway?" "I am Phelps—Kevin Phelps—Kevin to my friends." "All right, Mr. Phelps—" "*Doctor* Phelps." "Whatever. I'm to take notes on the facilities. Why don't you show me all the important stuff."

I was more inclined to wring her neck, but her company appealed to me for irrelevant reasons, so I went along with her ill-mannered request. I pointed out items of interest, describing them at length, while she scribbled suspiciously short fragments in a little notebook. Occasionally she asked questions, none of which indicated the slightest knowledge of physics or physics laboratories. Her voice was lovely, but she didn't seem to care what she did with it.

Then there appeared her employer, or patron, or whatever he was. "Professor Anton Vorchek," he boomed, extending a jabbing hand as he strode briskly forward. "Is this Phelps?" he asked the girl. "Indeed; very good. Pleased to meet you, Doctor Phelps. Shall we begin?" He was quite tall and lean, a striking, middle-aged fellow, well if not fashionably dressed in a long, open dark coat, tailored trousers and expensive shoes. His dark hair, partly concealed by a large floppy hat pushed back on his head, was tinged with iron-gray at the temples. His eyes were bright and piercing, his nose strong, his mouth firm and, at the moment, set in an amused, all wise grin. His speech, I discovered, was flawless and perfectly modulated, but bore a trace of an indefinable accent.

"One thing I must expect of you," he said crisply, "is complete data. Really, Doctor, there is no getting around it: you withheld pertinent information. Not realizing the kind or rate of progression we have here, I delayed coming by almost forty-eight hours. In matters such as these, time can be precious. Let us agree not to make the same mistake again."

"Oh yes, let's," I grumbled. "Doctor Vorchek—I see; you prefer Professor, do you?—Professor Vorchek, it will be easier to comply if you tell me exactly what you want, easier still if I know exactly why you're here. Due to an oversight, I suppose, your relevant credentials are still unknown to me. You aren't a physicist, are you? Forgive me, sir, but I still don't understand why my lab requires your presence in these trying times."

"I am an expert on mysteries," he proclaimed, after a studied delay while he puffed alight his pipe, "having devoted my long career to matters weird and unusual. Your situation is right up my alley, being composed, as should be apparent by now, of layers of mystery upon mystery. The truth must be ascertained, facts revealed, darkness banished. I beam probing light into these circumstances; I shall study and explicate, and in the course of time, if the evidence be ample, resolve. Now, to work."

Somehow he had managed to tell me nothing, for I still knew little concrete about him. To work we went, however, and for the next several hours he toured the scene, puffing jovially on his pipe, with me as his guide, and with Theresa in tow, she scribbling notes and interjecting unhelpful comments as we conversed. I described the sequence of events in the fullest detail, while in return he plied me with curious questions. "Are you familiar with Koppermeyer's writings on

228

inter-dimensional boundaries? Was attention paid to Helvetius' theories on the efficacy of second-level defense mechanisms? To the best of your knowledge, are any of your staff members of mystic cults, or devotees of odd religions?" These questions and dozens of others, senseless or meaningless to me, he continually hurled, along with many others which impressed me by their intelligent directness. It bugged me to admit (to myself) that he really did have a good grasp of the project and the principles underlying it. There were people working for me who didn't know half as much about the science.

During a lunch break I sought Cunningham, pressing him for further information concerning Vorchek. I wanted to know how my boss had come by the fellow. He told me. "Do you recall hearing of that business, a couple of years ago, at the Planetary Research Foundation? They had put together some of the instruments on one of the NASA probes to Jupiter, and were in charge of acquiring and analyzing the data. Something went wrong. A problem arose, something pretty nasty if the reports that leaked out were true. They kept it very hush-hush, and officially it never happened, but if the rumors were correct those folks got themselves into a pickle over telemetric data, if you can believe it. There suffered casualties, of a sort never specified, that sent all the big brains into a tizzy. Well, they brought Vorchek in, or he stepped in, and he straightened out the mess that had everybody else bamboozled. He's an eclectic thinker, a kind of supreme generalist, self-trained I understand, who knows how to solve puzzles that span multiple disciplines. Maybe he is an oddball, but I thought he might serve us well in this case, since what we have on our hands is a hell of a lot more than just a problem in applied physics. I want the pieces put together, I want this wretchedness put behind us. Talk to him, Phelps, work with him; satisfy him, and then the both of you satisfy me. Get the job done."

"I will," said I, "but I'm convinced we're dealing with a kook." After lunch I rejoined Vorchek and Theresa, and then, back at the lab, the professor had his first encounter with Gerald Steen. My colleague was hunched over a console, his normal behavior these days, recording endless strings of seemingly random numbers pouring out of the central computer, inputting his own variants, obsessively recording his results.

"Pleased to meet you," said the professor, his hard, inquisitive eyes belying his warm smile. "I see that output continues. Would you call it data or noise?" Steen glanced up, his mouth pursed sourly, his countenance radiating what I thought I must have mistaken for frank

229

hostility. "So you're Vorchek," he growled, "here to tell us what's what, are you?" "If I may be of service." "No doubt," Steen sneered. "I've been working on this without a break, concentrating on what counts, the heart of the machine, while others entertain guests." He looked at me and grinned coldly, then swiveled his chair out of the way to stare maliciously at our visitor. "See for yourself, Vorchek. It's all there, waiting to be read. Why don't you give it a whirl?"

"You honor me, sir," replied the professor. He bent over the monitor, perused the ever changing figures. What he saw appeared to captivate him, for he mumbled equations to himself and calculated with his fingers. "Miss Delaney," he called, "take this down: cohesive sine, enhanced logarithms incorporating linguistic patterns, and volatile, implosive energies feeding the system. Got that?" "I don't get it," Theresa responded, "but I wrote it down." "Fair enough. Dr. Steen, do you see it as I see it?"

Steen was visibly dumbfounded. He began to reply in an angry, cracking voice, then managed to control himself. "Well, that's a start, Professor. I suppose I ought to be pleased to meet a mind that can comprehend any of it. There's more in there, you can be sure of that. Given time, I'll break the code and get inside the machine."

"That may not be altogether wise. One must consider what may be waiting for you within." Vorchek brooded for a moment, then said, "I trust, Dr. Steen, that you will keep me abreast of your findings. I beg you to consult me before you take action." Steen leered, the professor shrugged and turned away. "Come, Phelps; let us finish the survey, at which time we shall take stock."

Much about this moment perturbed me. That Steen, of all people, could be making progress that I couldn't follow galled terribly, but I'd assumed he was whistling in the dark, generating bluster rather than results. Vorchek, however, had also seen something, and he'd caught it right away, without any great effort on his part. Maybe he was a big faker as well, or perhaps there was something to all this that was beyond me, something for which my training had left me unprepared. In that case, though, how had Steen—not my equal in smarts, much less my superior—begun to figure it out, as he kept hinting? What inner capacity gave him a leg up?

That evening, at Vorchek's polite insistence, he, Theresa, and I dined together. We ate at Tony's Seafood in town, sitting in a quiet, secluded back booth, on the table of which the professor had heaped the girl's notes and a bunch of requested documents which I had provided. During the fine meal I had little to say; Vorchek was subdued, occasionally flipping through papers; Theresa engagingly chatty, though her attempts at conversation seldom impinged upon weighty matters, and yet it was her casually blunt comment which instigated serious discussion.

"It's a screwy situation, all right," she said. "Everything's gone wrong, but nobody knows why, and what's happened since doesn't connect with what started it, and everybody's dying. That's the silly part. I mean, too bad about these technical problems, but it's not worth killing yourself for. Am I right, Professor?"

"On the latter point you are correct," said Vorchek heavily; "I am not, however, so certain about the rest. Indeed, on the basis of the fragmentary reports I received before arrival, I had already formulated a weak theory, one which has received modest confirmation from those curious deaths. If so, then Steen's work may also fall into place. I begin to see the shadow of the answer. I must come to grips with the substance, which will be supremely difficult, for there are unspeakable dangers involved."

"It's about time you included me, Professor," I said loudly, enough to startle a patron at the bar opposite. "I'm supposed to be a bright guy, but I don't know what you're driving at, and your very presence tells me I'm at sea. You're some sort of sociologist, or anthropologist, or antiquarian, or whatever, but you're brought in to repair damage at a multi-billion dollar physics lab, and what's more, I hear you've done this sort of thing before. Talk is you've garnered customer satisfaction in the past, handling dirty affairs like this one. Doing what? What do you know, what have you deduced? What is the problem, and what is the answer? Give me a break, and let me in on the big secret."

"Certainty and deduction are mixed at this stage," said he, "although I may expound basic ideas. Do not chide yourself, Doctor, for failing to grasp the essence of the problem. You are an expert on nature, while the source of the difficulty lies, I believe, in the realm of supernature. I am acknowledged by some an authority on the supernatural, that sphere which lies above or beyond the domain of standard science. There are whole swaths of reality which cannot be approached by conventional means; I, therefore, employ my own."

"So you're a New Age wacko made good," I snapped. "You gaze into crystals, count your beads, face east and sing a little song, and somehow that solves my problems. That's wonderful. To have gotten this far, you must have a great P.R. man working for you."

"You're as wrong as only a bonehead can be," Theresa cried, that lovely girl half rising from her seat and leaning towards me. "The professor is rock solid, as true blue as they come, and I would match him against any team of common scientists any day. If you'd just shut up you'd learn a thing or two." With that she leaned back, lit a cigarette and puffed furiously, pretending to ignore me.

"There is my public relations," Vorchek said with a boyish smile. "My dear Miss Delaney, you are very good to me. If you did not exist, it would be necessary—for the sake of my ego—to invent you. Seriously, Dr. Phelps, I have no more use for the childish formulations of popular beliefs than you do. The bizarre claims peddled on uncritical television programs or in weekly newspapers plucked from grocery store stands mean nothing to me, being generated solely from the hopes, desires, and fears of an ignorant public. My studies focus on genuine arcana, the esoteric mysteries that must arise at the rim of the known. At any given moment in the sweep of intellectual history, there are frontiers of knowledge. It is the glory of our age that we have pushed those frontiers to encompass a near totality of the natural world. We know it, or we can conceive it, or we can at least ask intelligent questions about it. There is, on the other hand, that vast beyond, the supernatural, about which we know little more than our credulous forebears who squatted in caves or who begged alms from the tops of temple pyramids. The realm of supernature exists; it is real, as real as anything you see and touch. My work has occasionally brought me into confrontation with it. That overarching mystical universe, largely unexplored to this day, can be approached at the margins by a man armed with prerequisite knowledge, and that universe can, at times, under special conditions, approach our own as well.

"That, indeed, is the situation we face. Allow me to describe chronologically, and to explain generally, based upon my previous experience, the recent sequence of events. You and your bright, superbly educated group set out to break down the final logical barrier which separates the macroscopic world from the microscopic. Physicists before you had delved down to what might be deemed a sub-atomic wall; you wished to knock down that wall, and make use, hopefully for profit (certainly for wisdom), of the latent energies beyond. A sound plan, within limits; think, however, of that analogy of the wall. A wall may form nothing but an obstacle, a challenge to be overcome. Such was your thinking. Yet it may also constitute a reasonable, proper barrier which protects us from harm or delineates units of property, be they homesteads or kingdoms. In the world of men, in the give and take of regular life, we rightly pause before a wall, for we suspect that it has been erected with the intent to keep us out, or otherwise mark a boundary of importance. That wall may be a dyke which, if broken, allows the flood to cascade upon us to our destruction; it may comprise a warning of enemies beyond, from whom we had best keep our distance. Walls may serve many purposes, so long as they remain intact.

"To the extent that it could, your experiment succeeded. You cracked the final barrier of materiality, and in so doing broke a tiny hole in the ultimate substratum. Unfortunately, you had given no thought to what might lie beyond. You had, in fact, opened a minuscule doorway from the natural to the supernatural, an egress and regress into another dimension. Yes, Dr. Phelps, you did it, without knowing what you did. You created a peephole into a boundless, unseen world, with no thought or care for the possibility that someone or something might peep back at you.

"There was more still, I regret to say, to your unpleasant surprise. At that moment an incredibly powerful stream of mysterious energy shot through the hole that you had fashioned. There are several ways to explain that: you stimulated an energy source beyond the dimensional layer, or unleashed a pent up tide of energy flow, or (as you may have hoped) initiated an unexpectedly powerful nuclear reaction within the substratum. The latter we may dismiss forthwith— by your own account you had passed the barrier, which I accept as given—and the other two possibilities do not jibe with my previous observations of such phenomena. Granting your data, there is only one explanation I will allow, that a force of awesome magnitude burst through the doorway so soon as you opened it.

"I do not refer to blind energy of the $E=mc2$ variety. Entry into our domain was gained by a violent but controlled, directed field, an act of purpose, of will. In evaluating what comes next it is wise for you to clear your mind of preconceptions and prior associations; when I speak of purpose and will, please do not fall into the error of thinking I speak metaphorically. The intruder was an organism, an entity, a living thing as such are understood in its domain. To grasp the enormity of the being you have awakened, we must note that the smallest crack in the wall fostered immediate access. We may posit that you suffered the grotesquely bad luck to puncture the barrier at the entity's precise location in its universe, in which case we are dealing with a potentially minor and manageable being. Such an outcome, while the happiest possible for us, is also the least likely, defying all conceivable odds. We must consider a direr possibility, that the thing was able to enter our plane at once, without delay, because where ever you broke into its realm, there it would be, waiting. Ponder long what we are describing: a being the size of a universe, one which makes up the entirety of its universe. Science has no term for such an entity, but philosophy and theology do, and that word is 'deity.'

"Now we wrestle with the cruelties of logic. I postulate the influence of a god, which I should not in a physical context, yet I must, for the facts demand it. 'God' is such a slippery term, one which excites sterile debate, now, ten thousand years ago, perhaps ten thousand from now. Is there one god, or are there two, or a dozen, or a hundred? Do we deduce his nature from nature, or from inherent ideas? We could discuss all night, we could argue the rest of our lives, without approaching proof or accuracy. It is well for us that we need not. Whether it be the one and only god, or merely an aspect of same, or a separate, competing deity among a crowd of similar types, it is still true that 'godness,' if you will, has invaded our world. That being so, we enjoy the rare opportunity to judge the nature of this god by its direct actions and the consequences of those actions. Here we come to an analysis of the events following the collapse of the experiment.

"Its first act was to seize control of your main computer. You must see that such control has been established, and you can hazard guesses as to why as well as I. The computer is the most powerful, energy-filled corporeal object within reach, one crammed with information, one connected, in some degree, to every form and field known to man. Our formless visitor took upon itself a body, a material shell within a material world. Numerous legends mention demonic possession and strange cosmic enlightenments; we experience a modernized version of the same. The god has taken complete charge of the machine. You do not know how the instrument continues to power itself, but I do. The god sustains itself in its new body, is its own source of energy. You cannot make sense of the data streaming from the machine. Of course you cannot, for the pre-existing contents have been wiped clean—it breaks my heart to tell you this—wiped utterly clean, and replaced by a fresh universe of data. The computer now embodies the god, the sole denizen of a cosmos alien to ours, and its output, until such time as we learn the rules of communication, must come across to us as gibberish.

"The meaning of later developments still requires examination, but the indications are ugly. Since the god erupted into our universe, people have begun to die, in every case by their own hand. The signs

234

are disturbing. I fear that sweetness and light are not to be counted on from this deity. We deal with a fearsome god, one which craves and demands sacrifices. There is something inherent in its nature which lures the victims to their destruction. Conversely, though this need not negate the first point, there is something inherent in the nature of the victims which renders them amenable to self-sacrifice. You have told me that the deceased were people oppressed by the trials of life; let us assume, then, that the god is a sort which feeds upon the miseries of mortals, or one which acts to induce deeper despair among those already afflicted in some manner."

"That's a huge assumption," I exclaimed. "Granting everything you've said—which of course I don't—you're going way out on a limb. The history of theology is chock full of broad arguments from effects to causes, most of them without merit, and it sounds to me like you're heading down the same endless road. You could prove anything that way."

"I could posit anything," Vorchek corrected; "what I can prove depends on the evidence, admittedly incomplete. I am not prone, whatever you may believe, to spinning wild theories or leaping at shadows. Versed by study in these questions, I have at my beck valuable source materials. Miss Delaney," he said, turning to the girl, "among the files you packed you did bring that fragment from Bleek, as I instructed?"

"It's with the other papers in our quarters," she replied, referring to the adjoining guest rooms they occupied at the facilities, a conjugation which made me wonder about them. "I took the liberty of reading it, and vile stuff it is, too. It's horrifying to think that it might have anything to do with this business."

"I don't know what you're talking about," I said pointedly.

"Nor should you," said Vorchek. "The matter falls beyond your purview, Dr. Phelps. Jacob Bleek, the mystical philosopher of old, in his day collected and mastered a great deal of information drawn from the esoteric wisdom of the ages. Only portions of his work survive. He specialized in the blacker types of knowledge, devoting an entire chapter of his writings to a particularly vicious deity who interests me considerably at this time. The indications are favorable, if you will excuse the word, but I wish to say no more at present. First I must gain confirmation."

That was that, for the time being. The professor would say no more, and my brain was swimming in such a fog that I couldn't intelligently pursue the matter. We left the restaurant (I noticed that

Vorchek charged the meal to an APP account) and retired to our beds.

I came to work oddly late the next morning. I had slept poorly, and after awakening sat hunched for a lengthy span over my coffee and toast, mulling over the incredible story Vorchek had told at dinner. It was strange; I didn't accept it intellectually, but his reconstruction of facts mesmerized me. He really had, after his own lights, tied everything together into a coherent whole, and he alluded to confirmation, the life's blood of science, without which his claims were futile and wasteful. Did he really expect to get it, and if so, how? He seemed awfully confident for a charlatan, but then, I supposed they often were. I would wait and see what he produced.

So I arrived late, and was one of the last to hear the news: Laura Ellsworth had killed herself. I had known her slightly—she worked in an ancillary unit, operating out of a separate laboratory in the complex, mixing novel chemical solutions for testing—but I hadn't known her well enough, it seemed, for I'd never guessed that she would off herself that way. She had always been a subdued and frowny sort, and I heard after the fact that real life had thrown her a few too many curves, yet nothing I was now told explained why she suddenly, at this particular time, decided that life was too much for her, and that she should sneak into her lab before opening time, activate a high intensity laser used for stimulating and busting molecules, wriggle on her back onto the small dais in the laser chamber where samples were serviced, and methodically burn off her own face, relentlessly and ruthlessly holding herself in place, despite the terrible pain, until such time as life departed from her mutilated body. Unexpected, monstrous, impossible; it couldn't be, but it happened, and another of our personnel bit the dust. Her colleagues found what was left half an hour later.

This extraordinary discovery jarred me emotionally, of course, and while imbibing the news I thought of Vorchek and his extraordinary theory. I could imagine him chortling and rubbing his hands with glee, while his sexy pet Theresa egged him on, cooing words of enthusiasm for his genius. Every death, he would claim, supported that much more his dismal vision of our situation. These tragic losses were unbearable, they were senseless, and I wasn't going to be the one to explain them, but was he capable or qualified to do so? At this moment of weary depression I experienced a remarkable feeling of revulsion against that man, who appeared to be feeding upon our misery. He wasn't right—he couldn't be—and what had become of the proper scientific principle of considering commonplace solutions first? People killed themselves all the time, without set pattern or interval,

236

through periods of drought and periods of storm, and the grim figures averaged out, if at all, only statistically. In a large group of our size, how many suicides were predicted in the span of a year or ten years? The recent crop seemed, I couldn't deny, an overly generous surplus, but who among us had calculated the odds? There were subsidiary factors worth counting: I thought of the initial troubles with the experiment and its aftermath which might, I supposed, have increased ill thoughts in shaky minds, and there was the copycat effect and the like, emotional and social instabilities which fed upon one another and were wont to cause wretched progressions to flourish. I thought of the shop worn concept of "the madness of crowds." I wasn't a psychologist, but that seemed as reasonable a framework as any in which to place our sad tidings. I thought of something else, too.

It occurred to me on the instant that the professor was wrong, decisively, stupidly wrong. I went in search for him, finding him in the computer room with Theresa. He looked dapper as always, showy rather than professional; where the rolled up sleeves, the rumpled trousers, the scruffy shoes of my co-workers? She, dressed to the nines, like something out of a fashion magazine; why didn't she wear pants and dirty tee-shirts, like every other woman I knew? They were keeping company with none other than Gerald Steen, with whom they were conducting an animated conversation. I interrupted brusquely. "Vorchek, I must talk to you." He nodded, chipper as ever, and followed me from the room, with Theresa in tow, clutching a sheaf of papers and dangling pad and pencil, Steen left behind grinning weirdly at me. I led the pair to my office, closed the door behind us, motioned to them to take seats. I settled into my big, comfortable recliner, gripping it by the plush arms. Vorchek said evenly, "What may I do for you, Dr. Phelps?"

"You can listen," I began, waving an accusatory finger at his face. "You're all wet, Vorchek; I've figured out that much. This time you rode your hobbyhorse too far. There is no supernatural mystery here, nothing that requires extreme explanations. We're not under attack from a god, but from bad luck. How do I know? I know because of the pattern of the deaths; the pattern that isn't there! You made a big, howling blooper, Vorchek, which blows your theory to smithereens. You speculate that weak, dark-minded folk are being targeted from outside, and build rickety castles on that foundation, but you've gone out of your way to overlook the obvious exception, the man who doesn't fit the picture, even though you spend half your time talking to him instead of me.

"I mean Gerald Steen. If you'd paid any attention to genuine facts, you'd have noticed that he's the most pathetic, broken, and miserable fellow in the bunch. He's got everything your theory demands, every trait that should've destroyed him quickly. He ought to have been the first to die, but he's very evidently alive. He's in good health, getting along just fine. I've never seen him more lively! If you're right, he's already dead; if he's alive, then you're an ass, here to make fools of us all and grab as much cash as you can. It's a great racket, Vorchek, one that's taken you far, but now it's blown up in your face, and I'm throwing the dynamite. I'm going to speak with Cunningham, and we're going to run you out of here."

I settled back into the haven of my chair, wiped my brow. "Have you solved," asked Vorchek presently, his vaguely foreign voice knifing the stillness, "the mystery of the computer?" "No mystery," I snapped, "only mechanical unreliability." "The curious readings?" "Fried circuits," said I, "spewing noise. We'll fix it." "And the news from the city?" he quietly queried. I sat up straight and asked, "What news?"

"My dear," he said to Theresa, "please update Dr. Phelps on the preliminary results of your investigation." "Gladly, sir," she cried, ruffling her handful of papers, which were indeed, as I now saw, copies of local newspapers. "At Professor Vorchek's request I examined the public reports of criminal cases in the vicinity for the period since the failure of your experiment. It turns out there's plenty going on. So far this week there have been seventeen suicides in the city, whereas there were only two recorded for the previous month. The authorities are frantic about it. All of the victims were likely types, but the numbers are at an all-time high, and in all but one case the manners of death were quite unusual. There are no overdoses or shootings in the temples among this lot. See, I've marked the summaries, and I've got three burnings, two multiple stabbings, drinking of acid from a car battery, a partial decapitation, and much, much more. Look them over for yourself." She tossed the papers onto my desk.

"Those are suicides?" I screamed.

"Every one," said Vorchek. "The plague spreads from this geographical point. Now, Doctor, is the time for calm heads to prevail. It is impossible to sweep this cohesive phenomenon under the rug. It exists. Everything links. Uncharacteristic morbidity radiates from your laboratory and, so we must conclude, specifically from your computer. We must sever all ties to the outside world until we resolve this ghastly business. To what outlets is your computer connected?"

"There aren't any," I said. "It did draw power from the city

238

supply, but that's shut off, as you know. It's operating on its own." I felt sick when I said those words. In my fervor I hadn't asked myself how I was going to explain that.

"Of course," said Vorchek impatiently, "but there are still physical connections, and telephone hookups, outlets to other machines at this complex and to other research facilities."

"Yes, there are. That's the way of the world these days. Everything connects to everything else."

"Break those connections," he commanded, "break them by brute force if necessary. Get yourself a pair of garden shears and cut every wire leading out of this building. Isolate the machine, totally. It appears that the influence has not yet reached out aggressively. Let us head it off, blockade it here, and fight our enemy on just one front.

"Now, as to the morose Dr. Steen, I must inform you that I have been closely observing him. He is the sort of man you think he is, as I learned quickly enough. I have not ignored him nor, despite appearances, failed to incorporate him into my equation. On the contrary, he forms an integral part of the sum. I ask you, Dr. Phelps, to grant my thesis for the moment. We derive the conclusion that potentially suicidal individuals are being driven over the brink by a malevolent force, yes? Yet Steen, our prime candidate, exhibits no tendencies in that direction. Given the premise, what would you deduce?"

"That in his case, another factor is in play."

"Necessarily so. You know him; you have observed him; can you deduce that factor?"

I took my time in replying, but I already knew the answer, had known all along. "He enjoys it," I said, "he's getting what he wants from the experience. He's carried self-loathing to such a level that it's all he lives for. He can't get enough of it. Steen doesn't want to die; he wants to wallow in misery."

"Simplistic," said Vorchek, "but accurate, so far as it goes. You describe him to a fair degree. There is more to him, however. The man is positively dangerous. His every waking moment is spent attempting to contact the god in the machine. We must know his precise reasons, whether they be wholly personal, or somehow directed against the wide world. If the latter, then we must shut him down and send him away."

"Shouldn't we do that anyway?" asked Theresa. "If he's a menace, let's send him packing."

"I have the authority," I pointed out.

"Not yet," advised the professor. "Steen progresses. He verges on results, and if it be safely allowable, I want those results."

Little more was said at this meeting. Nothing was settled, no plan of action was agreed upon, but I made no more threats, nor did I consider doing so. I would wait and see what developed. Vorchek left, bowing courteously and shaking my hand before he went. Theresa followed, turning to me at the door, staring into my face with her bland blue eyes and saying primly, "You're the ass," before scurrying away.

Later that day I requested, and received, a loan of the ancient document written by the philosopher Jacob Bleek. These were photocopies of what I could see was a translation or transcription, fourteen closely typed pages presenting an account which began in mid-sentence and broke off abruptly at the end. The text, curiously, consisted of verse, a very long and rambling poem explicating intricately abstruse concepts. Vorchek warned me about that, assuring me that in olden times such presentation was common among learned men. The bulk of the material related what I would call a legend or myth, although the author clearly considered his account to be no less than epistemologically coherent truth. It was a hideous tale, one that kept me awake long that night pondering its implications, one I couldn't make myself forget; one that I never shall.

Jacob Bleek, this old scholar with the euphonically apt name, had conceived after much study a harrowing view of the world and of man's place within it. The natural universe was a realm influenced and overshadowed by a greater realm where mighty forces ruled, a higher dimension within which alien and unfathomable intelligences operated according to their own wills, and in accordance with their own designs. These were the gods—or the aspects of godhood, as the case might be—absolute masters of space and time and fate. So vast and magnificent were they (Bleek routinely capitalized: "They," the "Gods," the "Lords of All Things") that the cosmos and its various substances and inhabitants, including man, could be viewed as no more than playthings at their command, when those majestic entities deigned to notice the infinitesimal bubble that we think of as all reality. For the sake of logical organization and understanding Bleek accepted the conventional wisdom of elder days, that there were many deities jostling for power or eminence, and in this fragment devoted his poetic treatise to a particularly reprehensible god, one whose properties were such that (as the author noted in a fey allusion) he must needs be portrayed in popular religion as a devil.

This Blug—an ugly, distasteful designation derived, so it was claimed, from mysterious records predating conventional history—represented or fostered everything vile and crude and corrupt in the universe. I couldn't glean from my twisted source whether Blug merely made use of and fed upon that which was nasty and squalid, or whether he served also as the ultimate originator of same, but he clearly dominated that aspect of existence, to the detriment of all concerned. This King of Filth, so ran the assiduously collected stories, ruled from a dark throne at the center of a dreadful region outside of the world, a rancid, stinking mire never to be found on any map, but co-existing, in that strange higher realm of being, at all points with the world of matter, energy, and man. The seat of Blug's primordial, everlasting kingdom was styled the Black Swamp, and it contained within its blasphemous, indefinable boundaries everything putrid, toxic, and loathsome. There Blug governed, and from there he whispered insidiously to all those oppressed by the burdens of life, all who hopelessly despaired, all whose hate or contempt or fury turned inward upon themselves in black mindless madness, calling to them and drawing them into himself, seeking to make them his own, stoking their self-destructive tendencies and thereby satiating himself with their inner darkness, as well as gathering unto himself an eternal, endless legion of sycophantic acolytes and craven, fawning worshippers, those who would dedicate their ruined dead souls to his glory for so long as eternity should endure.

Blug demanded debasement from the world, and he got it. Where his power impinged, there was squalor and decay and meaningless death. In that sense he was nothing but a symbol for everything wrong under the sun, a dull, dirty, tarnished emblem of entropy, and his name had been invoked in that regard, so I read, by thinkers of ancient times. There was more, however; according to Bleek, sinister Blug had gathered round himself on earth a degenerate cult of men who knew him for what he was, who knew what he wanted and were willing to pay the fearful price he exacted in return for adoring him. These were men who, in some sense, made up the lowest elements of humanity, men whose healthy virtues were well-nigh extinct, though they might otherwise be rich or educated, even respected for their works. People whose minds dwelt in black swamps of their own devising were the meat and gravy of Blug, their masochistic (my word) inclinations dragging them down into pits of joyous mental agony, from which they could look up to the face of Blug and find shocking solace in what they saw.

The Blug cult, ever present, had emerged from the shadows at certain points of history, mentioned, so I learned, in the writings of Artocris, Plato, and Augustine. Everywhere shunned and condemned, for its grisly practices as well as its ideas, it nevertheless persisted, for there were always the weak and miserable ready to grant obeisance to their chosen lord. Bleek wrote of notable events, culled from awestruck sources, which described specific irruptions of Blug into our universe, events on a small scale, but with the most deleterious of social and personal effects. Blug's power could reach forth from his nightmare kingdom, when foolish men had opened doorways for him, and under such circumstances his intrusion could lead to cumulative dismay and tragedy.

Tread not with thy soiled soul into the murk
For amidst the slime final perils lurk
Give not Blug His due lest ye be held fast
In quick'ning mud where horrors brooding last.

So said Jacob Bleek, or so ran Vorchek's transcription; that, and much else besides, all of it gloomy and ominous and, I couldn't help but think, oddly pertinent to current events. I despised what I read, despised myself for reading it, was like to kick myself for believing it, but in some fashion, down deep, I already did. Blug, or something like him, had broken into the modern world, as a result of my own honest actions, and now laid waste to the sadder minds among our people at APP and, I must accept, others as well. I came down very early in the morning, before dawn broke, to the administrative office, and there I gave orders (after clearing them with the incredulous but, oddly amenable Cunningham) to the maintenance staff to rip up every electrical conduit and telephone line leading into the accelerator building. Be sure that they asked plenty of painful questions, but they agreed to get onto it right away. Then I strode over to the ruin of my laboratory.

For once I caught up with Steen, who had been beating me to the punch every morning since the unpleasantness began. He looked a wreck, and glumly informed me that he had finally knocked off for a snatch of sleep, explaining that he could afford to since he was "so close to the ultimate breakthrough." He made a sneering comment about my new hours, then stopped short upon our approach to the structure, gesturing before him. Professor Vorchek and Theresa were already on the scene, performing some act by dim lamplight in the gloom.

I guess I might have expected them to be drawing a pentagram or similar occult device, but it wasn't that, or it didn't look it. What they were doing was painting a circle around the entire building, a broad white line that curved around from the back, to which they were just now putting the finishing touches, filling in the final gap. They were using long-handled mops, dipping them into a big double-handled pot. Up close the stuff didn't look like paint, being unusually viscous and slightly luminous in the fading dark. Vorchek had shed his hat and coat, but his natty tie still flapped in the breeze. Theresa had come down in fashion, but she still looked good, better than any girl I knew. I wished I had a private secretary like that.

"What trickery is this?" whined Steen. I asked the same, in a friendlier manner. Vorchek and Theresa paused and rested on their mops, forming an image like a new version of *American Gothic*. "Instituting safeguards," explained the professor. "No, this is not paint, but rather a composition of my own, one intended to repel extrusions of wicked influence. This fluid has been known to work effectively in less formidable cases, and I thought it worth a try here. Go on in, you two. We will join you in a minute."

"Useless rubbish," Steen muttered unhappily. He made straight for the computer room, while I detoured briefly to my office in order to update some files. When I finished and came after him, I found that our visitors had joined him, all three looking extraordinarily busy. Steen and the professor were deep in discussion at a console, while Theresa hovered about, taking notes and ostentatiously observing. "Three, one, four, one, six," she called out, "and a funny squiggle." "That is 'delta,'" said Vorchek. "Delta," repeated the girl, "and four, one, and a seven . . ." On she went in a sort of singsong recitation. I said sharply, "Somebody tell me what's happening."

Vorchek smiled and said, "Dr. Steen has cracked the code. It is a modified binary, groupings of ones and zeros, with other signifiers mixed in. The latter caused the most grief, but now that we know the language being employed, it is not too difficult to master."

"The language?" I cried. "Do you mean the computer language? It isn't anything like that."

"I refer," he replied, "to the underlying language which the machine is presenting to us in computer form. It appears to belong to a derivative of the antique Rhexellite tongue, a dialect not spoken on this earth for tens of thousands of years. I had previously noted certain patterns in the data which provided clues. A consultation of my library, which I keep on disc, confirmed my suspicions."

"Professor Vorchek has been most helpful," said Steen, his ungracious tone undercutting his words. "I'd worked out the code two days ago, but it didn't scan in English or any language I knew. He provided the final key. Now I'm actually reading the thoughts of the computer mind."

"An awful lot has been going on behind my back," I grumbled. "So, what have you learned?"

"It is an entertaining discourse," said Vorchek. "Here is a snatch which I have translated." He held out to me a sheet on which a paragraph had been scrawled. I took it and read. I started, gasped, could barely keep on to the end. It was the foulest, most degrading conglomeration of sordid, raving insanity I'd ever come across. I felt defiled to my soul by those mere characters on paper. I handed it back to him. "That's inside my computer?"

"It isn't your computer anymore," sneered Steen. "It's His."

"I wish you'd let me read it," said Theresa.

Vorchek grinned, but said soberly, "It is not edifying material for a sweet young girl. What do you think, Dr. Phelps?"

"I read Bleek," I replied. "I suppose this nails it down."

"It does; this, and a symbol which appears repetitively. Yes, you can see it here." He tapped the monitor screen. "That character, the one resembling a lambda, translates from the Rhexellite as a single hoarse, guttural sound, an unconventional word. Your perusal of Bleek should tell you what it is."

"It's true," I whispered, "this is really happening." Then, loudly, "You've had enough of that filth, Steen. Get away from there."

"Not nearly enough!" he screamed. Suddenly his basic nastiness evaporated, replaced by a tone of desperate supplication, a look of agonized woe. "It won't be enough until I've gotten in there and embraced Him. I'm almost ready to begin. I only need ten more minutes. Vorchek, you promised me."

"The promise stands," said the professor. "Your promise doesn't bind me," I cut in hotly; "I say no deal, whatever you have in mind." Vorchek shrugged, saying, "Dr. Steen, continue until all is set for our little experiment. Miss Delaney, maintain your records. Dr. Phelps, let us step outside." I followed him into the hall. Just then one of the maintenance guys showed up, delivering the message that all outside connections had been severed. "We had to rip up the asphalt," he fumed. I dismissed him. The professor enthused, "Everything comes together nicely." This was getting to be too much for me; too much, too fast. I rounded on my companion. "Vorchek, are you nuts? We've got to suppress that maniac before he does something awful!"

"Steen constitutes no threat to us," he announced. "I have

satisfied myself on that point. I had a long talk with him, man to man, a candid discussion, in which I learned exactly what he seeks. It is for Dr. Steen, as I surmised, a personal odyssey of self-fulfillment on his part, rather than aggressive megalomania. We may humor him with his experiment, which may prove unusually rewarding in its own right, while we commence our own, which should end the matter. The building is sealed, and an unbroken circle of countervailing force surrounds us. That should contain the sinister energies until we attack and defeat the source. In a few minutes we may begin." "Begin what?" I queried, and Vorchek replied, "To drive the great god Blug out of your computer, which it has possessed." Then he told me precisely how we would accomplish that. I nodded dumbly. I was adrift at sea, but maybe he knew what he was talking about.

We returned to the desolate computer room, where everyone got busy. Steen carried on with his mysterious endeavors, flashing fresh pages of strange text one after another on his screen, at times chuckling weirdly to himself. In a far corner, behind a low wall of consoles where we had some privacy, Vorchek, Theresa, and I labored to deploy a battery of complicated mechanisms which the professor had produced from his magician's hat. These were odd, spidery gizmos on tripods, linked by electrical cords, which he hooked into our internal power via a boxy transformer of homemade appearance which he also provided. "We fight force with force," he explained to me, "thrusting back the influence with an antagonistic, repulsive charge. All going well, we will hurl Blug back to whence he came, and stop up the mouse hole you made. It should be as simple as that." "Piece of cake," Theresa opined.

I urged Vorchek to activate his devices immediately but, inexplicably, he advised delay. "One more scene of this drama must be enacted," he said mysteriously. "Miss Delaney, bring the satchel, if you please." She hefted that item and they walked over to Steen. I tagged along shortly, to hear my colleague complaining, "It's a nuisance. I don't have time to waste on that." "A deal is a deal," said Vorchek authoritatively. "Put it on."

"It" consisted of an awkward headset and cumbersome goggles, confusingly wired with many tiny cables into a portable device, another rough and ready unit by the look of it, which the professor placed on the table top at Steen's elbow. I had to hand it to Vorchek; despite my first impressions, he had a penchant for machinery, and mighty exotic stuff at that. He seemed to be a man of many parts. Steen ungraciously donned the headset and goggles, connecting the pads of the former to his temples and scalp, strapping the latter to his eyes, then buckled down once more to his work. "Any second now," he breathed, but he cared nothing for us, had forgotten our presence in that moment. He spoke to the demons within his mind, and perhaps to one without.

As I was obviously impatient to speak, Vorchek drew us away from Steen. I asked, "What's he doing now?" The professor said, "Making contact, I expect. He has the means, and the knowledge; it can be done, if the party on the other end is willing. I think he is." "So what do we do?" "We wait, just a little longer. My specialized recording device, now attached to his brain and eyes, is storing all data, exactly as he sees and experiences them. That is pertinent information, sir, which we must retrieve for future analysis. Miss Delaney?" "I'm with you, Professor." "Miss Delaney, I want you on the switch. When I call out, throw it, and do not hesitate for a second. Dr. Phelps, you and I will observe from this intermediate position."

Theresa assumed her station, holding in her hands a control device wired to the professor's instruments. Vorchek and I remained where we were, watching Steen's hunched back. I wondered why we held back from the scene of the action. It occurred to me that it might not be safe to hang closely to Steen, and I wondered why that might be. The thought bugged me, but in the quiet tension of the moment I couldn't bring myself to ask.

Something happened. The computer began to generate sounds, unusual noises of mounting intensity, as if great activity churned within. Steen gasped, pushed away from his console. With his movement I caught a glimpse of the monitor. From about thirty feet away I couldn't see well, but could tell that the output had changed. No longer did the strange text flash on the screen. Instead, there was something else: murky suggestions of form, visual images appearing out of the heart of the machine. Observation of detail was impossible at this remove, and yet I didn't care for the little I saw. Sight of the screen was cut off by Steen's head as he leaned forward, soaking up every bit of the inexplicable imagery assaulting his senses.

Then Steen threw himself up out of his seat, shrieking a strange word as he did so. It wasn't English, wasn't any language I knew, or that I would have expected him to know, but he spoke it wildly, ecstatically, over and again, rapidly. There came a shrill cry from the man, a horrifying wail, and he collapsed back into the chair, sprawling limply, his arms and legs splayed in an ugly arrangement. The hard jostling dislodged the pads from his skull. I noted, instantaneously, that his screen had gone black.

"Miss Delaney," Vorchek cried, "hit it now!" She flipped the switch on the control box, Vorchek's odd devices activated, and all hell broke loose. A roaring emanated from the computer, a wholly non-machine sound, more like the bellowing of a big, angry animal. The room darkened slightly, and the floor shook. No, the building shook; a forgotten coffee cup tumbled from its perch, and a framed document toppled from the wall. The roar abated, transformed into a low, monotonous growling, less animalistic in nature, more like the sound of steel balls rolling continuously on a hard surface. Computer panels began to bulge and pop open, emitting sparks and black puffs of smoke at the joins. The growling became a thin, irritating, whistling whine, rising to a piercing crescendo, and then several panels of the computer blew out entirely, and—despite everything, I still couldn't believe what I saw—the whole massive machine sagged and began to crumple like tin foil. The destruction progressed at a dazzling rate; within mere seconds that modern wonder of solid circuitry and space age appliance deteriorated to scattered bits and jagged fragments of trash, a pile of junk viewed through belching gouts of steam and flickering, dwindling flames. The whining ceased.

"It is finished!" shouted Vorchek. "Miss Delaney, break the current." He said to me, "Sorry about the machine, Dr. Phelps. It was only a shell at this stage, of course. Blug had eaten out the interior to make room for the intrusion of his substance." He forthwith raced to the pathetic shambles of my computer, to where Theresa immediately followed and engaged him in lively, congratulatory conversation. I made for Steen. I pulled his head up by the hair and gazed into his face. I didn't have to be an expert to know he was dead. Oh God, he was the deadest man I'd ever seen. There wasn't a mark on him, and yet I couldn't conceive of a more lifeless corpse. The body was cold, beyond the absence of living warmth, a clammy chilliness, as if the life had been sucked from it. The eyes stared dully, the mouth contorted into a sickening, frozen smile. Steen had died happy, and that horrified me more than anything that had happened.

I joined Vorchek and the girl. "He's dead," I said flatly. Theresa said, "That's too bad." Vorchek muttered, "Predictable, really, just one more aspect of the tragedy." "You knew?" I asked. "It was written," he replied. "Steen has gone to meet his god, the only thing he really wanted. His eternal soul has found the only sort of belonging it would accept." He strode briskly to the dead man, gathered up the various components of his recorder. Theresa swooped in efficiently with the satchel to haul away the stuff. I stood immovable, calling out, "Why did he die, Vorchek?"

"I am no medical man," he said curtly.

"I mean why did it have to be? You set it up this way. Your sweetie here could have snapped that switch ten minutes ago, and we'd have obtained the same results, only Steen would still be alive. That's the truth, isn't it?"

"Possibly. His cooperation may have distracted Blug while we operated, which may have been a benefit to us. I do not know."

"It all came out in the wash," Theresa observed. "The problem's solved. Tough luck about that guy, but he was asking for it. Don't sweat it now; you're home free."

"Shut up, you," I snarled. "Silence, please, from the cheering section. Vorchek, tell me why."

"Because I need that information!" Vorchek thundered. "Only Steen could provide it, unless one of us volunteered to take his place. You do not understand the peculiar qualities of my recorder which he wore. It develops mental images and readings from the subject, what he experiences within the caverns of his mind. It functioned until the moment of Steen's death. Do you realize what that means? Can you imagine the data contained within that instrument? It is all there, as he lived it in those incredible moments. I can manage and massage those data, break them down, build them up, put them on a graph or transfer them to video. Much can be learned. Fear not, Dr. Phelps; I will see to it that you receive a copy of the results."

"I don't want it," I said disgustedly. "I just want you two out of here."

Within half an hour they were gone. Applied Physics Processing took a big hit, naturally, but it's a wealthy company, and all equipment got replaced in time, with much hand-wringing and references to the bottom line. Somewhat to my surprise I kept my job. Cunningham, amazingly, ever acted as if he partly understood the weird nature of what occurred that unspeakable week. He had always taken Vorchek seriously, and that fellow got with him and straightened out everything, for which I confess gratitude, and my boss saw to it that no blemish remained to fester on my reputation. The day came when I was back in business running experiments, as if nothing had ever happened. One particular experiment I studiously avoided, and no colleague ever suggested it to me again.

This morning a package arrived from Professor Anton Vorchek, without accompanying message, containing a video disc. I knew what it was and thought to throw it away or destroy it, but I couldn't do that; I'm a scientist, after all. This evening I inserted it into my player and watched it on my big screen wall panel television. It might be a fake (at one time I wouldn't have put a self-aggrandizing hoax past Vorchek) but I don't think it is. I'd like to know the secret of the professor's recording machine; it must be a marvelous instrument. Hours have passed, the time nearing midnight, yet I'm still shaking over what I saw, my comfortable, front seat view of the final moments of Dr. Gerald Steen, the man who craved for himself nothing but total and eternal abasement to the power of his chosen lord.

The picture began with a brief, clear-cut image of that well remembered monitor screen. Within moments the text vanished from the monitor, to be replaced by a vague, unfocused vision of formless shapes crowding into sight. Then everything went black for an instant—I wondered if that was all—only to have the picture return, but affording a completely different view. The monitor was gone, along with any trace of a laboratory setting. I and Steen were impossibly, unimaginably elsewhere.

Through his eyes and mind I gazed upon a dark, murky landscape of dense growth, a sea of alien shrubs and stunted trees with spiky branches and malformed leaves, rising from a plain of filthy-looking gray-black mud. There was little color to the image, as if I viewed everything through dark tinting, and the picture was smudged, a minute trace of blurring which obscured fine detail. Nevertheless, I saw enough to astound and grip me. The view of the muddy terrain seemed to thrust at me, and I knew that Steen was advancing, running into and through the scene. Damp, thorny fronds slapped at his face, my face, as he pushed into the grim wilderness. Thin, tentacular branches reached out as if grasping at the passerby. I think those plants possessed inherent motion, for there was no obvious evidence of wind. The progression into that mysterious land—shall I call it the Black Swamp?—continued. Occasionally I glimpsed living objects nearby in the ooze, awful creeping things I didn't recognize, while more often I spied what appeared dead things, incomplete and rotten. I shuddered to note that many of the living organisms looked less complete than the dead. One larger mud-caked specimen, which rolled hastily away into the slime beneath a thick, morbidly swaying bush, bore a disturbing similarity to a flayed human being.

The advance went on through that abysmal landscape for a considerable period, far longer than I could have calculated from the time frame of Steen's death. A kind of temporal expansion was taking place; much information had been packed into that short period while he retained a minimal connection to our world. Then the nearest bushes receded from view on both sides, exposing a broad clearing within which bubbled and steamed a shallow lagoon. A low island lay in the misty distance, with something large and black looming upon it. The image pushed forward again, haltingly, as if the source of the vision slogged through the oily gray water. Moving forms tossed and floundered in the muck, and they were terrible to see. Some were passably human; others might once have been human, but had undergone loathsome changes; others could never have been human at all. When these naked beings weren't rolling and splashing in the scummy liquid, as if in agony or distress, they were staring with gaping mouths and fawning toward the central island.

The island attained, the image paused, as if for a gulp of breath, or from fear or some other, less sane emotion. Something dark and tremendous loomed through the roiling vapors, something that heaved and quivered repulsively. Before it, on the soggy level ground, there sprawled, staggered, and danced a nightmarish horde of naked monstrosities that made the denizens of the lagoon look wholesome. I couldn't accept that such men or beasts lived, but they did, and in a lively manner. Those that had faces bore expressions of pious, ineffable joy. The scene zoomed suddenly, as Steen ran at the massive black bulk, and the source of all that unspeakable delight came clearly into view. Atop a crude, unadorned throne of apparently native rock, gray and unchiseled, squatted a ponderous, amorphous entity, shifting and squirming on its great seat, dripping grease onto the stained rock, an entity which I know must be or represent the foul and squalid Lord of Decay. There sat Blug, and there he governed his miserable empire, calling to those who could know no hope save in him. Smaller beings crowded around the base of the throne, where the substance of the horror slopped down. These beings were, in the main, quite human, men and women (many women), appearing less corroded than the outlying specimens, some still wearing shreds of clothing. They pressed up against that reeking (my imagination readily supplies that detail) mass, their hands sinking into the black gel. What were they doing? The image approached my shocked eyes.

From the lower fringes of Blug's heaving mass there bulged and grew frightful appendages, wet, glistening protuberances spouting intermittent streams of an abominably viscous, white, sticky fluid. I thought of unholy teats—God help me I did, may a sane and decent god help me—and I recoiled from the television screen in revulsion and desperate disbelief when I beheld the sickening confirmation. These poor, doomed, damned people, once the born kin of mine, once

250

alive to the same possibilities and dreams, bowed down and took those swelling protrusions into their mouths, greedily sucking at the thick juice than dribbled down their chins. I screamed, screamed again and averted my eyes when the image of one elongating teat swelled before me. In another moment the incredible video image gave out forever, but not before I realized that Steen, in his ultimate act of degradation, was bowing down to drink of the soul-destroying nectar exuded by his chosen god.

Facts in the case of Jeffery Scott Sims:

A degreed anthropologist, wilderness enthusiast, and photographer who makes his home in Arizona, Jeffery Scott Sims is a writer of fantastic and weird fiction. He is the creator of popular characters such as Professor Anton Vorchek, investigator of strange mysteries; Sterk Fontaine, self-serving dabbler in the supernatural; Jacob Bleek, the obsessively questing medieval wizard; and the combative and colorful heroes of ancient Dyrezan.

His publications include the collections *Science and Sorcery*, *Science and Sorcery II*, *Science and Sorcery III*, *Eerie Arizona*; the novels *The Journey of Jacob Bleek* and *The Journey through the Black Book*, plus well over a hundred short stories of the bizarre and the macabre. A number of these tales are set in the exotic and mysterious wilds of Arizona, or in imaginary lands of far times and places, ranging from forgotten eras to the distant future.

The author maintains a literary web site, *The Weird Writings of Jeffery Scott Sims*, which in addition to providing useful information on his works also offers an ever growing collection of entertaining essays devoted to unique or unusual topics related to the weird tale. This material may be freely accessed at
http://simsweird.infinityfreeapp.com/index.html